# ILLUMINATIONS
## OF THE *Heart*

A HISTORICAL ROMANCE NOVEL

# ILLUMINATIONS
## OF THE *Heart*

A HISTORICAL ROMANCE NOVEL

## JOYCE DIPASTENA

For Janet, my favorite *sorella* and best friend

Walnut Springs Press, LLC

110 South 800 West

Brigham City, Utah 84302

http://walnutspringspress.blogspot.com

ISBN: 978-1-93521-726-8

## Acknowledgments

My deepest thanks and appreciation to the following people:

Sara Fitzgerald, the first to "believe" in *Illuminations of the Heart*.

Lisa Messegee, Anna Arnett, Sarah Albrecht, Cindy Williams, Kari Pike, Kristine John, and Jennifer Griffith for their invaluable critiques of this work.

The sisters of ANWA for offering valuable suggestions during a time of significant struggle to know how I should proceed with this book.

Janet DiPastena, for going above and beyond the call of sisterly duty by her painstaking review of my manuscript (while jazzing me a little on the side).

And to Linda Prince and Amy Orton, who went to bat for me in a big way to bring you *Illuminations of the Heart* in the form that awaits you in the pages ahead!

# Author's Note

As I wrote this book, I strove diligently to be as accurate as possible when including historical events, descriptions, etc. However, when detailed research information eluded me, I sometimes had little choice but to fall back on my imagination. Such, for example, was the case with the ducal palace in Poitiers as described in *Illuminations of the Heart.* My word paintings of the palace and its gardens were inspired by Amy Kelly's biography *Eleanor of Aquitaine and the Four Kings.* (See my Suggested Reading List for bibliographical information on Kelly's book.) While Ms. Kelly did not draw me a floor plan, I nevertheless built upon her hints of sumptuous comfort to "create" the palace and gardens through which my characters pass.

As I confessed in my previous medieval romance, *Loyalty's Web,* I also took the historical legend of the Plantagenets' sinister ancestress, Melusine, and created a mythical emblem for Duke Richard of Aquitaine: the serpent-woman of his pendant and his servants' badges. The quip "From the devil they came, and to the devil they will no doubt go" is originally credited to St. Bernard of Clairvaux, but from all I have read of Duke Richard Plantagenet and his siblings, I can easily imagine them cheerfully turning this insult into what they may well have chosen to view as a compliment.

As for the tale of Rauolin and Mylisant, all credit for this romance must go to Acelet de Cary.

# Chapter 1

Poitou, Summer 1179

Donna Siri, cover your head."

Siriol de Calendri caught the fear in her companion's voice as the older woman nudged her mount close enough to reach out and whip the hood over her mistress's head. Regrettably, the action hindered Siri's view of the band of armed knights who had burst from the forest to surround her traveling party. Their shields, their surcotes, even their helmets lacked any crest or insignia to give a clue as to their identity. She had seen their blades leveled at the men of her guard before her companion's action had veiled her face. Siri knew from experience that it was safer to keep herself hidden, yet . . .

She started to draw back the edge of her hood to grant herself just a peek at their captors, but she felt Lucianna's fingers on her hand.

*"Carissima,"* her companion hissed in warning, *"per favore."*

Siri reluctantly left her hood in place. But she heard the hard warning in the male voice that rapped out, "Drop your weapons, if you hope to see your wives and children again."

There was much cursing in the Italian tongue, challenged by several threats in French, before she heard the soft clumping of swords being dropped onto the road.

"Now stand aside. Let us see what fortune has brought us today."

The Italians gathered around the two women, abandoning the wagons to their captors. For a time the robber-knights devoted themselves to ransacking the trunks and chests and ignored the travelers. Siri imagined the pleasure with which their captors must be discovering the rich fabrics of her gowns, the combs, the mirrors, the wreaths of silver and gold, that denoted her a lady of the first rank. Her late husband had endowed her too generously. The discovery of her jewels would undoubtedly lead these knights to conclude that she might reasonably be held to ransom for twice the amount with which she traveled.

But first they discovered the wine—her brother's best, a gift to sweeten the surprise, perhaps unwelcome, of her return to the land of her father's birth. Shouts of glee, recognizable in any language, punctuated the finding. Only then did alarm overcome Siri's curiosity. Men enflamed with the heat of wine were far more dangerous than the cold, calculating greed of knights simply bent on a little plunder. Nervously, she fingered the jeweled hilt of the slim dagger attached to her girdle. If they decided to seek more than ransom, they would find they had a hornet in their grasp.

The muttering of her guards at last provoked their captors into detaching several of their own number to surround them. Sensing Lucianna's distraction, Siri finally stole a peek from beneath the confines of her hood. She saw the dissatisfied posture of the French knights as they watched their comrades freely enjoying the bounty of the grape. Much good wine was drunk and spilled before their leader returned his band's attention to the more pressing business at hand. Siri marked him well. Though a dull, uncrested helmet concealed his face, the bold confidence of his commands confirmed his authority.

"Load it all back into the wagons. We will examine the spoils at the castle. We must be gone before Lord Fauke's devilish patrols begin."

"What about them?" One of their captors jerked his head towards the two women and their Italian guards.

The leader turned to weigh them with a steady gaze.

"Foreigners," he said, his derisive snarl muffled, like his voice, by the thick metal of his helm, "but apparently wealthy ones. One would have thought they would have guarded their treasures better."

He urged his mount across the space that separated him from his captives and pushed his horse between Siri and Lucianna, forcing them apart as he rode in an arrogant circle around the older woman. A dust-stained wimple concealed Lucianna's hair but revealed a set of handsome features, their smooth youthfulness belying the truth of her forty-odd years. Siri caught the sharp flash of Lucianna's eyes to hers and hastily ducked her head.

Her movement drew their captor's attention.

"And what have we here?"

He reached out a mailed hand and threw back the hood of Siri's cloak.

Siri was not surprised to hear his gasp. She had seen too many men stand stunned by her beauty. Their flattery she knew by heart: her glowing locks rivaled the liquid sheen of purest gold, her eyes dazzled like the sky on a midsummer's day, her cheeks bloomed with the blush of spring roses . . .

For all this and its accompanying effect she was prepared.

But she was *not* prepared for his companions' startled oaths, or the signs of the cross sketched hastily across mailed breasts.

"It's impossible!"

"But it is she!"

"My lord, it cannot be—"

"Silence!" their leader snapped, and Siri caught an impatient amber flash from behind the eye-slits of his helmet. "Of course it is not she. Look at me now, girl. State your name and origin."

Siri debated her answer. Some of his companions seemed to think they knew her, but she doubted that any of them could, unless they had passed through Venice, perhaps looking for transport to take them to the Holy Land. Her late husband had often aided such men, lending them money and arranging for ships for their voyage. But he had kept her hidden or veiled, fearful of her beauty's effect upon the intemperate crusading knights from the West.

"I am Donna Siriol de Calendri," she said at last, answering him in French as he had questioned her, "and I do not see why I should tell you

11

any more than that."

Again an amber gleam, this one amused. "Ah, but we have uncovered a spirited little minx. Come, girl, if we are to ransom you, we must know where lies your family. To whom do we send word of your capture?"

"There is no one," she said. "My parents and brother are dead and all I own in the world is in these wagons. Take what you will and let us go."

Her captor sounded skeptical. "Surely your family did not cast you alone upon the world? Nay, you did not leave your foreign land without a purpose. To whom do you go? Tell me—"

Just then one of his men, too far away to have been drawn into the surprise of her appearance, dropped one of the chests he had been loading back into the wagon. Out of it tumbled a bundle of vellum sheets, followed by several glass vials and a litter of brushes and pens. Siri watched in horror as he lurched drunkenly onto the sheets to reclaim one of the vials and hold it up to the light.

"Carissima, no!"

Lucianna grabbed for Siri's arm, but Siri evaded her and slid from her saddle. She ran, trembling with fury, and pushed the man away.

"You imbecile! You stupid, ignorant oaf!"

She was half the size of the robber-knight, but he nevertheless staggered back at her shove. She gathered up the sheets and tried in vain to brush away the stains from the figures painted there. Her eyes stung with tears at the desecration.

The man, apparently more intrigued with his discovery than offended by the shove, held the vial out to his master. "Look here, my lord. She's got it filled with sapphires!"

"That is paint, you fool, and don't you dare drop it. It is worth a fortune—"

"Carissima."

Lucianna's warning came too late. The leader rode to swoop the vial out of his comrade's hand and hold it up to the sun. The rich blue contents sparkled like jewels.

"A fortune, eh? For a vial of paint? And just who would pay to retrieve it unspilt?"

Siri could almost see the challenging cock of his eyebrow behind the iron helmet. She pursed her lips together in what she intended as disdainful defiance, but which she knew the bow-like cast of her mouth would translate into a pout. The man laughed, a bold, arrogant sound, and tucked the vial into his belt, then leaned down from his horse to take her chin between his fingers. The iron links that encased them were cold against her skin. The grip tightened painfully when she tried to pull away.

"Nay, carissima, you are in my power now. You will answer my questions, here or at my castle."

She met the amber gleam with scornful silence.

"Very well, then." He glanced at his men. "Is everything loaded?"

"Aye, my lord."

"Then my castle it will be."

His strong arm swept about her waist and lifted her off the ground. Siri had only seconds before she found herself planted before him on his horse, but in that space she moved like lightning. She twisted about in the same instant as she loosed her jeweled dagger. Her free hand flashed beneath his helmet to draw back the mail that shielded his chin. Before he could react, she pressed the point of her steel against his throat.

"You will put me back down," she said, her breath coming more rapidly than she liked, "and let my companions and me go, or I swear by my brother's grave, we will be the last innocents you will try to rob along this road." She imagined his sneering lips as his arm tightened about her waist. She thrust the point warningly up beneath his chin. "If you do not want your tongue pinned to the roof of your mouth—"

"Carissima," he murmured, "I think you have not the stomach for so grisly a task."

She nudged her blade higher and was gratified to see him roll his head back at the threat. "And I think you would be wise not to risk me proving you wrong. Now if you do not put me down and call your brigands off—"

"My lord," one of his men interrupted with a shout, "there are horsemen approaching!"

"Lord Fauke's men," cried another. "My lord, if we are

13

discovered—"

Her captor held her another moment, then slowly swung her to the ground. She thought she saw bemusement in the amber gleam that held her eyes for a weighing instant, but when he spoke, it was with the same swaggering arrogance he had used before.

"This round is yours, my lady. But the game is not over between us yet. We shall meet again."

He signaled to his men and they rode off into the trees, leaving Siri and her spoils standing in the road.

The fuming curses died in the flame-haired baron's throat as the full force of Siri's beauty seemed to strike him like a bolt of light. This was the sort of response to her appearance Siri was accustomed to, and she found it reassuring after the odd reaction of the robbers to her face. Their indications that they somehow knew her had been inexplicable for its impossibility.

"Bloody scoundrels," her rescuer muttered now. "They have been dogging these roads for months and when I catch them, I will skin their miserable hides from their backs. They did not injure you, I trust? Or any of your companions?"

With apparent difficulty he dragged his eyes from Siri and cast a glance at her traveling party, but almost immediately his bedazzled gaze returned to her face.

"My companions and I are unharmed," Siri said, "though I fear I cannot say as much for some of my belongings."

She glanced at the spoiled vellum sheets still lying in the road, but her impulse to turn her back on this gentleman and retrieve them was preempted by Lucianna's rebuking gaze. Siri hastily swept the man a curtsy. There could be no doubt from the quality and cut of his clothes that he was a gentleman of rank and wealth.

"Our thanks to you, sir. To whom do we owe our safety?"

The gentleman bowed and came up with a grin that set off a tiny warning in Siri's mind. There was a new gleam in his eyes as they raked the elegant curves set off by the tight bodice of her blue silk gown. Aye, this look she was too familiar with, and she drew the concealing folds of her mantle closer.

"I am Lord Fauke de Vaumâle, and I am pleased I could be of service to you. As I said, these brigands have been harrying hapless travelers for months. Duke Richard has charged me with their apprehension, but they are a wily, dishonorable lot, and so far they have eluded me." He paused with a darkling look. "When I catch them, there will be little enough of them left for the duke to exercise his justice on. I'll see to it their leader is naught but a bloody mass of—" He checked himself and his gaze again grew warm on Siri's face. "Forgive me, these matters are not for such delicate ears as yours. May I ask who it is I have had the pleasure of rescuing?"

"I am Siri de Calendri—"

"Donna Siriol," Lucianna corrected.

Lord Fauke looked perplexed. "Donna?"

"It means 'lady,'" Siri said with a rueful glance at her companion. "I gained the title through marriage, but my parents were not so nobly born."

"Ah." Lord Fauke looked disappointed. "Then you have a husband to whom you should no doubt be returned."

Siri hesitated, knowing the truth would bring that weighing desire back into his eyes, but she confessed, "My husband died two years ago in Venice, and my brother has but recently followed him to the grave. I have no other relatives, so my brother has placed me under the protection of a friend, one of your countrymen."

She stated the gentleman's name and the castle that was her destination.

Lord Fauke frowned. "Ah," he said again. "Then your brother chose ill. That 'friend' is in the duke's disgrace, and mine."

"You know him?"

"He is my own vassal—he and his neighbor, Sir Raynor de Molinet. The loyalties of both are suspect. Duke Richard is lord of Poitou and

Aquitaine, and those who think to turn it otherwise will find their heads on the block."

This fearsome threat dismayed her. Had her brother known this about his friend?

"I trust you are mistaken, my lord," she said. "I know little of these lands, save for rumors we encountered along the road. But I am certain my brother would not confide me to anyone of less than sterling honor."

Lord Fauke gave her a skeptical smile. "You are not like to find it in that gentleman. I would no doubt be doing you a service were I to ignore your brother's wishes and—"

Siri stopped him with a freezing gaze that had dampened, albeit never more than temporarily, more than one suitor overeager to sample her charms.

"I trust you will not do so, sir. I should be reluctant to have to call on my guards to defend me. They were some of the best swordsmen in Venice and had those robbers not taken us by such surprise, the brigands would no doubt be lying dead in the road even now."

The Italian guards had taken advantage of Siri's exchanges with Lord Fauke to retrieve their lost swords and awaited her command with their blades in their hands.

Lord Fauke gave an awkward cough and Siri noticed how the freckles on his face darkened when he flushed. "Now, now, naturally I will escort you wherever you wish to go. Pray," he added with a bow, "if I may help you to remount?"

"My vellum—" Siri began, glancing at the scattered sheets.

"My men will gather them up for you, never fret you, my lady. But it is growing late. We should be on our way."

Siri took note of the angle of the afternoon sun, but it was not until Lord Fauke signaled two of his men and she saw them respectfully gathering up her sheets that she allowed the red-haired baron to lift her back onto her horse.

Some hours later, Siri drew up her mount and stared dubiously at the rubble-filled ditch that encircled a razed stone wall that had formed an outer curtain to the soaring square castle beyond. A second wall nearer the keep, crenellated like giant gapped teeth against the sky and defended by four corner towers, rose smooth and untouched in the afternoon sun. A second moat surrounded it, this one filled with darkly roiling waters. Given the obvious threat of robbers in the nearby woods, Siri was not surprised to see that the twin-towered gatehouse beyond stood with drawbridge up and portcullis down.

Lord Fauke called out his name and immediately the bridge was let down and the gate opened. Clearly the guards had no inclination to challenge a man who was, as the baron had proudly informed Siri as they rode, a stalwart supporter and intimate of the king's son, Duke Richard. Lord Fauke told her that he had inherited wide lands in Poitou from a great-uncle who had died the past year. From a nearby stronghold, he regularly patrolled the forest roads in search of just such malcontents as had turned their bullying avarice on Siri's party today.

He and his men escorted Siri's party now into the castle's bailey. Siri had grown weary of Lord Fauke's bedazzled gaze as they rode. Hoping to forestall—at least for the time being—similar gazes from the occupants in the bailey, she once again drew her hood over her head.

The yard was filled with a miscellany of servants. A girl with long, brown braids carried a bucket across the yard while another shooed a flock of cackling geese toward a timber lean-to inside the wall. Several men stood near the stables conversing with one who looked as if he might be a blacksmith, while a large, friendly looking hound dashed from one member of the group to another, receiving here a pat of the hand, there some small treat from a tolerant knight or squire.

The dog came yapping across the yard to greet the newcomers. One of the men detached himself from the group and followed with a halting limp. Siri drew the edge of her hood over the lower half of her face and watched as the grey-haired retainer bowed low before Lord Fauke.

"My lord, we had no word of your coming. My master is not here just now, but you are mightily welcome to come inside and partake of some refreshment while you await his return."

"Nay, Sir Balduin," Lord Fauke replied, "I will not so trouble you. We came upon these poor travelers suffering an attack by the thieves of the forest. The ladies named this as their destination, and we thought it wise to guard them safely here."

Sir Balduin gave the ladies a rather blank look. "I beg your pardon. My master did not inform me that we would be having guests. We have no room prepared." He cast a worried glance at the wagons. "Will—Will your stay be long?"

Lucianna replied to his frankness with an ill-concealed condescension. "Indeed, *signore,* we come to stay. I regret that we were unable to send messengers ahead, but the letter will explain it all."

Sir Balduin looked astounded. "Come to stay? But—"

"Signore," Lucianna interrupted, "we have traveled many weeks to reach this land. Donna de Calendri needs to bathe and rest. Can you not find us some accommodation?"

Sir Balduin looked so flustered that Siri lowered the edge of her hood and offered him a sympathetic smile.

"Ah, saints!" He staggered back, so pale that Siri half feared he was about to faint. Other servants drew near at her unveiling, nudging and whispering, some making the gesture of the cross, while others fluttered less Christian signs. "It is impossible—"

"Come, man, pull yourself together," Sir Fauke snapped. "Have you never seen a beautiful woman before? Do as the wench says. Find them a corner to sit in while you make ready a room and send word to your master—"

"My master—" Sir Balduin gasped. "But he must not see this! Forgive me, my lady, but you cannot stay here."

"But we have nowhere else to go," Siri said. "Please, sir, the letter will explain all to your master. He knew my brother. They journeyed to the Holy Land together, prayed together before the Holy Sepulchre. I know he would not wish to deny my companions and me his simple hospitality."

"There, man, she's right," Lord Fauke said. "If there is a problem, leave it to your master to deal with. Now let these women inside—or must I escort them to Poitiers and explain your master's rudeness to the duke?"

Sir Balduin seemed alarmed by this threat, and Siri sensed it held a significance she did not understand. "It will not be necessary to trouble the duke with my master's affairs. My ladies, if you will come with me, you may wait in the hall until—well, until something can be arranged."

Siri did not give him a chance to change his mind, but slid out of the saddle and followed him into the keep.

~&~

She bided the waiting patiently, silently reassuring herself over and over that her brother would not have sent her on so lengthy and arduous a journey to this strange castle, had he not been confident of her welcome. Lucianna, seated beside her, concealed any anxiety of her own by grumbling on and on in Italian about Sir Balduin's incompetence and the dismaying prosaicness of their surroundings. Siri knew her companion missed the luxurious hall she had come to enjoy during her charge's marriage to Alessandro. Sumptuous to the point of excess, it had been to Siri little more than a splendid prison.

She fancied she could be quite content in this simpler hall. Only four colorful shields adorned its high, polished stone walls, arranged behind the empty dais, where they framed a long silk banner bearing the emblem of a gilded rose. The room itself was relatively small. The narrow, arched windows set with bars, cast a pattern of shadowed latticework across the rushes of the floor. Siri caught the scent of sweet woodruff beneath her feet, rising with a fresh fragrance very much like that of new-mown hay.

The scent grew stronger as she left her seat, her soft-booted steps crushing the petals to release the full potency of their perfume. She wanted to examine the stone hearth built into the wall near an exit that she guessed must lead to the kitchens. A cunning zigzag pattern had been etched into a reddish decorative stone that formed an arch about the fireplace, but on so warm a summer's day any flames had been dispensed with.

"Carissima, come. Such curiosity has no place in a lady."

"I am only a lady by marriage," Siri replied to Lucianna's rebuke. Too often her companion seemed to forget that fact. Her mother had been a merchant's daughter and her father a simple craftsman, though his skill had won him some wealth and his art had rivaled the best of the masters of Venice.

"Yet your father had some noble ties."

Lucianna's insistence sounded more wistful than confident. There had been whispers of an aristocratic birth, and it was widely known that her father's origins had lain in the far-off county of Poitou. But Walter Geraud had done his utmost to squelch the rumors and settle happily into his foreign home with his beautiful Italian wife. Walter the Poitevin, as he had been known to his patrons, had died without either of his children knowing how much of the gossip might be true. Her mother had followed him a year later, and then six months ago her brother . . .

Siri blinked back the tears of memory and returned to her seat beside Lucianna. With a darting, nervous glance at Siri's face, a servant brought in a tray of cheese and bread. Sir Balduin brought them some wine, but he did not linger long enough to converse, other than to reply—to Lucianna's query—that he could not guess the hour of his master's return.

The shadows of latticework had lengthened across the rushes and begun to fade when a deep, quiet voice caught Siri's ear. She turned her head to look at the man stepping through the arched entryway that had earlier admitted her and Lucianna to the hall.

"De Calendri? She says I knew her brother? I do not recall any such name."

He stood with head tilted, his tall frame leaning slightly down to listen to Sir Balduin. The hound Siri had seen in the bailey trotted at the man's heels. The man carried some sort of packet under his arm and an inkwell in one hand. At his shoulder stood a fair-haired youth, slenderly built, with a dreamy, distant expression. The youth's gaze flitted to Siri first with an absent curiosity, then focused into the same sort of disbelieving shock that she had witnessed twice before upon this day. He mouthed some word which Siri could not hear, but which caused the taller man's head to jerk up and around. The man did not seem to notice as Sir Balduin took the packet and inkwell, but stood so long unmoving, gazing on Siri's face, that Lucianna finally rose in obvious annoyance.

"Signore, I am Lucianna Fabio, and I have been charged to deliver to your care a most priceless jewel. Stand up, carissima. Pray, signore, allow me to present to you Donna Siriol de Calendri—"

Lucianna broke off as the man strode abruptly across the hall and caught Siri's chin in his hand. Siri gasped a little as he forced back her head. She saw the way the blood washed away behind his tan. She had an impression of strong, passionate features and a mass of coal-black curls, before she found herself engulfed in the swirling agony of his eyes. They embraced her like two deep, ebony pools, drawing her into an eddy of pain so poignant that she thought she must drown in its depths. From some great ringing distance, she heard him utter a name, not her own, but one spoken on a breath like a prayer.

"Clothilde."

And then the dark eyes closed and he lowered his lips to hers.

# Chapter 2

His mouth covered hers in a soft but urgent caress, and in his kiss was a need so great that Siri had not the power to deny him. Curiously, she found that she had no desire to try, but allowed her lips to warm in a wonderfully spontaneous response.

"Signore, please!"

Lucianna's sharp voice pierced whatever mad fancy had seized this man. He lifted his head with an unsteady breath.

"Clo—"

Siri was certain no one could hear the whispered name but she. She felt a queer twinge of regret that she must disillusion him.

"I am Siri," she said.

"Siri—?"

"Siriol de Calendri. You knew my brother, Simon Geraud."

For a moment his fingers lingered on her chin, his dark eyes clouded with a mist of confusion.

"Simon." He released her and stepped back a pace, then raised his hand to rub at his eyes. "Of course. You must forgive me. Your resemblance to—someone I knew—is remarkable."

Siri offered him a pardoning smile. "There is no harm done. I take it you are Sir Triston?"

He lowered his hand, but she caught again a glimpse of unfathomable pain before his gaze flicked away, as though whatever he saw in her was too hurtful to be endured.

"Aye. You say you are Simon's sister?"

She nodded. "Simon spoke of you often, with warmth. He said you suffered the long pilgrimage to Jerusalem together and that you had proven yourself a true friend."

"And he to me. Has he come with you to Poitou?"

"No." She held her voice as level as she could when remembering her loss. "He died six months past in Venice."

In the strong cut of Triston's profile, she thought she saw genuine regret. "I am sorry to hear it. I had hoped one day we would meet again."

"Simon hoped for that as well," she said. "Our parents both died when we were young and there was no one among our acquaintances whom my brother trusted enough to leave me in their care. And so he has sent me to you."

That won her a glance of surprise. "To me?"

"Simon said I was too pretty to be left alone in Venice. He said I would be safer in Father's country. Our father was Poitevin, but you were the only one Simon knew from Poitou. He said that I would be safe with you and that you would—But Lucianna has a letter that will explain everything."

She motioned to her companion. Lucianna drew a letter from her sleeve and handed it to Triston. He broke the wax seal and carried it over to the dimming light of one of the windows. The hound, which Sir Balduin had been holding by the collar, shook itself free and trotted after Triston. He reached out an absent hand to its head, but otherwise remained immersed in the letter.

Siri had never been privy to the actual contents and felt a stir of misgiving at the cloud of dismay that descended over Triston's face.

"Great heavens! Had your brother lost his mind?"

"What does it say?" Siri asked.

"He names me your guardian and charges me to arrange for you a marriage in keeping with your birth."

Siri felt her face go red. Her brother had spoken glowingly of his friend, Triston de Brielle. His staunch confidence in a man Siri had never met had eased her fear of being placed in the care of a stranger. But this matter of marriage had never been broached with her.

"If that's what he wrote, then apparently he had. I assure you, Sir Triston, I have no desire to marry again. I have skills, learned in my brother's workshop, by which I hope to find employment in some illuminator's shop, perhaps in Poitiers."

Lucianna's protest of this brought Triston's attention around to the older woman, giving Siri an opportunity to study his face in the fading light. He had the kind of wildly handsome looks that took one's breath away. She wondered if his ebony curls were as soft as they looked and if that firm line of his jaw bespoke as much stubbornness as strength. She had observed in his movements a kind of tightly harnessed power. He stood listening to Lucianna with an air of such quiet control that one might have thought the discipline came naturally to him, were it not for those passionate features. Siri sensed in the stormy beauty a latent heat, a turbulence of soul so keenly suffered and so determinedly buried, that it seemed inevitable that it must one day explode in frustrated fury to the grief of him who sought to deny its existence.

But Triston's quiet voice betrayed nothing of this silent struggle. "I remember Simon's skill with the pen," he said. "He used to draw the most fanciful creatures I had ever seen. His attempts to instruct me in the art by candlelight whiled away many a lonely night."

*Unbearably lonely,* Siri thought at the sad memory she read in Triston's face.

He turned abruptly to Sir Balduin. "Has a room been prepared for our guests?"

"Aye, sir," Sir Balduin said. "But we did not know where to bestow all their belongings. There are several barrels of wine, a scribe's desk with a high-backed chair, and a great many clothes."

"Take the wine to the cellars and the clothes to the chamber. As for the desk and chair—"

Siri spoke up. "I require a room with good morning light where I might practice my drawings."

"Of course. Sir Balduin, I think there is space in the east tower near the chapel where the Lady Siriol might ply her art. And if my ladies have not dined—"

"Then they will be staying, sir?"

Triston's eyes lingered carefully on Lucianna's face. "Simon Geraud made himself my friend on a day as dark as any I had then known. I will not dishonor that kindness now by betraying his last charge to me." He glanced again at Sir Balduin. "If you will see them to their room?"

For the first time the blond youth who had accompanied Triston spoke up. "I will do it."

Siri had nearly forgotten his presence. She saw now that he was older than she had first thought, nineteen or twenty at least, with pink-white skin that bespoke a dislike of outdoor activity, and shoulder-length hair so flaxen as to appear almost white. He started across the hall with an eagerness that contrasted sharply with Triston's studied restraint.

Triston caught him by the shoulder and crushed his enthusiasm with a curt, "No, Acelet. Take these things to my room."

Triston took the packet and inkwell from Sir Balduin with a movement that hinted of a hard-disciplined impatience and thrust them into the young man's hands.

Acelet's gaze fixed as hungrily on Siri as Triston's had formerly been tortured. "But Triston, can't you see—?"

"Acelet." Triston spoke quietly, but with implacable authority. "Go."

He gave the young man an unequivocal push towards the stairs. The force of it sent Acelet stumbling obediently out of the hall, but not before he had turned around three times to stare at Siri.

"Forgive him," Triston said with a rueful twitch of his lips. "He is my aunt's son and is the despair of us all. I have yet to find a way to bring his head out of the clouds long enough to instill in him the understanding that he must work if he is to win his desire for knighthood." His gaze flicked at Siri, as if testing the mastery of his own emotions, and finding it yet wanting, flicked away again. "Sir Balduin, our guests must be tired. Show them to their chamber, allow them to wash away the dust of their journey, and when they have rested, we will dine."

"Very good, sir. My ladies, if you will come with me?"

Siri cast a final glance at Triston, framed in the dimming light of the window where he scanned again her brother's letter. The hound nuzzled his hand, received another absent pat, then lay down at his master's feet. Even in the midst of that companionable scene, Triston's posture bespoke such loneliness that it almost made Siri's heart ache. Lucianna tugged at her sleeve. She turned reluctantly from her musings and followed Sir Balduin up the expanse of wide stone steps that wound away from the hall.

⚬

Siri luxuriated in the steaming bath. Days of dust and exhaustion floated away as Lucianna sponged her back, while a serving girl removed the luscious gowns from Siri's trunks and carried them to the painted wardrobe against one wall.

Siri brought her fingers again to her lips, marveling at the way they still tingled. She did not know what to make of her new guardian. His tortured eyes and tempestuous features contrasted bewilderingly with the quiet restraint of his voice and the disciplined control of his movements.

But his kiss she had thoroughly enjoyed.

"What do you think of him, Lucianna?"

"I think the man is mad, *si,* and dangerous." Lucianna splashed the sponge in the water. "Clasping you to his breast the moment he set eyes upon you! Have a care, Donna Siri. Remember that wicked apprentice who tried to ravish you in your chamber while your brother lay sick of a mortal illness."

Siri shivered. Her screams had brought Simon staggering from his sickbed to turn the lewd apprentice out into the night. The next morning, Simon had drawn up his will. No longer trusting even his own servants, her brother stated that in the event of his death, his highly profitable illuminating workshop was to be sold and with its proceeds his sister was to leave Venice, escorted by a company of knights selected by the shrewd Lucianna. Once in Poitou, he had no doubt his good friend Sir Triston would agree to stand her guardian.

The apprentice had not been the first to lust after her. Siri's beauty had bewitched men from the day she turned thirteen. She had stood at the heart of dozens of quarrels by hot-blooded youths hoping to win no more than a smile from her. Dignified craftsmen subjected her to the most foolish speeches, while noblemen showered her with trinkets and gold hoping to seduce her into becoming their mistress. She supposed it was no wonder that her husband, otherwise a kindhearted man, kept her veiled or shut away for much of their five-year marriage.

She scooped up a handful of water and watched it trickle through her fingers. She had been kissed innumerable times, both before and after her marriage, whenever some overheated "friend" of Simon's or Alessandro's had been able to back her into a shadowed corner. She was almost as deft at dealing out slaps as she was at drawing the saints. But for the first time in memory, her hand had not itched when she had seen Triston lowering his head towards hers.

"Who do you suppose he thought I was?"

"Carissima?"

"I don't think he was kissing me at all. I mean, not in his mind. He called me Clothilde."

"I tell you the man is *pazzo*. Mad." Lucianna tapped a finger to her head. She had cast off her dusty wimple and her rich auburn hair, winged with silver at the temples, framed her haughty face in thick, heavy waves. A companion of Siri's mother since childhood, Lucianna had accepted her brother's invitation to chaperone Siri after their mother died.

Siri stared down at her own lengthy tendrils, swirling like dark tentacles in the water. "I do not think he is pazzo at all, but he looked very sad. I think he must have been very much in love and that someone hurt him deeply."

But once Lucianna formed an opinion, she clung to it tenaciously. "I do not care what your brother said, I do not trust this *Signor* Triston. The sooner you are married and away from here, the better it will be for us all."

"But Lucianna, I do not want to marry again."

"Si, I know, you have some silly notion that you can live here as you did in your brother's house. He should never have permitted you to take up pen and brush. A donna such as you was never meant to labor for her bread. Your husband would not have been pleased at what you did after he died. He adored you, carissima."

Siri sighed. Yes, Alessandro *had* adored her. He had been smitten with her from the day he had walked into her brother's workshop with a commission for an illuminated Psalter and seen her gilding a fanciful page of mythical beasts. She and Simon quarreled over the rich nobleman before Simon left on pilgrimage. Her brother had been shocked on his return to find that she had defied his orders and married the old man. He had not believed her insistence that Alessandro, having outlived three wives and with a dozen grown children, looked on her as a daughter rather than a would-be lover. Marriage, she said, had been the only way for Alessandro to protect her from men, including her own servants, less honorable than he.

But Simon had refused to listen. He called it an abomination, an execrable waste of her beauty and youth. For a time, her softhearted brother refused even to speak to her. He would not believe her insistence that, although Alessandro doted upon her as he did over all his expensive trinkets, he had never touched her in the way of a man with his wife. Finally, after enduring months of Siri's unhappiness, Alessandro had confronted Simon himself. Their meeting had taken place in private, but whatever Alessandro said had finally convinced Simon they were both telling the truth, and reconciled him at last to his sister.

During their marriage, Alessandro bought her a richly furnished house in Venice and lavished her with jewels and gowns. But she had chosen to pack away her wealth at his death and return to her brother's workshop, rejoicing once more in an affection as fond and indulgent as any her husband had showered on her.

"Thank you, that is enough." Siri waved away the servant before she could pour more water into the tub. "I am ready to dress."

The servant dried her off with a fresh linen cloth, then Lucianna rubbed Siri's body with an oil pressed from the petals of violets grown in Alessandro's garden. Lucianna had gathered as many vials of oil and perfume as she could before Siri had closed the house for good on the day they had left for Poitou.

"Shall you be wishing to bathe as well, milady?"

Siri watched the way Lucianna puffed with pleasure at the servant's query. No one had ever called her "lady" in Venice.

"Do, Lucianna," Siri urged. She used a corner of the linen cloth she had wrapped herself in to rub briskly at her wet scalp. "I will sit by the fire and dry my hair while I wait for you."

Lucianna acquiesced and allowed the servant to fetch fresh water for the tub. Once Lucianna was settled, the servant replaced Siri's linen wrap with a chemise of sheerest lawn. Siri then had the girl bring a pillow from the bed. She used it as a barrier between herself and the hot stones of the floor as she arranged herself in front of the fireplace.

"May I comb your hair for you, milady?" the servant asked.

"Yes, please . . . what is your name?"

"Audiart, milady."

Siri guessed the dark-haired girl to be a little younger than her own four and twenty years. "Yes, thank you, Audiart."

Audiart had found Siri's comb along with the chemise in one of her trunks, its ivory rim carved and painted with leaves and roses. She knelt beside Siri and employed the tool with practiced skill to ease away the tangles and knots from her streaming tresses.

"It is passing strange," Audiart whispered. "Even your hair is like hers."

"Whose?" Siri asked.

"The Lady Clothilde's. Sir Triston's wife."

"Wife?" Siri twisted her head about on the word, inadvertently causing a yank on her hair that made her eyes water.

"Forgive me, milady." Whether Audiart apologized for the surprise or the pain, Siri was not sure. "I should have said, his late wife. She died a year ago, almost to this very day."

"And she resembled me?" There could be no other explanation for Triston's reaction.

"Indeed, milady, 'tis more than a resemblance. Had I not seen her poor body laid out myself, I would think you were she in very deed."

"That is ridiculous," Lucianna snapped from the bath. "People do not have a double, unless of course they are twins, which Siri is not. It is merely because the light is so poor. When you see her in the daylight, you will see how foolish you all have been."

Siri remembered Sir Balduin's greeting in the bailey. There had been plenty of light then, and the mere sight of her had caused him to stagger back in alarm. He must have thought he had seen a ghost.

"Pray fetch me my mirror," she said. "It is under some linen in the same trunk where you found my comb."

Audiart obeyed. An ivory frame encircled the glass, the back painted with the same flurry of leaves and roses as decorated the comb. In the center, nestled inside a painted heart, Siri's name glittered in gilded letters. A gift from Alessandro on a day when she had been particularly chafing at her restraints, and a prohibitively expensive one for anyone of less wealth than he.

Siri concentrated on her reflection. It seemed very commonplace to her. Her eyes appeared almost as dark as Triston's in the muted light, naught but the barest ring of vivid blue showing around the dilated pupils. She could see nothing remarkable about her nose that should send men into transports, nor understand why her small, full lips should tempt men into the most disconcerting assaults upon them.

"Did men strut like idiots after her as well?"

Audiart giggled. "Indeed they did, milady. I remember the days before she married Sir Fulbert—her first husband—how men would come to Pennault Castle to try to win her regard. Half of them were too tongue-tied to speak, the others oozed with eloquence, and all of them bore the most wondrous gifts to try and win her heart."

"She was married before?"

"Aye, but—" the merriment left Audiart's voice— "he was much older than she and—they were not very happy." She made as if to rise. "Perhaps I should not be speaking of this."

"No, please." Siri caught Audiart's arm. "Tell me more about her."

Audiart hesitated, then brushed her fingers against a flowing strand of Siri's hair. "Her hair was just like this, soft and smooth as silk, and this same bright color. Like the gold on the altar of Saint Hilary's when the sunlight catches it and makes it glitter like something alive."

"How did the Lady Clothilde come to marry Sir Triston?"

"The Laurants and de Brielles have been neighbors for generations. Sir Triston was always in love with her—one saw that in him even as a boy. But Vere Castle is all he owns and Sir Fulbert was a wealthy, powerful man. But Sir Fulbert must have been dreadfully cruel to her, because afterwards she—"

"She what?" Siri prompted as Audiart stopped.

The servant looked suddenly frightened. "Please, milady, I should say no more."

"Why? Has Sir Triston forbidden you to speak of her?" Perhaps he grieved for her so deeply that he could not bear to hear her name.

"No, milady, but—'tis not my place. Please, if you wish to know more, you must ask the master."

She rose before Siri could stop her, and Lucianna began such a tedious rebuke of her charge's curiosity that Siri let the matter go.

# Chapter 3

$A$t least Siri better understood the meaning of Triston's pained glance as she entered the hall to dine. He looked quickly away, but Sir Balduin and Acelet seemed unable to drag their eyes from her. She hoped it was more than merely her resemblance to the Lady Clothilde that riveted them. Her extravagant green silk gown with its gay floral pattern woven in gold, and her blue silk mantle adorned from shoulder to hem with an infinity of silver half-moons, had been the height of fashion on Venice. She had caught up her hair in a crespine of gold net with tiny rubies glistening amid the mesh. Only reluctantly, at Lucianna's insistence, had she attached to her girdle her jewel-hilted dagger. Lucianna would not credit that Siri could bear more than a passing likeness to Triston's late wife, and her suspicions of their host's intentions were strong after what she called Triston's "lascivious greeting."

Triston welcomed them both courteously, but Siri noticed that he carefully avoided looking her in the face as he took her hand and escorted her to the table that had been set up on the dais. A tremor, bewilderingly similar to the pleasure she'd felt when his lips had lingered on hers, washed through her again at the quiet strength of his clasp. The pleasure vanished too soon as he seated her beside him at the table and withdrew his hand.

*What foolishness,* she chided herself. She was merely overtired from their journey. She had been courted by many handsome men, and had not felt her heart tempted by even the most dashing. Not that Triston appeared to have any interest in courting her. His stiff posture exuded naught but discomfort at being forced to sit by her side.

Why that fact should ruffle her, she did not care to examine. She sought instead to distract herself with a survey of the table. When she had lived with Alessandro, they had always dined on gold or silver plates. In her brother's house, they had used wood. But here she saw thick slices of dry bread, cut into large squares and set out on a clean white tablecloth as trenchers.

Other than Acelet and Sir Balduin, they were joined only by Triston's chaplain and her Italian guards, who would be dismissed on the morrow.

"The rest of my household dined before noon," Triston explained. "I hope these few dishes will meet with your satisfaction."

Siri allowed him to place on her trencher a slice of roast salmon in an onion sauce, some broiled chicken with a spiced mince relish, some lentil crisps, and a spoonful of delicate gillyflower pudding. Siri, fond of sweets, discovered that the latter had been made with a generous measure of cinnamon. She ignored Lucianna's rebuking gaze and consumed three generous servings.

"Sir Balduin informs me that you met with some unpleasantness along the road," Triston said, casting a sidelong glance at her hand as it plunged the spoon yet again into the pudding.

Lucianna whispered fiercely in Italian, and Siri reluctantly took the spoon out again.

"Some armored knights tried to rob us," she replied, sliding the spoon's cup in and out of her mouth to lick away the last traces of the pudding. "But Lord Fauke interrupted them and guarded us the rest of the way here."

"You were not harmed?"

"Oh, no. They thought to hold us for ransom when they saw all my jewels and gowns, and they were very pleased to find the wine, but they had not time to do more than spill a little of it before Lord Fauke arrived."

She nibbled on a lentil crisp. The crunchy, delicate crust held a cheese mixture stuffed full of raisins, almonds, and dates.

"Did they wear a crest?"

"The robbers? No. I looked and looked, but I could see nothing by which I would know them again." She wondered if she should mention that they had appeared to recognize her resemblance to the Lady Clothilde, which must mean they had known Triston's wife, but Triston preempted her.

"They have been harrying the roads for the last three months. Duke Richard has charged Lord Fauke with their apprehension and has placed a price on their heads—one hundred gold coins for their leader. If you wish to ride out from the castle, you must tell Sir Balduin, and he will arrange for someone to escort you from the garrison."

"I will remember," she promised. "We owe a debt to Lord Fauke for rescuing us. I understand you are his vassal?"

Triston's face darkened, but after a brooding moment, he said only, "Aye."

Sir Balduin volunteered from where he sat beside Lucianna, "Lord Fauke is of Aquitanian birth, a longtime companion of Duke Richard. He became heir to Lord Roger, his great-uncle, when both of Lord Roger's sons died. Fauke made a brief tour of his future Poitevin lands eight years ago, but spent most of his time then lingering at Belle Noir Castle. As soon as he could, he returned to Duke Richard's court, until Lord Roger died last fall."

Aquitanian birth. Eight years ago. That, Siri thought, must explain why the baron had not reacted to her face like all the others. His "brief tour" of his future lands must have taken place before Triston married Clothilde.

Having finished off the sweets, Siri sampled next the broiled chicken. But their journey had been long and tiring, and with the bracing effects of the bath worn off, she felt her eyelids drooping. Even through her exhaustion, she continued to sense Triston's stiffness from where he sat beside her. She guessed that had etiquette allowed it, he would have arranged for Lucianna to sit between them.

His sober brown tunic contrasted starkly with her elaborate gaiety, but she noted that the cloth was of good quality and the cut set his broad shoulders to advantage. It flitted into her mind that the shoulder nearest her might be very pleasant to rest her sleepy head upon.

She actually felt her head drifting towards it before she jerked herself up with a blush. Thank goodness he was not looking at her now!

His tight sleeve revealed a ripple of muscles as he reached for a silver flagon with a finial in the shape of a five-petaled rose. Perhaps some wine would revive her. She waited for him to fill his goblet, then held out her cup.

"May I have some, please?"

He hesitated, then signaled a servant, who brought forward an elaborately etched pitcher.

She frowned and placed a hand over her cup before the servant could fill it. "What are you having?"

"Something far less pleasing than what Guy is waiting to serve you. Acelet has tasted your brother's wine and assures me that it is far superior to anything I have in my cellars." He motioned again to the servant, but Siri continued to block her cup with her hand.

"But you are not drinking it."

"No."

"Why? Simon sold all his other barrels, but the Vernaccia from Tuscany he kept especially for you. He said he had taken several bottles on his pilgrimage, and that he had shared them with you and that you had grown particularly fond of the wine and—"

Triston glanced at her now, just a glance, but the rest of her statement shriveled in the flash of his eyes.

"I no longer drink wine, my lady." His voice was quiet, composed, as though her words had not touched the delicate spot she knew they had.

She wanted to ask him what he drank instead, but Lucianna's toe tapping against her ankle warned to keep quiet. She let the servant fill her cup with her brother's red wine.

Several awkward moments of silence passed until Acelet broke it. "We shall have to make some changes, Triston. Lady Siriol will not be wishing to dine in gloomy silence like this every day. You should hire a troubadour to entertain us all. I heard one on the road to the village yesterday, singing the songs of Duke William, the queen's grandfather."

Acelet launched into a melodic recitation, singing the words in a clear, true voice.

Triston interrupted him before he could begin the chorus. "Duke William may have been called 'the Troubadour,' but he was also a knight of formidable ability. If you wish to emulate his ways, you might begin by devoting a little less time to your romances and a little more to your sword practice."

Acelet flushed at the rebuke.

Siri said with a smile, "A little music must always be welcome. Why, Sir Triston, Simon said you used to boast that Poitou was the very birth-seat of poetry. Many of the tales I have heard chanted and sung at both abbey and inn along our way here have credited their origin to the courts of your queen Eleanor."

Her remark appeared to revive Acelet's spirits. "My mother was a young girl at her court in Poitiers. She sat in some of the Courts of Love and heard the Countess of Champagne deliver her verdicts on matters of fealty between men and women. Of course, those days ended when King Henry imprisoned the queen in England."

"She is not in prison," Triston said. "She lives quite comfortably at Winchester Castle."

"Which she is never allowed to leave. Would you not call that a prison, my lady?"

"Indeed, I would," Siri said, thinking of her own comfortable confinement as Alessandro's wife.

Triston looked impatient. He exchanged a glance with Sir Balduin, though he addressed his words to Siri. "King Henry has restrained the queen with good reason. Not long past, she stirred up their sons to rebellion against their sire and sent them off to start a war which resulted in a good deal of misery for us all before the king crushed it with his usual efficiency. He has placed the queen where she can do no more harm and, with her seditious influence out of the way, has managed to re-establish peace with his sons."

"Peace!" Acelet exclaimed. "You call the terrors Duke Richard has inflicted on us 'peace'?"

"Take care how you speak of him, Acelet. He is governor of these lands and is my liege lord."

"He has razed our castles, burned our towns, dishonored our women. It is shameful to serve such a man. If the Young King were our liege, things would be very different."

Triston's chair scraped harshly as he pushed himself to his feet. For a moment, Siri thought he was going to shout something at Acelet. Then she watched him master the anger with that same unyielding discipline she had recognized in him at their first meeting.

"So long as you are under my roof, Acelet," he said very quietly, "your allegiance is to the duke. You will not speak of the Young King again." He turned and bowed to Siri. "If you will excuse me, my lady, I have some matters that I must attend to. Sir Balduin, see to our guests "

Siri stared after him as he strode from the hall. After a moment, the chaplain rose and followed him out.

Sir Balduin leaned across Lucianna. "You must excuse Sir Triston, my lady. He is walking a thin line just now between King Henry and his son, Duke Richard. Triston's sympathies have always lain with the king, who seeks to extend the peace he has established through law in England to the unruly barons of our land. But Richard's attempts to enforce his father's will have sometimes been high-handed."

"High-handed?" Acelet snorted. "He lets his mercenaries pillage the land when he is not employing them to level some poor knight's castle."

"Some blatant rebel's castle," Sir Balduin rebuked him. "Triston is loyal to the duke, but he is not blind to Richard's arrogance and has no stomach for his cruelty." He shifted his gaze between Siri and Lucianna. "Triston sided with those barons who advised the duke against the siege of Pons. In truth, he questioned only the wisdom of beginning so difficult an assault just before Christmas when the ground lay heavy with snow, making it nearly impossible to replenish our supplies, while the fortress we besieged sat secure with its winter's store. Those who opposed the assault proved to be right, but Duke Richard has ever since suspected our loyalty."

Siri, comfortably sated on the sweets and broiled chicken, leaned back in her chair and sipped her brother's wine.

"Pons did not fall?" she asked. Lord Fauke had said Sir Triston was in the duke's disgrace. Was his counsel against this siege the reason?

"Nay," Sir Balduin said. "The duke was finally forced to go after other game. He marched to Taillebourg the Impregnable and took it with terrible cunning. Triston and I both fought with his forces that day." Sir Balduin patted his right leg. "At the struggle for the gate, I suffered a blow that shattered my hip and has left me with this painful limp. I would surely have died like so many others, had Triston not stood over me, defending me with his sword. We forced our way into the town, but the savagery with which the duke loosed his forces to sack and burn it, the viciousness of his revenge upon the defenders of the castle . . ."

Sir Balduin looked like a battle-weathered soldier, but he shuddered at the memory.

"Triston stayed until the bloody end, but he refused to go any further with the duke. Duke Richard has not forgotten the desertion, though Triston's open rejection of the rebels' cause has so far protected him, and us, from royal retaliation."

Disturbed at the images of violence roused by Sir Balduin's tale, Siri sat up and placed her wine aside.

Acelet said, "The duke claims he is Poitevin. He quotes Poitevin poetry and sings Poitevin songs, but he treats our barons like slaves. Now if the Young King were our lord—"

"The Young King," Siri interrupted. "That is King Henry's eldest son and heir?"

"Aye," Sir Balduin said, "named Henry like his father. The king crowned him as co-regent when the lad was only fifteen. Three years ago, the king sent him to help his brother, Duke Richard, pacify the rebels, but he grew bored and when the spring tournaments began in Flanders, he was off for a season of jousting. He enticed a number of Poitevin youths to follow him, among them Sir Triston's young brother, Etienne."

Acelet said passionately, "He is a most worthy prince. Generous, courteous, gracious, the soul of liberality—"

Sir Balduin snorted. "Shallow, vain, and improvident is more like it. Heaven help us all if he should become our lord!"

"He said he would come back if we wanted him," Acelet insisted. "And if Richard does not begin to show us some respect, he may find the rebellion taking on a fraternal edge."

"Hold your tongue. If your cousin hears you speaking so—"

"I don't care what Triston says. He is a coward and a bully and—"

"A coward is he? 'Twas no coward's sword which defended an old man at Taillebourg."

Acelet's blue eyes sparkled with scorn. "He hates Duke Richard and he is afraid to say it. I call that a coward. And he has not even the courage to look at the Lady Siriol because she looks like Clothilde and he is ashamed that he shed not a tear when she died."

"Now that is enough."

Sir Balduin's voice came sharper than even Triston's had. He stared down the young man's angry challenge until Acelet's gaze dropped sulkily to his trencher.

"You must forgive the boy, my lady. He prides himself on his pretty manners, but he has too many romantic notions in his head. Although I fear—" Sir Balduin hesitated with a troubled look "—he is right about the Lady Clothilde. Your resemblance to her is nothing short of extraordinary. You must be patient with my master, my lady. He loved his wife very much, and having you here is bound to be difficult for him."

"I understand," Siri said, although she was not at all sure that she did. She smothered a yawn behind her hand, then turned to her companion. "Lucianna, if you are finished, perhaps we should be going to bed. We have had a very long journey."

"Will you be requiring anything before you retire?" Sir Balduin asked.

"Thank you, no. We—"

She broke off as Acelet sprang up and dashed with unseemly haste to pull out her chair for her to rise. "May I escort you to your chamber, my lady?"

She smiled at him. "Thank you, but Lucianna and I remember the way."

She held out a hand to Sir Balduin. "Pray thank Sir Triston for the meal and tell him I hope I will see him again in the morning. Good night."

Acelet seized Siri's hand before Sir Balduin could respond and placed on it a kiss. "Good night, Lady Siriol."

It was a very courtly gesture, but a sudden shyness in his smile offset his gallantry. Siri bade him good night, then took Lucianna's arm and led her companion out of the hall.

⟨⟩

Exhausted, Siri fell asleep almost as soon as her head touched her pillow. Tangled dreams of battling knights, blazing buildings, and shrieking victims blurred her fatigued visions. An uncoifed knight with tumbled black curls, sliced his way through the enemy to reach someone lost in the crowd. She could not see his face, though he appeared repeatedly in her dreams of the night, always fighting, always struggling, always seeking . . . she never knew quite what. Her heart pounded oddly, not with horror or fear of the battle, but with an intense longing that the one the uncoifed knight fought for might be she.

How long she slept before the screams awakened her, she did not know. Her eyes flew wide, and she lay confused for a moment as to whether or not she still dreamed. The fire in the hearth had turned to embers. For several minutes, she could not remember where she was. The bed felt strange and Lucianna was beside her, although the cries had aroused her too. Then the memories flooded back. Vere Castle . . . Sir Triston . . .

The last shreds of slumber vanished as Siri slipped from the bed. "What do you think it is?"

She pulled her chemise over her head and ran to the door to open it.

"Siri, come back. It is no business of yours."

"But someone is in distress." She listened again. The screams were shrill, like a woman's yet different, and she now heard in them the quiver of a sob. "A child," she said suddenly. "It is a child, and it is terrified."

"Siri, come back!"

But Siri flew out the door in her bare feet.

# Chapter 4

Triston awoke in a cold sweat, the shout of horror still vibrating in his throat. He was sitting up in bed, hands outstretched as if somehow he could reach her, stop her, draw her back before she was gone forever . . .

Isobel . . . Clothilde . . .

He shuddered and covered his ears, trying to block out the screams.

"Forgive me," he whispered. "Clo, forgive me."

The screams lowered and thickened, then sank to hysterical sobs. Triston pushed the heavy curls from his dampened forehead. A deep breath, and then another. Not Clo's screams. Perrin's. Another nightmare.

Triston swung himself out of the bed and tugged on the clothes he had tossed off a few hours before. Breeches, hose, loose linen shirt—there was not time for more. He moved in swift silence, following the childish cries to the room at the end of the passageway. Already they had begun to quiet, dissolving into gulping sobs. He hesitated before entering the open doorway.

"Mamma, Mamma!" the child wept.

"Hush, now, don't be afraid," a sweet voice soothed. "It was only a dream. You are safe now. Hush, child, hush."

He knew the voice, yet he did not. Young and clear as spring water, it held a timbre both familiar and strange. He stepped inside and experienced a shock. A woman sat on the floor, her golden curls tumbled about her shoulders in exquisite disarray, the skirts of her lawn chemise spread out around her, while the child buried his head and wept into her lap.

"There, now, there." She stroked his dark curls. "You will make yourself sick if you do not stop. There is naught to be afraid of now."

The child lifted his head and Triston saw the small hand tremble as it reached to touch the woman's golden mane. "Mamma, I thought you were gone. I thought he hurt you. I thought I would never see you again."

*Nor I,* Triston thought. His jaw tightened and he covered his eyes with an unsteady hand. He must not be carried away by the child's vision. In the darkness of the room, illusions were too easily succumbed to.

"Shh. Lie down and close your eyes. I will hold you until you go back to sleep."

"You promise?"

"I promise."

"And you will be here when I wake up?"

Triston held his breath.

"You mustn't worry about tomorrow. Just lay your head down here—" she pulled him back into her lap— "and think the sweetest thoughts you can."

The child's protests dissolved as she sang a low lullaby. The words were intriguingly familiar to the French that Triston spoke—*dolce, carissima, bello, amore*—yet of such different accent that he could not be sure he knew them. The child gave a hiccupping sigh and snuggled down into the woman's billowing skirts.

She sang one lullaby after another, stroking the boy's curly head. At last, apparently convinced that he had fallen asleep, she raised her head and stared straight at Triston.

"I do not think I can lift him back into the bed," she said quietly.

Triston hesitated, then moved to lift the child out of her arms. The sturdy boy of daylight hours now felt small and fragile, his curly head rolled against Triston's breast. A reflexive tightening of his arms caused the boy to stir and murmur. Triston forced himself to relax his hold. If the boy awoke, this rare, sweet moment would be lost. Siri had already crossed the room to smooth the sheets and plump the boy's pillows. Triston followed her and reluctantly surrendered his burden to the bed.

"Is he your son?" she asked, observing the caressing brush of his fingers against the boy's cheek.

"Aye," he said softly. "Perrin. Seven years old last autumn."

He gazed down at the sleeping boy. Time was, it was he who had held his son, he who had sung, not tender lullabies, but hardy ballads of knights and battles and courage and love that had set his son's eyes aglow and chased away any but the brightest, happiest dreams. Before Clothilde died.

Before Perrin had become afraid.

"Thank you for coming to him," Triston murmured.

"He is a beautiful child."

"His mother was beautiful."

She stood so near that he could feel the warmth of her body, smell the fresh, clean scent of violets on her skin. Clo's scent. Clo's hair, Clo's face . . .

Even before he turned towards her, he knew he was making a mistake. If once he looked into her eyes . . .

He tried to look somewhere else instead. At her small, white hands, so easily and wonderfully lost in his large, brown palms. At the smooth curve of her arms, softer than the silk of the clinging blue gown she had worn that day he had loved her in the woods. At the riot of gold hair and the soft, quivering chin and the bow of her honey-sweet lips—

He did not realize he was caressing each one of these features until he had to move his fingers to kiss her. It seemed the natural thing to do. He always kissed his wife after she or he had sung their son to sleep.

But it did not take five seconds to realize that this was not his wife. This mouth did not yield to his with soft passivity, but sprang to life beneath his own, firm and strong and eager. He pulled away, startled not only by the energy of her response but by the thrill that ran though his veins.

"Forgive me, Lady Siriol. That was—unpardonable."

Her hands on his waist burned through the thin fabric of his shirt, and the smile she gave him almost swept his senses away.

"Don't apologize. You looked as if you needed the comfort."

Dismayed by a rush not of comfort, but desire, he pushed her away from him, then felt a quick pang of alarm when she stumbled and fell across the bed.

"Did I hurt you?" he asked sharply.

She sat up and shook her head. Her voice lowered but remained steady. "I'm sorry. I'm afraid I was—overbold."

"Nay, the fault was mine. I—"

He stopped as Perrin rolled over and opened his eyes. "Mamma?"

Triston stepped back into the shadows and watched as Siri bent over to reassure him. "I'm still here. Go back to sleep, Perrin."

The boy gave a sleepy nod and turned over.

"You must forgive us both," Triston murmured, resisting the impulse to approach the bed again. "I'm afraid in the dark, he—and I—became confused."

"I know," Siri murmured. "No sooner had I stepped into the room than he flew into my arms, calling me 'Mamma.' I'm sorry if my presence here is going to upset him."

"In the daylight he will be able to recognize his mistake." Siri said nothing, and after a moment he told her, "Don't feel that you must continue to sit with him. I can send for one of the servants—"

"I don't mind," she said. "I would like to stay a few more minutes."

"As you please. Then I will offer my thanks and apologies again, and bid you good night, Lady Siriol."

"Good night, Sir Triston."

He left her with her golden mane fallen forward over her face like a veil.

❧

Triston tried to look attentive as he sat in the hall, listening to Sir Balduin run down the list of matters to be dealt with at the next manor court. He had thought to divert himself for a few hours this morning by immersing himself in matters of estate, but his thoughts perversely continued to betray him. After he had left the Lady Siriol sitting with his son, he had spent the remainder of the night pacing his bedchamber. Even had she not borne such a disturbing resemblance to Clothilde, her brother's will was insane. There could not be more than four years

44

difference between his and the Lady Siriol's ages. And where on earth he was supposed to find her a husband . . .

". . . and the de Molinets are renewing their claim to the pasture land on the east side of the forest."

That brought Triston's attention around to Sir Balduin with a snap. "The devil they are. Sir Drogo and I settled that matter three years ago."

"Sir Raynor is challenging it. He says as joint heir, he should have been consulted."

"Then he should have been here, not off frittering away his inheritance in Flanders with the Young King."

Triston's irritation carried a smoldering edge. Now that his brother, Sir Drogo, was dead, Raynor had come home to assume control of the inheritance. Triston had no doubt that Raynor was bent on stirring up trouble wherever he could. He still held a grudge against Triston for Isobel, while the memory of Raynor and Clothilde—

Triston nearly choked on the bitter image. Determinedly, he thrust the memory away.

"That land lies on our side of the river," he said, "and I have the documents to prove that it was purchased back at full price. If Raynor complains, show him the rolls."

"He says his brother was tricked. He is threatening to take the case before Lord Fauke."

"Let him," Triston snapped. "The record will bear us out." He and Raynor each held their respective lands from Fauke de Vaumâle, and both were subject to judgment from his seignuerial court. Triston rose and paced across the dais and back before swallowing his anger. "Is there any other business I need to attend to? Have you seen our guests this morning?"

"Lady Siriol is setting up her workshop in the east tower. I found some space near the chapel, as you suggested. The room is small, but the light in the mornings is excellent, and she said it would be satisfactory."

"Thank you, Sir Balduin. That will be all for now."

Sir Balduin rose with a bow, gathered up the rolls he had brought for his master's review, and limped out of the hall.

Triston continued to stand for several minutes beside the table, battling his reluctance to go and speak to his new ward. Surely now in the morning light, the likeness would not be so strong. Surely he would be able to gaze on her, converse with her without wanting to smother her in his arms, to cover her face with kisses while he groaned out his love and begged her forgiveness . . .

He ran a hand through his hair, setting his curls in disarray, then tried to smooth them back down. This was absurd. He could not possibly have seen what he thought he had. It was impossible that two people should look so entirely alike.

But when he stepped through the open door of the tower chamber and saw her sitting bathed in a glow of morning sunlight, he felt the breath again sucked out of his throat and the painful thudding in his breast.

She sat in a high chair, bent over a tall, slanting desk, rubbing a piece of pumice over what looked like a sheet of parchment. She looked up at the sound of his footstep. Her soft mouth quivered up at the corners in what he recognized as a brave attempt at a smile, an attempt he knew was going to fail. In another moment those lips would droop back into a pout, or worse they would start trembling and tears would well up into those big blue eyes. He would have to sweep her into his arms and cradle her to his heart and whisper over and over again that he would make everything right . . .

"They have ruined it," she said. "I have tried and tried to clean it, but the stains are too deep."

There went her mouth, and the tears— He took a step towards her, but she rubbed them away with a briskness that startled him into stopping again.

"I'm sorry. I know it is foolish to be so mournful over a mere painting. But it was one of Simon's."

Triston moved cautiously closer to the desk, where she had neatly set out several vials of paint and a row of pens and brushes. She looked like a small burst of sunshine herself, draped in a vibrant yellow gown with her shimmering gold hair flowing loose in rich, curling waves down her back. That sorrowful face he knew, but the bright strength springing even through her tears . . .

Unaccountably disturbed by that subtle foreignness in a countenance he knew as well as he knew his own heart, he looked away from her to the scatter of sheets on the desk. Vellum, not parchment, and a very fine quality, much better than the inferior stuff he used for his scribblings. Some of the stained sheets were blank, but he knew that her tears were for the few that bore her brother's paintings.

"Simon loved his craft, I recall that well," he said. "I don't think I ever saw him without parchment and quill tucked into his belt, and that tiny inkwell he always carried about on a chain. It seemed as if he could not sit still without being about some drawing, detailing the strange plants and creatures we saw on our pilgrimage, or creating some new monstrosity from the vivid realms of his imagination."

He gestured at the vellum where a winged blue ram charged a green bear with tusks and red, curling antlers like a deer. It was a measure of Simon's talent, Triston recalled, that he had been able to draw such oddities in fully plausible shapes, if not in convincing colors.

"Yes," Siri said, "Simon did take especial delight in transposing various animals' heads with other animals' bodies and attaching to them the wings of birds. It started when he drew his first bestiary. He wanted to prove to our father that he was ready to be advanced from apprenticeship. Simon worked morning and night, drawing and painting, scarcely pausing to eat, until the project was finished. He said when he slept that night, he dreamed the animals all jumbled up in his head, and the next morning he drew his first staglion—a stag with the head of a lion."

She laughed, although he heard a small catch in the sound. Triston could not remember the last time he had heard laughter at Vere, even tinged with sadness, as hers was.

He resisted the impulse to look into her face again, but said, "Surely your father did not apprentice you, as well?"

"No, but he allowed me to watch the others and sometimes gave me cast-off scraps of parchment to draw on. One day I sketched my name and decorated the 'S' with three vines and a veritable garden of flowers. Father said it showed talent, so he began instructing me, and then he gave me a brush and taught me to illuminate as well. Sometimes he would even let me help with a patron's commission, but I was never allowed to sit and draw in the workshop until after he and Mother died."

"You learned French from your father?" Triston asked.

"Yes. He never learned Italian well. His apprentices had to translate until Simon grew old enough to work in the shop."

"And you do not know from what part of Poitou he hailed?"

"He never said."

Triston nodded. "I'm afraid I am unable to restore your brother's paintings, but I will send to Poitiers for fresh vellum to replace the blank sheets that are spoiled."

"Thank you. Naturally, I will pay for it."

"Nonsense. Consider it a gift, Lady Siriol, to show how pleased we are to have you with us."

He stole a glance at her. A mistake. The brilliance of her smile banished the last threat of tears, but it also sent such a shaft through his heart that he turned away quickly and walked over to the window.

"It is those clumsy oafs who waylaid us who should pay," he heard her complain. "It is a wonder they did not break any of my vials of paint, although their leader stole the most valuable one. A blue pigment made from lapis lazuli. Simon said it came from mines in the east, and I know it was terribly expensive and difficult to obtain. I don't know how I shall be able to replace it."

"Is it urgent that you do so?"

"Oh, no, I suppose not. I still have my reds and greens and even my gold, but . . ."

"I will make inquiries at the monastery at Limoges. They have an impressive library there. My cousin borrows their books from time to time. Perhaps the monks will know how we can obtain some more of this lapis lazuli for you."

"Thank you. And I *will* pay for that. Alessandro left me very well provided for, so I need not be a burden upon you at all, save for the inconvenience—"

"'Tis no inconvenience, Lady Siriol. But I admit, I am concerned about my ability to fulfill your brother's wishes for you."

"You mean the marriage? I have told you, I've no desire for another husband. I wish to find work in some illuminator's shop."

Triston groaned silently at the naiveté of this response. Clothilde had never quite grasped the power her beauty held over men either. The thought that Siri could sit side by side with some Poitevin calligrapher or artist day after day and not find herself carried off and ravished before a week was out was a fantasy he knew it was his duty to crush.

"Simon's instructions to me were quite specific. There is no question that a marriage must be arranged," he said firmly.

"Simon would not have forced me to marry against my will."

She spoke equally firmly, but sounded a little cross as well. If she were as much like Clothilde as she looked, pressing her would only plunge him into the heart of a stormy tantrum. He had no desire to risk that until he had found her a suitable partner. And find her a partner he would. There would be no escaping the memories until she was gone from Vere.

"I must apologize to you again for my behavior last night," he said, staring down through the bars of the window into the corner of the bailey it overlooked. He saw Sir Rollo leaning on his sword, looking hot and displeased in the summer's sun. "I'm sure that someone has informed you by now of how much you resemble my late wife. In the darkness, I'm afraid that I—"

"You have already apologized. It is not necessary to do so again."

If possible, he thought she sounded even more cross than before, but he was too relieved at her willingness to let the matter go to question her response.

"I appreciate your forbearance." He forced himself to turn back towards the desk. "We wish your stay here to be a pleasant one. If there is anything you require, you have only to ask Sir Balduin and he will—"

He broke off as a scampering of footsteps and a yapping bark announced the arrival of his son and the hound, Talbot. The hound darted over to greet Triston, then ran to back the boy.

"Talbot, come." Triston called him sharply and the hound obediently trotted back to Triston's side. Triston glanced quickly at Siri's face, tensing for the alarm he expected to see there. But Siri only smiled.

Perrin stared at her, his dark curls uncombed, his small tunic hiked up over his twisted belt, his blue eyes bright with a feverish excitement. His delicate features flushed, then paled.

"Mamma," he whispered.

"Perrin," Triston said.

He saw the shrinking way the boy stepped back at the sound of his voice. Triston linked his hands behind him so that no one could see how tightly he clenched them.

"Perrin, this is the Lady Siriol de Calendri. She is our guest. Come here and let me straighten your tunic, then you may give her a bow."

Perrin hesitated at the command to approach his father, looking as if he had just been ordered to enter a dragon's den and become the main meal—a perhaps not-so-laughable fear to a seven-year-old boy. Certainly, Triston found nothing amusing in his son's round, frightened eyes. But the boy had to learn to obey.

"Perrin, come here." Triston kept his voice calm but firm.

White-faced, the boy came and stood as his father untwisted his belt and pulled down his tunic. But when Triston ran a hand over the boy's curls, he so openly flinched that Triston let him slip away with his hair still disheveled.

"Now go make your bow, and see you do it properly."

Perrin took several running steps across the room, whether eager to escape his father or to speak to Siri, Triston preferred not to ponder. He watched with some pride the grace of his son's obeisance.

"Lady Siriol?"

"Yes," Siri said brightly, "but most people call me Siri. I hope you will as well."

"You look like my mother."

Siri's smile grew gentle. "I am not your mother, Perrin. But I hope we will be friends." The boy looked so sad, that Triston was grateful when she added cheerily, "Would you like to see what I am about to draw? It is going to be a dashing hound like that one over there by your father. Perhaps your father can hold you up to see . . ."

Triston saw the boy's terror at this suggestion, as Siri must have, for she trailed off with a startled look. The desk stood too high for Perrin to view what lay atop it.

Triston said quickly, "I will get a chair."

But Siri stopped him. "No, I have a better idea. Did your mother have a garden, Perrin?"

The boy nodded.

"Then perhaps you will show me where it is and I will take my imagination there. It is such a beautiful day. You may carry my box with the pens if you like."

"Can Talbot come?" Perrin asked.

Triston's stomach knotted. He started to rebuke his son, but Siri forestalled him.

"Of course he may. It is his portrait I shall be drawing. He must come, don't you think?"

Triston stared at her. Clothilde had been terrified of dogs. But Siri called the hound to her and laughed when he leapt up to lick her face.

The contradiction of that happy sound with the woman he remembered sent Triston out of the room, overwhelmed by confused emotions.

Contrasted in his mind with Siri's welcome of the hound lingered Clothilde's frightened screams every time Talbot had come near her, and her panic whenever she had seen the hound romping with their son. Perrin had always turned to Triston for reassurance from his mother's outbursts. The removal of the dog and a few soothing words from Triston had usually restored Clothilde to trembling smiles. Once quiet again, Perrin had gone happily into her arms, for he had adored his mother and been the best of friends with his father. Or so Triston had always thought.

It had been nearly a year now since he had first seen his son shrink from him. It had taken Triston completely by surprise. He tried to lay it down, like the nightmares, to Perrin's shock at his mother's death and had thought that both would surely fade in time. But they had not. Triston was no nearer knowing how to solve Perrin's fears now than he had been when they first appeared. And he could not help but wonder whether Perrin's healing might be helped or hindered by that golden stranger with his mother's face.

"Good morning, Sir Triston."

"Denis." Triston greeted his man-at-arms as they met on the stair. He took the opportunity to turn his troubled thoughts to another subject. "Have you seen my cousin this morning? I saw Sir Rollo standing alone in the yard."

"Aye," the man answered. "I saw him a bit ago, headed for one of the mural towers with a book in his hand."

Triston felt a surge of impatience at this information, but he determinedly swallowed it. The burning memory of what a momentary flash of temper had cost him in his youth had thus far prevented him from dealing with his cousin's delinquencies as his nature urged him to. But one way or another, he was going to shake some sense into Acelet's ramshackle head.

He found his cousin on the battlements, propped up in the space between two merlons on the curtain wall, his cloak spread beneath him to ward off the dust of the stones where he sat. He wore a bright green tunic with slashes in the sleeves to expose a red silk lining. A wide-brimmed felt hat protected his delicate complexion from the warm summer sun, while he held a leather-bound book tilted back against his knees. From the way Acelet twisted a tendril of hair about his finger, Triston knew that he was deep in the throes of some romantic dream.

"You were supposed to meet Sir Rollo in the yard after breakfast."

The young man jumped at Triston's voice. "Cousin, I—"

Triston snatched the book out of his lap. A quick scan of one page revealed it to be some tale of a mystical maiden and her love-stricken knight. Triston had a deep respect for the written word and was not averse to spending an evening with a book himself. But daylight hours were meant for action, and for a squire that meant training in the yard with the best swordsman Vere Castle could afford to hire.

"Sir Rollo came dear to these walls," he said. "I did not begrudge the expense for you and Etienne, and now that my brother is gone, I expect you to make Sir Rollo earn his keep. Don't tell me you've misplaced your sword again?"

Acelet reddened. "It is in my room."

"Then go and get it. And while you're at it, change out of those ridiculous clothes. I'll thank you to stop cutting slashes into the sleeves of every tunic I buy for you. If the seamstress wants the lining to show through, she will put them there herself."

"I have asked her to," Acelet said, "but she said that you will not allow it."

Triston had less success swallowing his exasperation than he had his former anger. "Because it is a ridiculous fashion. I don't care how the young men dressed when your mother attended the queen's court at Poitiers. She has outgrown such foolishness and has pled with me to help you do the same. You said you wanted to be a knight."

"I do! But—"

"You're not going to become one frittering away your time like this. Go fetch your sword and get down to the yard. And you will apologize to Sir Rollo for keeping him waiting. If I hear any more complaints from him—"

Triston recognized the sullen crumpling of Acelet's face as he slunk off the wall and knew what his response would be even before he spoke.

"There is more to being a knight than knowing how to bully an enemy with a sword. There is honor and courtesy and liberality of soul—"

"When the king calls upon you to fulfill your knight's service and your enemy swings a sword at your head, courtesy and liberality will not spare you from being sent to your Maker, if you do not know how to deflect it. We have been through this a hundred times before. Acelet, I am trying to be patient, but—"

Acelet gave a jeering laugh. "You? Patient? That's a jest! I suppose that is why your son is so afraid of you and why your wife—"

Triston's jaw clenched. "You will leave Clothilde out of this."

"Aye, you would like to forget her, wouldn't you? Forget her tears, forget her anguish and that you were the cause of it all!"

"Acelet—"

"I loved her too! I would have laid down my life for her, but she loved you and only you."

Triston saw a glisten of tears in the young man's eyes. He had not been blind to Acelet's infatuation with his wife, an attachment he had dismissed as harmless, if annoying in its cloyingly worshipful manifestations. He had never rebuked the young man for it and remembered Acelet's shattered sobs the horrible night she died. It was why Triston took a deep breath and forced himself to speak evenly now.

"I know you cared for her, Acelet, as I did. Let us not mar her memory with a quarrel."

But Acelet's pink-white skin flushed darkly beneath the brim of his hat. "You never loved her, you never cared! You claim it was an accident, but sometimes I wonder."

Before Triston could suppress it, a flame of anger flared up. He tried to choke it back down, but his voice shook as he warned, "Acelet, leave it alone."

"No, I am not going to let you forget. You never treasured her. She was your brightest jewel—an angel, an innocent lamb who adored you as if you were some god—and when she learned about you and that harlot in the village—"

Triston's hand flexed into a fist. "Acelet, stop."

But Acelet jabbed on. "You think you can bury your guilt? That the whole of Vere does not know the truth? She died hating you, Triston, hating you for what you had done. You thought you could sweep the memory out like soiled rushes, but now she has returned. Every time you look at the Lady Siriol, you will remember how you betrayed Clothilde, how you broke her heart as well as her neck—"

Triston's hand swung up, only at the last instant his fingers spreading so that they landed with a slap rather than a brutal blow across the young man's face. Still, there was enough strength in his arm to send Acelet back against the wall. He leaned there slumping, his head turned away, his hand pressed to his reddened cheek.

Triston's chest rose and fell in quick, angry breaths. "Go. Get your sword and get down to the yard."

Acelet straightened. He sent a glare of bitter hatred at his cousin before he threw his cloak over his arm and walked away.

# Chapter 5

"Twas an accident, my lady, and let no one tell you otherwise."

Sir Balduin sent a challenging glance at Acelet, seated beside Siri in the grass. The grey-haired retainer had come with a request from Triston to fetch Perrin from the garden and send him to his lessons with the chaplain. After many whining protests Perrin had finally gone, taking the dog Talbot with him. But before Sir Balduin could excuse himself to Siri, Acelet joined them and took Perrin's place at her side.

Siri resisted the impulse to smile at the young man's hat and the rather inexpert slashings of his sleeves. But her amusement faded quickly when she saw the faint but fresh bruise on his cheek. She laid her drawing board aside to exclaim over it, but her sympathy had prompted a startling accusation.

"Accident, my eye!" Acelet said now. "I saw him—"

"You saw nothing more than the rest of us. She lost her footing and fell down the stairs." Sir Balduin turned to Siri. "It was late and we had all retired to our beds when the quarrel began. I don't know what she was accusing Triston of this time, but apparently she ran out of their room making some shrieking threat and Triston followed, trying to calm her. But she never would calm when she was in a fit like that. Triston caught her at head of the stairs, there was some sort of struggle, she lost her balance and fell."

Acelet gave a derisive snort. "Fell—or was pushed?"

Siri's mind echoed Sir Balduin's obvious shock. "How dare you, Acelet! Triston worshipped every hair of the Lady Clothilde's head. He would have given up his own life to bring her back."

Acelet sprawled in the grass, his elbows planted in a sprinkling of violets and periwinkles.

"Triston pretends to mourn her," he said, "but 'tis guilt, not grief, that tortures his conscience. Her fragile nature had become tiresome to him, her sensitive beauty a burden. He preferred the bawdy wenches of the village to her pure embraces, and when she caught him in a flagrant betrayal, it was too much for her trusting, innocent heart."

Sir Balduin growled, "If you do not mind your tongue, 'tis my hand you'll be feeling across your face. To be spreading such scurrilous tales about your cousin is shameful after the way he's taken you in, provided you room and board and training for that knighthood you claim is your heart's desire. Why aren't you out in the yard with Sir Rollo, rather than trying to stir up trouble here?"

"And what will Triston do when he learns I've disobeyed him? Hit me again?" Acelet rolled onto his side and looked at Siri. "He is a dangerous man, my lady, and guilt for the Lady Clothilde may turn his anger on you. You are so like her . . ."

His gaze slid over her face with wonderment.

Siri bowed her head so that her long hair fell over her face. She did not want him to see how deeply his talk of Triston had disturbed her. She dismissed Acelet's accusations of disloyalty on Triston's part. The memory of Triston's hands sliding up her arms, his fingers at her lips, set her quivering again, even in the heat of the sun. A man who caressed his wife with such tenderness, who kissed her with such longing, surely would not seek pleasure with "bawdy wenches." Siri knew it with unerring certainty.

But she could not ignore the bruise on Acelet's cheek. With Triston's gentle touch still lingering on her skin, she could not believe that Triston might ever have set his hand to his wife with anything but love. But Perrin? She had seen the boy's fear of his father—nay, more like terror. Triston was a large man and she had sensed in him anger and frustration.

Had he vented it on his son?

Yet that, too, seemed so unlikely. She had seen only affection in the way he had straightened the boy's rumpled tunic in her workshop. And when Perrin had flinched from his father's touch, Triston's dark eyes had held not impatience, but a bewildered confusion.

She tilted her head to gaze again with puzzlement at the faint bluish mark on Acelet's face.

Sir Balduin must have guessed her thoughts and misinterpreted them, for he said, "Do not listen to him, my lady. Now tell the truth, Acelet. Did you ever, in all the time you have lived at Vere, see Triston abuse his wife either in word or deed?"

Acelet hesitated. "Nay," he said at last, "but that does not mean—"

"Nay," Sir Balduin cut him off. To Siri, he said, "Triston is the most honorable man I have ever known. I stood with his father when word came of his birth, I watched Triston grow up, and witnessed his tears twenty years later when his mother died. It was his love for his mother that took him to Jerusalem in fulfillment of a vow to pray for her soul. That choice parted him from the Lady Clothilde and nearly shattered his heart. But Triston had sworn an oath, and love or no, he would not break words spoken to God."

"Like his vow to drink no wine?" Acelet derided.

"If your cousin chooses to abstain from that temptation, he should be praised, not mocked."

"Like you praise his tears for his mother. You do not mention that he had not one drop to shed as he stood staring down the steps at the broken body of his wife."

"He was in shock. And I suspect that in private, he has wept tears enough to satisfy even you."

Acelet looked skeptical. "You always defend him, but I have heard the stories of his youth. He was no paragon of virtue then. Why don't you tell the Lady Siriol about his affair with Isobel de Molinet? Or worse yet, the Lady Osanne—"

Siri stiffened, but Sir Balduin cut Acelet off with a curt warning.

"I think the Lady Siriol has heard quite enough from us both. Get out to the yard and pacify Sir Rollo before he complains of you again to Triston. You are sorely testing the limits of your cousin's indulgence, Acelet. If you are not careful, you will find yourself packed off home to your parents."

This prediction apparently bore more weight with Acelet than any former threat had done. He got up with a scowl, then turned to Siri. "May I escort you back inside, my lady? Out of this heat?"

She set her pen once more to her drawing board. "Thank you, but I have a bit more to do here. Perhaps, Sir Balduin, you will sit with me and tell me more about my new home?"

Sir Balduin began, with an apologetic cough, to excuse himself from this request, but at that moment Lucianna joined them in the garden, carrying some embroidery in her hands. She greeted Sir Balduin with a cool nod and seated herself on one of the low wattle walls that enclosed the garden.

"I should be glad to stay, my lady." Sir Balduin addressed his words to Siri, but she was quick to catch the way his gaze lingered on Lucianna.

Siri smiled, then saw Acelet's hesitation and said, "Don't worry, I shan't let Sir Balduin say anything unkind about you in your absence."

When Acelet had gone, Sir Balduin sat down beside Lucianna with a respectful distance between them. While he endeavored to draw Lucianna into conversation, Siri dipped her pen into her inkwell and traced on a sheet of soiled vellum an arc-necked swan floating on some squiggly waves. Here the eye, a line or two there to define the feathers . . .

Lucianna did not seem inclined to converse and when Sir Balduin lapsed into silence, Siri asked, "What was she like?"

"My lady?"

"The Lady Clothilde. Did you know her as a child, as well?"

"Aye," he said, "the Lady Clothilde's family lives at Pennault Castle, near enough for the children to all grow up together. Even as a child, her beauty made her the center of everyone's attention. It was a nervous kind of beauty, but beauty, nonetheless. Everyone adored her, and men came from every corner of the land to court her. And Triston was just as smitten as the rest."

"But she did not marry Triston at the first."

Siri stated an obvious fact, but to her surprise, Sir Balduin hesitated. His grey brows lowered over the bridge of his nose.

"Her mother had higher ambitions than a lowly knight's son. Sir Fulbert de Merval was a powerful man and coveted the Lady Clothilde, while her mother—" His mouth hardened. "The Lady Gwenllian is a sly, calculating woman. Welsh. And the Welsh are all mad, as we know. She would not have Clothilde as Triston's wife, and while Triston was on his pilgrimage, she forced Clothilde to marry Merval by means of a cold, sinful act."

Even Lucianna glanced up at the harshness of his words. What had the Lady Gwenllian done to make Sir Balduin look so grim?

"It must have been very painful for Sir Triston to return and find her wed to another," Siri said.

"Aye. I'm afraid he consoled himself with too much wine and with— but that's neither here nor there. Merval died during the king's wars with his sons. Triston won Clothilde back then . . . but it was never the same."

Siri watched as Sir Balduin's face grew darker still.

"My lady had changed. The poor lass's spirit had never been very strong. Her beauty, as I said, was of the nervous sort. One moment she would be wreathed in the most brilliant smiles, the next plunged in the depths of despair. But it was not until after her mother's crime that she became unsettled."

"Unsettled?"

Siri's startled query checked him. He slapped his thighs and abruptly pushed himself to his feet.

"'Tis too fine a day to be speaking of these sad matters. None of it can be mended now. Forgive me, my ladies, but I have duties I must attend to. If you will excuse me?"

He started to turn away, then paused and looked again at Siri.

"I'm afraid Acelet was right about one thing. You look so much like Clothilde that I fear Triston may have some difficulty reminding himself that you are not she. Be careful, my lady, or you may find Triston head over ears in love with you all over again."

Siri watched him leave the garden, then resumed work on her swan. But before many minutes, the drawing blurred and her pen grew still.

"Is something amiss, carissima?"

She glanced up at Lucianna. "What?"

Lucianna nodded at her neglected drawing. "I hope you have not let Signor Balduin put ideas into your head. Signor Triston is a man of great physical beauty—si, even I can see that. But I do not trust him. Do not be so foolish as to fall in love with him."

Siri blushed at Lucianna's words. "Don't be absurd. I scarcely even know Sir Triston, and I certainly do not mean to fall in love with him."

She forced her pen into motion once more, but she could feel Lucianna watching her, perhaps with more reason than Siri liked to admit. She had sat for hours last night beside the sleeping Perrin, her mouth glowing warm from Triston's kiss. Over and over she had told herself that her reaction had nothing to do with the man himself, only with his manner. It was her newfound discovery, nearly doused by her experiences in Venice, that there did in truth exist men with the capacity to discern love from lust, which had made her want to lose herself so thoroughly in the kisses that Triston dealt her.

For a breath's moment, Siri slipped back into the memory of the night. The nearly irresistible temptation she had felt to thread her hands through Triston's thick black curls, the yearning to see his sensitive mouth curve up into a smile, his ebony eyes drowning her, not with pain, but pleasure . . .

But there had been no pleasure in his eyes when he had spoken to her in her workshop this morning, only that same unfathomable anguish that had engulfed her at their first meeting. Acelet had hinted of other women in Triston's past, but clearly only one held his memory and heart today. Clothilde. Siri shook herself firmly back to reality. No matter how much she wished to find love, the humiliation of finding it with a man who would forever view her as someone else was unthinkable. So long as she shared Clothilde's face, Triston must remain naught but a hopeful pattern for her future.

Siri settled quickly into her new home. In time, she meant to begin an investigation of illuminating workshops in Poitiers, where despite Lucianna's resistance, she still hoped to eventually establish herself. She had been dependent on others—Simon, Alessandro—for too long. She had married Alessandro when she was only sixteen, too young to know how to fend for herself. Since then, with the experience she had gained at driving off unwelcome advances and with her jeweled dagger at her side, she felt certain she could protect herself quite adequately.

But for now, she sat in the garden every morning with Perrin. She had always wanted children of her own. Until she found a satisfactory union to give them to her, she contentedly passed the hours with this bright seven-year-old boy, sketching animals, birds, and flowers for his delight. Before long, she had Sir Balduin fashion a smaller version of her drawing board. She cut in half one of her spoiled vellum sheets, gave Perrin one of her pens, and, guiding his small hand with hers, helped him to trace a figure of his own.

Lucianna sat watching them from one of the wattle walls, her auburn hair veiled, her expression stern over her stitchery as the boy begged to be shown how to draw another and another. Some mornings Siri would do so, on others Perrin snuggled up against her and watched in silence as she practiced and refined her own skill.

She saw little of Triston during those days. One morning, a fortnight after her arrival at Vere, she found on her artist's desk a packet of fresh vellum sheets with a note indicating that it had just arrived from Poitiers. He'd signed the note with a flaring 'T.' Siri admired both the energy and grace of the inscription. Triston had once mentioned that her brother had taught him something of the family art. Gazing on the brief note, she wondered if Simon's pupil had not shown more aptitude than her reticent guardian had admitted.

She did not have the opportunity to inquire of him. Triston was too preoccupied in matters of estate to have time to spare for his new ward. He had to prepare for the upcoming manor court, Sir Balduin told her, oversee the washing and shearing of the sheep, and review the early plowing and the mending of the barns.

Siri could not but admire Triston's industry, but she guessed that even on a manor as small as Vere, at least some of these duties could have been delegated to some deputy. She had seen no more than a glimpse of the laborers' fields the day they had arrived at Vere Castle. Curious to know more about her guardian's interests, she sought out Sir Balduin and requested a guide from him.

"Of course, my lady," the grey-haired retainer replied. "I will ask one of the men to—"

"I will do it."

Siri caught Sir Balduin's quick frown. Acelet had entered the hall in time to hear her request and now joined them with an eager smile for Siri.

"Shouldn't you be at practice with Sir Rollo?" Sir Balduin said.

Acelet waved the reminder away. "Lady Siri wishes to see the manor. Sir Rollo can wait a few hours until I have shown it to her."

In the last few weeks, Acelet had spent almost as much time with Siri in the garden as Perrin had. When not regaling her with some romantic tale, he sat in a dreamy silence and sighed and simply gazed upon her face. She suspected he was drawn more to her likeness to his former mistress than to her own uniqueness as Siri, but there was something so boyishly ingenuous about his adoration that she could not find it in her to be offended. She accepted Acelet's arm and allowed him to whisk her away to the stables before Sir Balduin could protest again.

But to her chagrin, she quickly learned that her choice of Acelet as guide had been a poor one. Rather than answering her questions as her gentle grey mare cantered alongside his bay past his cousin's fields, he kept drifting off into other, dreamier matters, preferring to regale her with a lyrical account of the latest romance he had read than to speculate on what sort of crops his cousin planted or where the sheepfolds might lie. Siri at last gave up asking him anything and let him lead her where he willed, enjoying a few hours of freedom from the castle's confining walls.

Acelet guided her through a rambling village, occupied at this time of day only by a few women and children gathered about the well. They emerged from the village onto the forest road. Siri nervously fingered her dagger's hilt, glad that she had strapped it on before leaving the castle. But unpleasant memories of her encounter with the band of robber knights faded when they left the road after a short distance and followed a path that ended beside a river.

With some relief, Siri allowed Acelet to lift her to the ground. She had forgotten how wearying riding a horse could be. Raised in the great city of Venice, she was more accustomed to gliding the smooth currents of a canal than being jostled about on the back of some beast. She hurried down to the riverbank and dropped into the grass, breathing deeply of the familiar scent of water misting upwards on a hot summer's day.

"I did not realize Vere stood so near to the river," she said.

The high bank fell rather steeply away to the waters below. Small, foaming crests attested to the speed of the river's flow.

"Have you heard the tale of the squire Rauolin?" Acelet asked, dropping into the grass beside her. "While on a quest for his master, he fell into a treacherous river and might have drowned but for the saving arms of a water nymph, Mylisant. She carried him to land and held his head in her lap, stroking his dripping locks until he opened his eyes and bethought he gazed upon an angel. She promised to be his love and come to him each evening to that spot beside the river where she had saved him. But he was never to speak her name to others or boast of her beauty. For many long years he kept her faith. But one day, when his master mocked him for shunning the pretty wenches of the castle and cast a slur upon his manhood, Rauolin forgot his pledge and blurted out the story of Mylisant. In that instant, he saw her face before his eyes, streaked with silvery tears and heard her whisper a reproachful good-bye. Ever after he haunted their trysting place beside the river, but he never saw her more."

Acelet placed his elbows on his knees, propped his chin in his hands and stared wistfully across the river.

Siri watched him with amusement. She wondered if he ever had a thought in his head besides romance.

A clopping of hooves, echoing against some wooden frame, made her look around. She had not noticed before a bridge that spanned the river several yards away. A horseman rode across it. When he saw the couple seated on the bank, he turned his mount and approached them.

"Good day to you, Acelet."

The dreaminess left Acelet's face, replaced with a bright, eager look as he sprang to his feet. "Good day to you, Sir Raynor."

"You are in delightsome company today." The gentleman flashed an admiring grin at Siri from the depths of a well-trimmed russet beard. "Who, may I ask, is your exquisite companion?"

Acelet held down a hand to help Siri to her feet. "This is the Lady Siriol de Calendri. She is our guest at Vere."

The gentleman swung himself off his horse. "I am delighted to meet you, Lady Siriol. I am Sir Raynor de Molinet, a neighbor and friend of Sir Triston's."

A small, stylish hat of red felt capped the russet waves of the gentleman's hair. He wore a forest green tunic, falling only to mid-thigh and slashed up the sides nearly to the hip. A short red mantle draped his shoulders, clasped at the breast with a circular diamond brooch.

Siri smiled politely and extended her hand. He took it in his bejeweled fingers and set a kiss upon it. Only as he raised his head once more did she register the unusual color of his eyes. She gasped a little at their deep amber shade. In an instant her mind flashed back to the robber on the forest road and his mocking, yellow eyes. Instinctively she stepped back a pace, her free hand going to her dagger. Then she stopped. His brows lifted at her reaction. Did he recognize her, too? Or was she mistaken? She supposed if one man might have eyes of such a color, another might as well.

Still, the coincidence left her suspicious. She drew her fingers away from his. "You say you and Sir Triston are friends?"

He answered with a smile less brash than before. "Perhaps that was an exaggeration. Triston was somewhat older than I. My brother and he were friends, though, and I used to tag along whenever they would let me. I have been away for some years with the Young King's court, but my brother's death forced me to return. I have not yet had the opportunity of renewing my acquaintance with Triston. Had I known he was harboring such a jewel at Vere, however, I would certainly have found one 'ere now."

The smile widened on the words, regaining a cockiness familiar from her days in Venice. But Siri was listening too hard to his voice to care. She tried to place it with that of the robber's, but failed. Her assailant's bravado had been too muffled by the unmarked helmet he had worn. Still, this gentleman's manner seemed very odd. If he had known Triston from boyhood, he must have known Clothilde as well, yet he had not given the least indication of surprise at Siri's reputed resemblance to her.

"I have not been at Vere long," she said, wishing to test him. "A little over a fortnight. And a rude welcome we had to your lands, being set upon by a band of villainous knights not ten miles from our new home."

Raynor's face reflected nothing but sympathetic concern. "Aye, the roads have been so troubled of late. I hope you suffered nothing more than a little fright at their hands? Word is they seldom harm their victims, preferring merely to relieve them of whatever valuables they might carry and, in rare instances, hold a nobleman or two for ransom."

"We were fortunate that a noble knight rescued us and drove the knaves off before they could do more than tumble my clothes into the road. I understand that your duke has placed a price on their leader's head."

"No doubt," Raynor said dryly. "Richard prefers to be the only tyrant in these lands. But you say that Vere is your new home?"

Acelet spoke up with the answer. That he admired Raynor and wished to be noticed by him was clear. "Lady Siri is Triston's new ward. Her brother was an illuminator in Venice, and when he died his will sent her to Vere."

"Ah, then it seems we have both shared a similar recent loss. My condolences, my lady. Who was your brother, and how did Triston come to know him in far off Venice?"

"My father was Poitevin," Siri said. "Walter Geraud, a skilled illuminator who traveled to Venice as a young man and married a Venetian merchant's daughter, my mother. But my father claimed he had made a vow before his marriage to visit the Holy Land, and his failure to keep it always troubled him. When his last illness was upon him, he was so riddled with guilt that Simon, my brother, promised to fulfill the vow for him, and only thus did he die in peace. Simon made the pilgrimage a year later, and met Triston along the way. They became good friends, such good friends that he has trusted Sir Triston with my protection now that the last of my family is gone."

"But Acelet said your name was de Calendri."

"A married name. I am a widow, Sir Raynor."

"I see. And now you have returned to the land of your father's birth. But are you sure there are no Poitevin cousins whose claims to your care might supersede Triston's?"

Oddly, that thought had never occurred to her. "Simon never spoke of any, and I suppose he would have known."

"Perhaps he trusted Triston to know. You say your father's name was Geraud?"

She nodded, an uncomfortable tightness spreading through her stomach. Of course, she did not intend to stay at Vere forever, but leaving of her own accord was one thing. Being forced away by strangers . . .

"I will inquire if you like, to see if anyone knows the name—"

"That is not necessary." Realizing she spoke too quickly, she tried to moderate her tone. "That is most kind of you, Sir Raynor, but I'm sure Triston will see to such matters, if he has not already."

Raynor gave her a keen glance, then grinned. "If I were Triston, I would make it a point to do no such thing. In fact, I would do everything in my power to keep your charming face close by and hoard your beauty to myself. You see, my lady, I speak my ignoble thoughts quite freely. Let us hope that Triston is more honorable than I."

The gleam in his eye baffled her. She could not quite tell whether it bespoke the kind of audaciousness that usually accompanied a bold desire to seduce her, or whether he simply teased.

"Raynor's castle is across the river," Acelet piped in, "to the north of here. If you stand at the very edge of the river and crane your neck just so, you can see the edge of some of his fields."

Acelet demonstrated the necessary position. Siri, not wishing to seem disinterested in the proximity of their neighbor's lands, stretched her neck politely as well.

Raynor said, "You will have to stand closer than that if you wish to see them. Like this, my lady." He took her arm and before she could resist, propelled her down to where the bank fell away steeply to the river. "It would help if you were taller, but if you stand on your toes and look right there . . ."

Siri obediently rose up onto her toes and stared in the direction of Raynor's pointing finger. She strained to see what he wanted her to see through the gap in the bushes on the other side.

"I can't—"

"No, you're not looking right. Over there." He pushed her a step closer to the edge.

"I'm trying, but I can't see—"

"There."

"I— Oh!"

She gasped as the edge of the bank crumbled away under her feet. She struggled to catch her balance and step back onto firmer ground, but her heel slipped on the grass and she felt herself sliding with the earth towards the rushing waters below.

# Chapter 6

Raynor's hand clamped on her arm, jerking her back to safety a bare instant before she heard Triston's voice ring out.

"Lady Siriol!"

She whirled her head and saw Triston thundering towards them on a gleaming black horse, panic in his face at the sight of her danger. She stumbled against Raynor, trembling and unsteady from her near misstep.

Triston drew his mount up so sharply that the beast reared, its hooves flailing at the air. Before the hooves finished descending, he hurled himself out of the saddle, strode down the bank, and wrenched her out of Raynor's grasp. Only then did she see the white fury that had replaced the panic in his face. He shoved Raynor so hard that he would have landed on the ground had Acelet not been behind him to break his fall.

"You vicious cur!" Triston shouted.

"What are you doing?" Siri cried when Triston jerked Raynor out of Acelet's arms by the front of his tunic.

Triston responded by giving Raynor so fierce a shake that Siri heard Raynor's teeth bang together. Appalled, she grabbed Triston's arm and tried to pry him off. Whatever mystery lay behind him, Raynor had saved her from what might have proved a tragic misstep. It took Siri a second jerk on his arm before Triston paused in the string of curses he had loosed on Raynor, then released him with another shake that sent him stumbling into Acelet's arms again.

Siri rounded on Triston. "Have you gone mad? Had Sir Raynor not caught me just now, I would have landed in the river."

"I've no doubt that's exactly what he intended," Triston shot back.

The accusation stunned her. "Triston, it was an accident."

"The devil it was. I knew he'd be back out for mischief the moment I heard he'd returned to Belle Noir." He pointed an unsteady finger at the now rumpled knight. "If I find you anywhere near the Lady Siriol again—"

Raynor pulled himself out of Acelet's hold, his face as red as Triston's was white. "You've mistaken the matter, Triston. I was only—"

"Nay, it is you who have made the mistake. I know what you have in your mind, but it will not work, Raynor. You cannot harm me through her. She is not Clothilde."

The implications of this ominous allegation troubled Siri as much as the mocking smile that broke across Raynor's mouth, but she said, "Triston, he was not trying to harm me."

"No? Then how was it you came to be standing so near the water with him at your side?"

"He was showing me his fields."

She thought the sneer that curved Triston's lips ill-became him. "Indeed. No doubt he believed you could see them more clearly from beneath the waves."

"It was an accident, as she said," Raynor insisted. "Acelet mentioned my fields and she slipped as we were trying to show them to her." Again that smirking smile. "You understand how accidents happen, don't you, Triston?"

A rush of color stained Triston's pale cheeks. He swore again and took a step forward, but stopped when Siri refused to move out of his way.

"These are my lands," he snapped at Raynor, "and if you do not want to be thrashed off them, you will remove yourself now. If I catch you here again, or anywhere near my lady—"

Raynor made some show of smoothing down his sleeves, as though determined not to appear intimidated by Triston's threats. Another slow smile curled up his mouth as he turned to Siri. "My lady, it was a pleasure to meet you. And provided Triston does not lock you up in some tower at Vere, we will meet again.''

Triston's muscles twitched as if he intended to challenge this promise in some physical way, but then he stilled, his powerful frame rigid with a simmering rage as Raynor retrieved his horse and rode back across the bridge.

"Come," Triston said then. He seized Siri's arm and pulled her over to where they had left their horses tethered. "You are not to ride down to the river again or speak further to Sir Raynor. Do you understand?"

Siri pulled herself out of his grasp. The whole scene between him and Raynor seemed ridiculously overreactive.

"You will not tell me what I may or may not do, Sir Triston. I may be your ward, but I am not your slave. I will go where I please and make friends of whomever I will."

"Not of that miscreant you won't, unless you wish to find yourself headlong in the river next time."

"He was catching me, not pushing me. How many times must I tell you that?"

"Raynor de Molinet is a black-hearted villain. He will not hesitate to stoop to the basest means to win his obsessive goal. Think, my lady. How was it in truth you came to be standing so near the water's edge?"

"We told you. Acelet said we could see Sir Raynor's fields and—'' She broke off at the sharp flash Triston shot Acelet's way.

Triston's eyes narrowed on his cousin's flushed face, but he only said, "So Acelet spoke of the fields and you went to the edge of the bank to look. Did you step there yourself or did Sir Raynor guide you?"

She hesitated. "Well, he . . .''

Triston looked grim as she trailed off. "Just so. Take care, Lady Siriol. Sir Raynor is not the innocent neighbor he wishes to appear. He means nothing but harm by you."

"Why should he wish to harm me?"

"Because—"

She caught the quiver of pain that flashed over the anger in his face and finished the answer for him. "Because I look like the woman you loved?"

She forced herself to ignore the little stab in her heart when he gave a curt nod. "I cannot help my face, Sir Triston. And I cannot understand why that should make me a target for Sir Raynor to injure you—unless you have formerly injured him in some way?"

Triston's mouth tightened, but he did not answer. Instead, he placed his hands on her hips and tossed her up into her horse's saddle with no more effort than had she been a troublesome puppy.

He turned to Acelet. "See my lady back to the castle. We will talk of your part in this escapade later."

He waited only long enough for Acelet to sulkily mount his horse, then dealt Siri's horse a slap on the rump that sent it trotting away from the river.

Triston did not even pause to remove his spurs before retreating to Vere's chapel. The metal clicked against the stone floor as he paced the length of the room, once, twice, thrice . . . He had ridden back to the castle slowly to avoid Siri and Acelet, then had come straight to the chaplain, hoping for guidance, comfort . . . he was not sure what.

Father Michel watched Triston's agitated pacings for several moments before saying, in his calm way, "Perhaps you should tell her the truth."

Triston stopped and ran a hand through his hair. "She must know about Clothilde by now," he said. "Someone has surely told her."

"And about Isobel?"

Triston shook his head. Had Siri known about that, she would have reacted far differently to his quarrel with Raynor today. But whom would she have believed?

"Sit down, my son, and try to calm yourself."

Even in his agitation, Triston felt a smile tug the corners of his mouth at the chaplain's determinedly paternal manner. Father Michel could not be older than Triston's own twenty-eight years, but he was very earnest in his calling. His optimistic view of God's mercies had proved a sorely needed balm to Triston's unhappy soul. Most of what he knew of Triston's past

71

had come only through Triston's confessions, as he had been employed at Vere for less than three years. But his rebukes, though unrelenting against sin, were always softened by encouragement and quiet forgiveness.

Forgiveness. Triston closed his eyes and sought to imagine that blissful state. To be free of the memories, the guilt . . .

"I'm afraid, Father," he said abruptly. He opened his eyes and stared at the gilded crucifix on the altar, its jewels winking in the light of the candle beside it. "Afraid of what Raynor might do. Afraid of what I might do to Raynor. I have tried to forgive, as you counseled, have tried to forget, but every time I hear his name, I see them again—"

"You must pray, my son."

"I have, as hard as ever I prayed over my sin with Osanne. But it is not the same. That sin was mine and I bore the consequences of it. But Clothilde was innocent, and because of him she—"

"Quiet. You must not relive it. You have no power over another man's hate, only over your own."

*Hate.* That was what Triston had felt today in all its explosive, familiar force. Once assured of Siri's safety, his impulse had been to throttle the life out of Raynor, to put an end to his miserable, vicious mischief once and for all.

"Why is it you fear for the Lady Siriol?"

Triston made an impatient gesture. "You have seen her face. Her resemblance to Clothilde makes her an obvious target for Raynor."

"But you said he already had his revenge."

"Aye, but he does not know that. Raynor was not here when Clothilde died, and I have taken good care that he should not learn the reasons for that night's tragedy. Though he knew how her death would hurt me, he is sure to believe it no more than an accident, completely unrelated to what he did and said that Christmas before I threw him out of Vere."

He resumed his pacing.

After a few moments, Father Michel again broke the silence. "Eight years is a long time to hold a grudge, even such an one as you suggest Sir Raynor has held against you. You say his brother accepted your story then. Might Sir Raynor not have had time to reflect during his service in the Young King's court and lay his hate aside?"

"You do not know how he loved Isobel," Triston said. "You did not see his grief when I pulled her from the water. He did not believe me then and he will not believe me now." His jaw tightened, as it always did when he forced himself to face an unpleasant truth. "I do not disclaim the part I played that day. Had I not lost my temper— Nay, Father, I do not pretend to be innocent in his loss. She haunts me to this day. Sometimes I think—"

He stopped again, but the insightful chaplain seemed to know the silent groan that rose from his heart.

"That you will never escape the mistakes of your past? You have confessed them freely, my son, and I have absolved you of them all. Your repentance has been sincere, as is evidenced by your faithful keeping of the vows you made over your sin with the Lady Osanne. Have you not kept yourself from wine and lust as you swore to do?"

"The wine is easy. Memory alone is enough to slake my thirst for that. But the other—"

For the first time, Father Michel frowned. "You find yourself tempted with a woman?"

Triston did not answer, but the chaplain discerned the obvious truth himself.

"The Lady Siriol. You desire her?"

Triston gave a crooked smile. "What man would not? Her beauty is incomparable."

"And her likeness to the Lady Clothilde uncanny."

A sigh escaped from deep within him. "Aye. But she is not Clothilde, and I have sworn to touch no other woman."

"Nay, my son, if you told me truly, that was not exactly the terms of your vow."

Triston turned, surprised.

"As you told it to me," Father Michel said, "the wording of your vow was to touch no woman 'save she who is in His sight my wife.' Though I trust it has held you from engaging in any more illicit affairs such as you—er, enjoyed with the Lady Osanne, it does not preclude you from marrying again. Young Perrin needs a mother and is fond of the Lady Siriol. And if she contents you as well . . ."

The temptation ran like fire through Triston's veins, but he was not so insane—nor so unjust—as to succumb to it. What life would that be for Siri, to be loved for her likeness to another woman?

Nay, that was not the answer to his dilemma. The illusion, however much he wished to believe it, was not real. She was not Clothilde. He had seen it today over his confrontation with Raynor. Clothilde would never have rounded on him with those formidable sparks in her eyes, berating him for what must have seemed to her an irrational suspicion. Their quarrel would have thrown Clothilde into hysterics, the kind of shrill, frightening fit that he had come to dread.

He forced himself to push that memory away and remember his wife in her quieter moments, sweet and smiling in his arms.

He shook his head. "I could not love the Lady Siriol fairly, as a man should love his wife. Clothilde would always stand between us. I will find her a suitable partner, as her brother wished, and send her away from Vere. Then Raynor will not be able to harm her, and we shall all have some peace."

Father Michel nodded, but Triston knew he was no more convinced of the truth of that than Triston was himself.

⊷

Days passed and the altercation between Triston and Raynor was not mentioned again. Siri saw Triston only at dinnertime, when of necessity he always took his place beside her at the table. There he responded to her attempts at conversation stiffly, always avoiding her eyes.

Also attended by the castle's chaplain, Sir Balduin, and several other old soldiers of the garrison, the meals at Vere would have been silent, dreary affairs had not Acelet made up for his cousin's reserve with a constant stream of prattle. Triston often looked impatient, and more than once Siri saw him open his mouth as if to utter some rebuke. But he always closed it again without speaking, and the only time he actually snapped out a word was when Acelet drifted into extravagant praise of the Young King.

Politics were never spoken of at the table. But Acelet knew no such restraint when he joined Siri in the garden.

"I caught a glimpse of him once," Acelet said one morning.

He lay sprawled in the grass beside the dog Talbot, while Perrin leaned against Siri and watched her sketch a swarm of honeybees hovering over an array of flowers. This time Acelet had added vertical slashes to the breast of his surcote as well as the sleeves, exposing the bright green tunic beneath. It was, he had informed Siri earnestly, the way the young knights had dressed at the Court of Poitiers when his mother sat in the queen's circle. Lucianna muttered over her stitchery that they must have looked like devils. Siri thought *lunatics* a more apt word. She distracted herself with Perrin before the laughter that bubbled inside her could escape.

"Soon I will show you my paints," she told the boy. "Then we will turn these flowers yellow and red and green. Who did you catch a glimpse of, Acelet?"

"The Young King. Three years ago, just after I came to Vere. Triston had been commanded to join Duke Richard's siege of Chateauneuf, but he was ill, so he sent his brother, Etienne, in his place. The Young King was at Chateauneuf as well. When word came that he left before the siege was over and that Etienne and some other Poitevins had left with him, Triston sent me to inquire as to the rumor's truth. I found Etienne with Sir Raynor de Molinet in the Young King's camp. Etienne refused to return, and as I watched them ride away, I saw the Young King in the forefront."

His voice hushed, as if in awe of his memories. "He was glorious, rubies sparkling from his coronet, his gold hair gleaming in the sun, his tall frame draped in scarlet and gilt . . . His every movement was one of charm and grace, and when he turned his head and I saw the beauty in his face—"

"Why did you do that, Lady Siri?" Perrin pulled on Siri's sleeve as she finished drawing a small crown over one of the bees. She guessed that he had heard his cousin's breathless recital too many times before to be impressed with it now.

"Because bees are led by a king, as are we," she said, ignoring the resentful glance Acelet sent at the boy. "He is a most benevolent ruler, leading by example and never turning his sting upon malefactors. He has only to demonstrate to them the error of their ways, and in shame they will turn their own stings upon themselves."

"Papa says King Henry is a benevolent ruler."

"Ha!" Acelet's scornful laugh woke the dozing Talbot. The hound gave a bark. Acelet pulled gently on one of Talbot's ears, but said, "The old king is a tyrant, crushing our people through his war-hungry son. We were a free people before the Angevins came. Now they seek to take away our liberties, and because we do not want to surrender them, the king sets Duke Richard to ravage us like a wolf among the sheep."

"Papa calls Duke Richard the 'lion's cub.'" Siri had to stop drawing as Perrin leaned across the board in her lap to better view his cousin. "I heard him tell Sir Balduin that the king will give us law if we will let him and that it is the rebels' fault the duke is allowed to be so bloody. He says if we would lay down our arms, King Henry would rein the duke in and—"

"There is a word for men who would sell us into the Angevin power. Some would call them traitor."

"Papa is not a traitor!" Perrin rose up on his knees, his vivid blue eyes flashing a son's indignation.

Encouraged by the boy's reaction—surely he would not rise so quickly to the defense of a man who abused him—Siri agreed, "Of course he is not. Shame on you, Acelet. There now, Perrin, you are quite right to maintain your father's honor. You love him very much, do you not?"

To her dismay, he pushed her board aside and buried his face in her lap. She stroked his dark curls and found him trembling. But before she could try to elicit the reason, the serving girl, Audiart, entered the garden.

"Milady, I beg your pardon, but the master is asking that you attend him and Sir Gavin in the hall."

"Sir Gavin?"

"I do not know him, milady," Audiart said.

Perrin looked up at Siri and she felt his hands clutch her gown. "Lady Siri, must you go?"

"I must, if your father commands it," she said. "Perhaps you would like to come with me?"

Ordinarily, Perrin would have leapt at the invitation to remain in her company, but he shook his head vigorously now.

"I will escort you, Lady Siri."

Acelet sprang to his feet and held down a hand to her, but Lucianna gathered up her embroidery and rose.

"If you wish to be of use, young man, you will take this child and that dog away. Donna Siriol cannot go to an interview dressed as she is. Come, carissima, we must make you presentable for Signor Triston's guest."

Perrin looked as resentful as Acelet did to be palmed off thus on his cousin.

"Here," Siri said. She held out her drawing board and pens to Perrin. "Perhaps you will take these to my workshop for me. Do you think you can carry the inkwell too, without spilling it?"

"I'll carry it," Acelet muttered, seeing the boy fumbling with all the objects he took from Siri's hands. "Come, Talbot."

The hound jumped up, but only so he could thrust his head into Siri's lap. She laughed and scratched him behind the ears.

"There, you scamp, now be off with you," she said.

Talbot gave a reluctant whine, but at Acelet's second command, followed him and Perrin out of the garden.

# Chapter 7

$\mathcal{S}$iri changed her grass-stained gown and veiled her hair before entering the hall with Lucianna at her side. Triston stood with another man just below the dais, but he turned at the sound of their entrance.

Siri felt her breath catch away, as it always did on those rare occasions when he gazed at her full in the face. He looked as if he had just come in from the fields, his brown tunic layered with dust, his dark curls tousled as if recently tossed by the wind. She experienced again that same quivering sensation she had known when he had first set his lips to hers.

But in that same instant, she recognized again the anguish in his eyes. It deepened as his gaze swept the length of her blue cendal gown. She had chosen the color because she knew the hue enhanced her eyes to a deep and brilliant sapphire and set off the smooth ivory sheen of her cheeks.

Surely it had been a trick the Lady Clothilde employed as well.

She cursed herself for falling into so obvious a trap, but Triston had already turned sharply back to the other man.

"Sir Gavin—" she heard the shaken note in Triston's voice— "allow me to introduce you to the Lady Siriol de Calendri and her companion, the Lady Lucianna Fabio."

Siri sank into a curtsy as the gentleman bowed over her hand. He was shorter than Triston, and had a pleasant if rather bland face and drab brown hair that brushed against his sage green mantle.

"You were right, Triston," he said with a look of awe. "The resemblance to the Lady Clothilde is incredible. I'm surprised you are willing to give her up."

Siri's eyes narrowed at this remark, but Triston answered curtly, "She is not Clothilde. I have explained to you her origin and the charge her brother gave me concerning her."

*My brother's charge. To find me a husband?*

Sir Gavin's response sealed her suspicion. "Aye, and remembered how earnestly I courted Clothilde before her mother gave her to Merval."

He circled Siri, looking her up and down in what she considered a highly impertinent way.

"Exquisite!" he exclaimed. "It will be Clothilde all over again. There is not a man within a hundred miles who will not be clamoring for her hand."

"That is what I am trying to avoid," Triston said. "I'll not have her set up like some prize at a fair. I wish to settle the matter quietly, in keeping with her dignity and mine."

Siri sent him a seething glare, but he would not meet her gaze again and hence missed her warning. She had no intention of standing meekly by while they discussed her as if she were some inanimate object, subject to the whims of their determination.

Sir Gavin stopped in front of her and inquired, "You are part Poitevin?"

Invited to speak, she returned his regard steadily. "My father was Poitevin, but my mother was Venetian."

"Noble?"

She heard the hope in his voice and sighed. "Alas, no. My mother was a merchant's daughter. My father did not speak much of his family, but there is no reason to think—"

"There were rumors," Lucianna interjected, "that he did have noble blood. Though he became an artisan, many remarked that the grace of his hands betrayed his true birth."

Siri swallowed her irritation at Lucianna's interruption. Lucianna had always held too much admiration for noble titles.

Sir Gavin looked encouraged by her remark. "Your first husband was a knight, was he not?"

"Signor Alessandro de Calendri," Siri admitted, "but he also dabbled in merchandising, which is how he maintained his wealth."

This confession seemed to check Sir Gavin somewhat, as she had hoped it would. Trade was an occupation no Poitevin noble would have deigned to engage in.

Seeing his hesitation, Triston said, "Her first husband left her a generous dowry, and she is doubtless possessed of many exemplary talents. She has presided over a large household and must be skilled in the management of servants."

Siri shook her head. Sir Gavin raised a brow.

"My husband's housekeeper managed our servants," she said. "Alessandro had complete faith in her judgment and did not wish me to interfere. My husband doted on me, Sir Gavin. I had nothing to do all day but to sit on silk pillows and be waited upon. I'm afraid I am odiously spoiled."

Triston frowned at this. "She is nothing of the sort. She is most industrious with her needle and her embroidery is excellent. Every morning she sits in the garden and executes some cunning design."

She sent him a look of reproach. "Ah, Sir Triston, you know that is not what I am doing in your garden. My mother sought in vain to impart that talent to me. I have not the least aptitude for it. My stitches come out crooked and I invariably pull the thread so tight that it ruins the cloth." She gave Sir Gavin one of her brilliant smiles. "I can't mend clothes either, and I've no knowledge of herbs or healing. I can't even make a proper tune on a flute, though I daresay my singing would not make a man wince. As a wife, Sir Gavin, I have naught to recommend me but my dowry and my beauty, and the latter is quite enough to make you the envy of every man from here to Venice."

Sir Gavin blinked.

Triston looked grim. "My ward is very frank, but I trust you will account such honesty a virtue. I am sure she exaggerates her shortcomings and will quickly master whatever skills you deem necessary in a wife."

"Well," Sir Gavin said, taking in one last sweep of her beauty, "I suppose a man might make a few allowances when the prize is to be so otherwise felicitous. I shall think on it, Triston—carefully."

He bowed to Triston and again to the ladies, and left the hall.

No sooner had he gone than Siri rounded on Triston, so angry that his handsome face blurred through the steam of her vision. "How dared you try to sell me to that man! I am not your property, Sir Triston—"

"No, but you are my ward," he reminded her stiffly, "and I have a duty to your brother to see you respectably established."

"I have told you that I do not wish to marry again. If you are so eager to see me gone from Vere, then I will be gone, but in my own way. Lucianna—" she turned to her companion— "begin packing our belongings at once."

"Donna Siri!"

"Don't be ridiculous," Triston said. "Where would you go?"

"To Poitiers. Surely there is some illuminator who could use another artist. I would match my skill against any Poitevin."

She saw the impatience surge into Triston's face and the difficulty with which he reined it back in.

"It would be worse than irresponsible of me to allow you to try such a thing," he said. "I have heard about your mirror, Lady Siriol. I suggest you look in it again and remember your brother's apprentice."

His words momentarily checked her temper. Simon must have included an account of that episode in his letter to Triston, perhaps to serve as a warning in just such a confrontation as this. Simon had known of her reluctance to remarry. He had indulged her wish while he lived, but he was no longer here to protect her.

Still, she said stubbornly, "I can take care of myself."

"What, with that little dagger you sometimes carry?"

She flushed at the mockery in Triston's tone. Her fingers brushed the empty space where the blade used to nestle against her skirts. She had abandoned it days ago, not liking to wear it when she spent so much time in the garden with Perrin.

Nevertheless, she said, "That dagger stood me in good stead when we were set upon by those brigands on the road. I had it at their leader's throat before he could even think about laying a hand on me."

"Aye," he returned, "a man might be disarmed by that once, but he would not give you a second chance. His guard will go up, and yours will inevitably go down. Just look at you now. Your dagger is in your chamber and if I had a mind to sample those pouting lips of yours, I would only need to—"

"What?" she challenged as he broke off. She lifted her chin. "What would you do?"

She felt a stab of disappointment when he did not answer. She threw him a scornful look before she turned away.

"This."

She gasped as Triston jerked her back around. She stumbled against his chest and found herself staring at the dark brown broadcloth of his tunic. Not until that moment had she realized how vastly taller he was than she, her head not quite reaching his shoulder.

"Signor, this is outrageous!"

"Stay back," he warned Lucianna. "I merely wish to drive home to your lady a lesson."

Siri looked up into Triston's flushed face, her arm throbbing beneath the strength of his fingers, her breaths coming quickly. "And what would that lesson be?" she asked.

His dark eyes, fixed on the bow of her mouth, smoldered with something other than anguish now. "Just this. If I wanted to dishonor you, Lady Siriol—" one hand stole round to the small of her back, pressing her against him with a quiet, determined power— "there would be very little you could do to stop me."

Lucianna protested again, but her outburst sounded as no more than a faint echo in Siri's ears, drowned out by the wild thudding of her heart and the hot rush in her veins. The strength with which Triston held her was so overwhelmingly superior to anything she had experienced before, that even had it occurred to her to struggle, she would have had as much chance to escape as a lamb being embraced by a bear.

She should have been afraid. When her brother's apprentice had held her down, she had rent the air with her screams. But now, trapped in

Triston's much more powerful hold, all she felt was a thrilling fire and an aching anticipation as Triston eased his grip on her ever so slightly and lowered his head towards hers.

She closed her eyes and lifted her lips for a kiss that never fell.

"I trust you see the danger?" His voice was husky, his mouth so close that she could feel his breath on hers.

Frustrated at the failure of a caress she had anticipated with eagerness, and with the promising source so temptingly near, Siri succumbed to an impulse. She pushed herself up to complete the kiss.

Their lips clung together for only an instant and she would never be quite sure whether his warm response was real or imagined. With the same quick thrust he had used that night beside Perrin's bed, he shoved her away. By the time she caught her balance and opened her eyes, he had already retreated to the window.

"Your pardon, Lady Lucianna," he said, in a gruff effort to soothe her companion's indignation, "but I knew not how else to overcome my new ward's stubborn blindness."

He stood with his back to them both, depriving Siri of any opportunity to read his expression. From the way Lucianna continued to rail at Triston, she clearly had not discerned whose movement had been responsible for the kiss. Siri listened with no small shame as Triston manfully took the blame for her misdeed.

"I trust 'tis an offense I shall not have to commit again," he said. "I hope I have convinced your lady that her dreams of independence in some illuminator's shop are unrealistic and can only end in disaster."

His words cut off the rest of Lucianna's protest, but she indicated her continued displeasure with an angry sniff. "Indeed, signore, I have told her again and again that the safety of one so bella lies solely in marrying some knight worthy to protect and cherish her."

"Exactly," Triston said. "I asked Sir Gavin here to acquaint your lady with him, not to force him upon her. Sir Gavin is a good, honest man who is in favor with the duke. He is young and moderately handsome, so the ladies say, and I thought she would not find him entirely objectionable."

"I haven't left the room," Siri said, annoyed at again being discussed as if the issue were of no immediate concern to her.

She rubbed the arm that Triston had held with such fierce strength. Her flesh still throbbed, but she knew she would find no bruise there. There had been too much hard-honed discipline in his grasp to hurt her. 'Twas not pain, but a still-pulsing pleasure, that resonated through her.

She stared at his broad-shouldered back. No man had ever caused her heart to beat so wildly with only a glance, with the mere touch of his hand. How could he kindle such fire in her, and not taste it too?

Suddenly, employment in an illuminator's workshop seemed far less desirable than a lifetime of this man's kisses.

Gracious, what was she thinking? *Siriol Geraud, don't you dare be so foolish! Yes, he is the most handsome man you have ever met, and yes, he sets your heart racing, but physical attraction is not the same as love. What do you know about the man himself? Practically nothing.*

Nothing. Except that he placed the safety of an aging retainer over his own when pressed in the heat of battle. That he preferred a quiet life, tending the affairs of his manor, to blindly following a bloodthirsty duke. That in spite of an inherently impatient nature, she had seen him repeatedly exercise the self-restraint of a saint in the face of Acelet's dreamy, careless ways. And that he appeared to grieve as deeply over his son's baffling fear of him as he did over the loss of that precious son's mother.

This was a man, at the very least, to respect. But to love? Only time could tell her the answer to that. Time to test her own feelings. Time to make him see beyond the memories stirred by her face and demonstrate to him her own unique spirit as Siri.

Time . . . But how to win it? Triston professed himself anxious to marry her off. How pleased would he be to stand by and watch her being courted?

"Very well," she said. "I daresay you have made your point, Sir Triston. If marriage is the only way, then I shall marry—"

Triston tossed her a hard look over his shoulder. "Have I your word on that?" he demanded before she could lay out her conditions. For the first time, his eyes gazed unflinchingly into hers. "No more absurd talk about illuminator shops?"

Siri hesitated. Her word. He had not asked for a vow of the sort Sir Balduin had described in the garden, the one that had caused Triston to sacrifice the woman he loved to keep a pledge to his mother. But she thought of her father. Whether spoken to God or man, Walter Geraud had never considered his word to be less than his absolute bond. Should his daughter prove less honorable than he?

It was not too late to retract her rash promise. But those ebony eyes gazing so directly into hers well nigh knocked the breath straight out of her. Was it worth the gamble?

"Yes," she gasped, answering her own question aloud. She cast her die, knowing there would be no turning back. She tilted up her chin and steadied her voice. "You have my word. But only if you agree to allow me to choose my own husband."

She suffered an almost physical pang as Triston turned his head sharply away, breaking off their brief, rare connection.

His shoulders lifted in a shrug. "Now that Sir Gavin has seen you, he is sure to spread word of your remarkable beauty all over the county. If you wish to subject yourself to a host of pretentious knights tripping over their feet and their tongues trying to win your hand, that is entirely your own affair."

She felt Lucianna's shrewd gaze on her face and hid a smile, but she puffed with satisfaction within, just the same. If such a contest did not win her time and opportunity to test both their hearts, nothing would.

"Thank you, Sir Triston," she said. "I'm afraid that is exactly what my vanity requires."

## Chapter 8

Laurant. That is the Lady Clothilde's father?" Siri asked Sir Balduin. She sat with him in the hall at the table set up on the dais, reviewing the list of names she had asked him to compile of eligible bachelors in the area.

"Aye, my lady," Sir Balduin replied. "He is not, of course, looking for a wife himself, but he is Sir Triston's father-in-law and a near neighbor, and for such a banquet as you have in mind, it would only be proper to invite him."

She nodded, ignoring the old retainer's dismay at her insistence that they continue with plans for a feast over Triston's objections. Triston had growled that his household would be upset soon enough with a deluge of slack-witted suitors and he saw no reason to turn her choice of husband into an exhibition. But Siri was determined to make her courting as extravagant, and as public, as possible.

"Are there any others here like Lord Laurant?" she asked. "Necessary to include, but not interested in a wife?"

"Lord Fauke. He is not married, but he has a . . . lady . . . and has shown no interest in replacing her with a wife. But he is Triston's lord and would be slighted if we snubbed him."

Siri fancied she understood Sir Balduin's hesitation over the term "lady." She had recognized Lord Fauke's licentious nature, and there had been too many men who wished to make her their mistress behind her husband's back for her not to suspect Sir Balduin's meaning.

"Then that leaves only eighteen," she said disappointedly.

"There might have been more had you not set the feast so soon. But Triston will not spare us more than three messengers and I think they will not be able to ride further than this in the time you have allowed."

She had chosen the end of next week for her banquet.

"What about Sir Raynor?" she asked abruptly. "He is not married, is he?"

"Sir—" Sir Balduin almost choked over the name. "My lady, you are not thinking of inviting him?"

"Why not?" she asked, curious to hear his reply.

"Triston would have Sir Raynor's head if he stepped across Vere's threshold again!"

She was quick to pick up on the word. "Again? Then they have not always been enemies?"

Sir Balduin hesitated.

"If you do not tell me, there will be someone who will," she said, not as a threat, but as a simple statement of fact.

He seemed to consider his words before he spoke, but finally said, "Triston was not always as—disciplined as you see him now. As a youth, he had an impulsive temper. But he was also very handsome and had a dashing way with the women. Isobel de Molinet, Sir Raynor's sister, fell desperately in love with him, but Triston was only twenty and had not a mind to bind himself to her. One day they had a terrible quarrel as they stood beside the river near Belle Noir Castle. It was wintertime, and the river but newly frozen.

"I have only Triston's word for what happened that day. He said that when he spurned her advances, she attacked him in a fit of frenzy and when he thrust her off, she fell onto the ice. The ice was thin and it broke beneath her weight. Triston had worn a shirt of mail that day, hoping to engage some of the young men of Belle Noir in a little friendly swordplay. By the time he stripped it off and plunged into the water, it was too late to save her. The poor lass drowned. Most accepted it as a tragic accident, including her elder brother, Drogo. But Raynor, the younger, blamed Triston."

Siri could feel Sir Balduin watching her closely. She said only, "And Raynor still blames him? After all these years?"

Sir Balduin looked grim. "Indeed. I have no doubt it was in revenge for that perceived crime that Raynor enticed Triston's brother Etienne to desert the siege of Chateauneuf and ride away with the Young King. He knew such a desertion to the duke's cause would set Triston's loyalty in serious question. The de Brielle name was already in disgrace because of the actions of Triston's father."

"What did his father do?" This was the first she had heard anything spoken of Triston's sire.

"He made an ill-advised alliance with the French against Angevin interests in Poitou, then died and left Triston to bear the consequences of his treason. Triston won a pardon after his subsequent actions helped to foil the plot in a critical moment. But Duke Richard has never forgotten the stain on our house's honor. Triston was too ill to attend the siege of Chateauneuf himself, but as soon as he recovered, he was forced to swear a humiliating oath of repentance and future faith to the duke."

"But if Sir Raynor deserted the siege as you say, his honor should be in disgrace as well."

"It no doubt is in the eyes of the duke, but so long as Sir Raynor has the Young King's protection, there is little Duke Richard can do."

"And Raynor never forgave Triston for his sister's death?"

"Nay. A year after Chateauneuf, Etienne brought Raynor to Vere for Christmas. Raynor baited Triston endlessly during that fortnight, but Triston held his temper until one night after everyone else had retired. What Raynor said then must have gone beyond the bounds, for swords were finally drawn and Triston spilt a little of Raynor's blood. The Lady Clothilde must have come upon the scene, for her hysterical shrieks roused the household. Triston was in a terrible rage. He threw Raynor out into the snow and Etienne went with him. They returned to the Young King's court. But three months ago Drogo de Molinet died and Raynor came home to inherit Belle Noir."

Siri considered all this. "You do not know what they fought about at Christmastime?"

"No, my lady. Raynor insisted to Etienne that Triston's attack was unprovoked, but only a fool—or a misguided boy like Etienne—could believe that. Triston had changed after Isobel's death. It was clear to everyone who knew him that he blamed himself almost as deeply as Raynor did. His attempts to bury the temper he had succumbed to that day were painful to watch, and thereafter he seemed to shun women entirely. At least until after his pilgrimage and his affair with— But that was an aberration, for he never looked at her or any other woman again. It came as a complete shock to us all to learn that he had married the Lady Clothilde without any of our knowledge, especially when one remembered how we had all thought her the Lady Merval."

"What?" Siri asked, startled at this odd statement.

Sir Balduin looked abashed, as though he had spoken something he should not. "Please, my lady, I do not know all the reasons for Triston's anger. I know only that Raynor provoked him terribly. It would be worse than unwise to invite him to your banquet."

She nodded, remembering the ugly confrontation beside the river. She pushed her curiosity about Raynor away. She wished she could dismiss her next question as easily, but though all she had witnessed contradicted the fear, Sir Balduin's words compelled her at least to ask. "Does Triston ever lose his temper with Perrin?"

Sir Balduin seemed genuinely surprised. "With Perrin? Of course not. I have never even heard him raise his voice to the child, not even to reprove him for slipping away from his lessons with Father Michel to sit in the garden with you."

Siri blushed at this mild rebuke. "Yet Perrin is afraid of his father. He looks terrified every time his father touches or speaks to him."

Sir Balduin's face grew grim. "Aye, I have seen it," he admitted. "Triston knows it too. It seemed to begin after the boy's mother died, but we can none of us find an explanation for it."

Siri brooded over this for a moment, then shook her head in puzzlement and returned to her plans for the banquet.

With Lucianna's assistance, all fell satisfyingly into place. Men were sent out to hunt the necessary game, her brother's wine was marked and set aside, and troubadours and other entertainers were hired. Arrangements were also made to obtain the abundance of flowers Siri wished to decorate the hall, for the Lady Clothilde's small mead with its low spreading flowers was not sufficient to obtain the effect she had in mind.

"Tapestries," Siri said to Lucianna. "We will place them there and there—and there, between the windows."

She pointed at three of the four walls of the hall as she swept up and down the rush-strewn floor. Her dagger bumped against her leg in rhythm to her movements. Lucianna, outraged over what she termed Triston's second assault on her mistress, had threatened to lock Siri in their chamber if she did not strap the weapon back around her waist and leave it there. Siri had reluctantly done so, mostly to stop the nagging, for it had become clear as day to her that rather than posing any threat to her virtue, Triston's only objective was to avoid her as completely as he could. She had scarcely seen him since they had clashed over Sir Gavin, not even at dinner, for he had begun to send excuses by Sir Balduin that he was too busy to attend.

She stopped so abruptly that Perrin, who had been following at her heels, nearly collided into her. She put her arm around the boy as she turned to stare at the wall behind the dais, the only one with any adornment. Its four colorful shields framed a banner with a gilded rose, the emblem, she had learned, of the de Brielle house.

She glanced at a servant passing through the hall on some errand. "What do you think, Audiart? Does this room not need a little cheering?"

Audiart paused and studied the hall's empty walls. "Indeed, milady, a little more color in here would be welcome, and a tapestry or two would undoubtedly cut down on the drafts. Sir Triston's father removed all of his wife's handiwork after her death and stored them away in the wardrobe connected to what was his and is now Sir Triston's bedchamber. But the wardrobe caught fire three years ago, and all the tapestries were destroyed."

"Not all of them," Perrin piped in. "Papa has two of Grandmama's tapestries in his chamber, and Uncle Etienne had one as well."

Siri looked down at Perrin's curly head. He could not always have been so afraid of his father, to speak with such familiarity and eagerness of the contents of Triston's chamber.

"'Tis true," Audiart admitted. "Triston had preserved two of his favorites in his former bedchamber and they thus escaped the flames. They hang in his new chamber now. But I do not think Triston would wish any of them removed to the hall."

"What about the Lady Clothilde?" Siri asked. "Had she any tapestries, perhaps brought with her from her parents' home or woven during her marriage?"

Audiart hesitated. "There was only one, and it was—flawed."

"I will not mind a misplaced thread or two. Where is it?"

"In Sir Triston's chamber. But—"

"I will show you, Lady Siri." Perrin grabbed her hand and tugged her across the floor to the stairs.

"Donna Siri," Lucianna protested, "you cannot invade Signor Triston's chamber!"

"Perrin, Lucianna is right," Siri said.

"But Papa is out about the manor someplace. He won't know. Please, Lady Siri? You will like Grandmama's tapestries. I want you to see them!"

The temptation to learn more about Triston's wife by viewing some of her weaving, and to see Perrin's grandmother's, teased Siri's curiosity, but she told herself it was only for Perrin's sake that she set her foot on the first step. He must have visited his father's chamber many times without fear, to be so urgent to take her there now. Surely she should encourage whatever tenuous thread this boldness still reflected between them.

"We shall just take a quick peek," Siri promised in response to Lucianna's renewed protest. "If I like the tapestries, then I can devise some way to ask Triston about them and persuade him to lend them to me. Yes, Perrin, I am coming."

She heard the rustling of Lucianna's and Audiart's skirts behind them as she followed Perrin up the stairs.

⁓

Siri had every good intention of only peering sufficiently around Triston's door to see the tapestries on the walls. But with the same determined force he had used in the hall, Perrin tugged her over the threshold.

Once inside, she could not resist the impulse to take some stock of the room itself. The modest chamber held a curtained bed with the repetitive emblem of the gilded rose shimmering forth from some of the drawn-back folds. A table stood nearby, with a basin and pitcher, and an unlit candle. A carved, cushioned chair, and two tapestries on the walls completed the decor. The open shutters admitted enough light for Siri to study Triston's mother's handiwork. One tapestry portrayed a hunting scene, the other boaters on the river, an image that stirred some homesickness in Siri's breast. Both had been wrought with skill and elegance, achieving a balance of color and form that she could not but admire.

"They are beautiful," she said. "They are the very things we need in the hall. Triston must let us use them. But there are three walls and we will need a third. Where is the Lady Clothilde's?"

"Sir Triston keeps it in his wardrobe," Audiart replied. "But, milady, it is nothing like these and will not suit your purpose at all. Perhaps the one in Master Etienne's chamber—"

"I will see this one first. Bring it out into the light."

Audiart hesitated, as she had below in the hall, then whispered fervently to Siri, "Sir Triston shut it away because he did not wish Perrin to see it."

Siri felt her brows arch, but she merely turned to the boy and said, "Wait here for us, Perrin." She stepped towards the wardrobe door, but Perrin clung to her hand.

"But Lady Siri, I want to see it too!"

She urged him into his father's chair before she loosed her hand. "Of course you do. But Audiart does not want to risk dragging it through the dust. It is quite large, and I must help her carry it out, so that we may view it by the window."

He did not appear to have caught the words of Audiart's whisper, and Siri was relieved when he accepted her lie. She turned again towards the door, which opened into a separate dressing chamber.

"Milady," Audiart hissed, "Sir Triston did not wish anyone to see it."

Siri felt an uncomfortable stir of conscience, but she deliberately squelched it. She had already allowed Perrin to lead her thus far into temptation. Besides, her intentions were honest and the result would be for Triston's own good.

"I understand," she answered softly, "that it must cause him painful memories of his wife, but he cannot mourn her forever. You told me it has been a year since she died. Triston has got to stop glumping around and face life again. Setting this tapestry out with the others will be a first step. Lucianna," she tossed over her shoulder, "light that candle on the table and bring it into the wardrobe."

The small square room held several wooden chests, some carved, some not, of differing sizes and lengths. The larger Siri guessed held Triston's clothes, the smaller whatever jewels he might own. A stray garment or two lay strewn over a chest here and there. Various cloaks hung on pegs in the walls and shoes lined up along one side of the floor. The wall directly opposite the door held the tapestry, but it was not until Lucianna brought the candle that Siri's breath sucked in.

No wonder Triston had locked it away from Perrin's gaze! The nightmarish colors and shapes could only be a reflection of a disordered mind. What might have been intended as flowers suddenly distended into a grotesque series of irregular circular patterns woven in a bizarre combination of reds and yellows and greens and blues. They altered abruptly from one color to another with no thought for balance or form. But it was the frequency with which a distorted black pattern shot amidst the colors, offering an impression of Stygian lightning, that set the seal on Siri's conclusion of madness.

"I told you it was flawed," Audiart murmured.

Siri was too dismayed to even speak. Audiart was right, Perrin must not be allowed to see it. Not now. Not until she could answer his inevitable questions about its contorted designs. Too disturbed to gaze on it any longer, she turned away and caught sight of what looked like a sheet of parchment atop one of the taller clothing chests. There was a drawing on it.

She picked it up without thinking. "What is this?"

Lucianna brought the candle closer. Again Siri's breath caught.

If the tapestry had been unique for its chaotic disharmony, this image was almost unnatural in its perfection. Siri had drawn and illuminated many women, from saints to serfs, but always in the traditional pattern of smooth faces with stylized noses and mouths, and eyes that spoke nothing of the heart. But she had never seen a drawing like this. This face had planes and angles, like a real woman's would, her high cheeks set off with subtle shadings, her delicate eyebrows feathered over wide-gazing eyes, her bow-like mouth sketched in a melancholy droop . . .

"Donna Siri, it is you, " Lucianna whispered.

But Siri shook her head. "No, it is the Lady Clothilde. Isn't it?" She looked at Audiart.

"Aye, milady. There is a clearing in the woods where Sir Triston sometimes goes and draws her. Do you think—" the servant sounded afraid. "Milady, you are an artist. I have never seen anything like the pictures he draws. They are so—real. Do you think it is the devil's power which lends him such skill?"

"Nay," Siri replied, "such talent as this could only be a gift from God."

But it was not his talent alone that riveted her gaze to the drawing. It was the likeness of this face to the one she saw when she looked in her mirror. Until this moment, she had not believed that what others claimed was truly possible. But there was no doubting the evidence before her eyes. It was her face, yet it was not.

The discovery held her so enthralled that she only dimly heard Perrin's small squeak of alarm, answered by a deep, startled voice, followed by the scampering of fleeing footsteps. Not until another, stronger footstep trod nearer and Audiart exclaimed, "Sir Triston!" did Siri's head bounce up.

His powerful frame loomed in the open doorway to the wardrobe.

"I trust I am not intruding? When last I recall, this was still my chamber."

His cutting irony caused a wave of color to sweep up into Siri's cheeks. "Sir Triston, we— I—"

"What are you doing here?"

Embarrassment to be caught in this awkward position flustered her. "I— I was looking for some tapestries to decorate the hall. Audiart mentioned that your mother had—"

Triston's gaze flicked over her head to his wife's tapestry. His cutting voice went hoarse. "Perrin— Did he—?"

"No," Siri said quickly. "He didn't see it." She knew the fleeing footsteps must have been the boy's. "Triston, what does it mean?"

When Triston's eyes returned to her, their blaze threatened to spring out and consume her.

"Get out."

He seized her arm to force her from the wardrobe and saw the drawing in her hand. His face went white.

"How dare you?" He tore the parchment from her hand and flung it back onto the chest where she had found it. "How dare you go prying through my things like this?"

"I was not prying! I was—" She broke off, for prying was exactly what she had been doing.

He dragged her out of the wardrobe and pushed her towards the door. "You've no business being here. Now get out."

Indignation at this manhandling nearly overwhelmed Siri's guilt, but before she could speak again, Lucianna pulled her out of the room and Audiart shut the door behind them.

# Chapter 9

Triston slammed the door of his wardrobe and turned the key to lock it. His hands trembled with rage as he withdrew the key and flung it onto the table. The presumption of the wench! To go snooping through his room for such a trivial excuse as a tapestry—

The tapestry. He dropped his head into his hands with a groan. In the space of a few seconds he'd experienced surprised pleasure at seeing Perrin in his chamber, followed by a heartbeat's gratitude for whatever trick Siri had employed to lure him here. But in the next instant, as Perrin fled, gratitude crumbled to disappointment so keen that he'd vented it on Siri with the snapping tongue he struggled so hard to keep in check, a sharpness he had immediately regretted . . . until he'd seen her standing near Clothilde's tapestry.

Panic had fueled his white-hot anger then. Panic at what questions it might have roused in Perrin's young mind had he seen it. And saints, what must Siri herself have thought?

Clothilde had woven it three years ago, just after he had brought her to Vere. He had still been recovering from the wound in his chest and had been naive enough to believe that the fits she had suffered in her parents' house would cease once he had her free of her mother and Pennault Castle. He had watched her at her weaving during those long weeks of his convalescence, so reassured by her domestic endeavor that he did not question the constant, slightly dissonant humming that accompanied her task.

The shock when she finally spread her work out for his view had numbed his mind with horror. There could be only one interpretation of so bizarre a pattern, but it was one he could not accept. Not when she stood there glowing so proudly at her achievement, her eyes soft and guileless as the dew on the grass, so trustingly eager for his praise. He had voiced it hoarsely, praying she might not see his alarm, and had been relieved beyond thought when she had climbed onto the bed beside him and nestled into his arms.

She had not complained when he had locked her work away. With it, he had tried to lock away the truth, a truth he shrank from even now. A truth from which he had sworn to protect Perrin.

Anger surged again as he thought of the risk Siri had taken by leaving the wardrobe door open while Perrin sat so nearby in his chamber. Then it ebbed away nearly as quickly. She could not have known. How could she ever have imagined she would stumble across a weaving so monstrous? She should not have invaded his chambers, but might he not have given away more by his own exaggerated temper than had he settled simply for a stern rebuke?

He retrieved the key from the table and went to reopen the wardrobe door. He picked up the drawing and carried it out into the light. And this. Why had he panicked to see this in her hand?

Sweet Clothilde. He never seemed able to capture the smiles he had so loved in his youth. From the first hour Simon Geraud had encouraged him to try his hand at drawing, his inspiration had been Clo. He had drawn her in infinite poses, had detailed her in every shade and every plane, but when it came to her lips, his pen persistently traced them in this despairing droop.

Sadness. Mere sadness. Surely Siri could not have guessed anything amiss from that.

He laid the picture aside and returned to the wardrobe to fetch more parchment. Today would be different, he told himself. Today when he sat in the clearing, he would think of nothing but the love they had shared there. He would remember Clothilde in her innocence and would draw her wreathed in smiles.

He took up the small chest where he kept his pens with the inkwell that had been a parting gift from Simon Geraud, and slid it under his arm with the parchment. Another's face flitted, unbidden, into his mind. Simon's sister. Did Siri know how often he passed by the garden when she sat there with Perrin and Acelet, how often he lingered to watch his son? Did she know how his heart warmed with relief and gratitude to see Perrin happy again? Or how her own laughter, less bell-like than Clothilde's, more full and rich and irresistibly infectious, judging from how easily Perrin and Acelet joined in her merriment, stirred long-buried memories in him? Memories not of his struggling days with Clothilde, but of those bright, peaceful, loving days when his mother had lived, filling their hall with her cheerful spirit all the days and nights of his childhood and youth.

He pushed the pang away. Nay, he would not think of his mother now, or Siri either, that golden impostor whose own brilliant smiles sometimes threatened to cast Clothilde's into pale shadows. Later he would apologize for the temper with which he had flung her out of his room. But just now he would go to the clearing. And he would dream only of Clothilde.

Siri thought constantly about Triston's drawing through the remaining days leading up to the banquet. There was no further denying of what she had not wanted to believe. She and the Lady Clothilde shared a face so similar it was eerie.

What must have lain behind that other face disturbed her, but she kept her questions to herself for now, declining to challenge Audiart's repeated descriptions of her former mistress as a "quiet, gentle girl." Quiet, gentle, or otherwise, with Triston's drawing fresh in her mind, Siri knew she must take some bold step to differentiate her likeness to his late wife. Audiart confirmed Siri's suspicion that the Lady Clothilde's meek nature had been reflected in the simplicity of her dress. Then Siri determined to appear just the opposite.

She began her transformation the day of the banquet by selecting for the evening a flowing tunic embroidered with elaborate diamond shapes running between bands of scarlet silk. A wide gold-chain collar was attached to the gown, studded with a single ruby positioned to lie just below the hollow of her throat. She laid out the gown on her bed before she bathed, together with a lawn chemise, a girdle sprinkled with rubies and pearls, a light silk mantle also embroidered in scarlet and gold, and her jeweled dagger. Neither Lucianna nor Siri trusted a hall full of Poitevin strangers.

Siri almost made a blunder after her bath. She rubbed herself with violet oil, then donned her chemise before allowing Perrin to come in and watch her comb out her hair.

"You smell like Mamma," he said with a happy sigh.

Immediately, Siri pushed him back out of the room and bathed again, replacing the violet oil with one distilled from lavender.

After being readmitted, Perrin sat on the bed and watched her don her exotic gown and girdle.

"Mamma never looked like this," he whispered as Lucianna pinned up Siri's bright hair so that it covered her head in a mass of golden curls.

Nothing could have brought a sunnier smile to Siri's face. If Perrin thought so, then she had surely succeeded in her task.

She kissed the boy. "Thank you, Perrin. Now run off to your supper and I promise to save you some sweets from the feast tonight."

Perrin hugged her and ran off with a grin.

✥

Siri descended the stairs a few hours before the banquet. To her surprise, she found the formerly empty walls of the hall adorned with the two tapestries she had seen in Triston's room. A third one she guessed must have belonged to his brother, Etienne.

She caught Audiart's arm as the servant hurried through the hall. "Did Sir Triston say anything when he sent the tapestries down?"

"Nay, milady," the servant replied. "Beg pardon, milady, but I must go and supervise Perrin's supper."

She dashed off before Siri could question her further. Siri sighed and turned about to examine the hall. Trellises woven with lilies and roses stretched up along the spaces of the walls not covered by the tapestries. She had had the same flowers, coupled with daisies, twisted into garlands and stretched down the centers of the white-clothed tables. The blooms' heady fragrances mingled in the air with the scent of rue and basil, the latter strewn among the rushes.

She crossed the hall to survey the tables more closely. Metal goblets, knives, and spoons had been set out, as well as trenchers tinted pink with sandalwood. While the musicians tuned their instruments, she strolled past the sideboards set up against the wall, pausing before one that held an array of pitchers and flagons filled with wine, ale, and sweet ciders.

She recognized the silver flagon with a finial in the shape of a five-petaled rose. It was the one Triston was always served from. On an impulse, she poured its contents into one of the goblets set out nearby, determined at last to solve the mystery of Triston's thirst.

No sooner had her eyes rounded in surprise at the cool liquid that flowed into her mouth than a disdainful voice spoke from behind her.

"Excruciatingly insipid, is it not? Water."

Siri swallowed, then turned, startled to see Lord Fauke. While their other guests had set up tents in the fields that stretched below Vere's walls, room had been found in the castle for Lord Fauke and, as Sir Balduin had termed her his "lady." Lord Fauke was alone now, richly dressed in a dark crimson surcote with a heavy banding of gold about the chest. Despite the wealth implied by the silk and gilt, Siri thought the choice of color a poor one, for it doused his fiery hair to an uncomplimentary orange and heightened the freckles on his face.

"My lord." She sank into a curtsy, still holding the goblet. Lord Fauke took it from her and filled it with one of the wines.

"I think you will find this more bracing," he said, sipping it first before returning the cup to her. "One of our excellent Poitevin vintages."

*One of my brother's excellent* Tuscan *vintages,* Siri thought. She set the goblet back on the sideboard. "Thank you, my lord, but I will wait until the food is served."

He shrugged and held out his arm. "Then allow me to escort you to the dais."

She hesitated, but it would have been rude to refuse. She took his arm and let him accompany her to the high table.

"Does Triston never drink wine?" she asked. She attempted to draw her hand away as they reached her chair, but Lord Fauke laid his fingers over hers and held them where they lay in the crook of his arm.

"Not since an overindulgence led to the sullying of his conscience with my lady." He continued with a sneer and a frankness that showed precious little respect for Siri's sensibilities, "It was a sin, Triston told her, though I say when one finds a wench so willing, one is a fool not to avail himself of her. Of course, I did not know the lass then, but she has told me of their—pleasures."

His pale eyes traveled the length of Siri's scarlet gown, as though he envisioned finding such pleasures with her.

She popped her hand out of his arm so abruptly that it succeeded in bringing his eyes back up to hers. She turned away, her back straight, and made a show of rearranging the utensils on the table. Triston and "my lady"? Surely Lord Fauke did not mean the dark-haired beauty who accompanied him to Vere. She dismissed the leering insinuation in his voice as quickly as she had Acelet's remarks about Triston and "the bawdy wenches of the village" Lord Fauke's dislike of Triston reverberated too strongly to give credence to words most likely spoken in spite.

"I understand you come from a family of illuminators, my lady?" If her rebuff had offended him, it did not sound in his query.

"My father, Walter Geraud, and my brother Simon were both notable illuminators in Venice," she replied.

"And I am told that you have some skill yourself."

"Who told you that?"

"Word gets around. I heard that Triston is trying to find you some paint to replace that which you lost to the robbers who attacked you on the forest road."

"The lapis lazuli," she said, hopeful enough to turn towards him again. "Do you know where I can find some?"

"Perhaps. My clerk is transcribing a new psaltery for me and I am looking about for an illuminator to execute the miniatures along the borders. I might be able to locate some of this lapis lazuli if you think it would enhance the text—and if you would consider doing the paintings yourself."

Siri struck a cautious note. "I do not know if I am sufficiently skilled . . ."

"Allow me to be the judge. You have a pattern book, do you not, of your work? Perhaps you will let me see it?"

Siri could think of no objection to this request. "Certainly, my lord. Perhaps tomorrow or—"

"Why not now? It will give us an excuse to escape the squall of these musicians. I promise I will have you back in good time to greet Triston and his guests."

He had her hand through his arm again before she could protest. Siri could not believe that he intended any serious misconduct with the start of the banquet so close, but she was nevertheless comforted by the bump of her dagger against her thigh as she led him to her workshop.

The room was dark except for the light flowing in from a torch in the corridor. All within the workshop was as Siri had left it, her paints neatly capped in their vials and set out in a row across the top of her scribe's desk, her pens and brushes lined up just below them, a pile of blank parchment sheets stacked to one side. The vellum was too expensive for common use, though she liked to keep some on hand, for one never knew when one might receive an important commission. But she used parchment with Perrin, and the drawings she had allowed him to paint this morning had been laid out to dry on the bench just below the shuttered window.

"My pattern book is over here," she said. She had left the leather-bound collection on her tall scribe's chair, where she had set it down after showing it earlier to Perrin. She would have left Lord Fauke's side to retrieve it, but again he clung to her hand and instead pulled her over to the bench.

"Let us examine these first," he said.

The area near the window was particularly shrouded in shadows. With the same quick action she had used in the hall, she jerked her hand free and went to light the candle on her desk.

"Those are a child's paintings. I am instructing Sir Triston's son. I think this is what you wish to see."

Lord Fauke followed her across the room and stood uncomfortably near as she picked up the pattern book and opened it. The pictures within were mere drawings, though expertly rendered, the colors being left to the patron's discretion.

"If you will tell me what you have in mind?" she queried. "These were done by my father, but I can reproduce or modify them in any way you please. These are our initials." She turned to a page of flourishing letters, some with flowers twined about them, others with tiny animals or people sketched inside. "Here are our saints' figures and other biblical images. These are our plants . . . our beasts . . . our birds . . . and here we have—"

Lord Fauke reached around her and closed the book in her hands. "You were right," he murmured into her ear. "Let us look at these tomorrow."

He leaned over her shoulder and blew out the candle, then turned her around. He caught the back of her head and jerked her towards him. Her hand flew up, but not in time to ward off the greedy lips that descended on hers in a raw, lurid kiss.

## Chapter 10

Triston entered the hall in an irritable mood, still dogged by his frustrated failure in the clearing some days before to capture the memory of his wife in her youthful gaiety. In the end, no amount of determination had succeeded in forcing his pen to turn those tragic lips into a smile. He had been greeted on his return to the castle by the sound of Siri's rich laughter as she and Lucianna sat in the hall, weaving garlands for the banquet. Any impulse to apologize for his behavior in his chamber had vanished in a flash of resentment. Clothilde had never laughed quite so merrily as that, yet she had looked so like Clothilde in her simple dandelion gown, her golden hair flowing o'er her shoulders, her bewitching blue eyes all a-sparkle . . .

He choked down the lump in his throat as he stepped now through the arched entryway. He could not bear this likeness much longer. The sooner Siri de Calendri was gone, the better it would be for them both.

It was still early, the hall filled only with servants putting the finishing touches on the tables, musicians tuning up their instruments, jugglers practicing their acrobatics in anticipation of their antics at the feast. Triston paused and gazed around the altered room. This was how it had been while his mother lived. The castle filled with music and laughter, the hall ablaze each night, warmed by those familiar tapestries on the walls . . .

"Ah, Triston, I hoped I would find you here."

He stiffened. He recognized the woman's voice even before he turned to face her. His gaze flicked over her sultry features, her raven locks caught up in two sleek loops on either side of her head, her voluptuous figure set off by a clinging gown of deep green silk.

"Osanne." He ignored her outstretched hands.

Her ripple of laughter was so familiar that it made him wince. "What, no welcoming kiss for your stepmother?"

Triston met her mocking eyes with a tightened jaw. This glistening temptress had married his father less than a year after his mother's death, and following his father's crippling, had made herself free with every handsome man her wanton eye had lighted upon. Triston had lusted for her too, or so he had been told. His wine-muddled brain recalled little of those months following his return from his pilgrimage. There were only images remembered in an indistinct haze, but scorched so deeply into his conscience that he had never questioned their truth.

"Come, my dear," she purred, "for old time's sake."

He made no move to resist when she slid her arms around his neck and pressed a kiss to his mouth. No amount of sensuous skill on her part could raise a response in him now. As hot as he may have been for her once, her embrace now left him empty and cold.

"Does your lover know how you serve him behind his back?" he asked when she finally drew away with a dissatisfied frown.

She laughed again, though crossly, her arms still around his neck. "Fauke is indulgent of my weaknesses, as I am of his. Our passion for one another is exhilarating, but it is not . . . exclusive."

"I suppose you must keep him exhilarated, lest he re-examine the part you played in the conspiracy against his master."

Osanne's finger traced a seductive line down the side of Triston's neck. "Fauke knows I lied when I said I was bullied into joining your father's plot against Duke Richard and King Henry. He has protected me only because I agreed to become his mistress. I have kept him intrigued enough not to regret it, though occasionally he may wander a bit. That pretty little ward of yours, now, she has caught his eye. Tell me, is it true—" her finger stole round to his chin, and up to his lips "—what the rumors say? That she reminds you so strongly of Clothilde that you have seduced her and locked her up in a tower?"

He pulled her hand away. "I am holding this banquet to marry her off, and she will leave Vere as chaste as she came to it. Who told you I had locked her up?"

"Sir Raynor. He summoned us to Belle Noir yesterday to complain of you. He says you have cheated him of some land."

"I bought that land back from Raynor's brother three years ago. I have the documents to prove it, should your lord care to have a look."

"As joint heir, Raynor should have been consulted. He is demanding a seignuerial court from Fauke . . . but I might be persuaded to speak to Fauke on your behalf."

Triston still held her hand, but that did not prevent her from rubbing her other one suggestively over the rose embroidered on his tunic's breast. His gaze lingered on the wanton, waiting lips she tilted towards him. He reached up to caress her throat.

"My father never forgave me for what we did," he murmured. "He died hating me for that."

He fondled her throat more boldly, eliciting an ecstatic little gasp from her. But her drooping lids lifted in alarm when his fingers wrapped around the column with a sudden, ominous pressure.

"Signor Triston!"

He released Osanne at the startled cry, but did so with a snap that loosed the pins from one of her loops and tumbled her black hair over her shoulder. Lucianna stood at the foot of the stairs, her hand on Sir Balduin's arm.

Sir Balduin shot a frown at Osanne, then said, as though in haste to distract the outraged look Lucianna had fixed on Triston, "We were looking for the Lady Siri. Lady Lucianna said she would be in the hall."

"I've not seen her," Triston replied. "Lady Lucianna, this is Osanne de Brielle—my stepmother." He saw Lucianna's shock as she surveyed Osanne. He exchanged a glance with Sir Balduin, then said, "Have you looked in her workshop?"

"S–Signor?" Lucianna seemed too dismayed by his brazen revelation to grasp his meaning.

"Lady Siriol. She and Perrin were working on some project in her workshop earlier today. Perhaps she has gone there to check on it."

"Fauke came down early, hoping to speak with you, Triston," Osanne said. She rubbed her throat, then smiled a vengeful smile. "He is looking for someone to illuminate a psaltery for him and heard that your new ward has some skill in the art. Perhaps he bore her off to her workshop to sample a bit of that skill."

Triston did not need the purring insinuation in Osanne's voice to alert him to Siri's danger. He knew his lord too well. He pushed his way past Sir Balduin and Lucianna and lunged up the stairs, his stomach coiling into a ball of cold panic.

At the top of the steps, he seized a torch from its bracket in the wall and swept down the passageway that led to Siri's workshop. He heard Lord Fauke's roar from the darkened chamber ahead. Siri shouted something back in Italian. Triston quickened his pace, a chill sweat prickling his skin, rage towards the baron warring with dread of the inevitable tumult of her terror. He stepped onto the threshold, muscles flexed to wrench her out of the brawny baron's hold.

Instead, he found her free in the center of the room, and for an instant, shock held him riveted. With his eyes closed, he had believed he could trace every inch of her from head to toes. But he had never seen this woman before, dripping with so much scarlet and gilt that it made him blink, her hair piled atop her head with the ends twisted into a mass of glittering rings, her face—aye, still Clothilde's face, but as he had never witnessed it before. Angry, indignant, defiant, but above all, in total and sublime control.

Lord Fauke sat sprawled across a bench near the window. His posture suggested that he had not landed there willingly. One spot on his cheek stood out redder than the rest. He leaned forward for a moment to clutch at one of his shins, then sprang up snarling and started towards Siri.

Siri had her jeweled dagger halfway out of its sheath before Triston strode between them.

"Put it up," he hissed.

"If he touches me again, I will spit him like a pig!"

Triston caught her hand and slammed the blade back into its sheath.

"Step aside, de Brielle," Lord Fauke ordered. "If that little cat thinks she can strike me and not feel the back of my hand—"

Triston turned so quickly that his torch swooped dangerously near to Lord Fauke's face. The Baron fell back, cursing, but Triston did not bother to apologize.

"This woman is under my protection, my lord. If she requires discipline, it is my prerogative to deal it. Name your offense and I will—"

"I slapped him and kicked him and shoved him," Siri said before Lord Fauke could answer. "And if he comes near me again, I will spill his blood on the ground."

Triston glanced over his shoulder and saw her fingers flexing on her dagger's hilt. "Stop it," he commanded. "I will deal with this."

Her bright eyes defied him for a moment, then narrowed, but her hand fell away from her blade.

"My lord," he said, turning back to the baron, "how is it you come to be alone in this room in the dark with my ward?"

Lord Fauke's face, already flushed, darkened still further. "I heard that the wench knew something of illumination. She offered to show some of her work to me and while we were looking at her pattern book, the candle blew out, and the next thing I knew, she—"

"Blew out?" Triston said. "With the windows closed?"

Lord Fauke looked confused for a moment, then answered blusteringly, "Nay, she closed them afterwards. Just before she erupted like a madwoman." He glared at Triston. "No doubt she is truly your wife resurrected again."

Triston's hand closed on the front of Lord Fauke's surcote. He had dragged the shorter man onto his toes before he felt Siri pulling at his arm.

"Triston, don't. You know he is lying. Let him go." She must have felt the twitching of his muscles, for she added in an urgent whisper, "And don't push him."

His habit of releasing his hold with a snap that usually sent his opponent staggering was not easy to master. But when Siri's hand stretched up to his, he relaxed his fingers slowly and allowed Lord Fauke to slink away.

"You are going to regret this, de Brielle," Lord Fauke growled, jerking his rumpled surcote down to smooth it. "When the duke learns how you have laid hands on me, how your wench tried to draw steel—"

"If you touch her again," Triston warned, "'tis my steel you will face. I know your ways, my lord. You lured her here hoping to seduce her in the dark, but she wants none of you. Leave her be. She is mine. And do not think you can take her from me by consorting with your duke. She is no heiress for Richard to claim guardianship of in protection of the royal interests."

"If I want her," Lord Fauke smirked, "the duke will give her to me, have no doubt of that. And despite your bravado, I do not think you will risk the duke's wrath by trying to deny me a worthless craftsman's daughter."

Before Triston could reply to this, a movement from the corner of his eye made him turn. Osanne had followed him and came forward now to take Lord Fauke by the arm.

"My lord, come," she cooed soothingly, "the guests will be gathering in the hall and you cannot appear before them with your clothes all rumpled as they are. Let us exchange them for fresh while Sir Triston thinks over his bad temper. He will apologize at the banquet and the question of this . . . tradeswoman can wait until later."

Triston bristled at the derisive way Osanne sneered the word 'tradeswoman.' He only remained silent because Siri pulled on his sleeve, and she had to pull even harder when Lord Fauke spoke again.

"Aye, I will be expecting an apology, Sir Triston. From you both." He sent a hard look at Siri, filled with anger and a still-simmering lust, before he allowed Osanne to draw him out of the room.

When they were gone, Triston turned and gazed into Siri's face, searching anxiously for signs of hysteria behind the anger. But though her gown and hair were ruffled, her lovely eyes betrayed no fear and her fury seemed to slide away with Lord Fauke's departure.

"Did he hurt you?" Triston asked.

She shook her head. "He only kissed me. A wet, disgusting kiss. So I slapped him. He howled, but he still wouldn't let me go, so I kicked him as hard as I could and when he flinched, I shoved him and he fell onto the bench."

She stopped, then to his surprise, she giggled. He observed the fascinating crinkles that appeared at the corners of her eyes.

"That lady didn't drag him off because of his rumpled clothes," she said. "It was the paint."

"What paint?"

"On the parchment. I had been showing Perrin how to paint his drawings. We laid them out on the bench to dry, but I'm afraid they hadn't finished when Lord Fauke sat down on them."

Triston placed the torch in a bracket beside the window and picked up one of the smeared drawings. "Perrin did this?"

It was amazingly good for such an immature hand. A dog painted brown and white like Talbot carried a bright red ball to a woman seated in the grass. A woman with long yellow hair. He might have thought it the boy's mother, had the woman not been smiling and reaching out her hands to the dog.

"He has his father's talent," Siri said.

"He's a bright boy," Triston answered with pride. "Father Michel says that he is reading well in both Latin and French, that he draws his letters beautifully, and that he is very clever with his sums."

Triston's own ability to read and write, solely in French, had been gained through his mother's loving tutelage. His father had thought such pursuits unmanly, certainly not to be sought by any knight who could afford to hire a clerk. But he had not forbidden the knowledge, as Triston realized he might have done. Triston had been permitted to learn his letters, but he had never mastered the higher learning of arithmetic and philosophy that his heart had craved. He hoped for better things for his son. But . . .

"I'm afraid Perrin has been neglecting his studies somewhat of late."

A glance at Siri showed a satisfying expression of chagrin on her face.

"I know. I should not let him sit with me in the garden so much. I do try to send him off, but when he gazes at me with those lost, frightened eyes and begs to stay—"

With her altered appearance he had less trouble meeting her gaze, though he braced himself for the question he knew was coming.

"Why is Perrin so afraid?"

"I should think the answer is obvious," he said. "You remind him of his mother. He is afraid of losing you, like he lost her."

That lower rosy lip of hers caught briefly between her teeth. He knew that had not been what her question meant, and that he had not given her the answer she had hoped for. But the truth was, he had no idea why Perrin was afraid of him.

"I have not heard any more cries in the night," she said. "Have his nightmares gone?"

"Aye." He added reluctantly, "Since you have come."

"I could stay," she offered suddenly. "If it would be a comfort to him. I have no real need to marry again."

His fingers curled into the parchment he held, causing a brittle, crumpling sound against the silence. "I think that would not be wise," he said after a moment.

"Not wise for whom? For Perrin—or for you?"

Those jeweled eyes of hers met his with a disturbing directness. It was not an expression he was accustomed to from her. Or rather, from the face that he remembered.

"For any of us," he replied. "You are not Perrin's mother. The sooner he accepts that, the sooner he can deal with the pain of her loss. And you deserve a household and children of your own, not to live in another woman's shadow."

He felt her searching his face. At last she nodded, but he saw the trembling of her lip before she caught it again between her teeth. She moved to the door, then paused. He expected to hear a tremor in her voice when she spoke again, but there was none.

"Thank you for coming to my rescue with Lord Fauke. I hope I have not caused you any serious trouble with him."

"Nay," he said. "I rather think you spared me from my own

recklessness. It was one thing for you to have shoved him onto the bench, but had I pushed him, as I was tempted to do—"

"Aye, I did not think he would take that well. Will you apologize to him?"

"For rumpling his surcote, perhaps. Not for defending you."

"Nor I, for defending myself."

"Beware of him, Lady Siriol. He is a vengeful man, and he lusts for you. I will protect you as best I can, but his forces far outnumber mine and with the duke's support, if he should decide to seize you—"

Her fingers went to her dagger. He wished he could convince her how inadequate that weapon would prove against a man like Lord Fauke.

Her sweet voice hardened. "I am sorry for the trouble I have caused you, Sir Triston. I will try to choose a husband soon and be gone from Vere as quickly as possible."

"There is no need to be—"

. . . *hasty.* Triston swallowed the word. Siri had already opened the door and was gone.

❧

In fact, she had heard Triston's parting protest perfectly well. It gave her a ray of hope that his heart was not as eager to see her gone as his words implied. She had seen his pain and did not doubt that it was real. But perhaps it was not, after all, insurmountable.

Lord Fauke's preeminent position as Triston's lord placed him in a position of honor at the high table and placed Siri to his right, but for the most part he haughtily ignored her. On the few occasions when he did glance at her, she met his glares with an increasingly contented smile.

Lord Fauke's assault on her had enraged her far more than it had frightened her, but it had also accomplished something she had nearly despaired of. The rigid tenseness had left Triston's body as he sat on her other side. He actually conversed with her in a quiet, natural manner, directing this dish or that to be served onto her trencher and seeing to it that her goblet was never left empty. When she asked him about his manor, he even went so far as to look her directly in the face, something he had never deliberately done before this night.

Was it the gown? The way she had done her hair? Had she succeeded in making herself different enough from his wife? Or had it been her reaction to Lord Fauke? What, she wondered, would Clothilde have done, had some man other than Triston tried to kiss her?

Of course, Siri could not know the answer. But the aftermath of her own experience was proving so propitious that when Lord Fauke growled a warning in her ear that he had not forgotten her offense, she chirped out a reply that somehow managed to sound like an apology without actually being one.

"He thinks he's won," Triston muttered as Lord Fauke turned away with a satisfied smirk.

"Let him," she said. "And don't start glaring at him again. If you can't pretend a proper humility, then just don't look at him at all."

Triston lowered his gaze to his trencher, but from the way he stabbed his knife into a slice of venison, she knew that he found both her advice and her example unpalatable. Hoping to divert him, she asked him a few more questions about his manor, then inquired about the way of inheritance in Poitou, which she had heard was unusual.

"The ancient custom is for the sons to inherit jointly their father's lands," Triston told her, "with the eldest brother's sons inheriting only after all of the uncles have died. My grandfather instituted a system of primogeniture for his lands when he was lord, but we remain a relatively rare exception, though it is rumored that Duke Richard hopes to impose the rule upon all of Poitou and Aquitaine."

"Can he do so?"

"He can try, but he will meet with some resistance."

He saw that her cup needed refilling and motioned to a servant, but Acelet intercepted the gesture. Amid the crowd of noble rank that Siri had assembled, the young man was acting as squire, cutting meat and serving wine at the high table on the dais. She observed that there were no artful slashings of his sleeves tonight. Like the other servants, he wore an elegantly simple forest green tunic embroidered on one shoulder with the de Brielle rose, the same insignia blazoned on the breast of Triston's tunic.

Triston frowned when his cousin took the bottle from the servant and filled Siri's cup, but he only continued, "Duke Richard swore that if he were our lord, he would respect our ancient laws and liberties. But the truth is, we have no law, and our barons want to keep it that way. We are a violent, unruly race, Lady Siri. Oh, we feign a facade of culture and civility. It is said that our poets and troubadours are praised as far away as your native Venice. But those elegant Courts of Love, which Acelet's mother so fondly remembers, were a symptom of a darker truth. Queen Eleanor thought she could tame our wild young men by imposing on them a gentler system, turning their thoughts away from spilling blood to making love. But it never became more than a game, one played in courtly halls but abandoned without to the harsh reality that power is bought at the point of a sword."

"You are wrong, Triston," Acelet said when his cousin paused. "We are a valiant, courageous people. If the Young King were our lord—"

"Squires do not speak while they are serving at the table," Triston interrupted sharply. He sent a glance past Siri to Lord Fauke, but the baron was conversing with the raven-haired woman on his left and had not heard Acelet's words. Nevertheless, Triston clearly thought it wise to shift the subject. "These strawberries in custard are excellent, my lady. I might have known you would commission such a sweet treat from my cook. Perhaps Acelet will fetch us some more, before he sees to our other guests."

Acelet's face fell sulkily, but he obeyed.

Siri whiled away the remainder of the meal basking contentedly in Triston's attention. She did not care a fig for all the admiring stares she received from the noble bachelors she had assembled. Several would-be suitors had brought their sisters with them. Siri understood their motivation, for as a widower, Triston was now considered eligible as well. She found herself leaning closer to him, as though she could deflect the ambition she read in the women's eyes. But Triston met it all with a shuttered look, which lifted only when he spoke to her, or occasionally when he conversed with the man on his right.

Triston had introduced this gentleman to Siri as his father-in-law,

Lord Laurant, of neighboring Pennault Castle. A blond, handsome man of some fifty-odd years, Laurant had blinked twice when Triston presented Siri to him, and pronounced in a slightly trembling voice that, aye, the resemblance to his daughter was strong, but not as complete as he had been led to believe.

Siri had glowed when he said it. She hoped that if Triston's wife's own father could see the difference, Triston could learn to see it as well.

The banquet lasted for hours, but at last the servants cleared the tables away and replaced the wine on the sideboards with fragrant waters set out in silver pitchers. Siri had learned in the early days of her marriage that it was wise to lock the wine and cider away before their male guests became so intoxicated as to forget their manners. She had left similar instructions tonight, for while the banquet might have ended, the entertainments had not and the hot desire in the men's eyes was too familiar.

To her pleasure, Triston did not shrink when she reminded him that protocol demanded that he partner her for the first dance. Always a handsome man, he was devastatingly so this night. His silk surcote with a gold-linked collar strained against the powerful breadth of his shoulders. Its deep green hue enhanced his wild beauty, and his ebony locks, still somewhat disheveled from the altercation in her workshop, tumbled over his brow in a cluster of negligent curls.

He held her hands lightly and led her flawlessly through the intricate steps of the dance, twirling her at the proper time beneath his arm and lifting her from the floor with an effortless strength that took her breath away. Each time he held her in the air, her fingertips just brushing the tops of his shoulders, a wild hope blazed through her that his hold would slip, that she might tumble downwards into his arms, that he might catch her against his chest and whisper an apology against her ear and—oh, if only the crowd would fade away, she would take his face between her hands and—

Triston set her down, light as a feather, as the music came to an end.

"I think the next honor should be mine, Sir Triston."

She felt Triston tense in the instant before his hands left her waist and he turned to face Lord Fauke. The baron stood at the fore of the group of men who had deserted their partners on the final note of the music and swarmed to seek Siri's hand for the next dance.

Triston's brow darkened. "My lord—"

"My lord is quite right," she said, preempting whatever unwise protest Triston had intended to make. "Come." She took Lord Fauke's arm. "Let us join the circle over there. Yes, and you shall be next Sir Gavin, and after him Sir Adam, and then . . ."

She led the baron across the floor with the others trailing behind them. She promised a dance to each one, and only glanced back at Triston once. She expected to see him glaring at her for having gone off with Lord Fauke, but to her chagrin, he appeared to have found a diversion in the company of Lord Fauke's sultry, raven-haired companion. The woman laughed up at Triston, one hand against his chest.

The music started. Lord Fauke took Siri's hands and pulled her into the dance, forcing her gaze away from Triston's reaction to the woman's familiarity. The baron had changed out of his unflattering, paint-stained crimson surcote into a robe of black and gold that seemed to turn his hair to fire. It agreed with his fierce expression, and the bold way he eyed Siri up and down made her feel as though her own drapery of scarlet and gilt had suddenly turned transparent. Despite her determination not to lose her composure again, her cheeks flamed and her hand itched to wipe the smirk off his face.

"I imagine Osanne will keep Sir Triston occupied for what remains of the evening," he murmured. "Come, my lady, let us slip away and go somewhere quiet where you can apologize to me again in some more—satisfying—manner."

"If you try to kiss me again, the only apology you will get is my dagger between your ribs."

Lord Fauke laughed and lifted her off the floor in time to the music. To her horror, he promptly did what she had longed for Triston to do and clumsily dropped her from the air into his arms. She pushed vehemently against his chest, but he held her firmly there, then lowered his head and rather than apologizing, bit her ear. By the time she freed herself, spitting with fury, the other couples were stumbling in their steps and staring.

Only Triston had not seen, for his companion had led him away from the dance and held his attention with his back turned to the circle.

Lord Fauke seized her hands and swung her, resisting, back into the dance. "Come, my lady, do not make a scene."

"If you do that again—"

Siri's fuming threat was cut short by a movement that forced them both to change partners. But her relief was short lived, for the man who now faced her, apparently emboldened by Lord Fauke's example, leered down at her and stuck out his foot, making her trip and fall against him. His hands slid suggestively over her hips, but no sooner had she hissed at him and righted herself than she was passed on to another who pulled a similar trick, and then another, and even Sir Gavin twirled her so hard that she fell dizzily into his arms.

The men's increasingly raucous laughter should have drawn Triston's attention, but he no longer seemed to be in the hall. His raven-haired companion was missing too, as were Lucianna and Sir Balduin. Laurant had left after the feast, and it was Acelet who finally whisked Siri out of the dance. He cursed the man who had been clutching at her in a thoroughly humiliating way, and pulled her out of the hall into the narrow passageway that led to the kitchens.

"Thank you," she panted, putting up her hands to tuck her hair back into place, for some of it had tumbled from its pins into her eyes. "Those *furfanti* have no manners at all. If Triston thinks I am going take one of them for my husband—"

"Your husband?" Acelet exclaimed. "Is Triston forcing you to marry one of them?"

"Well, no, not forcing, but—" She stopped with a cough. The smoke floating from the kitchen into the passageway tickled her throat.

But Acelet seemed as unaffected by the haze as he was by her defense of his cousin. "Then Triston is the—how did you say it?—the furfanti. What does it mean, Lady Siri? I hope it means 'fool.'"

"No, it means 'villain.' And *furfanti* is plural. The word you want for Triston is *furfante.* " Acelet looked satisfied at the definition, and she hastened to add, "But of course, Triston isn't one. He is neither a villain nor a fool."

"I say he is both if he is forcing you to marry someone you do not love. Aye, and a coward, too. He only wants to be rid of you because he fears the guilt you stir in him over Clothilde. How do you call a man a coward in Italian?"

*"Codardo,"* she said, "but don't you dare call Triston that. And don't accuse him again of pushing his wife down the stairs, for I do not believe it and Sir Balduin says that you weren't there."

"I was too! I heard her screaming and Triston shouting and I ran out of my room just as she fell. Triston just stood there, doing nothing, but I ran down after her, only—only it was too late." His voice quavered and Siri saw tears spring into his eyes.

"I'm sorry, Acelet. I know you loved her very much too. But I cannot believe that Triston—"

"She's right, Acelet," a husky, male voice broke in. "Accidents happen. You must learn to accept it—as I have done."

She spun about and stared with amazement through the haze into Sir Raynor de Molinet's amber eyes.

"How did you get in here?" she demanded. "You were not invited to my banquet, and Sir Balduin would never have let you in if he had seen you arrive."

"Then we are fortunate that he did not see me," Raynor said. "And I did not come to partake of your feast, but to simply gaze upon your beauty once more." To her impatient frown, he added, "Acelet let me in."

Acelet blushed at her accusing gaze. "Triston set only a perfunctory guard to watch the main gate, so I let Raynor in through a postern in the west wall and brought him into the castle through the kitchen. He just wants to talk to you, Lady Siri. He is not like those men in the hall. He is chivalrous and honorable, as all followers of the Young King are."

"Triston will have his chivalrous head if he catches him here. And yours too, Acelet."

"My lady," Raynor said, "I came only to return something that you had lost. Spare me but a moment so that I can give it to you and offer you my regrets, and then if you wish me to be gone, I will be gone."

"What is it?" she asked suspiciously.

"This."

He took something from his belt and held it up to the light of the torch. It glistened like a vial full of sapphires against the flame. No, not sapphires...

"Lapis lazuli! My paint. You have my paint!" She gasped. "Then that means that you are—"

Raynor grinned. "—the villainous knight who tried to rob you on the road."

# Chapter 11

ut why—" A coughing fit cut Siri short.

"Come." Raynor took her arm and guided her down the passageway towards the kitchens. "Let us get you out of this haze into some clean air. There is an exit through the kitchens into the bailey."

She pulled away. "I am not going anywhere with you, Sir Raynor. After what you have just confessed to me, I should call Sir Triston's guards."

"And watch them slaughter me on the spot? That would rather spoil your dance, don't you think?"

"I doubt very much that they would do other than lock you up somewhere and hold you for Lord Fauke."

"Provided Triston does not murder me first. You saw the way he nearly throttled me on the riverbank. He holds great hate for me, Lady Siri, a hate I'm afraid I have courted too often in the past. But I wish to set our differences aside, to restore peace between our houses." He took her hand and placed in her palm the vial of glittering blue paint. "Come, my lady, what real harm have I done you that you cannot bring yourself even to listen to my story?"

Siri considered him. She had heard Sir Balduin's version of his quarrel with Triston. She could not deny her curiosity to now hear Raynor's version. "Very well," she said at last. "But I am not going to be alone with you. Acelet shall come along just in case you decide to try to abscond with me again."

Raynor flashed her a grin—he had a very engaging smile—and denoted his acceptance of her terms by executing a bow of such perfect grace that Acelet's eyes glistened with envy.

Siri took the younger man's arm. "I know you admire Sir Raynor, Acelet, but I am trusting you tonight to guard me. Remember that he is your cousin's enemy and furthermore, is wanted by the Crown for highway robbery. He would have stolen me, had Lord Fauke not come to my rescue."

"He would not have harmed you, Lady Siri," Acelet insisted. "He and his men have never hurt anyone, though there have been many a barbarous mercenary who deserved it."

She stared at him. "Acelet, are you saying you have known all along that Sir Raynor was the leader of the robbers?"

Raynor winced as her voice rose in disbelief. "Please, my lady, can we not go somewhere else to discuss this? Someplace where there are not so many greedy ears which would benefit from my exposure."

Acelet said, "We can go out through the kitchen. Pull your hood back over your head, Sir Raynor. We will say that Lady Siri was overwhelmed by the crowd in the hall and needs some fresh air."

She let them lead her through the warm, bustling kitchen and through another passageway which led to the well house and ultimately into the cool, clean air of the bailey. Acelet was right, there were no guards on the curtain walls at the back of the castle to observe their trio, but those near the gatehouse surely remained near enough to come if she called. She breathed deeply, clearing her lungs, then turned to Raynor.

"Now then, sir—"

"Not yet," Raynor said. "Acelet, we must not keep my lady standing."

Acelet went scuttling around the wall towards the forepart of the yard in search of some prop for them to sit on. Siri stiffened when she found herself alone with Raynor. Her hand moved to her dagger.

"We should have gone to the garden," she said. "I had set candles out there."

"That was where I first wished to meet you, but Acelet found someone there before us. He said they were—amorously occupied—and doubted they would wish to be disturbed."

Siri's mind flashed back to her last view of Triston, with Lord Fauke's raven beauty gazing invitingly up at him from a bewitching face he could never mistake for his lost, adored wife's. She longed to ask just whom Acelet had seen in the garden, but the hot little stirring in her breast told her that perhaps it was better not to know.

Acelet returned, dragging several sheaves of hay tied up with twine into a bundle large enough for one person to sit comfortably on, two if they sat close.

"Shall I fetch another?" he asked.

"No," Siri said. She plopped down square in the middle of the improvised support. "You and Sir Raynor can stand. Now then, sir, speak your mind but be brief. You may start by telling me why you have been attacking innocent travelers on the road and remind me again why I should not have you hauled away for doing so."

It was Acelet who uttered in his passionate way, "They are not innocent. They are murderers and robbers and ravishers of women, all barbarous followers of the duke."

"Duke Richard?" she said in surprise. "You have been attacking Duke Richard's men?"

"For the most part," Raynor admitted. "He lets his mercenaries ravage the countryside between his campaigns to humble the Poitevin baronage. No one was safe upon the road until my men and I started patrolling it. We relieve them of their spoils, serve them with a warning and let them ride on their way. They do not often return for a second serving of our discipline."

"Acelet said you never harm anyone."

"No one has ever died at our hands. For most men a little humiliation does the trick, but I own that a few harder-headed mercenaries have had to learn their lesson a bit more harshly."

She frowned. "And Lord Fauke? He is no mercenary, but your own lord. Have you attacked him too?"

It was a moonless night and the darkness concealed Raynor's expression from her, other than the white flash of his grin. "I held him to ransom once. Blindfolded, inside a stinking peasant's hovel. His men took a bit too long coming up with the money. I heard that two of them received a rare beating when I finally set their master free."

"And you feel no guilt for that, Sir Raynor?"

"They were greedy, brutal men, like their lord. Nay, I do not mourn the suffering of such as they."

He sounded very virtuous, but Siri had another memory. "You attacked my traveling party, too. Are you going to pretend you thought we were some of Duke Richard's mercenaries?"

He shrugged. "You might have been. Your men babbled away in some unintelligible tongue, and Duke Richard has been known to employ armies of foreigners in his service."

"But Lucianna and I—"

"You would not have been the first women such scoundrels tried to abduct."

Siri kept one hand on the hilt of her dagger, while the other played with the neck of her vial of paint. She stared scornfully at Raynor's shadowed form. "You must think me a fool, sir. It was no rescue you attempted. In fact, you threatened to hold me to ransom. Would you have stuck me in a stinking hovel as well?"

He laughed, a rich, ringing sound against the darkness. "Very well, my lady, I admit to the lapse. Our reputation has become such that the pickings on the road have been slim of late. There have been no spoils to satisfy my men, and they were becoming restive. But I would not have harmed you—and I certainly would not have stashed you in some hovel."

She could not see his expression in the dark, but experience told her that he probably spoke this last with a leer. "I am far from convinced by your excuses, sir," she said, "but as you suggest, I've no wish to disrupt my own festivities by your capture. If you leave now and agree to cease your forays on the road, I will keep silent about what you have confessed this night. But if I hear of any more hapless travelers being robbed—"

"You will expose me to Lord Fauke? Fair enough. The game has begun to pall, in any event. I shall find some other means of support. My brother left me in some debt, you see, and short of selling off my lands, I see no immediate way of settling them. Unless I were to find me a rich wife . . ."

Clearly, Raynor knew the purpose of this evening.

"Are you suggesting that I marry you?" she asked.

To her surprise, Acelet sat down beside her on the edge of the hay bundle. "It would not be so bad, Lady Siri. He is in love with you and has been since the first hour he set eyes upon you. He would cherish you like the priceless jewel that you are, not maul you, panting, like those animals inside."

"Acelet—" she could not believe her ears "—you want me to marry Sir Raynor?"

"Unless—Unless you would rather marry me instead?"

The wistful hope in his voice touched her. "Dearest Acelet." She brushed his face with her fingers, then surprised herself by kissing his cheek. "You know I cannot do that."

"Because I am too young," he muttered. "Because I am not a knight."

"Because you are too young," she agreed, "but I could not care less whether I marry a knight or not."

"There are only four years between us," he insisted. "And you know that I—"

"Acelet," Raynor interrupted, "the lady has rejected you. Stand aside and give me a chance to press my own suit."

"It shall be just as vain," she said, dismayed when Acelet reluctantly stood up and allowed Raynor to take his place on the hay. She started to rise too, but Raynor caught her arm and drew her back down.

"Come, my lady, I've no intention of trying to ravish you, or even abduct you, though if I thought I could seduce you I would certainly do so."

"Well, you cannot," she said, "and I will thank you to release my arm."

"Only if you will promise not to run away until I have said my piece."

"I do not like this, Sir Raynor."

"You do not know me, Lady Siri. If you would only give me a chance, I think you would like me very well."

"My arm, sir."

Raynor shrugged and let her go. She edged away as far as she could without falling off the hay. She did not trust him, but she did not wish to appear a coward, either. She tucked the vial into her girdle, then shifted to face him.

"What is it you wish to say?"

He spread his hands. "I wish to plead for your help. I wish to end this feud between Triston and me."

"You think you can do that by marrying me?"

Again his teeth flashed in the darkness. "Nay, I desire you for yourself alone—and, of course, for whatever dowry you might bring me. A necessity, I fear, if I am to give up my income from the road. But Acelet was right. I have often scoffed at men who professed to have fallen in love at a glance, but since I first laid eyes on you, nothing has been the same. Your face, your hair, even the flash of your eyes when you held the point of your dagger to my throat—all have haunted me, waking and sleeping. My lady." He took her hand. His voice softened as he repeated the endearment he had heard Lucianna speak on the road at their first meeting. "Carissima, if you are looking about for a husband, I pray you will not choose before I have had a chance to prove to you my merits."

She drew her hand away, unmoved by this eloquent plea. "You cannot possibly think Triston would let me marry you."

He sounded rueful. "I know he will never do so unless I can make my peace with him. My desire for you makes it all the more urgent that I do just that. Please, my lady, you must help me. If not for my sake—then for Triston's."

For Triston. To ease some of the hurt and anger from his eyes . . . "But why me?" she said. "How do you think I can help?"

"Our quarrel was caused by a woman, and I fear it may require a woman's cunning to bring it to an end."

She made no attempt to feign ignorance of his meaning. "Your sister.

You blamed Triston for her death."

Raynor sighed heavily. "So, you have heard the tale. She was more than my sister, Lady Siri. She was my twin."

His twin! Sir Balduin had not told her this.

Raynor must have sensed her surprise. "Have you any idea what it means to be a twin?"

She shook her head.

"It means that you share one heart, one soul, as it were. One cannot think a thought, but what the other knows it, or feel a pain that the other does not share. It is a joined existence, and if one should die—it is an existence the other cannot bear to endure alone." He leaned forward, hands clasped between his knees. "When I realized she was gone—I tried to kill myself."

Siri gasped.

"My brother Drogo caught me with the dagger at my wrist. He wrestled it away before I could do myself harm, then locked me up like the madman I had become. For weeks all I wanted was to be with her in death. But at last my brother found a priest with the patience and persistence to convince me of my sin. Isobel was gone. If I killed myself, my soul would be lost, our reunion forever denied."

Siri's compassionate heart could not help but be touched by his story. She laid her hand on his arm and said softly, "Tell me what happened between you and Triston."

He appeared to study her gesture for a moment, then sat up and squared his shoulders. He continued with a dispassion that contrasted sharply with his former grief.

"Isobel and I were sixteen when she fell in love with Triston. Triston was twenty, my brother's age, and the two had been fast friends from boyhood. Drogo encouraged Triston's wooing of our sister, hoping for an alliance of our houses, but—" he paused and for the first time his voice hardened "—but Triston had not marriage on his mind. He seduced my sister's innocent heart, then cast her off and went after new game, which it did not take him long to find."

She drew her hand away, her caution stirred by his bitterness. "You have not forgiven him."

"For that, no," Raynor said. "I will never forgive him for the pain he caused Isobel, nor for the child he refused to acknowledge. But—"

"Child—?"

"Aye." He answered Siri's shock almost savagely. "It was that which precipitated the—accident. Isobel had been in despair since Triston abandoned her. I told her that he was not worthy of her love, but she was desperate to have him back, and at last she confessed to me why. She carried his child and could not bear to live with her shame alone."

Siri felt the blood flow from her cheeks and would have started to her feet, but Raynor caught her arm and held it hard.

"I confronted Triston, my lady. He denied it, but I knew he was lying. He had dishonored my sister, and I was not going to have her used and cast aside like a cheap village harlot. I knew he would not confess the truth to me. But I thought if he saw Isobel again, when he stood face to face with her and was forced to look into her eyes, that his lies would shrivel in the glaring light of his own conscience. I thought he would agree to do the honorable thing."

"You mean that he would marry her," she whispered.

Raynor gave a curt nod. "My brother Drogo knew nothing of Isobel's condition, and we decided it would be better if he should not learn of it. He and Triston were both within weeks of being knighted and often engaged in sword practice together. I persuaded him to invite Triston to Belle Noir for a match of their skill. Isobel and I met Triston down by the bridge that spans the river dividing our lands. We confronted him together. When he brazenly continued to deny he was the father of her child, Isobel sought to remind him of what they had shared with a few desperate kisses."

He rose from the bale so abruptly that Acelet, who had been standing beside them listening, started back a step. Siri saw the repetitive motion of Raynor's hands as he clenched and unclenched them, but her thoughts clung to his words.

Twice now, he had said it. *Triston denied being the father of Isobel's child.* Every fiber of Siri's body wanted to believe it. Everything she had witnessed, everything she had sensed in Triston bespoke a man of honor, a man of conscience.

*But he was not always a man,* a voice whispered in her mind. *Sir Balduin confessed a hasty temper in Triston's youth. Might his passions and judgment have been just as hasty then?*

She said through the sudden lump in her throat, "I understand the river was frozen that day."

"Aye," Raynor answered harshly, "but the snows had been light and the ice was thin. Rather than melting beneath her caresses, Triston cursed her and thrust her off. She fell onto the ice and—"

His voice strangled over the rest and he covered his face with his hands. Acelet started to lay a hand on Raynor's shoulder, but something made him draw back again.

"It was an accident," Siri said. Regardless of the doubts about Triston that had been stirred in her, she remained certain of that.

"Aye." The word came muffled through Raynor's fingers. "I know that now. But then, I was wild with horror and grief. Triston and I were both wearing shirts of mail that day, he in anticipation of his engagement with my brother, I because I had determined to beat the truth from him, if he refused to confess again. We both stripped off our mail and dove after her into the chilling waters. Triston found her first, but too late. The cold, the water—there was nothing we could do."

Raynor shuddered again. Then he dropped his hands and turned back towards Siri. "Others had heard our quarrel and joined us by then. Before my brother and the other young men of our castle, I accused Triston of murdering Isobel, of deliberately throwing her into the river to drown both her and her child. I drew my sword and leapt on him, and without his mail, my blade slashed his arm. My brother dragged me away before I could do him further harm, but not before everyone had heard my insane accusations. At first, I wanted Triston dead, like Isobel. But later—later, I knew his death would not be enough."

The bitterness in Raynor's voice momentarily quelled her questions about Triston's past. Nay, 'twas more than bitterness, more even than hatred. There was something approaching menace in his tones that caused

Siri to rise and draw near to Acelet.

Raynor's head turned with her movement and when he spoke again, the disturbing note was gone. "I am not proud of what I did, Lady Siri, and I confess it was done out of pure revenge. Isobel was the dearest thing in my life, and Triston took her from me. I decided to punish him by taking from him that which he valued most in all the world."

"What did you do?" she asked. Acelet must have felt her alarm, for his arm slid around her shoulders.

"One Christmas," Raynor answered, "I accepted his brother Etienne's invitation to spend the holiday at Vere. While I was here, I did everything in my power to seduce the Lady Clothilde into becoming my mistress, and when she resisted—I forced my kisses on her."

Acelet's arm tightened around Siri. She knew what must have happened next.

"Triston caught you, didn't he? That's why he threw you out of Vere."

"My lady, I have felt nothing but shame since that day. The Lady Clothilde had never done me harm. I had boyishly courted her in my youth. To try and use her in that way to punish Triston was worse than despicable. It is for that I wish to win his forgiveness—as I have finally forgiven him Isobel's death."

All these revelations threatened to overwhelm her. "What do you wish me to do, Sir Raynor?"

He stepped forward and seized her fingers in his. "I wish you to speak with him, to tell him of the tears I have wept in my shame, to convince him of my repentance—"

"If you do not release the Lady Siriol with your next breath," Triston's voice rang out from behind them, "the only one needing to repent will be me—for lopping off your filthy hands."

Raynor stepped back and Siri whirled. Triston's powerful frame towered even in the darkness.

"Triston, he was not—"

"Do not defend him, Lady Siriol. I swore I would see him dead if I ever caught him at Vere again."

Triston made a movement in the dark. She ran forward to catch his fingers, which had closed on the hilt of his sword.

"Oh, don't," she cried, desperate to avoid another violent confrontation like the one she had witnessed beside the river. Her mind raced. If she admitted the truth of Raynor's presence, she would have to implicate Acelet as well. Surely Triston would deal more gently with her than with a cousin already in danger of snapping his patience?

"It is my fault Raynor came," she breathed. "I—I invited him. I told Acelet to let him in and to fetch me away to meet him, because I knew you would not let him into the hall—"

"Listen to her, Triston," Raynor pled over her fabrication. "I have come to make peace."

"Peace?" Triston spat. "The devil you have. I believed your lies once when I let you ride through my gates with my brother. But it was spite you carried in your heart then, and 'tis the same you come bearing now."

Siri did not have the strength to restrain the vibrating force of Triston's fist on his hilt. He shook her off, knocking her into Acelet's hold, but when he closed the space between himself and Raynor, to her relief his fist flew through the air empty to land on Raynor's chin.

Raynor hit the ground with a reverberating thud, but he did not remain there long. Triston bent to grasp Raynor's tunic and drag him back to his feet.

"If I let you escape from me again—" he snarled.

Siri ran to pull urgently at his arm. "Triston, let him go, please. Raynor has confessed everything to me. I know how he has hurt you, what he did with your wife, but he is sorry now—as I know you are sorry for Isobel."

If it were possible, Triston's already tense muscles tightened still further. Then abruptly he thrust Raynor away, landing him once more on the ground.

"Get out!" Triston shouted at him. "Get out of my sight! If I catch you at Vere again, so help me, I swear I will kill you!"

"Acelet," she pleaded, "take Raynor away."

Acelet helped Raynor to his feet and led him off into the darkness.

Triston turned to Siri, closing his fingers on her arm in a grasp that made her wince.

"How dared you invite him here against my wishes? You knew I would not allow this, and you deliberately defied me."

"I—I wanted to know why you were so angry with him," she said, clinging to her lie as she sought to concoct a story that might appease him. "I had heard rumors—" she flinched as his fingers dug deeper into her flesh "—rumors about some land. That you and Sir Raynor were quarreling over it—" the painful grip eased "—and I thought it was a ridiculous thing to hate a man for, so I thought that if I could talk to him and learn his side of the story and then talk to you, perhaps I could persuade the both of you sit down and discuss it together in a calm and reasonable manner, and—"

Triston shook her. "Raynor did not come here to talk about land."

Siri's heart skipped. "He did! He—"

"Nay, that may have been why you asked him, but that is not why he came. He heard about your banquet, that you are looking for a husband. What did he tell you, Lady Siriol? That he fell in love with you that day he met you on the riverbank? That he cannot sleep for thought of you? That if you marry him, he will never forsake you for another? And what did you say in reply?"

"I said no, of course." She surprised herself by adding, "For now. But I must admit, I found him a deal more appealing than those knaves in the hall. Thanks to Lord Fauke's wretched example, the minute your back was turned they started pawing me like I was some wanton engaged for their pleasure."

This complaint successfully diverted Triston for a moment. He said grimly, "I warned you at dinner that our men are without discipline. Our counts and dukes have set a licentious example too many are eager to follow. They did not harm you, did they?"

"No," she said, "but if Acelet had not whisked me away, there is no knowing how far they might have gone."

"But where was Sir Balduin? Or Lucianna?"

"I do not know where they were. I do not know where you were—"

except that he had not been alone. The hour and the darkness lent an intimacy to her renewed vision of Triston and the sultry woman she had last seen him with.

"I was with Perrin. Audiart called me away to him. He had another nightmare."

"Oh." She blinked in surprise. Triston's hand relaxed so that she might have slipped away, but she did not do so. "But I thought you were— I saw you with— Then who did Acelet see in the garden?"

"I have no idea."

"You said Perrin's nightmares had stopped."

She was appalled when her statement came out laced with suspicion. But Triston's raven-haired companion had been missing too.

"They had, until Audiart told him that you might marry and leave us. Apparently he woke up screaming for his mother, and then he started screaming for you. Audiart called me to him, but he—he would not let me near him. So I came looking for you, hoping that you might be able to calm him. Only when I got to the hall you were gone."

His hold tightened again.

"Triston, I—"

"What did he tell you? My quarrel with Raynor is not over land. What did he tell you about me and Isobel?"

"I— Sh–Shouldn't I go to Perrin?"

"The child has probably cried himself back to sleep by now. Sit down—" she had no choice, as he pushed her onto the bundle of hay "—and tell me what he said."

She rubbed at her pulsing arm and chose her words carefully. "He told me that you fell in love with his sister, and then you fell out of love, and when she tried to woo you back you quarreled, and when she tried to embrace you, you—you pushed her and she fell onto the ice and it broke and—and she drowned. Triston—" even in the veiling shadows, she knew what lay in his eyes "—it was an accident. No one blames you for it, not even Raynor any more."

His ragged breath bespoke the pain she could not see. "That is not all. He told you about the child, too, didn't he?"

"Yes." She silently berated herself when the word came out in a whisper, then forced herself to remember the rest. "Triston, you were young, perhaps impulsive. If you and Isobel—"

"I owe you no explanations, Lady Siriol," he cut her off curtly. "What more did Raynor tell you? You said he confessed everything. Including what he did to Clothilde?"

"Raynor said that he tried to hurt you by seducing her, yes. But he regrets it terribly now, as terribly as you regret his sister. Triston, can you not forgive one another and—"

"Nay, Isobel was an accident, but what he did to Clothilde was cold and deliberate. Had it been any other woman, had it even been you— But Clo—"

The way his voice broke brought tears stinging into her eyes. "Triston, how long will you grieve for her? Sorrow will not bring her back— anymore than hate will. Raynor—"

"Raynor is lying if he says he regrets what he did. He laughed at me when I threw him out. He said he would win another day, and he sees that day come with you. Lady Siriol—" one step brought him before the bundle of hay "—he thinks he can hurt me again through you. I know his honeyed tongue, the ease with which he has seduced many a woman's heart, but you must not give it heed. It is not a marriage bed he wants you in—but a coffin."

She gasped. "Triston, that is outrageous!"

"It's true. I took Isobel from him. He took Clothilde from me—and now he is going to try to take you too."

He groaned into the darkness. Siri was not sure who reached out first, but suddenly she found her hands in his. She gasped again, this time with shivering pleasure when he pulled her to her feet and against his chest.

She had longed for this moment! To feel herself embraced fully, completely by his strong arms. But after his former, tentative kisses, the force of his mouth surprised a moan from her. His kiss immediately softened. He would have released her, but she rose onto her toes, her mouth clinging to his until the last possible instant.

"Don't," she whispered. "Please don't stop."

"But I've hurt you—"

"No—merely startled." She knew he could not see her trembling smile in the dark. She took his face between her hands and drew his lips back down to hers.

At first he met her mouth gently, but then it was as though something snapped inside him. Siri wound her arms around his neck, as their lips parted and came together again and again, his with a growing desperation, hers with delirious ecstasy. One of his hands slid up the back of her neck to loose the pins in her hair. She rolled back her head as her hair tumbled free, then gasped when he scattered a series of fiery, vehement kisses along her throat. His fingers twisted in her hair.

"I won't let him take you," he said in a fierce whisper against her ear. "I won't lose you again."

*Again.* The word struck Siri to the heart, but she clung to him a moment longer. She wanted only to surrender, to dissolve against him and through him until they were no more Siri and Triston, but a single, soaring being, never to be parted, never to know themselves without the other again.

She did not know where she found the strength to stop him, the strength to face the truth.

"Triston, I am not your lost love. I am Siri, and if you cannot want me for myself—"

Her voice broke. She gave a small sob when his hands fell to her shoulders and pushed gently her away. She sank back onto the hay and buried her face in her hands.

"Forgive me. Sweet lady, forgive me."

He knelt on the ground before her. His hands slid over the scarlet silk in her lap to rest upon her hips. He could not have seen her tears, but he must have felt them in the shaking of her body. He pulled her hands away from her face and brushed his fingers against the rivulets on her cheeks. Her lips trembled uncontrollably. She caught his fingers and kissed them.

"Lady Siriol—"

"No, please, do not say it. Do not say anything. Just let me—" she raised his face and spread her hands so that her thumbs brushed against his mouth "—kiss you once. A kiss from Siri. Then close your eyes and let me walk away."

She pressed her lips to his and let the taste of him flood through her again. It might be the last time and she must sear it into her memory forever.

Forever. She might have lost herself in the kiss that long, had the warm response of his mouth not panicked her. In that instant she knew he had drifted into the memory of his wife again. She thrust him away so quickly that he lost his balance and sat down hard on the earth. Then she fled, grateful that her streaming tears and pounding heart deafened the name he called out after her.

# Chapter 12

$S$iri."

Triston whispered her name again into the darkness. He sat where she had left him, on the ground beside the bundle of hay. He groaned and ran a hand through his curls. *Siri. Clothilde.* How had he grown so muddled?

When he first pulled Siri into his arms, he had known which woman he kissed. He would never have embraced Clothilde in that forceful way. Clothilde's fragile, sensitive spirit had reduced their marriage to little more than affectionate kisses at Perrin's bedside towards the end. But the three brief kisses he had already shared with Siri told him she was different. Within her burned a passion as frank as his own.

But fear, not passion, had driven his first impulsive kiss this night. Fear roused to an irresistible pitch by Raynor's presence at Vere and the threat Triston believed he posed to Siri. To have her merry laughter quenched by that villain, the bright strength of her eyes dimmed, to lose the hope her sweet lips imparted . . . Aye, it was Siri he embraced for a few soul-healing moments.

Then somewhere in the mingling of their lips, he had become confused. Perhaps it had been when he tumbled her hair over his hands. The feel of it had been so like Clothilde's. Suddenly, fear had shifted into pain again. It should have been Clo who was clinging to him, responding with the vibrance and strength he had wanted to believe lay somewhere beneath the tormented tendrils of her mind. For one fleeting instant in the dark, he had imagined that it *was* Clothilde, as she might have been, as she would have been had it not been for her mother . . . and Raynor.

The rebuke of Siri's tears had restored his senses and driven away the foolish vision. Clothilde was gone. And it was Siri's kiss that now lingered on his lips.

He closed his eyes and let the warmth of her wash through him.

"Siri," he whispered again.

An answering scream split the air. He shot to his feet, then stood uncertainly, unable to pinpoint the sound's origin as the piercing echo bounced off the castle's walls. Someone was hurt, in danger, but where—?

The second cry sent him rounding the keep's perimeter towards the front of the bailey—the same way Siri had gone when she had fled from him.

"Help! Someone help me!"

He quickened his pace, his stomach clenching as he recognized her voice. He was nearly to the foreyard when he realized he had gone too far. Her cries were behind him now. Back and to his right. *Over by the postern gate.*

Triston had ordered an end to the festivities when he had found Siri missing from the hall, but some of the guests still lingered in the yard, and several were carrying torches.

"Over here!" he shouted. "Bring a light!"

He strode back to the gate tucked so cunningly into the curtain wall that a besieger would never have guessed its existence. But someone had known of it, for it stood open, and Siri's frantic cries clearly came from the other side. Had someone attacked her and dragged her away to rob her, beat her, *ravish her*—?

He lunged through the gate, almost screaming her name. "Lady Siriol!"

"Sir Triston! We are over here. Oh, hurry!"

It was not easy to find her in the dark. The outside of the walls was covered with bushes and vines that had grown up thick around them. In the moonless night, he had to feel his way past them, calling to her over and over, holding his breath for each response, terrified lest whatever injuries she had suffered should cause her to faint before he could find her.

His mind filled with terrible visions of her fate, he was not prepared to have her rise up suddenly from the shadows and fling her arms around his waist.

"Thank heaven!" she breathed. "Oh, Triston—"

The fierce strength of her embrace should have reassured him. But . . .

His hands flew over her, feeling for lumps or cuts or—merciful heavens! Her palms were wet, sticky with something other than sweat.

Men with torches finally swarmed through the gate to join them, and Triston's knees went weak with horror. Blood. Her hands were red with it and there was a smear on her cheek and her hair was tangled and her skirts and sleeves were torn—

"It's not mine." She hurriedly wiped her hands on her gown. "Triston, the blood is not mine. It is Raynor's."

She pointed towards the bushes behind her. Still, it was not until one of the men who had joined them uttered an oath that Triston managed to drag his stricken gaze from her.

Siri sank to her knees beside Raynor's prostrate body. Even in the ruddy light of the torches, his face looked pallid, his eyes closed, his head rolled limply towards the men who had gathered around him. There was a rip at the throat of his mantle, as though whatever brooch had clasped it had been torn away, and the rings that customarily graced his hands were gone. Both Raynor's sword and dagger were missing, leaving empty sheaths strapped to his belt. Blood flowed from a wound near his hip, drenching his right thigh.

Triston knelt beside Siri and laid his fingers to a spot on Raynor's neck below his ear. A faint but unmistakable pulse fluttered there.

"How did you find him?" he asked.

She hesitated, then lowered her voice so that only he could hear her reply.

"When I ran away from you, I was crying. I could not see clearly and I stumbled against the wall and my hand felt the opening of the gate. Then I heard a groan and realized someone must be hurt. So I stepped through the gate to look. Only it was so dark I could only follow the sound. The brambles on these bushes tore my gown and then my foot struck something, and I reached down and felt—a man. He was still conscious then, barely so, but he spoke enough for me to recognize his voice as Raynor's. He said he had been attacked and robbed, but he fainted before he could finish. I was trying to feel him for injuries when my hand felt the blood and—" She shivered. "That's when I started screaming. Oh, Triston—" she turned towards him and pressed her face into his shoulder. "He has not said a word since and I could not even tell if he was breathing. He's not—?"

"No." Triston put his arm around her. "Not yet. But if he loses any more blood—"

"We must help him. We must take him into the keep and—"

"No."

She pulled her face away. "Triston—"

"No." He stood up. "The dog has got what he deserved."

"We can't just let him die!"

Couldn't he? Triston's mind flashed back to that Christmas-tide night when Clothilde's shrieks had brought him upon the awful scene. Raynor overpowering her terrified struggles, trying to smother her cries with his kisses. Triston had wrenched his wife free, then hurled a blow that knocked Raynor into the wall across the room. He did not recall actually drawing his sword, only that it had been in his hand when he had plunged through a reddish mist after Raynor. Raynor succeeded in drawing his own sword before Triston's blade slashed down on him. Their subsequent battle had sent them lurching into every corner of the room, steel clanging, wood splintering, Clothilde shrieking and shrieking and shrieking—

He had thought she would never stop. Even after his thrust caught Raynor in the shoulder, after he had thrown him bleeding out into the snow, Clothilde's frenzied screams had gone on—and on—and on. Only Triston's resolute strength had kept her from rending her tender cheeks with her nails, from ripping her hair out in fistfuls. He had held her writhing body hard in his arms, pleading with her to stop, frantic to know how to help her until the servant Audiart brought him a goblet with a sleeping draught. She poured it down Clothilde's throat while Triston held his wife's head fast. Still, it had seemed an eternity before the fit at last subsided and Clothilde fell into a drugged slumber.

And when she awoke, she had remembered nothing but Raynor's lies. Lies which had turned her against Triston, lies which had snatched her from his fingers and sent her tumbling down the steps to her death.

"Leave him," he said again. "Let the villain die, too."

"No!"

He turned and started back towards the gate.

"Triston!"

He ignored her cry. The men did not seem to know whether to follow him or not. Over their confused murmurings, he heard Siri's voice.

"You, there, tear off a strip from your mantle. We must bind up this wound. And you, we will use your cloak to lay him on and the four of you shall carry him inside—"

Triston swung about and shouted, "No!"

"I am not going to leave him here to die!" she shot back at him. "I don't care what you say."

"Then have someone fetch you a wagon and cart him back to Belle Noir."

"He has lost too much blood. We must get him inside and call a physician."

Fury exploded through Triston. "If you dare try to bring him under Vere's roof—"

Uncowed by his rage, Siri motioned to one of the men, who obediently tore his mantle and began binding Raynor's injured leg. Then she moved to Triston's side.

She spoke slowly, her voice low but steady. "I don't care what your quarrel with that man is. I don't care how he's hurt you, or how you've hurt him. He is a man and he is dying and he needs our help. And you are not the man I thought you were if you can let him die here, beneath your own walls, and not let the guilt of that haunt you for the rest of your days." She paused, then reached up and brushed one of the curls that lay against his ear. "Do you not suffer enough guilt as it is? Do not lay yet another against your conscience. Do not let him hurt you in this as well."

Triston closed his eyes, determined to shut out her face, to shut out the way her touch unnerved him. Was his pain so transparent? She was right. In the blaze of memory, he could watch Raynor die. But in the cold aftermath of silence, when he looked into his soul and realized what his inaction had wrought, the horror would overwhelm him.

He took a shuddering breath. "Very well. They may take him inside. But keep him out of my sight, and as soon as he is well enough to travel, you must send him back to Belle Noir."

Her voice warmed. "Thank you. You will not be sorry."

He opened his eyes, then caught her arm as she turned away to rejoin the men around Raynor. "No, let them take care of him."

"But—"

"We must get you cleaned up before Lucianna sees you like this. You have blood on your face, as well as your gown."

Siri rubbed at her cheek, but since she could not see herself, she entirely missed the smear. A reluctant smile tugged the corners of his mouth. He tried to wipe the smear away for her, but the blood had dried and clung to her skin. She moved her face at his touch, so that the soft curve of her cheek nestled warmly for a moment in the palm of his hand. Silken smooth, like Clo's, and sweetly scented...but not with violets.

He did not realize how near his lips were to brushing hers until he discerned the subtle fragrance of lavender on her skin. The unfamiliar scent should have stemmed this sudden, aching rush of longing. Instead, the last shreds of the anger and fear he had known in the bailey seemed to flow away as some power more irresistible than his own will brought his mouth gently down on hers. Her lips warmed instantly, ensnaring him in something so sweet and strong that it shook him to his core.

"Sir Triston?"

One of the men called to him from Raynor's side. He pulled his mouth away from Siri's, and experienced a pang of loss so keen that he actually gasped.

Saints! Had he lost his mind to embrace her like this before the men?

"Do as she says," he said gruffly, praying, for her sake, that the darkness had hidden his madness. "Bring Raynor inside. One of you find my man, Sir Balduin. He will tell you where to put him." He hesitated, then took Siri's arm again. "Come," he repeated, "I will escort you inside."

But she drew herself free. "Thank you, but I know the way. Good night to you, Sir Triston."

He knew the cause of her withdrawal. She feared Clothilde was in his mind again. Until he could be sure exactly who it was he ached for—Siri or merely a wistful image of what might have been with Clothilde—he must let her go.

The heat from the flames swept around Siri's numb body, penetrating the thin fabric of her sleeveless chemise. She knelt before the fireplace in her chamber, her stained gown in her hands. It was ruined beyond repair, good only as fodder for the flames, but she hesitated before casting it in. Her fingers traced the gold threads of the pattern worked into the scarlet of one of the torn sleeves. She had meant to make a new beginning this night. For a few moments in her workshop, and again at the banquet table, she was certain she had succeeded. Triston had gazed at her as though he had never seen her before, and that, she knew, was the first step to making him see her at all. Or rather, to making him see her as Siri, and not as his lost Clothilde.

But now everything was spoiled again. She cursed the darkness that had veiled her changes from him, which even now left her thrilling to kisses that were not her own.

"Donna Siri, what is this I hear about robbers at Vere?"

Siri turned, still on her knees. She kept the dress behind her back as Lucianna swept into the room.

"One of Triston's neighbors was attacked and beaten as he was leaving Vere tonight," Siri said. "He suffered a dangerous injury to his leg and was bleeding terribly when I— when he was found. Has a physician been summoned, do you know? Triston promised he would send for one, but I fear lest he should come too late."

She stopped as Lucianna's shrewd gaze slid over her still tangled hair—thank heavens she had washed her face!—then found the faint bruise on her arm where Triston had held her too hard in his anger.

"What are you holding behind your back?" Lucianna demanded.

Siri saw the steely intent in her eyes and tried to dodge, but Lucianna's hand darted behind her and came up with the torn and bloodied gown. The older woman's face went white. She swept Siri up and into her arms, clutching at her in horror and fear.

"Carissima! Oh, my *bambina!* What has that *diavolo* done to you?"

Siri did not need to ask whom she meant. Lucianna's suspicions had been too clear for too long.

"Lucianna, it is not what you think."

Lucianna's hand came under Siri's chin and forced her face into the light of the flames. Indignation sparkled through a glisten of tears in Lucianna's eyes, but a rigid sternness harshened her features. "Do not deny it, carissima. You have been with him. Signor Triston! That wicked Donna Osanne said he had gone looking for you when you left the dancing. I told Signor Balduin that we should follow! The *mostro*, the diavolo! Signor Triston has lusted for you from the moment you stepped into his hall, and now he has defiled you!"

"Lucianna, no! Yes, I was with Triston, but he has never laid a hand on me against my will. 'Tis true," she added to Lucianna's severe gaze, "that he kissed me tonight— I let him kiss me. I thought— I prayed—"

The tears that finally spilt over were Siri's own, hot and hurt and bitter. She jerked the gown from Lucianna and flung it into the flames.

"The gown— the hair—" She scooped the curling ends of her locks atop her head, then let them pour back over her shoulders. "It was all for nothing. Triston does not love me. He cannot even see me. Ah, Lucianna—" She sank to her knees with a choking sob.

"Donna Siri, do not tell me that you think you are in love with him!"

Siri shook her head. "Not think. I know it, here." She pressed a fist to her heart. "It is so deep inside me that I know it will be there forever. I promised him I would marry, but how can I give myself to another?"

"Have you given yourself to him?"

"No, I tell you, no. Lucianna, I swear!"

Lucianna motioned to a portion of the ripped gown that the flames had not yet reached.

"I tore it in the bushes when I was looking for Sir Raynor. The blood is his, as well. Lucianna, I swear it is true! I am the one who found Sir Raynor after he had been robbed and injured."

Lucianna stared at Siri a long moment. Then she bent and raised Siri up. "Very well. I know you would not swear to what is a lie. We will not talk of that again. But of the other we must speak."

Siri scrubbed at her wet cheeks. "If you are going to warn me against Triston—"

"Si, I am." Lucianna made her sit down on the bed, then sat beside her and took her hand. "Carissima, bambina, you have been as my own child. I could not look your mother in the face when I die were I to let you continue on this path. No, you will listen to me. Signor Triston is a wicked man. Tonight when I entered the hall, he was embracing a woman, the companion of *Don* Fauke, fondling her throat in a shameful, lecherous manner. When he saw me, he turned to me calm as you please and introduced her as—" Lucianna's hushed voice revealed the depth of her dismay— "Donna Osanne, his stepmother."

"His stepmother?" Relief swept over Siri. That the woman should be no older than Triston did not surprise her in the least. Had Siri not been a young wife to an old man too? "Then that is why she hovered around Triston all night and why she disappeared with him when he went to see about Perrin. She must have been worried about the boy as well."

Lucianna laid her hands on Siri's shoulders. "Did you not hear me? He was embracing her! No, not as a son should welcome the wife of his father, but as an— an *amante*, a lover."

Siri gasped. "Lucianna, Triston would not—"

"I tell you, you do not know him. I was suspicious. I drew Signor Balduin away to the gardens to learn more of her and him. Signor Balduin confessed to her wickedness, that she took many *amanti* while she was married to Signor Triston's father."

So it had been Lucianna and Sir Balduin in the gardens? Siri was surprised, but said, "That does not mean that she and Triston were lovers. I do not believe it. That would be a—"

"A sin, si. To defile one's father's wife is a vile sin indeed."

Siri sprang to her feet. A youthful indiscretion with Isobel might be regrettable but not unforgivable. But this—! "No. Triston would not do such a thing. I will not listen while you blacken him this way."

"It is true that I have no proof," Lucianna admitted. "Signor Balduin would not accuse his master, but his silence spoke loudly to me, as loudly as what I witnessed for myself in the hall. It is only further evidence of Signor Triston's wanton nature. Have you forgotten the wicked way he embraced you before he even knew your name?"

"Lucianna, he thought I was—" Siri stopped. Lucianna would never believe her. She had made up her mind about Triston, and there was nothing Siri could do or say to change it.

Just as there seemed to be nothing she could do to change Triston's.

She sat down again and rubbed at her temples. "I cannot think of this anymore tonight. My head aches—" and her heart ached "—oh, please, just let me go to bed." Tears welled up in her eyes again.

Lucianna's stern face softened. "Si, you are exhausted." She stood to plump the pillows, then nudged Siri into the wide, feather-soft bed. "Tomorrow," she murmured, as she tucked the blankets around Siri. "Tomorrow the men will come to court you again, and we will find you a husband to chase away these painful thoughts of Signor Triston. You will see, carissima. He will melt away like the lingering strands of a dismal dream in the light of the dawn."

Siri said nothing. But when Lucianna blew out the candles, she touched her fingers to her lips and knew she would never forget.

⟡

Siri passed a miserable night. Her dreams were all of Triston, and each time she awoke there were tears on her pillow. Then somewhere in the middle of the night, she started awake with thoughts of Raynor. What if she had found him too late, what if the injury was too deep, what if the physician had not arrived in time? Over and over the worries mingled with her pain to drive the last vestiges of sleep from her eyes. She rose with the dawn while Lucianna still slept and, pausing only to don a fresh white smock, hurried from her chamber without even stopping to braid her hair.

Sir Balduin stood guard outside the room where Raynor had been laid for the night.

"How is he?" Siri asked.

Sir Balduin looked grim. "The physician said he came very near to bleeding to death, but the wound has been stitched up and if it does not reopen or fester, the chances are good that he will recover."

"May I see him?"

She cast an anxious glance at the door, too worried to blush at Sir Balduin's disapproving frown.

"My lady," he said, "it was not wise to bring him here. Triston left the castle enraged this morning after the physician said it might be a fortnight before Raynor is well enough to return to Belle Noir."

"It was either bring him here or let him die. Triston agreed there was no other choice."

Sir Balduin nodded. "Aye, but it makes his presence no easier to stomach." He turned to open the door for her.

"Has Sir Raynor said anything about who attacked him?" she asked.

"Nay. I have sent men out to search the area, but I doubt they will find anything. The scoundrels have probably taken to the woods by now. 'Tis a disturbing turn, my lady. It seems our local brigands have tired of assaulting helpless travelers and now mean to prey upon us in our homes. Triston said the postern gate was open. It is possible that Sir Raynor was attacked here on the grounds, then dragged outside the walls. From now on guards will be watching the perimeter day and night, but I would caution you against straying too far from the safety of the keep. The garden should be secure enough, but I would go no further than that until the thieves have been apprehended."

Siri knew she should tell Sir Balduin about Raynor leading the robber knights and how impossible it was that they should have been their master's attacker, but she had promised to keep his secret for now.

A blast of heat and an almost suffocating fume of herbs and medicines welcomed her admittance to the chamber. A pot bubbled and gurgled over the flames in the fireplace, sending its cloying steam into every corner of the stifling chamber. Her eyes watered and her mouth filled with its thick, musty scent. She did not know enough of healing to dare remove the pot, but she did risk cracking open the shutter on the tall, narrow window to let in a little fresh air.

She moved to the side of the bed. Raynor was swathed in so many blankets that she could not tell whether his chest rose and fell, but she could hear his ragged breaths and see the sweat that streamed down his face and glistened in his beard. Beside the bed stood a trestle table with a clay basin and pitcher, a bottle of wine, and a few vials and cups, perhaps left behind by the physician. She found a cloth floating in the water-filled basin, wrung it out, then used it to wipe Raynor's cheeks and forehead.

His eyes fluttered opened. After a moment, the mist in them cleared and a faint smile flitted its way across his lips.

"Carissima," he whispered. "I have died and gone to heaven."

She supposed that with her white smock and trailing hair, she might indeed appear an angel to a man muddled from sleep or illness. She returned his smile, but said, "You have not died, Sir Raynor, and we mean to see to it that you do not. But you must lie very still so that your leg does not bleed any more and you must do everything the physician says."

He shook his hand free of the blankets and raised it to touch a strand of her hair. "Stay."

His hand trembled. She laid it carefully back down on the bed. "You must not exert yourself, sir. And I cannot stay. I only came to see how you are, and what I see is that you need to rest." She turned to Sir Balduin, who stood in the doorway. "Did the physician leave a sleeping draught for him?"

Sir Balduin shrugged.

She did not recognize any of the contents of the vials and cups and hesitated to administer an unknown medicine. She poured some of the wine into an empty mug.

"Drink this." She lifted Raynor's head and held the mug to his lips while he gulped down a few mouthfuls. "There. Now sleep. I am sure the physician will return again soon, then I will find out what all these concoctions are for. We will have you well before you know it, Sir Raynor."

Raynor moved his head sharply against the pillows, as though he sought to resist the dulling effects of the wine.

She quickly laid her hands on his shoulders to still him. "You must not thrash about, sir. Your wound—"

"Did they find him?" He spoke in a pant, winded by his movement.

"Who?"

"The man who did this—the man who robbed me. Acelet—"

"I have not seen Acelet this morning," Siri said. "I suppose he has gone out with Sir Balduin's men to look for the thief."

"No. Acelet— It was Acelet who robbed me."

Her breath came in a gasp. Then she saw the fresh sweat on Raynor's face. He was feverish, delirious. "Hush, sir. Acelet did not rob you and he certainly didn't stab you in the leg. Why, I imagine the sight of blood would make him shudder."

Thankfully, Raynor's continued insistence was too weak to carry to Sir Balduin in the doorway. "I tell you, it was Acelet."

"Why would Acelet do such a thing? He has no need of your jewels."

"He did it—for Triston."

*"What?"*

"For Triston—to avenge him—for Clothilde. Acelet said—he said—that Triston told him—told him to . . ."

Siri was torn between relief and regret when the wine finally numbed Raynor's tongue and closed his eyes. Surely he was not trying to accuse Triston of ordering his cousin to attack him! The very thought of Acelet attacking anyone with a knife was so absurd as to be laughable. Unless—

"Sir Balduin, have you seen Acelet this morning?" she asked.

"No, my lady, but I have been posted outside this door since the physician left just before dawn."

She turned away from the bed. "Sir Raynor has fallen back to sleep. A servant should be found to sit with him and bathe his face until his fever breaks." She could only hope that any feverish mutterings would be interpreted as delirium.

She closed the window and left the chamber with Sir Balduin, but no sooner had she shut the door behind them than the sound of a quick footstep made her look up. Triston strode down the corridor towards them. He had replaced his elegant robes of the evening with a practical knee-length brown tunic of the dark, sober color he seemed favor and of the simple cut that sat so admirably across his broad shoulders. His black curls looked wind-tossed and his left hand carried a rolled-up sheet of parchment, while his right held a pouch, which Siri guessed must hold his pens and ink.

He had been off somewhere drawing *her*—

She tried to smother the pang in her heart and lifted her chin in defiance of the flicker in his eyes when they lingered on her streaming hair.

He turned to Sir Balduin. "Sir Raynor?"

Sir Balduin gave a brief report on Raynor's condition. When he repeated Siri's instructions, Triston nodded and let him leave to carry them out.

"I knew I would find you here," he said when they were alone.

"Were you looking for me?"

"Aye . . . nay . . . aye—" He bit his lip.

She smiled at his confusion.

He fixed his gaze over her head on the door behind her. "Aye. I wished to apologize for my behavior last night."

"I'm sure Sir Raynor will appreciate that when he is feeling better."

Triston's dark eyes flashed. "Not about Raynor. That villainous dog can—" He stopped and steadied himself with a breath. "About before. In the yard. When I—" Again he paused, and this time he glanced down the corridor. "Can we go somewhere else and talk?"

"The gardens, if you like. I do not know how soon Lucianna will come looking for me there, but—"

Triston agreed with a nod and they started down the corridor.

When they reached the stairs to the hall, Siri stopped and touched the parchment still clutched in his hand. "Do you mean to bring this with us?"

He glanced down as she slid it from his fingers, but he made no attempt to prevent her from unrolling it. Had it been of anyone else's face, the drawing's realism would have fascinated her. The flowing lines that defined the lush and streaming hair, the soft curve of the delicate chin, the nose, the eyes, the brows—all except the mouth were hers. But the lips! Surely hers had never looked that sad, not even after Alessandro's death or Simon's. These bespoke something much deeper than grief for a loved one. These were a reflection of a spirit of desolate despair that Siri had never known.

"Please." She rolled the sheet back up and returned it to Triston. "Send it to your room."

Triston motioned to one of the servants in the hall and handed him the parchment and pouch with orders to take them to his chamber. The servant hurried off to obey as Triston led Siri out to the garden.

# Chapter 13

Siri's fingers flew through her hair, weaving the three thick bunches she had separated, into a single braid.

"There," she said when she was done. "Now can you look at me?"

She sat on one of the wattle walls in the garden, beneath a tall beech tree. Triston towered over her, his back to the sun so that she could not clearly see his expression. But his head was no longer turned away.

When he made no reply, she groaned. "Don't tell me she wore her hair like this, too?"

"No," he said after a moment. He did not ask who she meant. "But her sister did. Over her shoulder like that. Only it was longer and the color was different."

Siri had interrupted his awkward apology with a demand that he at least look her in the face if he were going to reject her again. He had obeyed so reluctantly that she had been tempted to make him wait while she ran to her room and pinned up her hair. She had tried plaiting it instead, and for a moment, despite his words, she was afraid that she had made a critical mistake. His fingertips swept a stray wisp at her temples, then brushed downward to her cheek. Siri dared not even breathe. If he should feel her tremble, he would draw his hand away and she would lose the thrill of his touch.

"Forgive me," he said, replacing the stilted words of his former apology with a simple plea. He tilted up her chin and rubbed his thumb across her lips. "I had no right to assault you as I did last night. 'Twas the act of a boorish churl."

"Nay," she whispered, "I did not mind the kisses. In fact, I . . . I would not object should you wish to kiss me again." She blushed at her own brazenness, but still held her breath hopefully.

Her heartbeat raced when he lowered himself to the wall beside her. A slow smile curved across his mouth. "You are the most maddening wench I have ever met. Has the Lady Lucianna any idea how you keep throwing yourself at me?"

"She thinks you are lusting after me," she confessed. "And I hope you do not think that I do this with every man? Because you are the first and only man I have ever asked to kiss me."

She drew a shivery breath when his hands encircled her face.

"Do not tempt me, sweet Siriol," he murmured. "I will only hurt you again."

"You did not hurt me," she repeated, as she had in the yard.

"Nay, not here." His mouth brushed across hers in a feathery caress. "But here." He pressed his palm against her softly throbbing heart.

"Triston—"

"Lady Siriol, I cannot love you as you wish me to. And I will not rob you of your honor for the sake of lust. Yours or mine."

She slid herself away from him along the wall. It was not lust that made her ache, but if that was all he felt for her, then he was right. It was not enough.

"Did you lust for Isobel, as well?" The question popped out in all its bitterness before she could stop it.

Triston's answer took a moment in coming. "For a time I thought I loved her, but it was never love I felt."

"Yet that did not stop you from robbing her honor?"

He stood up, his jaw tightening. "I was twenty years old, and I own that my blood was hot. But Drogo de Molinet was my friend. I never meant to harm his sister."

"I know her death was an accident," she said quickly. "But Triston—the child—"

"Isobel— Nay, I am not going to try to justify my actions to you. All you need to know is that I pushed her too hard, she fell on the ice, it broke, and she died. That is all that matters now, all that mattered then. I lost my temper and pushed her too hard."

The tremor that shook his voice brought Siri to her feet, but he waved her back.

"I swore on her grave," he said, "that I would never forget what my anger and careless strength had done. It is a vow that I have been far from perfect in keeping, but I have tried. I have *tried.*"

Siri longed to smooth those unhappy lines from his brow. "Perhaps you have tried too hard," she said. "Triston, it is good to control one's anger, but it may be dangerous to try to deny it." She paused. The lines in his brow only deepened. "Were you angry when you kissed me last night?"

Again she saw the tightening of his jaw before he answered briefly, "Aye."

"Why?"

She watched his hands curl into fists. For a moment, she thought he would refuse to speak. When he finally did, the tremor was still there.

"Because of him. Because of Raynor."

"Because I said I invited him here against your wishes? Were you punishing me?"

"Nay! Oh, aye, I was angry at you, but that was not why I kissed you."

She bowed her head. She wished that she had left her hair free, so that it might fall forward and veil her face. She knew that he would see her pain reflected there. "You kissed me—because you thought in the dark, you could pretend that I was her."

"If I could fashion you to be her again," Triston said, "I would do so. But I cannot. Lady Siriol, your brother was the best friend I ever had. And it slays me to the heart that I have been unable to give the sister he entrusted to me anything but pain."

She sank back onto the wall and linked her hands tightly in her lap. After a vain attempt to swallow the lump in her throat, she somehow managed to ask, "Tell me about you and my brother." He hesitated.

"Please. Sit down again and tell me. How did you meet? How did you become friends? Tell me everything you remember about Simon."

Triston did not move from where he stood. A moment passed before he answered. "We met on the ship that sailed from Venice. Simon recognized my accent and asked if I was Poitevin. I confessed that I was, and after that there was no shaking him off me."

She smiled. "He wanted you to tell him about Poitou, didn't he? He always wanted to come here. He even talked of moving us both to Poitiers and setting up an illuminator's shop there after Father died. And I think we would have done it if I had not married Alessandro."

"Aye," Triston said, "he told me of that."

"Of Poitiers?"

"Nay, of you and the Venetian nobleman. Simon was as terrified for you as I was for—" He stopped.

She slid along the wall, leaving space for him to sit without having to brush against her. "Tell me the rest."

He sat down on the opposite corner, so that his back and face were half turned away. "I never wanted your brother's friendship," he said. "I did everything I could think of to discourage it. I growled at him, I threatened him, I told him repeatedly to go to blazes, but Simon would not leave me alone. Finally he offered me the one temptation I could not in those days resist. He poured me a cup of wine, and he kept on pouring until I was so drunk that I babbled to him every secret of my miserable life. I told him about Isobel. And then I told him about Clothilde."

"You were in love with her even then?"

Triston laughed. It was the first time she had ever heard him do so, and it wrenched her heart that it should sound so bitter.

"I was twenty-one and had never loved anyone else. Isobel was a mere distraction to try to make me forget that Clothilde could never be mine. But I made her mine before I left, and I hated your brother for tricking that truth from me."

Siri stared at him, her mind tumbling in a series of sudden calculations. Triston had loved Clothilde at twenty-one. And Perrin— *Perrin*—

"Your son is seven years old!"

A rueful smile curled the corner of his mouth. "You have only just thought of that?"

Her cheeks burned at her humiliating stupidity. "Is that what you told Simon? That you loved the Lady Clothilde and got her with child before you left on your pilgrimage?"

He shook his head. "I did not know about Perrin then. I would never have left without Clo if I had. But my son was not conceived in sin and lust. She was my wife, Lady Siriol. I married her before I left Poitou, and I trusted her to wait for me."

"Married! But Audiart said— Sir Balduin said— Everyone says that she was married to a man named Merval."

Triston had propped his elbows on his knees, his hands linked together beneath his chin, but now he rolled his forehead against his fingers. "Their marriage was invalid. I married Clothilde in secret on the eve of my departure for Jerusalem. She and I both feared her mother's ambitions, but Clothilde would not let me tell anyone that we had wed. I pled with her, first to let me speak, then that she should come with me, but she refused."

"But you went anyway."

"I had to go. I had sworn an oath to my mother. But Clothilde promised she would wait for me."

Siri slid a little closer to him along the wall. "Then that is what you told Simon? That you had married the Lady Clothilde and left her behind in Poitou?"

She had not meant it as an accusation, but that was clearly how Triston took it.

His head came up. "She gave me no choice. I could not break my vow. I had sworn it on my mother's deathbed, before I even knew that Clothilde returned my love."

"She could not have loved you enough," Siri said, "if she betrayed you with another man."

Triston swung round on her, a dark blaze in his eyes. "She did not betray me. It was her mother who committed the terrible crime that destroyed her spirit and her—"

*—her mind?* Siri dared not speak the thought as he broke off, but the frantic swirls of his wife's tapestry rose up to her vision again.

In spite of his fearful blaze, she asked, "What did her mother do?"

He replied with the same sort of savagery with which he had confronted Raynor the night before. "That she-devil tore our son from her. The night of his birth, she ordered the babe abandoned in the woods, to conceal Clothilde's shame, so she said. She claimed Merval would not take her with another man's by-blow, but she knew the truth. Clothilde had confessed our marriage and my father's old chaplain could have confirmed it. But her mother was determined not to lose the alliance with Merval, and so she spoke the devastating order which cost me in one stroke my wife and my son."

Siri's voice went hushed with horror. "She abandoned an innocent child to the beasts of the woods?" Her generous mind could not conceive of so great wickedness. But the wrathful memory in Triston's face left her no doubt that it was true.

"That woman bears a stone where her heart should be. Had it not been for the pity of the servant to whom she commended the child, my son would have died before he had scarcely drawn breath. But the servant also knew of our marriage. She defied the order and carried the babe instead to an elderly couple who had once served my mother, hoping they would keep the child safe until my return."

Which they had faithfully done, as Perrin's presence at Vere proved. But— "The Lady Clothilde did not know, did she? She thought her child had died." It seemed the only answer for what had apparently happened next.

"Aye. It broke the last of her fragile will. Her mother succeeded in pushing through her marriage to Merval before I could return to claim her."

"But when you came back, you did claim her."

He groaned and dropped his head into his hands again. "I tried. But with Merval at her back, Clothilde dared not speak the truth. I begged and pleaded with her to confess our marriage. She stood there trembling like a leaf. She did not deny our marriage. She simply whispered that I must go away and never ask to see her again. What could I do? My father's chaplain had died during my pilgrimage. As long as Clothilde refused to confirm my word, I could not prove that we had ever been wed. So I returned to Vere—and drank myself into a stupor. It was not until after Merval's death that I finally won her back."

Siri had to curl her fingers into her palms to resist the impulse to touch him. "Triston, you could not have known when you left on your pilgrimage what would transpire in your absence. What befell Clothilde and Perrin was not your fault. You must not blame yourself as if it were."

For a long moment, he did not speak. Then he gave a heavy sigh. "'Not blame myself—' For a moment, you sounded just like Simon."

"Simon?"

"You come from cheerful stock, Lady Siriol. Simon always saw the light in the darkness, as well. Or almost always."

Hoping to distract him from his sorrow, she said, "Oh, please, tell me more about you and my brother."

He did not raise his head, but after a moment he answered, "I told you the trick he played me with the wine. He got me drunk as a piper and in a maudlin haze, I confessed everything to him, not just my marriage to Clothilde, but my guilt at having left her, my dread that she should not prove strong enough, that her mother would find some way to make her abjure our vows and force her to marry Merval . . ."

His fingers slid up to twist in his hair, then stilled as he took a steadying breath. "The next morning when I realized all I had said, I cursed your brother to high heaven. He perversely refused to take offense at the names I called him, and laughed when I demanded satisfaction with sword or dagger. So I landed my fist in his face. He just sat in the road with a blackening eye and grinned and said that he deserved the blow, for he had played me a paltry trick. I cursed him again and tried to stalk off, but Simon sprang up and blocked my path. When I threatened to darken his other eye, his grin vanished and he said with more soberness than I had ever heard him use, that I was not the only one being driven mad by fears for a woman. And then—" he paused, tilting his head to gaze at Siri "—he told me about you."

"About me?"

"Aye. I suppose he felt he owed me secret for secret to make amends for the wine. He told me he had a beautiful sister whom he had been forced to leave behind in Venice. She was being courted by a lustful old nobleman, he said, whom he feared might sweep her off her feet with his glittering wealth, and despoil her innocent youth."

Siri's cheeks warmed. "Alessandro had asked Simon's permission to marry me, and Simon had refused. Before he left for his pilgrimage, he tried to make me promise that I would have nothing to do with Alessandro, but . . ."

"He was terrified that you would not obey him." Triston straightened and shifted to face her. "I knew it when I heard the trembling in his normally cheerful voice. He was as worried for you as I was for Clothilde, nay, as haunted at the thought of what you might do. You were the most precious thing in his life, Lady Siriol."

"I know," she whispered. How could she explain? "But suddenly Simon was gone and there was no one to protect me. The servants—they turned out not to be as trustworthy as Simon and I had always thought. There were men who wished to—rob me of my honor." She chose the phrase that Triston had previously used. "And some of the servants were willing to help them for a price. Even Lucianna did not know what to do. But Alessandro—he was kind and he seemed to love me in a different way. I felt safe when I was with him. He never looked on me with lust, but with the sort of affection an old man might feel for a daughter." She hesitated, and Triston's skeptical gaze prompted her to add, "It is true. I was never a wife to him but in name. I told Simon that and he forgave me."

"Did he?"

"Yes. Alessandro treated me like a toy he found pleasure in showing off. He liked to kiss me and he liked to lavish presents on me, but he never— he never—" Her cheeks flamed beneath the directness of Triston's gaze. She turned her face away, then started when his hand covered hers.

"I am glad," he said softly, "for your brother's sake. Would that Merval had been such a man as your Alessandro. My homecoming might have been as sweet as Simon's. Instead, all the horrors of my dreams came true."

She twisted her hand about to clasp his fingers and squeezed them hard. "I'm sorry," she said. "But you did win her back."

"Aye, but at what price!"

She hesitated, then said, "I know how you have grieved for her, but—" She loosed his fingers to touch his arm, then caught her breath when his hand went to her waist. Surely it was only some unconscious gesture! But it set her heart to racing and lent a breathless note to the rest of her plea. "They are all gone. Simon, Alessandro, Clothilde—they are gone and our grieving will not bring them back. But you and I are still here. Can we not comfort one another?"

He answered with a smoldering gaze that slid over her face, then lowered to her braid. "I think it is not comfort you want from me," he murmured, "or that I want from you." She swayed towards him, but he caught her shoulders and held her away. "Lady Siriol—" his voice came low "—I would have to be more than a man not to desire you. You are so beautiful, so vibrant, so wonderfully warm and strong. But my heart does not lie with you, and I will not dishonor your brother's memory by offering you only my passion."

She closed her eyes and uttered a silent, desperate prayer. "Are you . . . sure there is nothing more?"

She gasped a little when his fingers slid into her hair, but kept her eyes tight shut as he worked to loose the links of her braid. His hands moved with a quiet strength, sending almost unbearable yearnings through her body at each gentle tug. But when he spread her hair about her shoulders, she knew his answer.

"Nay," he murmured, "there is too much that I can't forget."

She had to swallow hard twice before she could whisper through the painful pressure that threatened to close off her throat. "If my face were different?"

After an interminable pause, he whispered back, "I don't know."

She let the pain wash through her, then nodded and pulled her head away. The truth hurt, but not as much as it would were he to love her for the wrong reasons.

She opened her eyes and stood up. There was nothing more to say.

She stepped away from him, then stopped and stiffened. Lucianna came sweeping into the garden, Siri's dagger in her hands and her haughty face smug with suspicions confirmed at the sight of her with Triston.

"I knew I would find you here. If you think, signore, that I do not know what you have in your wicked mind—"

"Lucianna, Triston was only apologizing to me for last night."

Lucianna clearly did not believe her. "Come over here, carissima, come away from him. Now."

"But—"

"Now, I tell you. Strap this on and go back inside. I have a word to speak with Signor Triston."

"Lucianna, you are being ridiculous. He has done nothing—"

"Nothing? I have witnessed his lustful kisses myself. He thinks you are in his power, that because he is your master, he may defile you with no one to say him nay."

"Lucianna, he has not de—"

"Lady Siriol."

Triston's soft voice startled her into silence. The warning that underscored her name made her cast a quick glance in the same direction he was gazing. Perrin hovered at the entrance to the garden, the hound Talbot at his heels. The boy's wide blue eyes surveyed the three adults with concern. He carried something in his hand and from the way it trembled, Siri knew that he had witnessed enough to upset him.

"Lucianna, hush," she said, then held out her hands to the boy. "Perrin, come here."

Perrin hesitated, and she saw the frightened look he cast at his father.

"Perrin," Triston said, "do as she says."

Perrin sidled carefully towards Siri, his eyes on his father, then melted into the skirt of her smock. Talbot followed him with a soft whine.

"They say you are going away," Perrin whispered.

She leaned down to embrace him. "Who told you that?"

"Lady Lucianna. And Audiart."

Lucianna gave a haughty sniff at Siri's look of reproach.

"Perrin," Siri said, "I am not going anywhere just yet. I must find myself a husband first."

Lucianna said, "They are already gathering in the hall to court you, Donna Siri. The gentlemen from last night. It is not polite to keep them waiting. Come with me and we will make you presentable for them. I will settle this matter with Signor Triston later."

"Wait," Siri said. "Perrin, have you something to show me first?"

Perrin nodded and held up to her the sheet of parchment in his hand. "Someone has ruined it."

She studied the blurred drawings. "Oh, Perrin, I am so sorry about your picture. I'm afraid it was my fault. One of our guests visited me in my workshop last night and he did not see your pictures in the dark. He sat down on them before I remembered to warn him."

"Perrin—" the boy went stiff at Triston's voice "—may I see it?"

Perrin's eyes pleaded with Siri to help him escape, but she took his hand and said with a smile, "Yes, let us show it to your father. He will be so proud of what you have learned."

"But— But it's ruined," Perrin said, clearly hoping that this would discourage his father's interest.

"The paint is a little smeared, but the outline of your drawing had already dried and stands out quite clear. Come." She added in a whisper, "Don't be afraid. I will be right beside you."

"Carissima—"

"In a moment, Lucianna. Perrin, come."

Siri gave the boy no choice, but pulled him over to where Triston still sat on the wall. She was glad he had not stood up when Lucianna came. His height might have intimidated Perrin even more. Seated, their eyes were almost level, except that Perrin would not look his father in the face. Siri took the drawing from his hand and gave it to Triston.

Triston exclaimed over it as if he had never seen it before, admiring the skillful curves and lines and lamenting over the smeared paint. Perrin's body remained tense and his answers came in mumbles.

Perhaps, she thought, if he saw that *she* trusted his father he might begin to reconsider his fear. She sat down beside Triston, close enough to send another rush through her veins and to bring a protest from Lucianna.

Siri ignored her and reached out a hand to the hound Talbot's head as he trotted over to place it in her lap.

"Perrin," she said, "did you know that your father draws too?"

Perrin's eyes darted up in surprise.

"Lady Siriol's brother taught me," Triston said. "On the long voyage across the sea from Venice to the Holy Land, where I went to offer prayers for your grandmother's soul. Do you remember the stories I told you about my journey there? The strange animals I saw? You were little then."

Perrin hesitated. "I remember. The horse with the bumps on its back."

Triston smiled, and Siri noted that it held no bitterness now. "The camels. Lady Siriol's brother showed me how to draw them and many other things. But he never taught me how to paint like this. Perhaps one day you will teach me?"

Perrin dropped his gaze back to his shoes. It was a long moment before he answered, and his voice trembled. "Perhaps."

"Have you ever seen your father's drawings?" Siri asked.

Triston frowned. "Lady Siriol—"

"They are remarkable. I have never seen anything like them. You must ask him to show them to you one day."

"Lady Siriol—"

She caught the sharp warning in Triston's voice, but only whispered, "Surely you can draw something for him besides her." She stroked Talbot's head, then said to Perrin. "You have your father's talent. I have helped you to discover it is all, but I think only he can train your eye to see in the remarkable way his does."

Triston hesitated, then asked, "Perrin, would you like me to draw something for you?"

Perrin cast an uncertain look at Siri. "Will you come with us?"

"I—" She caught Lucianna's glance. "I cannot just now. I must go and see to our guests."

Perrin shook his head. "Then I do not want to go either."

"Perrin—" Siri's and Triston's protests came in unison.

"No." He backed away from them both. "I don't want to go with him. Lady Siri, don't make me."

It was Triston who answered. "No one will make you do anything, Perrin. Run to your lessons, then. I will let Lady Siriol show you my drawings later."

They watched him run off in silence. If Siri had needed further evidence that Perrin's fear had not been caused by his father's temper, she had just seen it in the patient way Triston had dealt with his son. There was naught but love in his eyes as he stared after the boy—love and a painful bewilderment.

"Triston, he didn't mean—"

A veil dropped over the tenderness, shutting Siri out. "Your guests are waiting for you, Lady Siriol. And Lady Lucianna is glaring daggers at me. You had better go too."

Siri shifted Talbot away and rose reluctantly to follow Lucianna, but she paused at the gate and looked back. Triston's head was bent in wistful study of his son's picture. The lines in his brow seemed deeper than ever.

❧

Triston stared at the drawing until the lines began to blur, then reached out a hand and lifted Talbot's muzzle.

"Why?" he whispered to the hound, as though the answer might lie in Talbot's liquid brown eyes. "Why is Perrin afraid of me?"

Talbot gave a sharp bark, shook his muzzle free, and rested his head on his master's knee. Triston sighed and scratched him behind the ears until the hound gave a low whine of pleasure.

Triston recalled how difficult Perrin's adjustment had been when he had first brought his son to Vere. Clothilde's tendency to clutch and weep over Perrin had frightened the four-year-old child. But once Triston had convinced her that Perrin would not be snatched away from them again, she had learned to smile—those soft, sweet, endearing smiles that Perrin, like Triston, had been unable to resist.

Only occasionally in those early days had she fallen into a hysterical fit in the sight of her son. Once had been when Perrin had fallen out of a tree in the garden and winded himself. Clothilde had knelt screaming over his little stunned body until Triston had stood him up, gasping, upon his feet and proved to her that Perrin was not only alive, but had suffered nothing more than a few bruises from the fall.

"The other times," Triston muttered, "mostly centered around you." He grabbed Talbot's muzzle again and shook it in a gentle rebuke. "I should never have given you to Perrin. I knew Clo was afraid of dogs."

Talbot gave a protesting bark.

"Don't you try to deny it," Triston said. "She screamed every time she saw you with Perrin." He thought briefly of the calm, easy way Siri always welcomed the hound's attentions.

The hound whined and shoved his head back into Triston's lap.

Triston patted him and sighed. "Nay, it is not your fault. Dogs, horses, hawks, even most people. Clo seemed to be afraid of everything, for as long as I can remember."

Even from girlhood. He had blamed her fears on her mother's oppressive abuse and had convinced himself that his love would be sufficient to restore her courage and strength, once he had her safely at Vere. But while sometimes months would go by without a disturbance, eventually something would occur to unsettle her again. And then in those last months, after Raynor's mischief, matters had spiraled until the days had seemed to become one endless hysterical round.

Perrin could not have been deaf to all his mother's wails in the night, but Triston had sought to shield the boy from the worst of the scenes. He had clearly succeeded, for it was not his sad, unstable mother Perrin recalled with fear. Somehow he had fixed his terrors on his father instead. Why? What had Triston done?

He ran a hopeless hand through his tumble of curls.

"What shall I do?" he asked Talbot.

The hound's head snapped up, then cocked to one side as if he were considering the question.

"Perrin is seven," Triston continued aloud. "Old enough to begin training as a page."

Triston had been six when his father had sent him to live with their liege lord, Lord Roger de Vaumâle. The road to knighthood began early, serving first as page, and then squire in another knight's household. It had only been the shock of Clothilde's death and Triston's hopes to repair the puzzling rift with their son that had prevented him from following the tradition with Perrin before now.

"Yes," Triston told Talbot, "it is time. Perrin will undoubtedly be happier away from me. He will not want to leave Siri, but that cannot be helped."

Or could it? Was she not with a host of suitors even now, weighing each for his prospects as a husband? She had promised to choose one soon, but none could wed her without Triston's consent. Surely the gentleman, in gratitude, would be willing to take Triston's son as well for training in his house.

"Aye," he murmured to Talbot "that is the answer. We will send them both away, and then, as I told Father Michel, we shall all of us be at peace at last."

## Chapter 14

Triston put Perrin's drawing away in his room, then went in search of Acelet. Thoughts of Siri had unhappily led him back into thoughts of Raynor. He wanted to know how that rogue had gotten into Vere last night, and he had a pretty grim idea that his cousin knew the answer.

He sought Acelet first in the bailey, where he should have been hard at swordplay with Sir Rollo. But the only pupils occupying the rugged swordmaster's time were a scraggly group of serving boys fighting a mock battle with wooden swords. It had become a familiar sight in recent days, the swordmaster drilling with a rabble of eager but clumsy children.

Triston motioned Sir Rollo away from the boys and asked, "When was the last time Acelet showed up for sword practice?"

Sir Rollo shrugged. "A week, ten days, I've lost count. Sir, I know I said I'd stay until he earned his spurs, but I fear you're being generous to a fault to keep paying me when all I do is sit, or at best, drill with brats like these."

"I know Acelet has been delinquent of late, but—"

"It's more than that, sir. I fear your cousin has not the fire for knighthood."

Triston frowned. "You said he had talent."

Sir Rollo pulled on the ends of his beard. "I admit, I've rarely seen a boy quicker on his feet than he. And he knows every position for defense and attack when engaged in swordplay with some imaginary foe. But when I am the one swinging the blade at him, he flinches."

"Flinches?"

"Aye. I can feel him wincing behind his shield every time my sword strikes it. He has not the heart of a soldier, sir. 'Twould be a kindness, in my opinion, to tell him that and send him back home to his mother." Sir Rollo spat on the ground, then added, "Lord Devereaux has offered me a goodly sum if I will leave you and come to instruct his sons."

Triston could not blame Sir Rollo for his frustration. That Acelet was annoying, rebellious, and maddeningly light-minded was beyond dispute, and had Triston not been so distracted with Siri last night, he might have thrown the young man out for letting Raynor into Vere. The calmer light of morning had taken the edge off Triston's temper, but he still longed to rattle Acelet's teeth with a good hard shake. There had to be a grain of sense in him somewhere, and Triston was determined to find it.

"Give it one more month," he said. "If Acelet has not mended his ways by then, I will release you from our agreement and you may go where you will."

Sir Rollo shook his head. "A year would not be enough time to whip the right spirit into that boy."

"Oh, he has spirit enough. I hope it is only the proper motivation he has yet to find. I have an idea. Let me try it. We can start today, if I can get her to agree."

Sir Rollo spat again. "You'll have to find the pup first. I've not seen him all morning."

Triston sighed again. "I have a pretty good guess where he is. I will fetch him. One month, Sir Rollo."

Sir Rollo shrugged, then muttered, "It's your money."

He turned to shout at the serving boys as Triston strode back inside the keep.

⚉

Siri sat at the center of her circle of admirers in the hall. Triston observed that she had again piled her shimmering hair atop her head, the thick tresses held in place with sapphire-and-diamond-studded pins. The tiny diamonds winking amidst the silver embroidered flowers sprinkled from shoulders to hem of her gown, made it look as if she had draped herself in several constellations-worth of stars.

With Lucianna seated beside her, he knew there was little likelihood that the liberties Siri had complained of the night before would be ventured again this morning. Apparently she had decided to forgive the men, for while he watched, she laughed and clapped her hands and quipped out merry replies to their extravagant flattery. But after several minutes, she caught Triston's eye. Lucianna followed her glance and gave a sharp shake of her head, but Siri slid from her chair. The crowd parted reluctantly for her. Several gentlemen insisted on kissing her hand as she passed, but at last she wove her way to Triston's side.

"Did you want me?"

He realized he was glowering at the men gazing covetously at her back. He hoped any fortune hunters among them would be warned off by his glare. He took her arm and drew her farther away from the men, to stand beside the empty hearth.

"I'm looking for Acelet," he said. "I thought sure I would find him here with you."

"I've not seen him. Perhaps he is with Sir Rollo."

Triston shook his head. "I have just come from him and Acelet was not there. He hasn't showed up to practice for a week or more. Sir Rollo is ready to wash his hands of him."

Siri apparently interpreted this as a complaint against herself. "I know I have been a distraction to him, as I have to Perrin. But I have promised you that I will marry soon and then—"

"Nay, I've not come here to rebuke you or discuss your marriage, but to ask for a favor."

"A favor?"

A tendril of gold hair had slipped from her pins. He was tempted to tuck it back into place, but linked his hands behind his back instead. "Sir Rollo is threatening to leave. He says Acelet's swordsmanship is too timid—that he will never make a knight."

Her eyes widened. "Not become a knight? But that would devastate Acelet. It is all he thinks about."

*Not quite all,* Triston thought, but he only said, "Aye, but if you are willing to help, Sir Rollo has promised to give him one more chance."

"You mean you want me to refuse to let him sit with me, instead of—"

"Nay, not that. I want you to come out to the yard when he is practicing, and watch." She stared at him. "Unless you'd prefer not to risk dirtying your gown—"

Her stare turned scornful. "As if I cared about such things. It is just that I don't see what good my watching Acelet would do."

"Think about it. Acelet is smitten with you, and above all things he wishes to impress you. He should not wish to appear hesitant or weak while you were watching him, but rather to show off to you his skill."

"You think my presence would lend him courage?"

"I think he would try very hard not to disappoint you."

To his surprise, she hesitated. He had thought her fond of Acelet and had expected a swift consent.

"He asked me to marry him last night."

Triston's jaw dropped.

She smiled and put up a hand to close his mouth. "Don't worry, I said no. I told him he was too young to be speaking of such things. But he thinks I refused him because he is not a knight. If I help him to realize his hopes, I'm afraid he may misinterpret my reasons."

Triston felt the grim tightening of his mouth. "First Raynor, now this. That boy is just begging to have his head knocked in."

She caught his arm as he turned away. "What are you going to do?"

"I am going to rattle Acelet's teeth and tell him to leave you alone. I am going to warn him that if he lends himself to any more of Raynor de Molinet's mischief, I will turn him out on his ear. And I'm going to tell him frankly that he had better start asserting himself with Sir Rollo or—"

"Are you going to hit him?"

"Hit him?" The question appalled Triston.

"I saw his bruise one day in the garden. He said you had hit him because he disobeyed you, and I saw the mark of your hand on his cheek. Triston, his affection for me is harmless, a boyish infatuation which he will soon outgrow."

Triston was too stunned to reply. Then he remembered.

"I slapped him." His face reddened. "I lost my temper and slapped him. He was jabbing at me about Clothilde, and I—"

He glanced away from Siri's worried eyes. How could he explain to her the guilt, the self-doubt? Clothilde had been a tiny woman, like Siri. Surely he should have been able to stop her, to catch her, to somehow prevent that tragic fall? He had tried. He *had* tried. But she had slipped from his fingers and afterwards he had found himself unable even to move.

He felt suddenly numb, like he had that night. "I loved her," he whispered. "Lady Siriol, I loved her."

Her fingers pressed hot against the cold of his cheek. "I know that. How could I, of all people, not know that? Acelet blames you for her death, but you are not to blame, anymore than you were with Isobel."

"Nay, I failed her. Somehow I failed her. Acelet is right. I should have been able to stop her from falling."

The ringleted ends of Siri's hair trembled with the shake of her head. "I was not there, but I know if you could have saved her, you would have. And the next time Acelet says otherwise, I will slap him myself." Her tentative smile failed to find a response in Triston. Her beautiful face sobered. "Triston, you must not let this guilt consume you. It will destroy you if you do."

He took her fingers and squeezed them, then let them go. He could not bear to gaze at her any longer. Could not bear to gaze within himself. "Thank you, Lady Siriol. I will see that Acelet does not bother you again, and I promise to do it with words, and not with the palm of my hand."

"Don't go," she pled when he started to turn away. "Come and sit with our guests. Listen to their stories and songs, flirt with their sisters. Let them divert your mind for an hour. Don't go away and brood."

Before he could reply, a new voice, low and sultry, purred, "Brooding is what Triston does best."

Triston stiffened as Osanne took his arm. He had not seen her entering the hall with Lord Fauke. His frown went from his voluptuous stepmother to the fiery baron who seized Siri's reluctant hand and pressed on it a shamelessly lascivious kiss.

Osanne traced a bold finger across the breadth of Triston chest. "You and I did not finish our conversation last night."

Triston scarcely heard her provocative words, so intent was he on glaring at Lord Fauke, but he knew to what she referred. Osanne had followed him to Perrin's room last night. She had been waiting for him in the passageway when he had come out, and she had tried several brazen tricks to seduce him into her chamber before he had managed to push her aside. Now as his fuming gaze encompassed Siri and the baron, he registered Siri's startled look at him, glanced down at Osanne's hand against his chest, and hastily shook it off.

His face warmed slightly. "You must excuse me," he said. "I have business in the village." With a quick step that left the baron looking flustered, he maneuvered Lord Fauke away from Siri's side and took her hand himself. "May I first escort you to your chair, Lady Siriol?"

"Thank you," she said, and her sunny smile melted away the momentary doubt from her face.

Her suitors cheered her return. Lord Fauke insisted on taking up the position closest to her chair, but with Lucianna at her side, Triston had no fears for her safety. He strode past the inviting glow in Osanne's eyes and made his way out of the hall.

❧

Triston returned to the castle in time to dine. Siri tried several times during the meal to coax him into conversation, but not until she drew his attention to Acelet's empty chair did irritation overcome his sober self-reflections.

"He is no doubt expecting me to blast him for letting Raynor into Vere last night," Triston said, "and is probably off hiding somewhere until my temper blows itself out."

"Has it blown itself out?" Siri asked.

"No," he answered briefly, and lapsed into silence again.

Observing the lowering cast of Triston's black brows, Siri was not sure she blamed his young cousin for fleeing. Yet she could not quiet a whispering fear that there was more to his absence than Triston believed.

Try though she might, she had not been able to forget Raynor's feverish accusation. Several times as she sat beside Triston at the high table, she came near to telling him of Raynor's words. Triston's unexpected concern to see his cousin successfully knighted had caused her to suspect that he was fonder of Acelet than he cared to admit. Surely he would not believe such a ludicrous tale as Raynor had told.

But when she bit off her words for the third time, she realized it was not lingering doubts of Triston, but of Acelet, that made her hesitate. Under ordinary circumstances, the thought of Acelet stabbing anyone would have been incredible. But she remembered the tight grip of his arm around her shoulders when Raynor had confessed his assault on the Lady Clothilde. Acelet had adored his late mistress, and Triston had sent Raynor off with Acelet. Was it possible that in some burst of outrage for his lady's distress, he had in fact seized a dagger and thrust it at the friend who, in the space of a few words, must have suddenly become in his mind a villain?

Other than Acelet himself, only Raynor knew the truth. As soon as the meal was over, she returned to Raynor's chamber, but found him still sleeping, so hot and flushed that she had not the heart to rouse him.

Another two days passed before there was any change in his condition. By that time she was truly alarmed, for Acelet seemed to have disappeared off the face of the earth.

"Aren't you worried?" she demanded of Triston after Acelet failed to appear yet again for breakfast.

"The boy has missed a few meals," he answered. "It won't hurt him."

"But no one has seen him between meals either. Where in the world would he have gone?"

"He is probably in hiding with one of our neighbors. He knows that at the very least, he is in for a severe tongue-lashing from me. He may even fear that I will send him home for thwarting my commands about Raynor. He is probably trying to think of some way to appease my anger before he shows his face at Vere again."

"Then why don't you send to some of these neighbors and ask if they have seen him?"

"Nay," Triston said, "let him sweat a bit. It will teach him a well-deserved lesson."

Thoroughly exasperated with this reply, Siri left Triston once again for Raynor's chamber. Perhaps today Raynor would be awake and lucid enough to tell her the truth. But as she reached out her hand for the latch, the door swung suddenly open and Lord Fauke strode out of the chamber.

His abrupt appearance so surprised her that she made no attempt to prevent him from seizing her hand.

"My lady." He swept her with an outrageously salacious gaze. "Ravishingly beautiful as always. I hope you will spare me a moment later, but just now you must excuse me. I have a word to speak with Triston."

The triumphant smile on his lips replaced her surprise with panic. No sooner had he left than she flew into Raynor's chamber, slamming the door behind her.

"What did you tell him?" she cried.

Raynor sat up in the bed, his fever gone, the flush on his cheeks replaced with a chalk-like pallor. He held out a trembling hand to her.

"Carissima. If you would only sit by my side every day, I should be well again in a trice."

She moved to the bedside. "I have been to see you twice a day, but you were too sick to know it. I am very glad that you are at last feeling better, but you must tell me what you said to Lord Fauke to send him off looking so smug."

Raynor's amber eyes glowed with bemusement as he took in her pile of glittering curls and her fanciful spring green gown where hounds and deer chased eternally in the silken weave of its fabric.

"Exquisite," he murmured, sinking back into the pillows, "but the color does no justice to your eyes." She pursed her lips and placed her hands on her hips. "Ah, but to be the object of such sweet wrath as beams from your face must make me the happiest of miserable mortals. I would ask only that I might spend the whole of my life in trying to coax those frowns into smiles."

"Sir Raynor—!"

"Carissima?"

Siri was hard put not to laugh. Even in his illness, the man was incorrigible.

"Come, now, that is better," he said to her reluctant grin. "The sight brings the strength flowing back into my limbs. Add to it a kiss and I shall stride forth from my bed with the energy of a hundred men."

"I am not going to kiss you, Sir Raynor."

He sagged against the pillows with an exaggerated sigh. "Then you may as well leave me to die."

"Don't be absurd. If you were going to die, you would have done it 'ere now."

His pale lips twitched in the depths of his beard. "You are a most hard-hearted angel, carissima."

"I haven't time to stand here and flirt with you. What did you say to Lord Fauke?"

Raynor shook his head. "I insist on snatching some small victory from my defeat. Sit down beside me and give me your hand and I will tell you."

"Sir Raynor—"

"Alas," he closed his eyes and moaned dramatically, "I fear I may be falling back into a swoon. In another moment I shan't be able to tell you anything at all."

Laughter bubbled out before she could stop it. "Oh, very well!"

She sat down on the bed and put her hand in his.

He opened his eyes with a satisfied grin. "Much better," he murmured, squeezing her fingers. "Ah, that they might lie here forever. Nay, don't go!

I will behave myself. What is it you wish to know about Lord Fauke?"

"Why did he come here and what did you tell him?"

"He wanted to know if I could identify my attacker. It seems he and everyone has assumed that the felon was the same as our slippery roadside bandit."

"Which is impossible, of course, since that bandit is you."

Raynor's expression was rueful. "The temptation to throw him forever off my trail was nearly too great to resist. But when it came to the sticking point, I'm afraid I felt compelled to tell the truth."

Siri's stomach flopped over. "What truth? You did not confess to the robberies on the road. What did you say?"

"I said—"

He stopped as the quiet air without the door splintered with a thundering curse. The next instant, the door banged open and Triston stood on the threshold, a reddish glow in his eyes and his nostrils flaring like some primitive beast preparing for the kill.

"You devil."

He lunged across the room, seized the front of Raynor's shirt and dragged him halfway out of the bed.

"Triston, stop it!" she cried. "Have you gone mad?"

Triston answered by swinging Raynor out of the sheets and dealing him a shove that sent him sailing into the nearest wall. Raynor's injured leg collapsed beneath him. He slumped onto the floor. Siri ran and knelt in front of him to shield him from Triston's fury.

"That's enough, de Brielle. Stand back from him."

Siri had never been so glad to hear Lord Fauke's voice, though the rest of his speech turned her gratitude into panic.

"If I needed further evidence of your guilt, you have just betrayed yourself in this dastardly attack on an injured man. When the duke learns of this—"

"You shall have your evidence," Triston swore, "when I choke the truth out of Raynor's lying throat." He dragged Siri away from Raynor and hauled Raynor onto his feet. "You vicious, mischief-making rogue. If you think anyone beside this slack-wit is going to credit this devilish tale you have told—"

Raynor's face was white.

"Let him go," Siri pled, terrified lest Triston's assault had reopened his wound.

Triston ignored her. He slammed Raynor against the wall and held him there. "If I wanted to kill you, Raynor," he snarled, "I would do it face to face in the light, not send some pathetic boy skulking about to catch you in the dark."

She stared at Raynor in dread. "Raynor, what did you say?"

"I say go to blazes!" Raynor hissed into Triston's face.

Lord Fauke roared, "Put him down, de Brielle!"

Triston spat a curse at Raynor and swung him about in a toss that landed him in a sprawl across the bed.

Siri ran to him and took his arm to help him sit back up. "Raynor—" she whispered.

"I told the truth!" he shouted. "That Acelet jumped me in the dark. When I drew my dagger to defend myself, he wrestled it away and tried to stab me in the heart. But I managed to twist away and the blade landed in my thigh instead. Acelet must have taken fright when he realized he had failed to kill me, or perhaps he hoped that I would bleed to death in the bushes. He gathered his wits sufficiently to take my jewels to make it look like a robbery and fled. But not before he confessed that Triston had told him to murder me."

"That's a lie!" Triston swore.

Siri said, "I don't believe it."

"Then where is he?" Lord Fauke demanded.

Triston hesitated and Siri froze.

"The boy," the baron continued with a sneer. "You told me in the hall that you have not seen him since the banquet."

"I do not know where he is," Triston said, "but he has not gone at my word. And anyone who knows Acelet would realize how ludicrous Raynor's story is. The boy flinches at every blow of my swordmaster's blunted steel. He did not engage Raynor in a wrestling match, unless Raynor instigated it in the first place. And he certainly did not stab anyone with a knife—"

"Sir Raynor has told me everything, de Brielle," Lord Fauke interrupted. "Your cousin foolishly betrayed you before he fled. Not only did he try to kill Sir Raynor, but he confessed your treason, as well."

The silence that greeted this announcement was so complete that Siri felt as if she had suddenly gone deaf. Raynor's body had been trembling, a reaction to Triston's violent handling, but even his tremors stilled. His amber eyes rested expectantly on Triston.

The silence exploded with a single gasping word from Triston's throat. "Treason?"

Siri felt her face go white.

"You thought you could speak words of fealty to Duke Richard," Lord Fauke said, "while in your heart you plot and pray that the Young King will usurp our good lord's name. You would make him our duke in Richard's place."

"Nay! I am loyal to Richard," Triston insisted.

"Yet your cousin is known to sing the Young King's praises, and your brother dances in his court."

Siri recognized the impatient clenching of Triston's fists. "My cousin is a foolish child, so addled with his own dizzy dreams that he does not know his left from right. And my brother did not share in my inheritance. Why should he not seek his fortune with the man who will one day be our king? Yours, my lord, and mine. Aye, and Duke Richard's, too."

"King, perhaps," Lord Fauke said, "but never master. Young Henry covets his brother's lands, but Richard is duke here, and he has sworn that no one, not the Young King, not the king himself, shall interfere with his governance of these lands. If you doubt his resolve or ability to fulfill his word, you have only to remember Chateauneuf." He paused, his heavy lips twisting into a smirk. "But you were not there, were you?"

Triston answered through gritted teeth, "I was ill. I sent what men I could, including my own brother, to fight beside the duke. When he summoned me to Pons, I came as a good liegeman."

"As I recall, you threw in your voice with those who counseled against that siege," Fauke remarked condescendingly.

"Because its planning and execution were poor," Triston interjected. "Even the duke was finally forced to admit that and when he turned his strategy to Taillebourg, I marched loyally beside him."

"And no sooner was the final blow struck for mastery there, than you deserted our cause, just as your brother deserted us at Chateauneuf. At the time, I thought it cowardice which sent you slinking back to Vere, but now I know you were already nourishing treason in your heart."

"Nay!" Triston said. "Richard cursed me for going, but he knew I was within my rights to withdraw. I had stayed with him far beyond the forty days' service required of any knight, and if I chose after that to return to my own affairs, he could not legally condemn me. I have never spoken against him or his rule in Poitou and you will not trap me now with this miscreant's lies." He jabbed a finger in Raynor's direction. "Where was he during the siege of Taillebourg? Where was he when the battle for Chateauneuf came to an end? You cannot charge me for my brother's actions with the Young King without charging Raynor for his own as well."

Not until he finished this speech did Triston appear to register that Siri was still clinging to Raynor's arm. He frowned and took a step towards them, but was checked by Lord Fauke's reply.

"Sir Raynor has owned that he once held sympathy with the Young King's cause. But he is prepared to renounce his former friendship and throw in his lot with the duke. That is why you sent your cousin to kill him. Because he was about to betray the conspiracy of which you had thought him a partner with you. When you learned that he meant to expose you, you decided he had to be silenced."

Triston's scornful glare swept past Siri straight into Raynor's eyes. "So, now it is a full-blown conspiracy he accuses me of. He fritters away his time with Flemish jousts and Flemish women, while I risk my life and that of my men beside the duke at Taillebourg. Now he comes home weeping tears of repentance, and at no more than his vengeful, uncorroborated word, I am to be charged with treason and condemned." His cutting gaze swung round to Lord Fauke. "You and Duke Richard may think that is enough, and in former days I would have been at your mercy. But King Henry has not completely relinquished his hold on Richard's leash, and the king is a man of law. You cannot charge me without witnesses and proof."

Lord Fauke did not look much concerned. "Oh, we shall have proof enough once we have found your cousin. And I would not place too much confidence in King Henry's law. If Richard determines in his own mind that you are guilty, he will have your castle in flames and yourself in chains before an echo of your name ever reaches the king's ear."

Triston's eyes narrowed in disgust. "You threaten like a bully, my lord. And you—" anger surged back into his face as he turned again to Raynor "—are not going to get away with this. You know that every word of it is a lie, spoken out of nothing but hatred and spite. I should have left you outside my walls to die." Siri's protest only caused his stormy eyes to engulf her as well. "You seem to have found uncommon accord with this fox. Take care, Lady Siriol, that it does not land you in the grave with Clothilde."

Siri found this warning so outrageous that she briefly forgot her indignation against Raynor. She released Raynor's arm, but said to Triston, "You are as bad as he, making accusations like that. Raynor does not mean me harm. And Triston is not a traitor. Raynor, you must tell the truth! You know that Triston is not involved in any conspiracy."

Raynor hesitated, his gaze sliding from Siri to Lord Fauke and back again. "It was Acelet who accused him," he said after a moment. "I only repeated his words."

This admission did little to comfort her, and her fear for Acelet soared nearly as high as her fear for Triston.

"Now will you send someone to look for him?" she demanded of Triston. "Might he with your father-in-law, or—"

"I will send men to search," Lord Fauke interrupted. "De Brielle would simply try to bundle him out of our reach before he can witness against him. Sir Raynor, you said that you would lend me some men from your garrison to aid in the search?"

"They are at your command, my lord."

"Then I will ride to Belle Noir and organize them to begin while I await the arrival of my own guard. And you, de Brielle, keep your distance from this room. If I learn that you have tried any further intimidation on Sir Raynor to make him retract his words, I will view it as further evidence of your guilt."

Siri left the bed and laid a hand on Triston's sleeve. "Come away," she urged. "Triston, please, we must talk."

To her surprise, he shook her off. "I have nothing to say to you, Lady Siriol. Stay here with your friend. You sought to protect him from my wrath. Stay and comfort him, tend to his wounds, listen to his slanders. You will not believe my warnings. Believe him, then. But I have nothing more to say to you."

He stalked out of the room behind Lord Fauke, leaving Siri staring after him in dismay.

# Chapter 15

Triston's determination to avoid her became painfully obvious after the scene in Raynor's chamber. Siri knew she was not helping matters by visiting Raynor each day, but Triston's violence had pulled Raynor's wound open again. She had hoped that while tending him, she might persuade him to retract his words against Acelet and Triston, but so far Raynor clung stubbornly to his accusation.

Seven days went by and the search for Acelet proved fruitless. The eighth morning, Siri slipped away from her circle of suitors and retreated to the garden, hoping for a space of quiet to reflect on the dilemma Raynor had cast them into. But she had not been there five minutes before one overly bold knight from her court invaded her refuge.

She tried to impart with a chill gaze how unwelcome his intrusion was. "Your pardon, sir, I came here hoping for a little privacy."

The knight responded with a saucy grin. "Privacy, aye, I have long hoped to find some of that with you."

"This is very impertinent of you, sir. I shall be choosing a husband soon, and if you wish to be considered in my decision—"

He cut her off with a laugh. "Wenches do not choose their own husbands. Men dispose of them where the greatest profit is to be had, and there is very little likelihood that Triston's choice will fall on me unless I provide him with a little incentive."

She tried to dodge past the knight. He flung out his arms and caught hold of one of her trailing sleeves. She jerked free and loosed her jeweled dagger.

"Ah," he said, eyeing her blade with a dangerous smile. "A challenge."

"Leave her alone!"

The boyish cry startled the knight. Perrin ran across the garden and planted himself between Siri and her assailant.

"Why, whose puppy is this?" the knight mocked.

Perrin's tangled hair and smudged cheeks made him look more like an errant serving boy than the dignified heir to Vere's master. He glanced up into Siri's face, then dug his heels still further into the earth.

"Lady Siri doesn't want you here. Go away."

He brought out a wooden sword from behind his back and waved it at the knight. It was proportioned to a slightly older child's height. The knight laughed. He grabbed the sword, wrestled it away from the boy, and slung it into the flowers.

"Now, then, whelp—" he grabbed Perrin by the scruff of the neck and pitched him after the sword "—be off with you. I've another game in mind than this, and I do not need you meddling with my pleasure."

"You are going to be sorry you did that," Siri said. "That is Sir Triston's son. Leave now and I will ask the boy not to tell his father how you've mistreated him."

The knight's gaze was hot on Siri. "Nay, but I will have a taste of you, first. Triston will be quick enough to give me your hand, once he realizes it is the only way to restore your honor—"

He broke off as a loud smack made him stumble. Siri craned her neck at the sound and saw Perrin swing his wooden sword twice more with a vigorous fury into the back of the knight's knees.

The knight should have struggled harder to stay on his feet, for when he lost his balance and dropped into the grass it placed him on an even stature with Perrin. The sword whirred around his shoulders and head like a swarm of maddened bees. The knight threw up his arms to try to ward off the blows, but each time he twisted about to grab at Perrin, Perrin sprang around to stay at his back and continued his vivacious assault.

It was the forceful and frequently mispronounced oaths Perrin shouted in accompaniment to his blows that finally brought someone else upon the scene. By then Siri was in the grass herself, shaking with laughter at the gentleman's wincing, exasperated and thoroughly ineffective attempts to drive the boy off.

Triston shouted, "What the blazes is going on here? Perrin, stop that! Come here at once!"

"Oh, d–don't scold him," Siri gasped. "He was r–rescuing me."

When Perrin refused to stop swinging his sword at his victim's head, Triston hefted him into the air and shook him. "Perrin!"

"He was trying to hurt her!" Perrin cried, clearly so angry that he forgot to be afraid of his father. "Lady Siri wanted him to go away, but he wouldn't go. I think he was going to do something bad to her, Papa!"

Triston's gaze shot past his still-struggling son to the knight who now staggered to his feet. Very slowly, he set Perrin down. Siri tried to stifle her giggles, for Triston's glare promised an unpleasant rebuke for the knight.

"Your whelp misunderstood me, Sir Triston. I was only—" The knight broke off with a nervous glance at Triston's balling fists.

"Lady Siriol, has this fellow injured you?"

"Nay," she said, "thanks to your courageous son."

Triston grasped Perrin's shoulder, but she saw his anger in the way his hand trembled against the boy. She guessed that it was only Perrin's presence that checked him from dealing the knight the chastisement he deserved.

Triston glared at the knight. "You, sir, have overstayed your welcome here at Vere. I suggest you leave at once, or what you have suffered here with my son's wooden sword will be repeated with my own of steel."

The knight apparently knew better than to challenge the fiery glint in his host's eyes. He muttered an awkward apology and limped hastily out of the garden.

A silence fell. Triston took several deep breaths. Then he looked down at his son. He pressed the boy's shoulder and Siri saw the lingering anger in his face tempered with affection and pride.

"Well done, Perrin," he said. "You acted most chivalrously to defend the Lady Siriol. I think you have the makings in you of a very fine knight indeed."

Perrin looked pleased, but he slid away from his father's hand. "Sir, may I learn to fight with Sir Rollo?"

Triston looked disappointed in his son's retreat. He said, "I'm afraid you are yet a little small for that. Where did you get that sword?"

Perrin hesitated. He shifted backwards another step when his father frowned

"Perrin?"

Perrin stared at the ground and shuffled his feet. "I took it away from some boys in the yard. Sir Rollo was teaching them. They are only a little bigger than I, and they are mere servants. Sir, why can't I—"

"Do not argue with me, Perrin. Why did you take one of their swords?"

Perrin's face went stormy, lending him a marked resemblance to his turbulent father. "They laughed at me. They called me a baby because I like to sit with Lady Siri, and they said I could never be a knight because you are making me learn to read and that is something that only clerks do. But I remembered that Father Michel said that King Henry reads both Latin and French and that I should be proud to share a royal talent. So that was not why I hit them."

Triston's frown deepened. "You hit them? Why?"

"Because— Because they said—"

"What? Perrin, tell me."

Perrin's mouth went mulish and he shook his head.

"Perrin—"

"No! It was mean. And it wasn't true!"

"Perrin, just because someone mocks you, that does not give you leave to—"

"It wasn't me! It was about Mamma! They said—"

Perrin put up a hand to his mouth. But it was too late. Siri saw in Triston's face a grim realization of what the boys might have said about Perrin's mother. He moved to touch his son again, but Perrin threw down his wooden sword and ran out of the garden.

Triston stared after him a moment, then turned and reached down a hand to help Siri to her feet.

"Perhaps you should go after him," she said.

"He does not want me. Lady Siriol, will you go?"

Siri steeled herself against the soft plea in his voice. She said, "He is your son. It is your duty to comfort him. Besides, I know nothing about his mother. You are the only one who can explain to him about her."

Triston's eyes narrowed, but he made no move to follow her advice about Perrin. He only demanded again, "Are you sure you were not hurt in any way by that fellow?"

"I'm fine. He would not have gotten far with my dagger between us. But I am glad Perrin distracted him before I had to use it."

He cast an annoyed glance at her weapon. "One day some man is going to snatch that dagger out of your hand, and no one is going to hear your cries until it is too late. Is that how you wish to enter your marriage? In shame?"

"I—"

"I have been very lenient with you, my lady, but I have had enough of these games. Your court is threatening to eat me out of castle and home, and those men are growing impatient. Don't think that braggart will be the last man to try to force my hand. If you cannot make up your mind for a husband, then I will do it for you. Sir Gavin is still eager to marry you."

"You promised to let me choose for myself, and I do not want Sir Gavin!"

"Aye, I fancy I know well enough who it is you do want. If you spend any more time shut away in Raynor's chamber, I shall be obliged to demand a wedding to restore your reputation."

This unexpected attack took her aback. In all her visits to Raynor, she had always been careful to have Lucianna with her in the room, or at least to leave the door open so that the servants outside could be sure that there were no improprieties taking place. Triston had no possible justification for laying such a charge at her feet.

No justification but one. Her affections were in no danger of being engaged by any of the swaggering swains in the hall. Did Triston suspect it might be otherwise with Raynor? And might there be a reason beyond their personal feud for him to care?

She murmured, "And what if I did want to marry him? Do you imagine that I would let you stop me?"

"I imagine," Triston said, "that the moment he is well enough to walk I will throw him out on his ear, if I don't murder him first for his vicious lies about Acelet."

She flinched at these words and thanked heaven that Lord Fauke was no longer at Vere to hear them. "But what if Raynor is right? Acelet heard Raynor confess his assault of the Lady Clothilde in front of me. What if Acelet attacked him for it and—" She broke off at Triston's scornful glare.

"Raynor's tongue must be more beguiling than I had supposed. No doubt you believed him when he said that I was a traitor, too?"

"Of course I did not! But—"

She stopped as a servant entered the garden.

"A messenger has come, sir, from Belle Noir castle."

Siri's heart jumped into her throat, and she saw the dismay in Triston's face. Lord Fauke was directing his search operations from Raynor's castle. Had Acelet been found?

Triston started to leave the garden, but she ran after him. "I'm coming with you."

He swung about, so incensed that he actually leveled a finger at her. "This does not concern you, Lady Siriol. And if you mean to stand by babbling your suspicions of my cousin, then I most assuredly do not want you anywhere near when I greet Lord Fauke's messenger."

"As if I would do or say anything that might bring harm to Acelet," she said indignantly.

"Then stay away. Go tend to your poor patient. And pray this is not the news we both fear it is, for I will cut Raynor's heart out myself before I'll allow Acelet to be sacrificed in his twisted scheme of revenge."

With this fiery threat Triston left her, and the blaze in his eyes as he made it sent her flying to Raynor's chamber.

To her surprise, Raynor was sitting on the edge of the bed. His white linen shirt fell just below the knees of his bare legs, its ties open at the neck to expose the reddish-brown hair on his chest. For the first time, awkwardness checked her arrival. Seeing him free of the blankets and in such a state of undress made her suddenly wish that she had sent for Lucianna to join her.

Raynor flashed her a grin. "Carissima, observe."

He pushed himself to his feet and it was then she saw that he had a wooden crutch beneath each arm. He wobbled a moment, then steadied. With a lurching movement that implied he had not yet mastered the use of his new aids, he swung himself away from the bed.

"Can I help you?" she asked.

He shook his head. "I must learn—to maneuver—for myself." He spoke in a pant and awkwardly advanced across the room to the open window. When he finally shuffled about to lean into its embrasure, she saw that beads of moisture had formed on his brow.

"You have exhausted yourself," she scolded. "It is too soon for you to be up."

"Nay, the physician said I have lain abed long enough and that I might begin to walk with these. Smile, carissima. I am very nearly well."

She hesitated, then turned and closed the door. She crossed to the table, found a dampened cloth, and carried it across the room to wipe his forehead.

"I am glad," she said. "Do you think you are well enough to return to Belle Noir?"

"You wish to send me away from you? You may as well banish me to some dismal abyss. Carissima, I thought you had forgiven me."

Siri stepped back and studied his face. He looked genuinely distressed, as he did every time they discussed this subject. "You did a terrible thing by accusing Triston to Lord Fauke. Triston is with one of his messengers now. I am afraid that Acelet has been found."

Raynor slumped off the crutches to sit in the embrasure. "Then Triston may be in danger indeed, but not from me. 'Twas Acelet who accused him. I have told you again and again that I was merely repeating his words."

This defense won little sympathy from Siri. "I have no choice but to believe you when you say that it was Acelet who attacked you, but I am quite sure you have muddled his words. You were badly injured and must have been quite dizzy from loss of blood. I don't see how you can remember it all so clearly."

Raynor looked stubborn. "I remember that Acelet said Triston had sent him to kill me."

"Acelet attacked you because of what you did to Clothilde. You should not have made your confession in front of him. And I own that he is angry at Triston as well, and may have said as much during his attack on you. But that you should draw from that that Triston ordered him to kill you can only have been a confusion caused by the trauma of that night. And if you hope to retain my favor, you will confess as much to Lord Fauke."

A gleam entered his amber eyes. "You mean if I tell Lord Fauke that I was mistaken, you will agree to entertain my suit for your hand?"

She hesitated. Raynor was not like the other men of her court. Only his exaggerated flattery ever tricked honest laughter from her, and that was because it was always spoken with a twinkle in his eye that betrayed his sense of his own ridiculousness. But the last few days there had been something else in the gaze he had occasionally let rest on her. Something cool and considering, as though he were weighing her. Or perhaps, somehow weighing himself.

She shook her head now. "I do not believe you mean that. Unless it is my dowry you want, because I do not think you are in love with me at all."

Raynor pressed a hand to his chest. "Carissima, you wrong me. It was for you alone that this poor heart of mine kept beating while my life otherwise threatened to flow away. Send me away from the bright beam of your smile and I shall dwindle and waste like a rose in the merciless snows of winter."

"Don't be absurd," she said. "You cannot stay here any longer. I do not think I can keep you safe of Triston's temper."

"Sooner would I take that risk than lose the sweet light of your face. Carissima."

He held out his hands. She did not know why, but she put her own in his. There was no laughter now in his eyes, but an earnest glow that startled her.

"You are the breath of my life. I knew from the first hour I saw you, when I unveiled your face on that dusty road, that I should never rest until I could hold you in my arms and speak to you every inadequate word of love from my soul. I will cherish you forever. Please—" he bowed his head and kissed her hands "—come with me to Belle Noir."

He sounded more fervent than she had ever heard him before. But . . .

"Come with you?"

He raised his head, and his mouth lifted in the depths of his beard. "It is customary for a wife to reside in her husband's home."

"You mean marry you? Truly?"

His smile grew rueful. "This shock of yours does not please me, carissima. Have I been so clumsy in my praises that you did not realize how deeply I am in love with you?"

"Clumsy, no. But I thought you were only teasing."

"And risk raising expectations in your mind that I had no intention of fulfilling? That would be the act of a knave." His eyes gleamed. For a moment there was the barest hint of something in his voice that made her wonder if these words were not aimed at someone beside himself. Then the gleam warmed back into a glow. "Nay, if you would condescend to have me, I would be the happiest, nay, the most blissful of men."

Siri had never imagined that he might genuinely wish to marry her. There was no question that she had been sorely disappointed in her other suitors. They had all proven to be just like that swaggerer who had confronted her in the garden. Eloquently, though respectfully, flirtatious before Lucianna's stern eyes, but as greedy in their gazes upon Siri as Lord Fauke whenever her companion happened to glance away.

Raynor was different. His flattery too was extravagant, but if lust simmered in his heart, he had taken care not to display it in her presence. But . . .

"I do not know if I am ready to leave Vere. What about—"

"Triston?"

Her face warmed as he completed her abruptly halted thought.

"He does not love you, carissima. Do you wish to stay with a man who will always see you as someone else?"

She shook her head, the lump in her throat making it impossible to form any other reply.

Raynor murmured, "He is more to you than I had hoped. Come away, carissima. If you stay, you may one day delude yourself into thinking that you have won Triston's eyes for yourself, that his memories have faded, overwhelmed by the vibrant reality of what makes you uniquely you. But you would be wrong. Clothilde was more than his wife, more even than his love. She was his obsession. And if ever he takes you for his own, it will only be because he believes that somehow he can reclaim her again through you."

Siri fought the truth for one more moment, then felt her final hope crumble away. What was it Triston had said in the garden, the morning after her banquet? *"If I could fashion you to be her again, I would do so."* Raynor was right. She had been deceiving herself, hoping that she had roused a flicker of jealousy in Triston's breast. From the day she had stepped across Vere's threshold, he had wanted only to be rid of her. Had he not said so again today? Then why did she continue to torture herself by lingering? Because she had rashly given Triston her word that she would marry, yet she could not bring herself to give her hand to any of those braggarts in the hall. The most painful emptiness in Triston's house seemed preferable to surrendering to a marriage based solely on a husband's wolfish hunger for her charms and her dowry.

But now an alternative held out its hand to her. She would be a fool not to take it, she told herself, a fool to remain at Vere and fall into the trap that Raynor's words so skillfully sketched.

She swallowed hard, but the lump in her throat refused to dissolve. She forced herself to speak through the ache.

"But Raynor—" it would not be fair to pretend with him "—I do not love you. I do not think I ever will. Are you sure you want a wife who comes to you with less than all of her heart?"

"If you brought me but a sliver, 'twould be more than most men find. And I will let time be the judge of where your heart finally comes to rest."

She freed her hands to encircle his face. She had never willingly kissed any man but Triston. It was with a shiver of doubt that she now pressed her lips to Raynor's. His mouth was warm and responded instantly to her caress, but she waited in vain for her pulses to quicken. There was nothing, neither pleasure nor revulsion. After several empty seconds, she drew away.

He must have seen her disappointment, but he did not seem offended. "In time," he said. "Only give me the chance to show you what may come in time."

The lump still burned in her throat. "But how shall we make Triston agree?"

Raynor hefted himself up from the window's embrasure. He leaned on his hale leg, supported by the crutch, and held out its mate to Siri. "I will walk better with your support, I think. Help me back to the bed and we will discuss what we should do next."

She took the crutch and passed her free arm around Raynor's waist. He was not as tall as Triston, but he was heavy limping against her. The weave of his linen shirt was thin and the heat of his body so close to hers made her suddenly nervous. She was not sure why, for he made no threatening moves.

Until they reached the bed. Somehow he stumbled then. They both dropped the crutches in an effort to restore his balance. She made a grab for his shoulders, but he reeled and pitched forward and to her horror, his weight carried her with him into the blankets.

Pinned beneath him, the memory swirled around her with sickening force.

"Let me up," she panted.

"Carissima," he said softly, "forgive me. I tripped. But now that we are here—"

She caught the cocky flash of his grin before his head swooped down to nuzzle her neck. His action sent her shuddering back into that night—the night she had awakened to the apprentice's lewd kisses. He had tried to stifle her cries with his hand, but she had managed to bite his palm, pull her mouth free, and scream. The same reaction now welled up in her throat. But this time it was not her brother who would come flying to her aid, but one of Triston's servants. And if Triston ever learned of this—

It was that thought that checked her. Raynor was not the wicked apprentice, she reminded herself. She had only to make him listen and surely he would stop!

"Raynor, please, I—"

His mouth smothered her protest, no longer gently responding to a kiss of hers, but with a fervent zeal. She sought desperately to stifle her panic. Raynor was not the apprentice. Even in his ardor, his kisses were coaxing. Not forcing, like the apprentice's had been. Nor tauntingly meant for another, like Triston's.

Like Triston's . . .

Raynor lifted his mouth, but all that escaped her now was a sob.

"Carissima?"

She must allow him a few more kisses. Just a few to reassure her, to convince her that she was making the right choice.

"Please," she whispered, "make me fall in love with you."

He murmured, "Carissima, I will try."

# Chapter 16

Triston stormed up the stairs, his relief that Lord Fauke's messenger had not come with news of Acelet's capture forgotten in his rage at the baron's outrageous command.

"My lord desires to engage the Lady Siriol's artistic services in the completion of his psaltery. Deliver her to Belle Noir before sundown."

Talk of manuscripts and illuminations did not deceive Triston. Lord Fauke wanted Siri away from Vere, or more specifically, away from Triston's protection. Triston had no intention of agreeing to so blatant a ploy, but the messenger insisted that Siri be brought before him to answer the summons herself. Triston saw no point in looking for her in her chamber. He remembered his parting shot to her in the garden and had little doubt but what she had run with his threat straight to Raynor. Had she not sought to protect Raynor from his rage before, when Triston had hurled him onto the floor?

Triston's blood hissed like boiling steam. She had professed her love for him, but it was his enemy she embraced and defended.

He knew that he had forfeited any right to care. He had rejected the heart she had so candidly held out to him. If she now wished to bestow it on some other man, he had no choice but to stand aside and watch her do so.

But not on Raynor de Molinet. Not on a man whose wooing could prove as dangerous to herself as it was undoubtedly aimed in revenge at Triston.

He wrenched open the door to Raynor's sickroom. Despite his earlier accusations, he knew how carefully Siri had guarded her reputation in Raynor's company. He expected to find Lucianna seated with her beside the bed. But both of the chairs were empty and the bed was occupied, not with a weak and wounded patient, but with a man vigorously recovered enough to be devouring the woman beneath him with zestful, ravenous kisses.

Triston needed no more than a glimpse of the gown he'd seen in the garden to know that the woman was Siri. Every muscle in his body twitched in a violent response, but his oath froze before it escaped his throat. He stood transfixed by a vision that suddenly tilted wildly between this scene and another.

Siri's gown slid down over her shoulder . . . Clothilde writhing in Raynor's embrace . . . Raynor's open and disarranged shirt . . . Clothilde's screams . . . Siri's gasping pleas . . .

"Raynor, don't— This is not what I meant— Please—"

The panted words from the bed turned the image red before Triston's eyes.

When the oath finally exploded from his throat, it was too late for Raynor to react. Triston hauled him off the bed and threw him against the nearest wall. He caught and pinned him there with one hand wrapped around his throat. Raynor could do no more than gurgle, and even that sound was cut off as Triston's fingers clamped down like steel bands. Triston could not even hear his own curses through the pounding in his head. The taste on his tongue was the same he had savored that other day, caustic and pungent, bitter as blood.

He heard an echo of a scream, but not until he felt his free hand being wrenched away did he realize he had drawn his dagger. Raynor clawed at Triston's hold. His eyes bulged, his mouth gaped in a helpless plea for air.

Triston shook off the hold on his dagger. He slid Raynor up along the wall, easing his grasp only enough to slide the point of his blade to the vein pulsing at the base of his captive's neck.

"Triston, no!" A set of delicate white fingers wrapped themselves around his blade and twisted it away from its target. "Ay!"

He released Raynor, turning in horror at the cry of pain. He pulled Siri's hand free of his steel. Blood bubbled up from the cut in her palm.

"Siri—" he croaked.

If she felt any pain from the cut she gave no indication of it, but pulled frantically at his hands. "Triston, please, you must stop. It is not what you think. I was helping Raynor back to the bed and he tripped and we fell and—"

Her face was so white that he feared she was on the verge of fainting. Her fingers in his felt like ice.

Her attempted explanation fell on incredulous ears. "Do you take me for an imbecile? That cur was raping you!"

He swung back towards Raynor, who had slumped to the floor and was raggedly gasping for air.

Siri sought to place herself between them. "Triston, no! He was not raping me, I swear it! Raynor asked me to marry him and I said that I would."

Triston gave a snarling curse. "The devil you did."

If it were possible he thought she went even paler, but she stood by her confession. "I did. And then he tripped and we fell, like I said, and he kissed me and I . . . I . . . k–kissed him back." Did she shiver on the word? "Then he got a little c–carried away, but he would have stopped— I know he would have stopped . . ."

She trailed off with another tremor.

Raynor rasped, "I was only sampling what will soon be mine. And for this, de Brielle—" he fondled his crushed throat and his amber eyes glowed "—I will see you in hell."

Triston shrugged off Siri's pleading tug and dragged Raynor back to his feet. "I will dispatch you there first, before I'll let you lay another hand on her. There is not going to be any marriage."

Raynor's teeth bared in a snarl. "Then murder me here, before her eyes. Go ahead. For that is the only way you will stop me from taking her from you."

Triston pushed him back against the wall. The arrogant face still wavered in a reddish mist. "If you think I will not—" He brought his dagger up beneath Raynor's chin.

"Do it," Raynor hissed. "Think how she will love you then. Or will your murderous rage drive her away, the way your coldness drove Isobel to her grave, the way your betrayals drove your wife mad?"

"Nay," Triston swore, "it was your lies that destroyed Clothilde. You have had your revenge on me, Raynor. Clothilde is dead—"

"And now you want her." Raynor tossed a glance at Siri.

In spite of himself, Triston glanced at her too. "No—"

"You want her," Raynor repeated, "but she will never be yours. I swear she will never be yours. I will see you in hell, Triston, a living hell, of such that you will pray for the soothing flames of death."

Raynor rolled back his head a bare instant before Triston punched his blade higher. Only Siri's scream stopped him from thrusting it clean through Raynor's flesh. Her uninjured hand darted up towards his dagger.

Warned by her sob, Triston jerked the blade away before her fingers could embrace it again. She reached out to catch his fist, still clenched about the hilt. With another broken sob, she pressed her lips against his white knuckles.

"Please," she whispered, "oh, please do not do this."

Her breath felt as cold as her fingers and her ashen cheeks streamed with tears.

He slid his knuckles under her chin and lifted her face up to his. Blazes! Raynor was right. He *did* want her. He wanted to kiss away the fear from her eyes, to cradle her shivering body to his heart. He wanted to mingle his lips with hers, not in angry panic, not in a regretful apology, but in a simple, aching need to somehow touch her soul.

And—curse him!—Raynor saw it and would use it to make his hurt seem but a shadow of his former pain.

He pulled his hand away and slammed his dagger into its sheath. He shoved Raynor onto the bed. "Get out of my house. I don't care if you have to crawl back to Belle Noir. If you are not gone within the hour, I will deal you such a thrashing as you may never walk again."

He grabbed Siri's arm, then saw the way she had balled her left hand

and was holding it against her midriff. He turned to the bed. Raynor sat up, tensing, but Triston only tore a strip of cloth from the sheets and used it to bind up her cut.

Then he dragged her out of the room.

"Where are we going?" she stammered.

"We are going to put an end to this farce once and for all."

He stopped just short of the head of the stairs that led down to the hall and rubbed his eyes with his fingers. Not until the reddish mist was gone did he trust himself to look at her again.

The mist threatened to swirl back. They could not go down like this. Her gown had fallen over one of her shoulders again and some of her hair had tumbled from its pins to cluster around her neck. He pushed the curls away, intending to restore her gown to some modesty, but his hand brushed against silken skin. Before he could stop himself, his rebuking touch turned into a caress.

Her flesh felt so cold. Impulsively, he stroked his hand up her throat and slid his fingers around to the downy tendrils at the back of her neck. Gently at first, then with a deepening pressure, he kneaded the tender skin there until the coldness began to ebb.

She rolled back her head with a shuddering breath. A flickering fear that her reaction signaled distaste at his touch was swept away when she melted into his arms.

"Siri—" His mouth drifted down towards hers. He almost checked himself when a sob broke from her in the instant before he kissed her. But her ingenuous mouth reached up to catch his and her clinging, urging, fervent response swept away the last of his doubts.

The coldness in her lips fled as he drank long and deep of their heady nectar. When he finally lifted his head, her lips were no longer pale and trembling. They were full and rosy and moist—and eagerly receptive to his second kiss.

This time her mouth was warm, though no less zealous in returning his caress. Fear, guilt, even grief slipped away for a few gloriously transporting moments. He felt her hands sliding up his back, curling into his shoulders.

"Triston," she whispered, "you know it is only you I want. Only you. And Raynor was right. You want me too!"

He froze, the fire in his blood congealing as if it had been doused with ice. Raynor. Not ten minutes ago she had been sharing these dazzling lips with *him.*

A souring taste of fury and betrayal filled Triston's mouth, flushing out the honey-sweet taste of his passion. He thrust her away so abruptly that she stumbled and came to a stop just short of the top of the steps.

"Nay," he said roughly, "it is not me you want. It is Raynor." He choked on the vision of them entangled on the bed. The world began to turn red again. "What more did you give him besides this—" he stepped closer and ran a finger over the bridge of her shoulder "—and this?" He touched the nest of her lips and found them still warm.

"Nothing." She caught his hand and spread his fingers against her mouth. "From the moment you first claimed them in your hall, they have yearned for your kiss alone. But you did not want them or me." She pushed his hand away and a light of dismayed comprehension burst through the tears in her eyes. "It is Clothilde. It is not me you want. It is still Clothilde. You were thinking of her when you kissed me just now."

To Triston's surprise, a denial sprang to his tongue, but he bit back the words. It was Siri he had kissed and it was Siri he ached to possess. But it was not Siri that he loved. How could he? She was nothing like the shy, trusting girl who had captured his heart and held it trapped in her own small hands for as far back as his memory stretched. Clothilde. Even when he had thought her an unattainable dream, his heart had beaten her name alone.

And now, here stood Siri. Her efforts to alter her appearance had been effective, but they had not erased the likeness. He had only to loose her pins like this . . . and this . . .

He spread the golden hair about her shoulders and there Clothilde stood again.

For an instant. Until her delicate chin jutted out and sparks flew from her eyes like blinding glances of sunlight refracted off lingering droplets after a rain.

"At least Raynor wants me for me," she said. "He does not try to make me into someone else. You bade me choose a husband and I have chosen. I am going to marry Raynor."

"The devil you are." Curse the wench. She was nothing like Clothilde at all, bending forward with her hands on her hips to glare at him. "You'll marry no one without my consent. You will make up your mind from one of those men below stairs and you will not speak de Molinet's name again."

This arrogant command replaced the pallor of her cheeks with a rush of angry color. "How dare you! You think you can kiss me like that and then dispose of me with no more thought than if I were a sack of flour?"

Triston had the grace to blush, but the kisses, charged though they were, had in fact changed nothing. Her presence remained a tormenting reminder of what he had lost, and he would never know any peace from his grief until she was gone from Vere.

He answered stiffly, "I have watched you play this silly game with these dithering swains of yours for weeks, and my patience with it and you is at an end. We are going downstairs now and find you a husband. And if you cannot decide—"

"I have decided!"

"—then I am going to give you to Sir Gavin. And there is where the matter ends."

He reached for her arm, intending to drag her downstairs if he had to, but she stepped back to evade him. Her heel dipped over the first step of the stairs. For a moment she swayed.

Triston's heart surged into his throat. If she fell— He caught her elbow and tried to pull her away from the danger, but she jerked her arm so vigorously to free herself that he released her and flung his hands behind his back. Just so had he lost Clothilde, in the very struggle to save her.

He moved quickly back so that she might not feel herself further threatened by him.

"There, I shan't touch you," he said hoarsely. "Come away from the stairs."

Whatever she saw in his face wiped the rebellion from her own. "Don't look like that. I am not going to fall."

He scarcely heard her. "Come away from the stairs. Please—"

He broke off, his mouth dry. A clammy sweat had broken out on his palms. His muscles twitched to pull her away, but he dared not make even a feint in her direction. If she shifted so much as an inch—

"Triston, I am perfectly steady. There is no reason to be afraid." She paused, then her head swiveled to glance behind her. Some sound below stairs must have caught her attention. When she turned back, it was with a murmured warning. "Perrin is watching us."

Perrin? Triston stretched his neck and saw his son hovering anxiously at the foot of the stairs. If Siri fell now—

"Lady Siriol, please."

Her single step was not enough to make him release his clenched breath. He moved back to give her more room, then turned when he heard his name called out from behind him.

"Triston."

He remained too wrought up in his fears for Siri to respond with aught but a blank stare to the sight of Raynor hobbling towards him on a set of crude crutches. Still somewhat disheveled, Raynor had nevertheless laced up his shirt and tucked it into a pair of breeches, cut loose to accommodate the bandages on his thigh.

"Triston," he repeated, "please, can we not talk? We both lost our tempers back there, said things we didn't mean. But if you will only give me a chance to convince you that Lady Siri and I are—"

Fury swelled up again, overwhelming Triston's alarm with a reignited blaze. "I have nothing to say to you, de Molinet," he snapped, "and neither has the Lady Siriol. Now get out of my house."

"I'm going. But can't we settle this first?"

"The way you settled with me using Clothilde?"

Raynor shook his head. "You wrong me, Triston. Why would I harm the Lady Siri? I owe her my life. You'd have left me to wallow in my blood the night of the banquet, and had she not pulled your blade away, you'd have cut my throat today."

"As I may yet do if you do not get yourself out of my sight."

Raynor's amber eyes darted to the diminutive figure poised just behind Triston. Instinctively, Triston edged closer to Siri.

His warning did not stop Raynor's advance. Raynor movements were jerky, suggesting that his leg was still weak and his skill with his new supports still less than expert.

"Triston, I pray you, if you would only listen—"

Almost at the same moment as Raynor spoke, Siri touched Triston's arm. "Triston, please. Hasn't this hate between you gone far enough?"

"Aye," Raynor said, "I am willing to bury our past. Let Lady Siri be the bridge of peace between us."

"Peace," Triston spat at him. "'Tis not peace you want with me, Raynor. I am not taken in by the glib plea on your tongue, when 'tis hate I still see in your eyes. 'Tis revenge you want for your lying wanton of a sister, but you are not going to win it through the Lady Siriol. Leave her be, or I swear by my soul that I will—"

Raynor's head went down before Triston could finish his oath. One of the crutches slipped and went spinning against the wall. Raynor's knee buckled. He pitched forward into Triston's chest, so hard that he almost knocked the breath from Triston's lungs. Triston could not stop himself from lurching backwards. He felt the strong bump of his body colliding into Siri's.

She gave a startled cry. He whirled about to see her teetering on the edge of the step where his impact had cast her. He grabbed for her arms, but they flailed out of reach, spinning wildly in a futile attempt to regain her balance. Her sleeve fluttered out of his desperate fingers, her skirt swung away from his clutching hand, even her hair flew defiantly from the fist he sought to close on it.

He had only time to scream her name before she was gone. He saw her falling and in the instant before his mind reeled into blackness, his heart pounded out *Clothilde*.

# Chapter 17

"Mamma! Mamma!"

Perrin's scream shattered the inky veil over Triston's mind, splintering it back into day, to this moment, to Siri stumbling, twisting, falling . . .

Perrin lunged up the steps, then stopped with his arms flung out as though he thought somehow to catch her.

"Perrin, no!" Triston shouted. "Get out of the way!"

He sprang down after them both, but again his desperate grasp met with empty air. Siri's head swooped down, away from his grabbing arms. Perrin vanished beneath her. Over and over they rolled down the stones steps, until they settled in a silent, motionless heap at the bottom.

Triston reached them in seconds. Siri sprawled face down, her hair spread around her like a tangled fan, her skirts billowed out so full that they nearly swallowed Perrin up beneath them. Only a whisper of dark curls showed from under her limply extended arm. Triston fell to his knees beside them, but shrank from touching her, even to uncover his son. What if her eyes were wide, like Clothilde's had been? What if her head lolled to that same broken, sickening angle?

Stunned and horrified oaths shook the air as men who were gathered in the hall, Siri's suitors, pressed round to stare at her immobile body.

"Is she. . . ?"

No one dared finish the thought. As one they fell silent, clearly waiting for Triston to speak, to act, to reassure or confirm their worst fears.

His hands trembling uncontrollably, he finally forced himself to push back the hair from her face. He saw a deep gash on her temple. The only splash of color against her alabaster skin, so white, so still that she might have been carved of marble. Except that her flesh was still warm. The heat had lingered in Clothilde's body, too.

He blinked away a burning beneath his lashes and carefully shifted Siri's arm. Perrin's face was unmarred, though the blood had left even his lips. The lids over his thankfully closed eyes shone like two tiny shells.

Two tiny, fluttering shells.

"Perrin?" he whispered.

He eased his son out from beneath Siri's body. The bright blue eyes flickered open. Triston crushed Perrin to his chest and heard him give a reassuring gasp. For a long moment Triston held him, rocked him, his face buried against his son's thick, curly hair while he silently uttered prayer after prayer of fervent thanks.

He stroked his son's curls and found a swelling on the back of Perrin's head. In alarm, he relaxed his hold and searched for other injuries. Perrin looked confused and dazed, but his bones seemed to be intact. Triston pulled him close again, but Perrin turned his head away.

"Mamma—"

Triston groaned and tried to shift Perrin around so that he could not see Siri. "Hush, Perrin, it is not your Mamma. Lady Siri has—"

"Mamma— Lady Siri— you made them fall!"

Perrin erupted in Triston's grasp, writhing so frantically that Triston loosed him, then sat back, stunned when Perrin fell on him with flailing fists.

"You made them fall! You made them fall!"

Triston scarcely felt the frenzied blows assailing his chest and shoulders. All he saw were the anguished tears flowing down his son's cheeks.

The stab of Perrin's words sliced straight through Triston's breast. "Perrin," he whispered, his lips numb, "it was an accident."

"No," Perrin screamed, "I saw you! I saw you push Mamma! And now Lady Siri— Lady Siri—"

The rest slurred away in an agonized fury, dissolving into sobs that became dangerously shrill.

Someone muttered, "His head. Someone should quiet the boy."

Triston's attempts to do so only aggravated Perrin's hysteria further.

"Blazes," he swore. "Someone help me. Take him away. Take him to Father Michel." Surely the chaplain would know what to do.

No one moved, the crowd of grown men apparently cowed by the little boy's fit. Triston stood up, furious at their inaction. He snatched Perrin up and thrust him kicking and screaming into Sir Gavin's arms. "Take him to my chaplain."

The flash in Triston's eye sent Sir Gavin springing up the stairs, Perrin held at arms' length so that the knight could escape his flying heels.

It was then, as Triston stared after them, that he caught sight of Raynor standing at the head of the steps. He leaned on the single crutch he still held, his bearded face pale, but otherwise devoid of emotion. There was no guilt, no grief on his features, nothing which might acknowledge either pain or pleasure at his deed.

Triston's world went red again. The caustic taste of murder flooded back into his mouth. Clothilde, and now Siri. May he burn forever in hell if he allowed the fiend to escape with his life again.

He pulled his dagger free and had started up the stairs when the only words on earth with the power to check him were uttered.

"Sir Triston! Lady Siri—she is alive!"

Triston turned sharply. One of her suitors had rolled her over and lifted her head into his lap. But not until Triston saw her chest rise and fall three times did he drop his dagger with a clatter on the stones and rush back to kneel beside her.

Except for the shallow evidence of her breathing, she lay so quiet that he almost doubted his own eyes. He scooped her limp body into his arms and murmured her name into her hair. Again his eyes burned, with relief, with a hesitant gratitude. He could not be at total ease until he had seen some stronger sign in her of life. A flicker of lashes, a flutter of fingers, even a whispery moan—

He took a deep breath to steady himself. "Find the Lady Lucianna and tell her what has occurred. I will take the Lady Siriol to her chamber."

He stood and swept with his sweet, injured burden up the stairs.

There was no avoiding Raynor when he reached the top. Raynor's face remained a mask, but he betrayed a hint of apprehension in the way he moved quickly back against the wall.

"De Molinet," Triston hissed without so much as a break in his stride as he passed, "if I see you again, you are dead."

⬧

Oblivion gave way slowly to a nagging discomfort, and then to great, white strokes of pain. Siri whimpered and pulled away the moist compress draped across her brow. She pressed the palms of her hands against her throbbing head.

"Carissima, bambina, lie still."

"Ah!" Siri cried. The pain pierced all the way from the front of her skull to the back.

"Can you not ease her?"

Triston's rolling tones seemed to enrage the former speaker, who even through her distress Siri recognized as Lucianna.

"Diavolo! I have warned you that if you do not leave this room, I will—"

"Peace, woman. You can tear my heart out later, after you have attended to your mistress."

"I would already have attended to her, had you not such slackards for servants. Where is that girl I sent to prepare the salve? If she has fumbled my instructions—"

"You should have gone with her. I told you I would stay with your lady."

"You ask me to leave the wolf to guard the lamb? You must take me for a fool!"

"Lady Lucianna—"

"Go away, signore! You have caused enough harm. I have seen my donna in tears because of you, and now I see her like this. She might have

205

broken her neck, and do not say that you had no hand in her fall."

Siri could not bear any more. She pushed herself up, then moaned. Her head felt like to split apart.

Someone tried to press her back down to the bed, but she pulled away. "It was an accident. Triston, tell Lucianna what happened. Tell her how Raynor fell and—" A wave of nausea hit her and she rocked forward until her head was nearly in her lap. "Ah, ah! Lucianna, make it stop hurting!"

"I will, bambina, I will. In only a moment or two. You must be patient until— At last! *Pronto,* girl, bring the tray here."

Siri bit her quivering lip and let Lucianna lift her head, but when Lucianna touched her right temple, she cried out and jerked away.

"Bambina, please, I must apply the salve."

Siri tried to sit still, but the former pounding was nothing to the streaks of agony that sliced through her head each time Lucianna touched her. She flinched away twice more and finally struck at Lucianna's hands.

"Signore—" even through the torturous buzz in her ears, Siri could hear Lucianna's reluctance. "Signore, you must hold her."

Siri felt the bed dip as Triston's weight joined hers. When his arms went around her, she burrowed her head against his chest, as though his embrace alone could bring her relief. He caught her chin and rolled it away, then held her face trapped in an inflexible grip while Lucianna mercilessly rubbed the salve into her wound.

Siri cried out again. Tears seared down her cheeks. But Triston's strength held her fast, until Lucianna had finished and wrapped a bandage around her head. Then his hand cupped her wet cheek and drew her head back down to his breast.

His touch felt cool against the burning stream of her tears, soothing the pain that ebbed from her head by excruciatingly slow degrees. Lucianna muttered something, but when Triston's hold on her slackened, Siri caught his arm and moaned a protest. His arm crept reassuringly back around her. She continued to cling to him, her fingers digging into the sleeve of his forearm until they found his muscles, hard and intriguingly large beneath her small hand.

"Carissima, you must drink this."

Lucianna's voice came as a vexing intrusion to the blissful warmth creeping upwards through Siri's body. Her temples still throbbed, but not as fiercely now, and she doubted that the tea Triston tilted into her mouth could promise a more powerful healing than his continued embrace. She opened her eyes to look at him, but his face swam so dizzily that she closed them again. She did not need to see him. It was enough to breathe his familiar scent, to nestle still deeper into his arms. She coaxed his fingers into that spot at the back of her neck that he had kneaded so gently earlier today, imparting to her such delicious shivers.

Not like those others, the ones she had suffered in Raynor's arms. Poor Raynor. He did not deserve the trembling dread she had rewarded his caresses with. Why was this so different? Why did she welcome Triston's touch, nay, ache to feel his hand, when Raynor's had left her cold and dismayed?

"That is enough, signore. Come away. Donna Siri must rest now."

"Don't go." Siri clutched at Triston when he started to draw away.

"But you must sleep," he murmured.

Her arms slid around him. "Then let me do it here." She moved her head until she could feel the strong beating of his heart beneath her cheek. "Hold me," she whispered, "please."

What sort of look he used to silence Lucianna she would never know, but he held her tenderly cradled against his breast until she drifted into sleep.

⁂

Triston was gone when she awoke. Siri felt his loss so intensely that tears started to her eyes. She sat up. Her woolen gown had been removed, leaving her garbed only in her chemise, and there was a bandage on her left hand.

*Her hand. Triston's dagger poised at Raynor's throat.* Her fingers flew to the bandage on her head as the memories swirled back.

"Lucianna!" She shook her slumbering companion. "Wake up!"

Lucianna's eyes popped open. "Carissima, what is wrong? Your head—"

"I'm fine," Siri said quickly. "It still hurts a little, but I'm fine."

"Then what is the matter?"

Siri hesitated. The tea Lucianna had given her must have been drugged, for she sensed that a good deal of time had passed since she had fallen asleep in Triston's arms. A grey, hazy light seeped in around the edges of the shuttered windows, and there was a feeling of dawn in the air.

"What happened after I fell?" she asked.

Lucianna's green eyes flashed. "After you fell? You mean after that mostro made you fall!"

"Made me—? Lucianna, that is absurd!"

"It is what the gentlemen heard his own son scream."

"Perrin?" With a rising horror, Siri remembered the little boy on the stairs, his arms spread out to catch her. "Where is Perrin now?"

"In his own bed, I presume, with a lump on his head the size of a goose egg, if I have heard aright."

"I fell into him," Siri whispered. "I could not stop myself. Raynor's crutches slipped and he fell into Triston and Triston fell backwards into me and I stumbled down the stairs and fell into Perrin. Was he badly hurt besides knocking his head?"

"The boy? I have no idea. Donna Siri, where are you going?"

Siri winced as she slid out of the bed. Every bone in her body ached. "To see Perrin. If he has come to harm because of me, I shall never forgive myself."

The fur-lined cloak she had worn to dinner still hung by the door. She pulled it around her shoulders.

"Carissima, stop. You are not well enough to be up."

She paused, swaying dizzily by the door, but she clung to the latch determinedly. "I will only see if he is safe, and then I will come right back. Lucianna—" she glanced over her shoulder, checked by the dread question that entered her mind. "What happened to Raynor?"

"Signor Raynor is no longer at Vere."

"Did Triston—"

"Signor Balduin escorted him away while Signor Triston and I attended to your injuries. I do not think Signor Triston saw him before he went. Carissima, at least wait until I can dress. I will accompany you—"

But Siri pulled open the door and was gone.

She supposed she should have expected to find Triston standing over his son's bed. He turned when she entered the room, his face pale and drawn. She imagined that his night had been a torturous one, worrying about Perrin, reliving again and again her fall—and Clothilde's. She knew his heart well enough by now to know that both incidents would have haunted him as one. She did not need to read the anguish in his eyes, to endure the painful way they swept her streaming hair, to know that she was right.

She was careful not to touch him as she approached the bed, careful not to do or say anything that might cross the line of confusion in his mind.

She nodded at the sleeping boy. "How badly is he hurt?"

"I don't know," Triston replied, his voice low. "Father Michel sent Audiart up to administer a sleeping draught. He has not awakened since. You should be in bed too."

"I'm fine," she insisted. "Did he break anything?"

"I don't think so. He was able to stand on his feet and scream and rail at me, so his bones must all be fine. But I worry about the blow to his head."

"Triston—"

A wave of dizziness hit her, and in an instant Triston's arms were around her. He swept her off her feet and lowered her into the chair where he had undoubtedly spent the majority of the night. It took all of her strength not to cling to him again. This was not the time to indulge her own whims.

"Thank you." She smiled weakly as he straightened.

He fixed his gaze carefully over her head and uttered flatly, "Perrin thinks I killed his mother."

She gasped.

"That is why he is afraid of me. My son thinks I killed his mother."

He sounded weary, as though the horror of his realization had numbed through an endless repetition in the night.

She could not resist grabbing his hands and squeezing them. "Surely you have misunderstood him?"

"Nay, I have understood him too well. He thinks I pushed you, too. And how do you imagine he will view me now, when he awakes?"

"But why would he think such a thing as that? He was watching us, so he must have seen the way you stumbled into me. And Sir Balduin said that no one saw the way Clothilde fell, except for—" She caught her breath at the sudden memory. "Acelet! He saw you. He said he heard you and Clothilde quarreling and came out to see what was happening. Triston, was it possible that Perrin heard you too?"

He groaned and pulled away from her to sink down on a nearby stool. His hands shoved back the thick curls from his brow. "You mean that he came out of his room? That he was standing somewhere in the shadows while I was struggling with her? She slipped. Lady Siri, she slipped! I tried to catch her, but—"

"I know," she said. "You tried to catch me too, but there was nothing you could do, then or now. Triston, if you can't believe that, how can you expect Perrin to?" She slid out of the chair to kneel beside him.

"There should have been a way. I should have found a way. You are so small and I was standing right beside you. How could I have missed?"

She laid her fingers to his lips, then pressed her palm into the cloth near his heart. "I know how it hurts you, here. I am alive and she is not. Why? I don't have the answer. Triston, sometimes there just aren't any." She drew down his hands and held them hard.

He sat for a long moment with his eyes closed, the planes of his face drawn tight. What thoughts might be taunting him now, she could not guess until he spoke.

"After she fell," he said at last, "I couldn't move. I just stood there, staring down at where she lay. She had been shrieking at me for days and suddenly—there was silence. I couldn't move. I couldn't think. I don't even remember seeing Acelet run down the stairs. He was just suddenly there, cradling Clothilde's body, screaming that she was dead and that I had killed her."

"Triston, if Perrin heard him—"

"He must have. He must have seen me trying to wrestle the dagger out of her hand, but he would not have known what our struggles meant. In the dark, in the confusion of his frightened six-year-old mind, perhaps it did look as if I pushed her. And then to hear Acelet screaming at me, accusing me—"

"But surely you tried to explain to Perrin afterwards what happened."

He freed one hand and plunged it back into his hair. "Nay, I left it to Father Michel. He told Perrin only that his mother had lost her footing on the stairs and fell. How was I to know that he had seen?"

"Oh, Triston."

"I know, I know. I should have told him myself. But I was so consumed with . . ."

"Guilt?" she said as he trailed off.

"Guilt," he repeated hoarsely, "for so many things. Lady Siri, I failed her in so many ways that I did not even know until it was too late. And now I have failed Perrin, too."

She brushed her thumb against the tight muscle of his cheek. "It is not too late for you and your son. It is not too late to tell him the truth."

"He will not believe me."

"Yes, he will—if you are honest with him. But I think you will have to tell him the truth about his mother."

He opened his eyes and cupped her face between his hands. He gazed so deeply into her eyes that she thought he must see to the very center of her soul. "His mother. Why could she not have been as strong as you?"

"Tris—"

He smothered her protest with a kiss, but the sheer pleasure of it could not overwhelm the warning her mind cried out. She moaned and pulled her lips away.

"Triston, please, I must know. When you held me yesterday, while

Lucianna bandaged my head—who was I to you?"

He kissed her again. "You were Siriol de Calendri. You will never be anyone else."

Her heart swelled and threatened to burst with joy. She started to slide her arms around his neck, but to her surprise he held her away.

"Sweet Siriol," he whispered, "that is just the problem. You will never be anyone else."

His meaning registered slowly, but when it did, it fell on her like a blow. If he had laid his formidable fist to her cheek, it could not have thundered more deeply through her body or with more finality.

"I have already spoken with Sir Gavin," he continued, meeting her stunned gaze with uncommon firmness. "He's agreed to a betrothal at the end of next week. I hope you and Perrin will both be well enough to travel by then. He's agreed to take my son for training as a page, and I think it best you await the wedding in Sir Gavin's house."

"Triston—"

"Whatever you need, whatever you want in the way of a trousseau, you have only to ask. I may not have your former husband's wealth, but there is nothing you could desire that I would not find a way to give you."

The generosity of this offer fell on bitter ears. "So, you think you can dispose of me, just like that." She snapped her fingers. "And Perrin too. You will send him away from you, still believing that you murdered his mother! Well, that poor little boy may have no choice in the matter, but I, Sir Triston, am not a child, and if you think that I am going to—"

A moan and a breathless voice interrupted her from the bed. "Mamma, Mamma."

Triston's head jerked towards the sound. Every thread of her being vibrated with the pain of his confession, but Perrin's pitiful voice made her push the wave of hurt aside.

"Go to him," she whispered to Triston. "Tell him—"

"I can't."

She touched his arm and felt his muscles drawn tight as steel. "Triston—"

"I can't. Lady Siri, it is you he needs now, to see that you are alive and well—"

She found his hand. "And standing unafraid beside his father. Let us go to him together."

"Nay, not now. Go. Help him, please."

She stood up slowly, for she sensed that Triston was making a mistake. But she went to the bed and sat down, lifting Perrin from the pillows into her arms.

"Hush, Perrin, I am not your mamma. I am Siri. We fell down, remember? And I don't doubt that you are as sore as I, but we are both safe and must thank Heaven for it. Your papa has been watching over you all night and has been very worried, but—"

"Papa is here? He made you fall!"

"No, he did not. I tripped—"

The small arms clutched at her. "He made you, I saw him! Make him go away!"

"Perrin—"

"Make him go away!" He buried his face against her breast and began to cry.

Siri threw a desperate glance at the stool, praying that Triston would understand the boy's trauma and not take his words to heart. But her glance met with empty air.

Triston had already gone.

# Chapter 18

Triston gathered up his pens and inkwell, his drawing board and a fistful of parchment sheets, and left the castle through the postern gate. The woods lay not far from the rear of the castle and the way to the clearing he knew by heart. Clothilde's Bower. His brother had named it when they were children. Memories of their youth swirled around him now as he turned his steps towards that familiar haven. Etienne had frequently resorted there as a boy with Clothilde's young brother to play at being dashing knights battling over the hand of the fair Queen Clothilde, who beamed on them from the tree stump that served as her throne.

Triston had observed their game from the fringes of the trees, for he had considered himself too old to join in such pastimes. Yet again and again he had been drawn to watch, as surely as if some sirenic spell held him in its thrall. As a squire of fourteen, he had not questioned why he found such delight in watching the ten-year-old girl with shimmering gold hair, or wonder why her bubbling laugh should set his heart aflutter.

It had been years and Clothilde grown into a woman, before he had dared to acknowledge the nature of the passion he felt. The childhood bower had by then long stood empty, abandoned by children now grown into adults. Yet it was here that he had found her weeping one mid-winter morn, newly pledged to Merval. Here that Triston had dried her tears of dread and fear and hesitantly confessed his love. And it was here that she had melted into his arms and wept that she loved him too.

That day now seemed a lifetime away, a lifetime of pain and betrayal and grief. Vows forsaken, his beloved despoiled, his child torn from him before he even knew of his existence. Clothilde's frail spirit had been too deeply battered, too cruelly abused to ever be restored to the delicate sweetness he had adored.

He paused to pull aside the shaggy bushes that hid the clearing from undiscerning eyes. Inside still stood the tree stump, covered with a moss as soft as the cast-off, fur-lined cloak his childish love had once used to drape her throne. He crossed to brush the moss with his fingers, letting the poignant memories flow through him again. This stump had served as their altar when they had married here in secret, with only God and his father's corrupt chaplain as witnesses. In this bower, Perrin had been conceived of their love. Here they had parted, and here reunited to find their innocence gone, their love tainted by the calculating manipulation of others.

Her image had never strayed far from his heart and mind, but it was here, in this clearing, that he still saw her most clearly.

As he had so many times before, he seated himself in the grass with his back against the stump and fixed a sheet of parchment to his drawing board. He uncapped the inkwell and dipped in a pen. With a few deft strokes she began to take form. The smooth oval of her face appeared, with just a hint of an ear that vanished beneath a mane of waving hair. A few feathery strokes defined her perfectly arched eyebrows. With the effortless skill of familiarity he traced in her wide, ingenuous eyes, her delicate nose, the two dainty bows that formed her lips, the lower one a bit fuller with the corners turned up . . .

He checked himself. That wasn't right. He had seen Clothilde smiling, of course, but he had never drawn her that way. Only once had he drawn her before her death, on the lonely journey home from Venice, but even then his guide had been his last memory of her, in tears at their farewell. The rest of his portraits had come after her death and had reflected her tormented despair.

He replaced the sheet with another and tried again. But his pen seemed to have a will of its own and when he was done, the enchanting mouth curved more merrily than before. Her eyes were not as wide either, narrowed in laughter, and after the briefest hesitation, he darted in the lines at the corners that defined the crinkles that gathered there whenever amusement rippled from her lips.

Siri. There was no doubt that it was she. Clothilde's eyes had never crinkled so, even when she was happy.

Triston pulled off the picture in anger and dismay. He wanted his wife, not this tormenting impostor. He tried yet a third time to draw her, only dimly aware of the way his jaw locked when he set himself to trace the mouth again. Try as he would, he could not recapture the melancholy droop he thought had been seared like a brand into his memory.

Frustration, tinged with something approaching panic, made him thrust the board aside.

"I have not forgotten you!" he shouted at the trees. "Clo, I have not forgotten!"

A responsive fluttering of leaves brought him to his feet, his heart pounding. Someone watched him from the edge of the clearing. Triston was acquainted with the stories of spirits, the souls of lost loved ones or enemies who returned from their graves to haunt mortals left behind on the earth. Clothilde had died believing herself betrayed, and though guiltless then, evidence that his loyalties now threatened to wander lay sketched in parchment at his feet. If she were watching him now, how would she ever believe that she remained his only love?

He reached the edge of the clearing in two strides and swept back the bushes with a slicing swing of his arm.

The blue eyes that stared back into his were no spirit's.

"Acelet!"

The young man bolted with a look of utter terror into the trees. No more than a moment of stunned inaction passed before Triston went after him. Acelet was faster than he expected. In the end, only a determined lunge by Triston finally tumbled his cousin to the earth.

Triston had to pin him there, arms clamped to his chest, for Acelet fought like a man deranged.

"Stop it!" Triston commanded. "Be still! I am not going to hurt you."

Acelet continued to thrash. Triston finally hefted him up by his arms, pushed him back against a nearby tree and held him there. He had not seen Acelet so white since the night that Clothilde had died.

"I didn't do it," Acelet gasped. "I didn't do it. Let me go."

"What didn't you do?"

"I'm not a murderer! And I'm not a traitor! I'm not! Triston, don't let them—don't let them—"

He broke off with a shudder and a muffled sob. Triston loosened his hold very slightly and viewed his cousin more closely. A soft growth of beard shaded the young man's cheeks, the bristles so pale, like his hair, that Triston had not observed it at first. Acelet still wore the forest green tunic with the de Brielle rose that Triston had made him don for Siri's banquet, but it was torn, stained along with his cream-colored hose, and twigs and grass clung in his long flaxen hair.

"Have you been hiding in the woods all this time?" Triston asked. "Acelet, in heaven's name, why?"

Acelet groaned. "N–Not all the time." His teeth chattered with what could only be fear on so warm a day. "Triston, p–please, d–don't let them find me. I kn–know I have said and done some— some f–foolish things— things you may never forgive me for. B–But I have not done *this.*"

"Acelet—" Triston hesitated at the sight of Acelet's eyes darting wildly left and right. Lord Fauke's guards. He must know they were searching the woods for him. "Come."

Triston held Acelet's arm so that he could not escape and dragged him, sputtering protests, back to the clearing.

"But if they find us here—" Acelet panted.

Triston pushed him down on the tree stump. "If you do not tell me the truth, and I mean every word of it, I may well give you into their hands. Do not try me further, Acelet. Now look at me, nay, straight in the eye, and tell me why you fled the night of the banquet."

Despite Triston's command, Acelet's gaze shifted away. His mouth took on a mulish cast that Triston knew too well.

"I'm not a traitor and I didn't try to kill anyone."

"Then why does Raynor say that you did?"

His eyes flashed up at that. "Raynor—? That's a lie! He never said—"

"Acelet, why do you think those men are looking for you? Because Raynor told Lord Fauke that you attacked him. He swears that I sent you to do it to silence the knowledge he has of some sort of plot you and I are allegedly engaged in to replace Duke Richard with the Young King as our lord. Your indiscreet paeans to the Young King's grace and my brother's presence in his court have made the accusation all too plausible for Lord Fauke. If we don't find a way to prove that Raynor is lying, you and I may both end up swinging from a traitor's rope."

Acelet dropped his head into his hands with a sobbing moan and began rocking as though he were in pain.

Suddenly Triston understood. "That's what you're afraid of, isn't it?"

Acelet sounded like he was strangling. "Not the hanging. But the other—"

There was no need to explain what he meant. Hanging was only the first step in the punishment for treason. Even so self-absorbed a young man as Acelet must have heard what followed next. The drawing and burning of one's bowels while still alive, and the dreadful knowledge of one's subsequent beheading and the dividing of one's body into quarters . . .

Impulsively, Triston bent down and laid a hand on Acelet's shoulder. "You'll not come to that, cousin. No one is going to waste such energy on a worthless puppy like you. Besides, you are not the one they want."

Acelet groaned again and said without lifting his head, "I hide up in the trees when they search for me, and sometimes I can hear them talking. One day Lord Fauke was with them and he was breathing out terrible curses against you. Triston, I admit that I have been angry and—and I wanted to see you hurt, the way you hurt Clothilde—but I never intended to be a party to anything like this!"

"Acelet, I cannot help either of us if you will not tell me what it is you have done." Triston pressed his shoulder harder and felt the young man shrink away from his fingers. "Acelet—"

"I—I helped Raynor fake the attack."

Triston frowned and straightened. "Fake it? How? And why?"

"He said he needed more time to court Siri but that you would not let him near her. But he said if he were injured, then you would have to let him stay at Vere until he recovered and that he might be able to contrive a way to see her while he was there. So he told me to take his jewels so it would look as if he had been robbed and—"

"And then you stabbed him with his own dagger?"

Acelet's head bounced up, his pallor now tinged with a sickish, greenish hue. "No! He wanted me to, but I couldn't do it, so he—he took the dagger and did it himself. Then he told me to take the blade and his jewels and to flee to Belle Noir and wait for him there."

"That is insane!" Triston exclaimed. "No man attacks himself with a knife."

"Raynor did! He said it would only be a flesh wound and that he would not mind the pain if it would save her from you."

"Save who?"

"Her! Siri!" Acelet grabbed up one of Triston's drawings that lay near his feet and waved it frantically at his cousin. He sounded dangerously near to hysteria now. "And I agreed to help him because I would sooner have seen her with him than repeating Clothilde's miserable life with you!" His hand clenched on the drawing, his fist distorting the delicate lines of her face. Tears slid out of his eyes into the pale bristles of his beard. "Why couldn't you just love her the way she deserved to be loved?"

There was no question whom Acelet meant.

"I tried." Triston fought back the wave of helplessness that always seemed to accompany his wife's memory. "Acelet, I tried. But you do not understand how she was."

"She was an angel, the purest vision to ever walk the earth."

"Acelet, she was mad."

The stark words startled Triston as much as they did his cousin. It was a truth he had long known in his mind and heart, but had never had the strength to speak before. But now he knew that for his own sake, for Perrin's—and for Acelet's—it was time he acknowledge the truth aloud.

"You sat with Clothilde when she was quiet and lucid, and knew only her beauty and gentle spirit. But when tormented by her demons, she was shrill and violent, a danger to herself and to any who stood near."

Acelet shot to his feet, the drawing still clenched in his hand. "Nay! How can you revile her like this? She was the kindest, sweetest, gentlest woman ever to draw breath! How dare you call her violent!"

Triston hesitated. Then he slowly unlaced the strings at the neck of his tunic and drew the cloth wide to expose his chest.

"Look." He laid a finger to the deep white scar that marred his flesh bare inches to the right of his heart. "You will recall when you first came to Vere, you were told I lay ill of a fever, that it was why I could not join in the duke's siege of Chateauneuf."

"I remember," Acelet growled. "But I don't see what that—or that—" he pointed at the scar "—has to do with Clothilde."

"'Tis her mark," Triston stated so flatly that Acelet looked taken aback even in his rage. "I suppose she thought she was protecting me. Three years ago when the English Earl of Gunthar was in Poitou, he once spoke a threat against me. Clothilde heard it and in a frenzied passion she seized her brother's dagger and attacked Gunthar. When her sister Heléne tried to distract her, Clothilde turned the blade on her, and when I intervened to save Heléne—this was the result."

"She stabbed you?" Acelet gasped.

Triston gave a grim, curt nod. "Oh, I'll grant she did not know what she was doing. I approached her from behind and she simply whirled and thrust. I'm told as soon as she saw me fall, she collapsed in remorse and tears."

Acelet looked stunned, his eyes riveted to the scar.

Slowly, with fingers that were not entirely steady, Triston laced his tunic back up. "Obviously, I survived her blow, but I had not yet fully recovered when the duke summoned me to Chateauneuf. I sent Etienne to serve in my place, and brought Clothilde to Vere. I told myself that her former outbursts had been an aberration brought on by her mother's abuse. I believed that if I could only keep her quiet and secluded, perhaps—perhaps the madness would fade. But it did not. The spells were infrequent at first, and I was able to shield you and Perrin from the worst of them. But after Raynor came, after he twisted what was left of her mind with his vengeful lies—"

Even through the painful haze of his memories, Triston was aware of the struggling emotions on Acelet's face. The dismay, the doubt, followed by a resurgence of anger.

"Nay, it was because you betrayed her that she ranted so! You shamed her with that harlot in the village!"

Pain flared into a frustration so sharp that Triston's hand closed on the front of Acelet's soiled tunic. "That harlot, as you call her, was naught but a poor serf's daughter who had been ravished by one of Duke Richard's lawless mercenaries. Because I was her lord, she came to me hoping for redress. But the man had taken his pleasure and fled. There was nothing I could do for her but to lend her food and clothing to see her through the winter and the birth of her child."

"Raynor said *you* were the father!"

Triston pushed him back down on the stump. "That was a calculated, bold-faced lie. He knew that Clothilde never left the castle and would have only his word or mine to rely on. Once he planted the seed, there was no stemming the poisonous results. Suspicion bred in her like a canker. When rational, she professed to believe my innocence, but when the madness was upon her—"

"Stop saying that she was mad!" Acelet sprang back to his feet. "*You* are the one who is lying!"

"You can ask anyone in the village. Ask the girl herself. Who would know the truth better than she?" Triston gripped Acelet's shoulders. "You might have learned the truth a long while ago had you not kept your head so smugly in the clouds. Come out of them now. It is time you faced the world as it is, and not as you wished it would be."

Hostility still glittered through the tears in Acelet's eyes. "But the night Clothilde died—I saw you push her."

"No." The anger suddenly flowed out of Triston, replaced by a weariness that nearly overwhelmed him. "You saw me struggling with her and you saw her slip from my grasp. She had taken my dagger and was threatening one moment to kill the 'harlot,' the next to kill herself. I was trying to wrest the dagger away from her and was so worried about the blade that I did not see how near we had come to the head of the stairs. One moment she was in my hands, the next she was—gone."

He spread his fingers as for one wrenching moment he saw her slipping away from them again. He sank down onto the tree stump that Acelet had abandoned and covered his face with his hands.

When Acelet finally spoke again, it was with a familiar complaint.

"You didn't even shed a tear when she died."

Triston groaned. "I have shed a great many tears since then. Not a night has passed that I have not ached to have her in my arms, and the sun has not risen on a day where I have not felt the racking emptiness of her loss."

He could hear his own heart throbbing in the silence that followed these words, a silence broken after several minutes by Acelet's softened voice.

"Until now."

Triston looked up to see Acelet smoothing out the crumpled parchment in his hand.

"You are in love with her, aren't you?" Acelet said. "With Siri."

Triston stared at the drawing. So Acelet saw the changes, too.

He uttered hoarsely, "I don't know. I seem to see her everywhere. But whether it is Clo's face or Siri's—"

Acelet studied the portrait, then said, "Clothilde never looked so happy as this." He knelt to lay the parchment back in the grass. Triston saw the nervous trembling of his mouth. "Did Raynor really say that I attacked him?"

"Aye," Triston said, relieved to let the former subject go. "But I think you already suspected him, didn't you?"

Acelet shrugged, but his voice and demeanor were subdued. "Raynor gave me a secret word to speak to his gatekeeper and told me the man would hide me until he returned to the castle with Siri. But then Lord Fauke came, and I overheard the gatekeeper talking to Raynor's captain of the guard. The captain said that I had tried to kill his master and that I was guilty of treason against the duke, and that when they caught me they would have proof of your guilt as well. I don't think the gatekeeper quite knew what to do, whether Raynor would wish him to continue to conceal me or surrender me to Lord Fauke, but I decided it was better not to stay while he made up his mind. So the first chance I got, I fled into the woods."

He rose and paced across the clearing, his hands fluttering together behind his back. "I told myself over and over that it was some sort of mistake, that Raynor would protect me as he promised to. At first I blamed you, but then I realized that was absurd. Lord Fauke was accusing you, too. And why would anyone else think that I was responsible for the attack? No one even knew that Raynor was at Vere that night, except for you and Siri."

Triston hesitated. "She thought you might have done it because of Clothilde."

Acelet spun about. "Siri thought that I—"

"Nay," Triston said quickly, "it was Raynor who accused you, and she never believed the part about the treason. But she said that Raynor confessed his assault of Clothilde in front of you. She thought it might have enraged you against him."

Acelet colored. "Raynor told me what he was going to say to Siri that night, but he told me it would only be a half-truth. He said that he had been in love with Clothilde, that he was trying to convince her to leave you and go with him to Belle Noir when you came upon them and in a jealous rage, drew your sword and tried to kill him."

Triston felt the grim setting of his jaw. "More lies. If his story were true, why he did not tell the same to Siri?"

"He said that Siri would not believe him if he reviled you, but that she would be impressed by his honesty if he confessed his own transgressions and behaved genuinely repentant for them."

Exasperation nearly caused Triston to clutch his head again. "Blazes, Acelet, what is it going to take to wake you up? Raynor knew if Siri caught him in a lie it would ruin his scheme to seduce her, so he brazenly told her the truth. Raynor has manipulated you every step of the way, and now he has betrayed you for his own selfish, vengeful ends."

Triston saw the struggle in his cousin's face.

"Come back with me to Vere," Triston said. "Ask Siri whose side Raynor has landed on. She will tell you that he has forsworn his allegiance to the Young King."

"Forsworn?" Acelet eyes widened. "Nay, whatever Raynor has done, he has not done that."

Triston stood up. He bit off the impatient rebuke on his tongue and repeated, "Come back with me. I own, Siri's head these days is none too clear where Raynor is concerned, but her honesty is intact and she will frankly acknowledge the words he has spoken. Ask her, if you will not believe me."

Acelet cast a sharp glance at the bushes. "How do I know this is not a trap—that Lord Fauke will not be waiting at Vere to arrest me?"

"You have my word." Triston laid his hands on Acelet's shoulders again. "Acelet, you are my own blood. 'Twould be a stain on my honor were I to let my kin come to harm."

He held his breath for Acelet's reply. Acelet had distrusted him for so long. What if he were not able to make the leap across his former delusions?

"I will listen to what Siri has to say," Acelet said at last, "but you must bring her here."

"Acelet—"

"No, returning to Vere is too dangerous."

"I don't mean to trumpet your presence there. We can enter by the postern gate and I can smuggle you into the keep."

Acelet shook his head and backed away. "No. I don't know what to believe. Raynor promised that he would find me a place in the Young King's court. He cannot do that if he has forsworn his allegiance, as you say, but I don't know that he has. Perhaps someone saw me running away that night we faked the attack. Perhaps you saw me—"

"And then accused myself of treason? Even you have more sense than that."

But Acelet's stubbornness reasserted itself in dismaying force. "Just bring Siri here. If she says that Raynor accused me, then I will believe her—and perhaps I will believe the rest as well."

"Acelet—"

"Tomorrow, at noon. I will be here in the clearing if I can reach it safe of Lord Fauke's guards. Now I am going—unless you mean to try to stop me?"

Triston saw the challenging lift of Acelet's chin. "If you are determined to spend another night tossing about on the ground rather than slumbering in your own bed, so be it. I will bring Siri here tomorrow. And I hope you do not fall into some snare before then."

Acelet's chin came down. Triston caught the flicker of renewed alarm in his eyes before he turned and ran out of the clearing.

⌘

"What do you mean, she is gone?"

Triston's words thundered in the empty hall. He had ejected Siri's suitors following her fall down the stairs, while Sir Gavin had returned to his castle to prepare for his bride.

Sir Balduin stood before Triston, obviously distressed. "Sir, I am not yet sure how it happened. Apparently she charmed a handful of your guards into saddling a horse for her and accompanying her and the Lady Lucianna to Belle Noir."

"Belle Noir? Siri has gone to Belle Noir?"

Sir Balduin limped a hasty step backwards, as though to escape the flash in his master's eye. "That is where one of the grooms heard they were headed. She gave him this. He brought it to me, but not until after they were gone. It is addressed to you."

Triston took the folded parchment sheet that Sir Balduin held out to him and stared down at the elegant rendition of his name. Then he flipped the parchment open and read the flowing script within.

> *Triston—I gave you my word that I would marry,*
> *and you vowed to me that the choice should be*
> *mine. I have chosen Raynor and I go to him to*
> *fulfill the promises I have made to you both. I plead*

225

*him forgiveness, for my sake, for the pain he has
caused you, and trust that you will not seek to
injure the man whose life now becomes my own.*

*May God grant you the peace for which your soul has
yearned. Remember me please as your sweet Siriol—*

There followed a wobbly dash, as though she may have intended
to end her message thus. But then she had added, in letters apparently
composed more in haste than with her usual elegant script—*"and know
that this shall always be yours."*

She had signed her name inside a painted heart.

"Sir, what do you wish me to do?"

Triston heard Sir Balduin's question, but he did not immediately
respond. He placed a finger over the "ol" in her name and gazed a long
moment at the familiar diminutive. Then his gaze flicked up to *Raynor*
and the whole letter blurred in a reddish mist.

"We are going to fetch her back," he snapped. "And if she thinks that
out of consideration for her I will not have Raynor's head on a charger—"
He pulled his finger away. "Assemble the garrison and tell them to arm
themselves. That wench is yet mine, and she is going to learn that if I
have to storm Belle Noir to teach her."

# Chapter 19

Siri braced herself for the encounter with Lord Fauke. She had known that there would be no way to avoid him at Belle Noir, but she trusted once he learned that she was pledged to marry Raynor, he would desist in his dishonorable advances. He strode out to meet her the moment she rode into the bailey. She allowed him to lift her off her horse only because she was too dizzy to stop him.

"My lady, I am glad to see you safe and sound. Sir Raynor told me of the spill you took."

"I'm afraid I am still a bit unsteady," she said.

She tried to draw away when his hands slid from her waist to her hips, but the journey, though short, had left her weaker than she expected. As always, his gaze fixed greedily on her face. She had rebelliously discarded the bandage about her head before she left Vere. Now she raised her bandaged left hand to push back the long strand of hair she had draped over the cut in her forehead. Her fingers told her that the flesh around it was still swollen and she imagined an ugly bruise must surround it as well.

Lord Fauke looked aghast at the marring of her beauty. He released her so abruptly that she swayed back against her horse.

"Regrettable, is it not?" she said at his dismay. "Lucianna fears it may scar."

"That would be most regrettable indeed." His gaze shifted away from the mark.

"Signore, if you please!"

Lucianna's imperative address might have set up Lord Fauke's hackles ordinarily, but he now seemed relieved to turn from Siri and lift her companion to the ground.

*"Grazie."* Lucianna shook out her skirts. "And now if you will escort Donna Siri and me inside? This ride has been madness for her. She should not even be standing yet, much less jostling about on the back of some beast. We must get her to a bed."

"Lucianna, I'm fine," Siri said, though in truth, her head had begun to ache again. "Raynor does not even know that I am here, much less that I plan to stay. Perhaps there is no room—"

A deep, roguish voice broke across her doubt. "Carissima, there is always room for you."

Raynor limped towards her across the bailey, aided by a single crutch. His speed surprised her, given that it had been his unsteadiness only the day before which had resulted in her fall.

"I saw your party approaching from the ramparts," he said, "and I have sent orders that chambers be prepared. Carissima, dare I flatter myself that you have come on my account?" He took her bandaged hand gently in his, then muttered a curse when he saw the cut on her brow.

"Does it spoil me for you as well?" she asked softly.

"Nay." He kissed her fingers above the linen. "My clumsiness might have cost you far more. I am quite sure Triston thought we had broken your neck."

She felt a stab in her breast at Triston's name. She was glad that she had not been conscious to see his initial reaction to her fall. It had been enough to see his drawn pallor this morning and to hear the anguish of memory in his voice.

"I must speak with you," she told Raynor, "alone. Is there somewhere we can go?"

"Of course. But do you not wish to rest first? You look weary."

"I will be fine, if only I can sit down. And I do not wish to put this off. Lucianna, pay these good men for their escort and send them back to Vere. Sir Raynor and I will not be long."

As they mounted the stairs inside the keep, she could not resist commenting on Raynor's remarkable recovery from the disabling wound in his leg. It seemed to her that his limp became more pronounced as she spoke and that he shifted more heavily onto his crutch.

"The pain comes and goes," he said. "It has been better today."

"When Lucianna told me that Triston had thrown you out of Vere—"

"He allowed me to leave in one piece, but only, I think, because he was so distracted with you. I thought it was better to escape with my skin than my pride. Sir Balduin kindly arranged for a cart to carry me off before his master could come seeking my blood. Triston blamed me, you know. He thinks I fell into him deliberately."

She sighed. "I cannot make him see reason where you are concerned. But I hope that when we are—"

She broke off as he threw open a door near the head of the steps and drew her across the threshold. At first she thought he had brought her to the chamber he had spoken of in the bailey. Then she saw the weapons hanging on the wall, the mail shirt slung across a chair and the emblem on the bed curtains that matched the shield on the wall over the bed.

Raynor flashed her a scampish grin. "You said you wished to go somewhere private."

"But this is your chamber."

"Aye, and I can assure you we will not be disturbed."

He tossed his crutch aside and before she could anticipate his intent, he swung her onto the bed and followed her down.

"I am much better today, you see," he murmured. He locked his fingers with hers and lowered his head to kiss her.

She twisted her head aside so that his lips met only her cheek. Her heart pounded, echoing the growing pain in her head. "Raynor, if you wish to ravish me, I am too weak to stop you. But I pray you will not begin our life together this way."

His mouth nuzzled her ear. "You were willing enough at Vere."

"I was not. You know that I begged you to stop. And if you had only listened to me, Triston would not have found us the way he did and he would not have dragged me from the room and you would not have come after us, and I would not now have such a headache that I can't even see straight."

He raised his head. "Ah, now you are blaming me too?"

"No, of course I am not. Only . . . only . . . Raynor, please." His renewed kisses, scattering down her throat, left her chest so tight that she could scarcely breathe.

He stopped, but his voice was impatient. "I do not understand your reluctance, my lady. Have you changed your mind about our wedding?"

"No. I have told Triston that I am going to marry you. But—"

Raynor sat up. "Then what is the problem? Why do you tremble so when I touch you? It is as if you find my caresses—distasteful."

"It is only my head," she said, as desperate to believe that herself as she was for him to do so. "Raynor, please do not be angry. I want to marry you. That is why I have come to Belle Noir."

"And how does Triston feel about our union?"

"I don't know—and I don't care." She sat up too, blaming her tears, like her trembling, on the pain in her head.

Raynor eyes narrowed. "You have quarreled."

She wiped her cheeks with a fiercely determined hand. "Oh, no, we do not quarrel. He simply reminds me again and again that I am not his beloved wife and there the matter ends. Well, I cannot endure it anymore. I want a man who sees me for me. Raynor, you knew her too. Can *you* see beyond her face into mine?"

She held her breath while his gaze roamed over her countenance. She had left her hair to flow loose because it hurt too much to pin it up. He lifted a strand of the gold and slid it between his fingers.

"We shall make Triston regret his folly, my lady. Whoever he saw in you, he should have kept you cherished to his bosom. Now he has lost you again—forever." He kissed her, so quickly that she had not time to shrink.

"Raynor—"

"There, I only mean that you will be my wife, not his." He stood up and pulled her to her feet. "I will show you to your chamber and you can rest. We will talk of this further when you are feeling better."

He led her to the door, but her dizziness returned in such a wave that she only dimly noticed that he now moved without any crutch at all. She stopped on the threshold and leaned into the doorjamb for support.

"I am afraid," she said, "if we do not marry quickly, Triston may try to stop us."

"Indeed," Raynor agreed. "At the moment, you are still his ward and without his consent, even a swift marriage might be undone at his word. Unless we convince him that a ceremony is necessary for your honor—"

She turned her head away when he bent towards her.

He gave a heavy sigh. "Very well, my little nun. We shall wait for the wedding night, provided I do not have wait too long. To have you beneath my roof and not taste of your delights may be a greater temptation than I can resist. But I have already begun to explore another way to win you, one which, if it proves fruitful, even Triston will not be able to thwart."

"What is it?" she asked, surprised.

"Ah, I will not raise your hopes until I am sure. It should be but a matter of days." He lifted her chin. "Just one more, to last me until then."

Siri let him kiss her. Her fingers curled into the wood of the doorjamb behind her, but the blunt hunger that had crept into his kisses at Vere and that she feared he had been about to repeat here on his bed, was thankfully absent. And if she could summon no response to his coaxing passion, at least, this time, she suffered no shivering dread.

"Eudes!" Raynor called.

A servant appeared.

"Show the Lady Siriol to her room and see that whatever she requires for her comfort is provided her. Until later, carissima."

He kissed her hand and Siri went away with the servant.

⁓

The servant escorted her up another flight of stairs and down a long passageway to a small, square bedchamber. He retreated with a bow and

231

a glance at the woman who paced the floor inside like a caged lioness.

"I told you we should not have come here!" Lucianna exclaimed, pausing only long enough to grant Siri a glimpse of the indignant fire in her eyes. "What do you think? That servant tried to put us in separate chambers, so that wicked *Don* Fauke might more easily seduce you. But I sat right down on that bed and refused to budge. No doubt the servant has gone to complain of me, but I will not leave you, not even were you to command me!"

"I shan't do so." Siri sank down on the bed Lucianna had gestured at so grandly. "Of course I want you with me, and I do not trust Lord Fauke anymore than you do."

She closed her eyes against the throbbing in her head. She tried to think of Raynor, but it was Triston she saw, his stormy face framed by its wild curls, taunting her against the shades of her lids. Tears welled up hot in her throat, but she choked them back down. *I'll weep no more for you, Triston de Brielle,* she vowed. But she had to curl her fist tight against her heart to keep it from bursting.

She felt Lucianna's hand brush the hair back from her temples. "Bambina, you are ill. Will you not let me attend to your cut?"

"Yes, please," Siri whispered. "And you may wrap my head up again, if you like, and I would like one of your draughts to make me sleep."

To sleep, to rest in oblivion, free of this persistent hurt in her breast . . .

Lucianna fetched the salve from one of the few bags they had brought with them. Siri sat tight-lipped while Lucianna worked the ointment into her cut, determined not to flinch and not to indulge herself with the memory of Triston's strong, comforting arms.

Lucianna muttered as she worked, "You know I do not approve of your choice of Signor Raynor, carissima. The man has great charm, si, but a very wild reputation. Some of the servants at Vere held him in great suspicion." She stopped and sighed. "I suppose we shall never see any of them again. I could not go back without you."

"Go back?" Siri said. "To Vere? I thought you would be glad to leave there."

Lucianna sounded cross. "Si, of course I am relieved to have you free of Signor Triston, but . . . Well, never mind." She paused, then said abruptly, "You will have no more need of me once you are wed. After the wedding, I will return to Venice."

Siri opened her eyes to stare at her companion. "Venice? Lucianna, you cannot leave me."

Lucianna was busy wrapping a new bandage around Siri's head and would not meet her mistress's startled gaze. "It will be for the best. Signor Raynor will not want an interfering old woman in his house."

"You are not old! And you did not interfere when you came with me to Alessandro's."

"Ah, you were only a girl then, and I liked *Don* Alessandro. But this Raynor of yours . . ." She bent and laid a hand to Siri's dagger. "He has not married you yet, and you must keep this near until he does. He would not be the first man to try to seduce a woman with promises he had no intention of keeping."

Raynor's restraint in his chamber had been evidence enough for Siri that his intentions were honorable. Still, the thought of Lucianna leaving her to return to Venice disturbed Siri more than it should have, more than she knew it would have had Lucianna been leaving her in Triston's care.

"Lucianna, I do not want you to go."

Lucianna had finished tying off the bandage and was on her way to the door. "Carissima, I do not trust these servants. I must go to the kitchen myself to prepare your draught."

"No, I mean to Venice! Lucianna—"

"Hush, bambina, we shall talk of that later. Now bolt the door after me and do not open it again until you hear me call your name."

Siri knew it was absurd. She would not have come to Belle Noir had she not believed that she would be safe here. Still, as soon as Lucianna left, she rose from the bed and slid the bolt into place.

⚜

Lucianna's draught proved powerful. Siri slept through what remained of that day and into the following morning. Her rest was dreamless until the early hours of dawn, when she slipped into fretful visions. At first they were of Triston, imparting emotions so elusive that she could not afterwards recall whether within them he had gazed on her with tenderness, betrayal, or the familiar anguish of rejection. Then the face quivered and altered, still Triston's, yet grown younger, the eyes lighter, filled not only with loss but with terror.

She pushed herself up with a gasp.

"Perrin," she whispered. "I did not even say good-bye."

She had held the frightened boy after Triston had left them in Perrin's chambers, but Perrin had been too distraught and too disoriented by his own injuries to believe her soothing words about his father. Again and again he had called her Mamma and wailed that his papa had pushed her. Siri, in dismay at his growing hysteria, finally summoned a servant to bring him a draught less powerful than Lucianna's, but no less effective. She continued to hold him until he fell asleep. Then she had slipped from the chamber, her resolve to leave Vere Castle already formed.

Triston's words to her in Perrin's chamber had snuffed out the last of her hopes. Nothing she had done, nothing she could ever do would succeed in winning away his love from his lost Clothilde. So be it. But she would not be dismissed like a piece of chattel, given in marriage to Sir Gavin, merely because Triston wished to be rid of the painful memories she stirred. She was in pain now too, but she would seek its healing in her own way.

It had pricked her conscience sorely to desert Perrin while he was still so confused, but she had known her only chance to escape would be while Triston was absent from the castle. Stubbornly, she had told herself that it was for the best. Triston would now be forced to confront his son himself, and in so doing, surely he would find a way to help the boy to understand the truth and regain his faith in his father.

But all Siri saw now in the early morning air was a child she loved, abandoned and afraid—and she had not even said good-bye.

A wave of stifling guilt urged her to go back, to try to explain and reassure him. But Triston would never let her return to Belle Noir if she did, and she was determined to marry Raynor.

"Lucianna, what should I do?"

She reached over to shake her companion awake, and found the bed beside her empty.

"Lucianna?"

Siri's gaze swept the room, but even in the dim morning light she could see that no one was there. She slid from the bed and dressed quickly in a fresh tunic, then ran to the door. It was unbolted and unlocked. She opened it and peered into the passageway. Had Lucianna been lured away? Was this some trick of Lord Fauke's to get Siri alone and indulge his wicked lust at last?

If so, she was not going to sit here waiting for him to come for her. She went back to the bed and pulled out her dagger from beneath her pillow, where Lucianna had made her lay it for the night. Siri strapped it around her waist, then slid on a pair of silken slippers and left the room.

She started down the passageway, but after several minutes, she stopped. She did not know which way to go. What if a turn brought her into the presence of the very man she wanted to avoid?

"My lady, may I help you?"

She whirled, her hand on the hilt of her dagger. A young man had appeared from a doorway a few feet away. Of slender build, he had a smooth, honest face and wore the sober robes of a clerk.

"Sir," she said, eyeing him cautiously, "I am—"

"Lady Siriol de Calendri." His gaze slid over her in awe. "Forgive me for staring. I had heard you were beautiful, but— I am Geoffroi Demari, my lady, Lord Fauke's clerk."

Siri's gaze darted suspiciously up and down the passageway, then narrowed at the room behind him.

Geoffroi smiled. "There is no need to fear, my lady. Lord Fauke poses no threat to you at the moment. He is not at Belle Noir."

"But I saw him yesterday."

"He departed shortly after you arrived, but he has left you a commission to fulfill in his absence. If you would please step this way?"

He gestured at the open doorway. Siri hesitated, but curiosity and his reassuring smile prompted her to obey him, albeit without withdrawing her hand from her dagger.

But no trap awaited her within the room. Both of the windows were shuttered, but there were enough lighted candles on the several tables to make the chamber as bright as noonday. She approached one of the smaller tables first; it was scattered with a half-dozen parchment sheets. Nay, not parchment. She reached out a delighted hand to touch the silky smooth surface of one of the sheets. Vellum, and of exquisite quality, white as ivory and almost as thin as tissue.

Geoffroi waved his hand in the air above the sheets. "These will suffice to complete my assignment. Another day, two at the most, and I will be done. The next step, my lady, falls to you."

He gestured towards a larger table in the center of the room. There dozens of similar sheets were spread, but each of these bore an elegantly written script, the letters printed out in beautifully rendered calligraphy.

*"Blessed are the undefiled in the way, who walk in the law of the Lord."*

Siri read the words inscribed on the nearest sheet out loud. They were the first of many verses known as the Gradual Psalms, recited by Jewish pilgrims as they journeyed to Jerusalem. She had watched her father and brother illuminate so many psalteries containing these verses that she had learned most of them by heart.

But the manuscript was not complete. The first letter of "Blessed" was but lightly traced in, designed to be painted over with an illuminated initial. Space had been left indicating that a large and impressive one was desired, and many more blanks had been reserved for miniatures.

"Lord Fauke spoke to me of his psaltery," she said, "and professed an interest in having me illuminate it for him. But I never agreed to do so."

"Indeed?" Geoffroi looked surprised. "He gave me to understand that you had. He said that you were to begin at once, as soon as you were rested that is, and that I was to provide you with whatever you needed to complete the task."

Despite her quarrel with the baron, the commission tempted her. It had been too long since she had employed her skills in anything but aimless sketching or tutoring Perrin's childish hand. The challenge of setting miniatures to actual words again, to integrating picture with text, was a prospect that sent through her a thrill of excitement. But . . .

"My brushes and paints are all at Vere. Someone will have to be sent to retrieve them."

Geoffroi hesitated. "Aye. Well, there may be some difficulty in that."

She glanced up from the psalm she had been studying, her mind already engaged in trying to decide whether the initial letter should be done in simple ornamentation or whether she should place some human or animal figures within the loops of the "B." She raised her brows at Geoffroi's remark and waited for an explanation.

Geoffroi gave her one of his pleasant smiles. "Sir Raynor said you were not to be troubled with the matter just yet. I brought a few paints of my own to Belle Noir—a red, a blue, and a yellow. Alas, no silver or gold. But they might suffice you for a beginning. And I presume you will first wish to draw your figures out? I have a variety of pens you might use, and plenty of black and brown ink."

She followed his gesture to yet a third table where all the tools he had mentioned and more were set out. Perhaps Raynor felt that Triston, in anger at her flight, would refuse to send her belongings to Belle Noir. She would sooner forfeit them all, including her paints and brushes, than risk the sort of confrontation that was sure to ensue were she to send Raynor to demand them.

Besides, Geoffroi was right about the work. There were weeks' worth of drawings to be done, judging from the number of manuscript pages already completed, before she would ever need her brushes.

"I wish I had my pattern book," she said. "But I trust my memory is sufficient to make a good beginning. Let me wash my face and comb my hair. I don't suppose I could arrange for a bath? The ride from Vere has left me feeling positively filthy."

"You don't look it," Geoffroi murmured with another smile, this one gone touchingly shy. "But I will see what I can do, my lady."

Clean and refreshed, her hair washed and shining and curling over the cut in her forehead—for her head felt so much better that she had cast off her bandage again—Siri set to work on Lord Fauke's psaltery. Lucianna still had not appeared when Siri left their chamber for the second time. The servants who brought up her bath said only that Lucianna was engaged with events "up above" and that she wanted Lady Siri to await her here.

But with Lord Fauke gone, Siri had no hesitation in awaiting her return with Geoffroi instead. His ready blushes and self-conscious smiles told her that he was as harmless as he was smitten.

She spared him only an occasional kind glance and otherwise plunged excitedly into her work, grateful that the cut in her palm lay in her left hand and not her right. She decided to open the psaltery with an image of David, clothed in his shepherd's robes, seated in the grass amidst his flocks. She would draw him playing his harp as he sang the words that followed: *"Blessed are the undefiled . . ."*

She picked up a silver-tipped pen and began to sketch in the young shepherd-king's form, then paused and tapped the pen against her lips. How did Triston manage to capture the planes of the human face? What sort of shadings did he use to achieve those high cheekbones, the soft, swirling hair, the large, tragic eyes . . . ?

She caught her breath so sharply that Geoffroi glanced up from his work.

"My lady?"

She shook her head, trying to drive away the image of Triston's drawings of Clothilde. "It is nothing. I think I will start with the sheep."

That proved a much safer task. The occupation did not entirely distract her from the nagging ache in her breast, but it allowed it to dull a little as she focused her mind on the project at hand. She sketched out a half-dozen sheep, darted in some blades of grass for them to graze on, lightly drew in the lines of a hillside with an opening that she meant to paint as the mouth of a cave. By the time she returned to the figure of David, her confidence in her own skill had reasserted itself and she sternly banished all thoughts of Triston and his art from her mind.

With the windows closed and in the unchanging light of the candles, she had no sense of the passage of time. Nor did she hear the opening door, so deeply immersed was she in her work.

"Take care, Geoffroi. If my lord catches you gaping at his wench like that, he will put out your eyes."

Siri swiveled about on her chair. The Lady Osanne stood just inside the threshold. She had left Vere Castle with Lord Fauke, and in her absence, Siri had allowed herself to forget about Lucianna's suspicions of an illicit love affair between Triston and his sultry stepmother. But those charges reared starkly back up as Osanne spared Siri a look of contempt before gliding over to Geoffroi.

"How much longer do you mean to keep me waiting?" she purred at the clerk. "You could not ask for a better opportunity. With Lord Fauke gone—"

The young man looked incensed. "My lady, you offend my office. Even were I not indebted to Lord Fauke for my position, I should not abandon my vows for you."

Osanne laughed her sultry laugh. "Virtuous men have always excited me. Their passion, once loosed, burns with such intensity that one fears being devoured by it." Her crimson lips pursed and she blew a breath at Geoffroi. "Perhaps it is because they have so much lost time to make up for."

She laughed again as Geoffroi flushed, then she stepped away to confront Siri. Her smile became a sneer. "Triston has much to make up for too. They say he has lived like a monk since his wife died. No doubt that is why he burns so hot for you."

Siri tried hard not to let her dislike of this woman show. "Triston does not burn for me. And I have come to Belle Noir to marry Raynor."

"You play the innocent well, my lady, but it is not merely Raynor you are after. You must have them all—Fauke, Raynor, even Geoffroi. And don't tell me you did not know that Triston would come storming after you. It is what you wanted, to see them at one another's throats, like dogs quarreling over a bone."

"Triston—?" Siri stared at her. "Triston is here?"

"Not here. There." Osanne waved a hand. "Outside the walls. He has not enough men to scale them, but he has enough to lay siege and is threatening to do so if Raynor does not give you up. Raynor has been defying him from the battlements all morning. He says Fauke will bring troops from the duke to relieve us before our food or water supply runs out. But if Triston obtains more men from his father-in-law and Sir Gavin, as he is threatening—"

Siri swung about on Geoffroi. "You knew! That is why you would not send for my paints. You knew Sir Triston was out there and you did not tell me!"

Geoffroi looked chagrined. "Sir Raynor commanded me to say nothing to you. He said he would deal with the matter—"

"Take me to him," Siri demanded.

Geoffroi hesitated, but Osanne said, "Allow me," and made an exaggerated bow towards the door.

Dozens of armed men paced the wall-walk. Seeing Siri emerge from the corner tower that provided access to the battlements, a soldier moved quickly to claim his master's attention. Raynor had been leaning through one of the gaps between two soaring, square-toothed merlons on the crenellated curtain wall, but he drew back at the soldier's muttered word and turned with a frown.

"Carissima." He placed himself firmly before the opening as Siri approached him. "There is no need for you to be here. I do not know what you have heard, but—"

"I heard that Triston is laying siege to these walls, and that it is all because of me! Raynor, I will not be the cause of further quarrels between you. Let me speak with Triston."

"I think that would not be wise. Bernard, escort the Lady Siri—"

"No." She evaded Raynor's soldier. "Not until I— Lucianna!"

She saw her companion farther along the walk and ran to her side.

"Donna Siri." Lucianna turned and took her hands. "Signor Raynor would not let me send for you, but I am glad you have come. It is time you see for yourself the depths of that diavolo's madness. Look."

Siri was so small that she had to stand on her toes to see where Lucianna pointed through the gap between the merlons. Thirty feet below, Triston had assembled his men, not an overwhelming force, but an effective one, sufficient to surround the walls and prevent all comings and going through the gates. Colorful tunics fluttered over mail armor that glittered in the late morning sun, but only a few men had donned their helmets. Most remained bareheaded like their leader. Triston rode at the forefront, astride a large, stamping stallion with a coat as black as its master's errant curls. At his side rode the grey-haired Sir Balduin. The faithful retainer looked up at the walls, but not towards the opening in which Raynor had formerly stood.

For a moment Siri thought he was staring at her. Then she realized her mistake. She turned in surprise towards Lucianna. Lucianna pressed a hand to her lips and drew back from the gap.

"Carissima," she whispered, "Signor Triston is threatening to assemble more men, to build war machines, to storm the walls and burn the keep. If there is fighting, some on both sides will surely die."

"Lucianna." Siri put her arm around the older woman's waist. "Why did you not tell me you were in love with Sir Balduin? I would never have made you come with me to Belle Noir."

Tears splashed down Lucianna's haughty cheeks, confirming Siri's amazement, but even now Lucianna would not speak her own heart. "You could not have stopped me from coming. My duty is to you, bambina, as it has been since your sweet, sainted mother gave you into my charge. If I could only see you happy and safe—"

Triston's sharp voice cut off the rest. "Where have you gone, de Molinet? If you think I have done with you . . ."

His familiar accents made Siri shiver with pleasure, but the brittle edge to his words colored her reaction with dread. She looked anxiously about and saw that Raynor had indeed drawn back from his gap in the wall. He appeared to be engaged in a heated exchange with Osanne. The raven-haired beauty looked smug, but Raynor looked furious, and a sharp gesture sent her off with a toss of her head back to the tower stairs. Raynor watched her go with a scowl, then turned and joined Siri and Lucianna with scarcely a hint of a limp at all.

"I wish you had heeded Lord Fauke's clerk and stayed below," he said, his voice low. "Carissima."

He plunged a hand into her streaming hair and jerked her mouth up to his. His kiss fell so quick that it smothered her gasp. Hard and hungry, he ravished her lips, then released her so abruptly that she fell into Lucianna's arms.

"A man could lose his way with you," he murmured, then turned to the opening she and Lucianna had abandoned. "The wench is here with me, Triston. She has come of her own accord. Withdraw now and she shall come to no harm."

"And I am to take your treacherous word for that?" Triston jeered. "You swore you'd repented once before, just before you assaulted my wife."

Raynor's face darkened like a thunderclap. "When the woman is yours," he shouted, "it is assault. But when she is mine, it is a private affair with which I am not to concern myself. So Isobel told me again and again. You had my sister so enamored of you that she would not listen to my warnings. I knew you would betray her, but until I saw her dead on the riverbank, I had not fathomed how base your heart truly was."

Her view blocked by the merlon, Siri could not see Triston's face, but his response sounded abrupt and impatient. "I have not come to thrash out the past with you, Raynor. I want only the return of what is mine. If you do not surrender my ward, I will knock down these walls and have you dragged to account before Duke Richard's court."

"Nay," Raynor swore, "but you shall pay for your crime first. You murdered her, Triston! Murdered my sister to conceal the shame of your own child! 'An accident,' you said, and even my brother believed your lies. But I knew the truth, then and now. I tried to seduce your wife, aye, and when I heard that she had died, I wept only that mine had not been the hands that pushed her. But now, Triston—now—"

Raynor moved so quickly that Siri had not time to register his intent.

One moment his hands were on her waist, the next he swung her up into the gap between the merlons. He held her firmly in the center of the empty space, with naught but his hands on her ankles to help her maintain her balance.

"If you want her, Triston, I will give her to you—with all the mercy you showed my sister."

# Chapter 20

Raynor, what are you doing?" Siri gasped.

Air rushed against her cheeks, and with a sickening lurch in her stomach, she felt herself swaying forward.

Raynor's hands jerked her upright again, but he shouted, "Well, Triston, do you want her?"

"So help me, Raynor, if you let her fall—"

Siri heard the hoarseness in Triston's shout. Below the walls yawned a deep, rugged ditch with a rubble of stones at the bottom. She knew that was where she would land if she fell, her body shattering against those stones. Triston knew it too, and he pushed his horse to the edge of the ditch.

"Back off, de Brielle. If you want this wench to live, then back off from my walls."

Triston withdrew a few paces, but held up a hand to stay any retreat by his men. His voice came grim with resolve. "Very well, de Molinet. What must I do to win her back safe and sound?"

"You do not understand yet, do you?" Raynor snarled. "You shall never have her back, not alive. You may thank the heavens that she has aroused my passions, or she would already be dead in that ditch. Now choose you, Triston. You may take her broken and cold if you will—or surrender her to me here and now for my wife."

Siri swayed again. Again Raynor righted her. Her heart had not left her throat since he had placed her on this precarious perch. After an initial squawk of horror, Lucianna had gone mysteriously quiet, but Siri remained too terrified to tear her gaze from the scene below.

Sir Balduin again ranged his horse alongside Triston's. He drew his master's attention with a hastily whispered word. Triston bent his head to reply and a furtive conversation ensued. It continued too long for Raynor's liking. With a muttered curse, he grabbed the skirt of Siri's gown and jerked her onto her knees. He wrapped his hand in her hair and pulled her head back until his mouth was against her ear.

"Tell him I mean it," he growled. "Tell him to consent to our marriage."

"If you think," Siri gasped, "that I am going to marry you now—"

He shook her, then snapped his hand free and pushed again towards the edge of the wall. She cried out and clutched at the stone rim.

"Tell him, or pray that you can fly."

With her eyes riveted on the ditch below, she did not have the courage to defy him. "Triston," she called, "Triston, please, you must go back to Vere."

"And give his consent," Raynor hissed.

"And—And you must let me marry Raynor! Please—"

Triston hesitated, and Raynor shouted, "Do it, Triston! Here, with all my men as witnesses, state that you freely surrender the Lady Siriol to be my wife."

Triston's voice rang out sarcastically, "And I suppose you will want the jewels of her dowry as well?"

"I could not accept a portionless bride. See that her trinkets are delivered to me. I guarantee your servants will not be challenged by our roadside bandits."

Again a whispered word from Sir Balduin and a curt nod of Triston's head.

"Very well, Raynor," Triston said, "you give me no choice. But my consent comes with a price."

"You are in no position to quibble with me, Triston."

"If you were so eager to see her dead, you'd have done the deed by now. I will concede to the marriage and surrender her dowry—but you must lend her back to me for a day."

"Lend her back?" Raynor gave an incredulous laugh, but he ceased abruptly at Triston's next words.

"Aye. I need her to coax Acelet out of the woods."

Raynor's hold on Siri so slackened that she was able to shift herself over to the merlon. He allowed her to lean against it, but when she sought to slide back to the wall-walk, he pushed her roughly back up.

"You know where Acelet is?" he demanded of Triston.

"I have seen him once. But he thinks I am in league with Lord Fauke and he fled from me. He will not trust me, but I believe the Lady Siriol could persuade him to surrender himself peacefully. Whatever crimes he has committed against you and the duke, I want him alive to stand his trial, not cut down by one of Lord Fauke's overzealous guards."

Braced by the stone merlon, a measure of security crept back into Siri's body. She turned her head to see Raynor's reaction.

His amber eyes narrowed. "What guarantee have I that if I agree, you will return the Lady Siriol to me once Acelet is in your possession?"

"You have my word."

Raynor gave a thin smile. "With Triston de Brielle, one need not ask for more. Still—I prefer to hear you swear it."

Siri saw the glance that passed between Triston and Sir Balduin. Raynor clearly saw it too.

"Swear it, Triston. 'I do freely surrender the Lady Siriol de Calendri to be the wife of Raynor de Molinet. And I will commit the jewels of her dowry to the knights of Raynor's household within twelve hours of the marriage.'"

Triston's gaze swept upwards to Siri. He was too far below to read his expression, but she could see his pallor and knew that he was trying to weigh her degree of danger. Raynor's hand closed on the back of her neck and thrust her head back over the edge of the wall.

Triston's voice rang out tense and angry. "I do freely surrender the Lady Siriol de Calendri to be the wife of Raynor de Molinet. And I will commit the jewels of her dowry to the knights of Raynor's household within twelve hours of the marriage. This I swear. Now, Raynor—"

"'And,' Raynor added, "'the Lady Siriol, being permitted to return to Vere to collect her belongings, shall return to Belle Noir twenty-four hours after departing therefrom.'"

Triston repeated the words impatiently.

"Swear it," Raynor demanded.

"I swear it."

"Nay, Triston, you must make it such an oath as I can trust you will not break. Swear it—on your mother's soul."

Triston's horse pranced backwards, reacting to its master's startled hand. "Raynor, I have given you my word."

"It is not enough. Not where the Lady Siriol is concerned. You will call it coercion and say you were justified in breaking it. But if you do, may your mother's soul never come to paradise, may she eternally suffer the torments of her sins in the purgatory of the accursed, and may your prayers and those of your brother never bring her mercy from the flames. Swear it Triston, or so help me I will forget love and greed alike and take my vengeance now."

He shoved her so that the upper half of her body went over the edge. She screamed and her hands flailed in the empty air. Raynor held her by naught but the skirts of her gown. If the fabric tore, if his grasp should slip . . . The scene below whirled into a dizzying darkness and a roar in her ears warned her that she was on the verge of fainting.

"Triston," Raynor shouted, "I will do it."

Triston's answer rang like a hollow echo. "No! Raynor, I will swear to all you have said! By the peace of my mother's soul—"

Raynor pulled Siri up and back, then dropped her in a shuddering heap on the wall-walk. She huddled there on the stones, the faintness giving way to slamming waves of nausea. She stuffed a fist in her mouth and let tears of reaction stream down her face. Triston and Raynor were still shouting at one another, but she could not comprehend their words through the buzz that filled her head.

Then all fell silent. Little by little, the buzzing ebbed. Her stomach ceased its heaving, but her violent trembling had not subsided when

Raynor touched her shoulder.

"Carissima—"

Terror gave way to fury at the sound of his voice. She sprang up spitting an Italian curse. She threw every ounce of strength she could summon into the swing of her arm and slapped him across his bearded face. Before he could recover from his surprise, she pulled her dagger free and flashed it straight at his heart.

Raynor twisted away just in time to evade it. He cursed too, loudly in French, and caught her wrist when the steel came at him a second time.

"Carissima, I do not want to hurt you, but—"

She lashed out with two stinging kicks to his shins. She tried to wrest her hand away when he winced, but he held her fast. He slammed her back against the wall, wrenching her wrist so painfully that her fingers flew open and the blade clattered to the stones at their feet. With a sob of rage, she tried to drive her nails into his face, but he caught both her hands and pinned them to the wall on either side of her head.

"Diavolo!" she screamed. "Triston was right all along! I was nothing to you but a means of revenge!"

She twisted wildly in his grasp, but he held her fast until frustration overcame her and she sagged against the wall.

"Carissima," he said softly then, "this was not how I wished to win you."

He looked so remorseful, so mortified by what he had just done, that she whispered, "Why?"

He shook his head and sighed. "I did not know what to make of you when I first saw you on the road, looking so much like Clothilde but with such fire of spirit. Clothilde would have swooned at the sight of us, but you! You berated my men like errant squires and had your dagger at my throat before I could blink. The differences between you were astounding! But the face was so similar—I own, the thought came to me then that there must be some way to use you."

"Against Triston," she said, unable to keep the bitterness from her voice.

"Aye," he admitted. "I did not yet know that you were in Triston's ward, and when I learned of it, I did not know how he would see you. Would your spirit be so unique that he would overlook the likeness? Or would your face be all that mattered? Would it be enough to make him fall in love with you all over again?"

Her face *had* been all that mattered, she thought, and it had indeed been enough—enough to divide them forever.

"That day on the riverbank," she said, "when I first met you as Raynor, you held me by the water's edge, and if Triston hadn't come, you would have pushed me in."

But again Raynor shook his head. "Nay, in truth, I was but attempting to show you my fields. It was not until Triston tore you from my hands and accused me of intending you harm to spite him, that I saw my way. You were Clothilde to him. And it seemed a fair recompense that you should die by my hands, as my sister did by his."

"Then why did you not kill me today?"

He gave her a rueful, crooked smile. "Because I fell in love with you, carissima, in those days when you waited upon me in my illness at Vere. I tried to resist it, I tried to remember Isobel's body laid out by the river— but when I was with you, all I could see was you, your enchanting face and bewitching smiles and the merry twinkle in your glorious eyes. How could any man not fall in love with you?"

He bent his head to kiss her, but she twisted her face away.

"You have a strange way of showing it. Knocking me down the stairs in a fall that could have broken my neck, and threatening to throw me off your battlements!"

Raynor nuzzled her ear through her tangled hair. "Triston should not have maddened me. Both times he spoke words that provoked me, and in such moments I forget all but my hate of him. That is why I wanted you to stay below today. I feared what I would do if you were near and he spoke of Isobel."

She sought in vain to escape his seeking mouth. Desperate to distract him, she said, "You were the only one to speak Isobel's name. All Triston said was—"

The nuzzling stopped. "I remember what he said," Raynor snarled. "My assault of Clothilde was in revenge for Triston's seduction of my sister, but I failed then, just as I failed to avenge Isobel's death. Clothilde should not have died in some meaningless mishap. There was no satisfaction for me in that! But with you—"

She held her breath, but the dangerous fire in his amber eyes slowly ebbed.

"Nay, carissima, I must have my revenge another way now. I will not harm you—unless Triston enrages me again."

"Then what will you do?" she asked. Clearly his professed love for her had in no way tempered his hatred for Triston.

"First, I will marry you, and let Triston burn with the knowledge that it was his oath of consent that surrendered you to my caresses."

Siri thought of the oath that Raynor had made Triston swear, an oath she knew Triston would never break. He had not broken his former vow to pray for his mother's soul in Jerusalem, even though that pilgrimage had surrendered Clothilde, the woman he adored, to another man. Then surely he would not break this one for Siri, who had failed to win any claim to his heart at all?

That knowledge brought her pain, but also relief. Triston would not come to her rescue, but neither would Raynor be able to harm him.

Raynor must have caught her unguarded expression. "Do not delude yourself, carissima. As I said, our marriage is the first step—but not the final one."

She stiffened. "What do you mean?"

"When I realized that I could not bring myself to conclude my revenge through you, I was forced to turn to another plan. One which, with Lord Fauke's all-too-willing cooperation, promises to come to a satisfying fruition."

The scene in Raynor's sick-chamber returned to her mind in a horrific shock. "The treason charge," she whispered. "But it is a lie."

Raynor shrugged. "Aye, but unfortunately for Triston, it is a plausible lie. Duke Richard's fears of conspiracy are not entirely misplaced. I know of myself that the Young King entered into several secret alliances with various Poitevin barons before he deserted his brother after Chateauneuf.

There is small doubt that Triston's brother knows of these alliances too, or that he has recruited Triston to join them. At least, that is the story I will tell. And as a former intimate of the Young King, you may rest assured that I will be believed." The cunning smile had never entirely left his lips, but now it turned cold, almost vicious. "When I see Triston's head posted on the gate of Poitiers—then I will be satisfied that Isobel rests in peace."

A tremor slammed through Siri, almost as violent as that which had seized her after he'd pulled her from the walls.

"But you have no proof," she said. "Triston says you cannot make that charge stick without proof."

"Oh, I shall have proof, once you bring me Acelet."

She stared at him, comprehension dawning. "You cannot trap Triston without him. That is why you agreed to let me go back to Vere. You need Acelet to make this devilish scheme succeed."

"It would facilitate matters considerably, if he were to confess his and Triston's part in the conspiracy."

"And if he does not?" As foolish as Acelet was, Siri could not believe he was involved in anything so wicked as treason.

"That youth will say what I tell him to say. If he does not, he will find himself under the executioner's knife, alongside his cousin."

"Acelet called you friend," she said in disgust, "but it is you who are the traitor. You have betrayed both him and me."

Raynor released one of her wrists to touch her cheek. "Carissima, someday you will—"

She turned her head and sank her teeth into the flesh between his thumb and forefinger. Raynor yelped and jerked his hand away, then stumbled back when her toes renewed their stinging assault against his shins.

Siri did not wait for him to recover from his surprise, but wrenched her other wrist free and lunged for her dagger. Raynor sprang after her, but her fingers found the hilt one instant before he caught her. He spun her about, then froze when she poised the blade's point against the hollow of his throat.

"I should not even hesitate," she said, holding his glittering eyes without fear. "I should drive it straight in—and I will if you do not drop your hands to your sides and keep them there."

Raynor's hands fell away from her shoulders. "Carissima, you have no stomach for murder."

"Not murder," she said, "but self-protection I am more than capable of. If you doubt me—"

"Ah, no." He rolled back his head at the warning nudge of her blade. "But how will you escape this castle, once I am dead? My men will never let you ride through these gates with my blood on your hands. They will punish you for my death—after they have enjoyed your beauty as only angry, lust-filled knights know how to do."

His words horrified her and for a moment the awful vision numbed her mind. That was all the time it took for Raynor's hand to flash up and snatch the dagger out of her hand. She made a desperate grab to retrieve it, but after holding the blade briefly in the air above her head, he startled her by sliding it back into the sheath at her side.

He gave the weapon a condescending pat, then caught her hands and held them out of temptation's way. "Come, let us leave it there for now. You might decide you need it on your wedding night."

Siri spoke through stiff lips. "I don't care what you have made Triston swear or how you threaten me, I will never repeat the words which would make me your wife."

"Oh, you will speak them, all right, and this is the last time you are going to threaten to use that knife on me. But if you wish to use it on Lord Fauke, I shall be quite willing to help you fabricate a defense, or better yet, accuse some jealous lover of bursting upon you while you were—"

"Lord Fauke?"

His cunning smile now held a hint of apology. "Alas, yes. Not knowing a few days ago that I should be able to win such an agreeable oath of consent from Triston, I'm afraid I entered into a rather unpleasant bargain with my lord. In return for helping me win your hand from the duke, Lord Fauke insisted that I grant him *jus primae noctis* with you."

Siri knew her Latin, but she did not understand Raynor's odd inflection of this phrase. "Law of the first night? What do you mean?"

"It is a right sometimes exercised by a lord over his serfs, but it is not unheard of for a vassal to surrender his wife to the same—er, honor. What it means, I'm afraid, is that Lord Fauke has the right to claim your . . . companionship . . . on our wedding night."

Siri had not thought it possible for Raynor to sink any lower in her eyes. But now she turned her gaze away, so filled with contempt and disgust that she could not bear even to look at him.

"Carissima—"

"Do not call me that. You sicken me. You claim to love me, yet you threaten to kill me in your rage, and in your sanity you promise to give me to another man's lust. If you let Lord Fauke touch me, I will kill him—and then I will kill myself."

"Nay," he said softly, coaxingly. "'Tis an ordeal you will forget when I hold you in my arms in the morning. I swear I will drive it from your mind, drive everything from your mind, until there is only you and me and the love we will share."

"I wanted to give you my heart once," she whispered. "I wanted to find a way to love you. But now you will not be able to touch me, that I shall not remember Lord Fauke, and I shall not be able to look into your face without seeing Triston's—"

She choked on the rest, but she could not fight back the vision. Traitors in Venice had been treated no more gently than traitors in these domains. Siri had seen the heads of the executed, set up high on bridges or walls as a warning.

Desperation forced her to make the only plea she could. "Raynor, spare him and I will do anything you ask. I will marry you and never cast my eyes on Vere again, never speak his name—"

But Raynor shook his head. "I cannot live with Isobel's ghost any longer. Forgive me, carissima, but this is the only way to lay her to rest."

Siri tossed back her head. "Then you shall do it without my help. I will not trap Acelet for you. I will not leave these walls."

"You will return to Vere, as I gave my word. And within twenty-four hours you will return, bringing me that very youth."

Siri pressed her lips together hard and shook her head again.

"Carissima, I regret that you should be so stubborn. I did not want to make matters still worse between us by making this threat, but I'm afraid you leave me no choice. Where do you imagine your loyal companion, the Lady Lucianna, is at this moment?"

Siri willed herself to maintain a haughty silence.

"I had my men bear her away and lock her in one of my towers. If you wish to help her, you will do exactly as I say."

Siri's facade of defiance slipped. "You would not dare to harm her—"

"I should think you would have learned by now that there is nothing I will not do, if it will win me my revenge."

Lucianna at this monster's mercy—

The trap snapped clean and fast around Siri. "What must I do?" she asked, her mouth dry.

"Bring me Acelet. That is all. Bring me Acelet."

# Chapter 21

Raynor carried her down to the river, set before him on his horse. Siri knew that he did it for effect, to demonstrate yet again to Triston how completely he held her in his power. Flanked by a handful of his guards and longtime companions in his mischief, they rode to the bridge that spanned the wide path of water that divided his lands from his neighbor's.

Triston waited on the other side alone, mounted on his black warhorse.

"Twenty-four hours, Triston," Raynor shouted the mocking reminder, "until your oath makes this wench my wife. I will leave it for you to wonder whether the ceremony will merely formalize what we have already enjoyed."

Raynor shifted Siri about in his supporting arm and twisted round her head with his hand. He set a hard, hungry kiss on her lips, her head held secure with a grip on her chin so fierce that she thought it might crush her jaw. The kiss, she knew, was meant to enrage Triston. When he at last allowed her to pull away, she rubbed her hand across her mouth and spat. He laughed, but angrily, and pushed her from his horse so roughly that she fell on her hands and knees in the grass.

Triston had ridden halfway across the bridge before he had mastered his rage and brought his mount back under control. But she could see the thunder in his face. She knew that if Raynor touched her again, it would mean his or Triston's blood. She stood up, her hands and knees tingling. Then she ran, her hair pouring back from her face in the wind, her silken slippers soundless against the wooden boards of the bridge, until she reached Triston.

He leaned down for her, his strong arm lifting her from the ground to set her before him on his horse. She buried her face against the soft cloth on his chest and wound her arms around his waist, glorying in this moment of safety. In her relief, she allowed herself to dream that the arm that held so tightly did so with love.

"Twenty four hours, Triston," Raynor's voice rang out again.

"I know!" Triston shouted back. His voice lowered and he repeated on a groan, "I know."

Raynor gave another mocking laugh, then Siri heard the clopping of hooves as he and his men rode away.

She did not turn her head to watch them. She clung to Triston like a frightened child, afraid that if she let him go she would slip away back to the terrors of Belle Noir.

"Has he hurt you?" Triston asked, his voice soft, his breath not far from her ear.

"No," she whispered into his tunic.

"Come, lift up your face and let me see."

He nudged his hand between them until his mailed knuckles came under her chin and tilted her face up to the light.

"He did not harm me," she said, knowing he searched for marks that might have been left by Raynor's hand. "He only frightened me a little." Triston's brows shot up. Her voice went wobbly. "Very well, more than a little. When he held me over his walls and threatened to—" She broke off with a shudder, then leaned her forehead against Triston's breast. "I have been such a terrible fool. If only I had listened to you. If only I had believed your warnings about Raynor."

He cradled her against him and murmured, "Nay, the mistakes have been mine. They have all been mine."

She glanced back up. The note of pain in his voice had become as familiar to her as the beating of her own heart. He stared at the dark waters that ran below the bridge, but his gaze looked hazy, unfocused, as if fixed on some taunting inner vision.

She turned her own gaze to the waters. "Is that where she died?" She did not need to speak the name.

"Over there." He nodded towards the bank on Raynor's side. "We were standing there, just to the north of the bridge. That is where she threw herself on me, begged me to give a name to her child—and that was where I lost my temper and pushed her onto the ice."

It had been a long while since Siri had allowed herself to remember that part of the story. "Triston, it is the only part I cannot understand. Young as you were, to deny your own child . . ."

Triston looked down at her, his dark eyes inscrutable. She watched for the clenching of his jaw, which so frequently betrayed his struggle with guilt. But there was not so much as a twitch at the corner of his mouth.

"I would not have rejected the child," he said, "if it had been mine."

Her eyes widened. "But Raynor insists—"

"Raynor would not believe me. I suppose I cannot fully blame him. Aside from Isobel's word, he had caught us a few months earlier sharing some rather indiscreet kisses. We used the meet there by the river, and there was one night when I burned so hot for her that I came very near to indulging our mutual desire the way Raynor clearly suspects me of doing. But I was within weeks of being knighted and my mind was filled with the lofty ideals of the title I would soon hold. Drogo de Molinet was my friend. To despoil his sister would have been an indelible stain on my honor. Had I succumbed to temptation, the only way to retrieve that honor would have been to marry her . . ."

Suddenly she understood. "Which you were not willing to do— because you were in love with Clothilde."

There was a moment of silence before Triston said, "I thought I could forget her with Isobel. But even on that night, I could not drive Clo's sweet face from my heart."

Siri had to bite her lip to stop its quivering, until curiosity overwhelmed her.

"Then whose child was it?" The question popped out before she could stop it. An expression flitted so quickly over his face, that less keen eyes than hers might have missed it. "You know, don't you?"

Triston cast another sweeping glance at the water, then abruptly wheeled his horse about and set the beast into a canter back towards Vere.

"Aren't you going to tell me?"

"It is none of your affair, Lady Siriol. And it changes nothing—least of all the way she died."

Siri stared into his grim face for a moment. Then she leaned against him again and tightened her arms about his waist. To be near him again was a pleasure she meant to savor to its fullest. She could not tell from the way he held her whether he found any joy in her embrace, but at the moment joy was the emotion uppermost in her breast. The darkness of her doubts slid away with his story of Isobel. What man but Triston would have forgone a beautiful woman's willing arms for honor and friendship's sake?

If only he could see the brightness of his own soul. But to this hour, all he seemed able to find in himself was failure and despair. She knew it from the way his gaze had lingered on the waters where Isobel had died. It was that memory he had chosen to nourish. Not the loyalty and self-mastery it had taken to resist a moment's lust, but the tragedy that had followed a flash of anger.

Justifiable anger, in Siri's eyes, for what sort of woman would try to trap one man with another man's child?

The walls of Vere rose before them and her hold on Triston grew a little more desperate.

"Triston, Raynor's plans for revenge do not stop with marrying me. He is obsessed with destroying you, but if he knew the truth—"

"I cannot tell him the truth," Triston said, "not all of it. I do not know if he would believe me, even if I did."

"Can you not even try?"

He shook his head and trotted his horse across the drawbridge, which had been let down at their approach.

His stubbornness bewildered her. "But Triston—"

His strong arm shifted her away from him before she could finish and lowered her to the ground inside the bailey. He dismounted after her and stood for a moment looking at her.

"Come." He brushed a mail-clad thumb lightly across her creased brow. "You are not wed to the villain yet. We have twenty-four hours. Let us make the most of them."

"Where are we going?" she asked, as he took her hand and began pulling her across the yard.

"To see Father Michel."

"The chaplain?"

"Raynor extorted my vow under arrant circumstances. Still, I spoke the words and cannot alter them, unless the chaplain will absolve me from my oath." He mastered the tremor of doubt in his voice. "Nay, he is an honest, merciful priest. When he understands the execrable way Raynor won my vow, he will—"

"Triston, stop." She tugged at his hand until he turned around and looked at her. "It is not enough. Even if he absolves you, I still must go back."

"Go back?"

"I must! Raynor has—"

He caught her by the shoulders, startling her into breaking off.

"What?" he demanded. His voice hoarsened oddly. "What has Raynor done to you?"

"Done to me?" she repeated. "You mean, besides dangling me over his walls?"

"No. I mean, he said—" Triston's grip tightened, then eased, then tightened again. "At the bridge, before he kissed you, he said—" The rest seemed to catch in his throat, as though to speak the words would choke him. She saw him swallow hard, twice, before he ground out, "He said—that a marriage would only formalize what the two of you have already enjoyed."

It took a moment for Raynor's meaning and Triston's interpretation to sink in. "Triston, you think Raynor and I are lovers?"

"When I caught him kissing you here on the bed, you defended him. And then you fled to him. Why? Why did you leave me to go to Belle Noir?"

Siri was not prepared for the hurt that flooded up into her throat. It rose like a thick, smothering wave. "Because you did not want me," she choked out the words. "And I did not know where else to turn."

She looked away. She could not stop her heart from aching for the response she knew would never come. She wanted him to tell her that she had been wrong, that he had always wanted her, that if she had only stayed another day, he would have—

He released her and stepped back. "I gave you somewhere to turn. I gave you to Sir Gavin. But instead of going meekly to an honest, decent man, you run to my worst enemy, a man who calls me murderer and traitor."

Siri felt her heart crack clean through. Even now, all he wanted was to give her away, to any man but Raynor. His anger bespoke, not the wound of a betrayed heart, but only of pride.

"That is why you want your vow absolved," she said bitterly. "So you can marry me to Sir Gavin."

"I did not say that. But what do you expect me to think? I saw you and Raynor with my own eyes—"

"Yes, I let him kiss me that day. He had asked me to marry him, had told me that he loved me—and just then, I was desperate to be loved. I prayed he could make me forget you. But—" She broke off, then ran her hands up and down her arms. "Perhaps he was simply too eager. When he kissed me, I–I felt so cold. I begged him to stop, but he would not listen. And then you came in and found us and would not believe me when I said—"

She stopped with a shiver. She expected Triston to be enraged, to challenge her, to accuse her of lying. She closed her eyes and waited.

"I remember."

His soft response startled her eyes open again.

"Your hands were like ice afterwards. I wondered then how you could be cold, when he was clearly so hot." He took her fingers and tested them with his lips, since his own mail-clad hands were unable to sense their coolness or warmth. "Like now," he murmured. "Why are you so afraid?"

"I don't know," she whispered. "Usually when a man tries to kiss me,

I go blazingly angry, like I did with Lord Fauke, but Raynor—"

"Tell me," he said as she broke off again. "I won't chide you if you tell me the truth."

She curled her fingers about his mail gloves and clung to them. "I was angry at your choice of Sir Gavin," she said, "and the other men—there was nothing in them but lust for me. But Raynor seemed different. I suppose it was a measure of his cunning that he was able to convince me that he honestly loved me. So when he asked me to marry him, I said that I would. That is why I did not struggle when he kissed me on the bed. I had made up my mind to be his wife. How could I then shun his caresses? But the fiercer his kisses grew, the harder he held me, the more overwhelming the memory became . . ."

"Memory?"

Her voice shook. "The apprentice in my brother's house. Did not my brother tell you of that in his letter?"

"Aye," Triston admitted, his voice grim. "Simon knew he would not live much longer and feared there would be others like the apprentice, ready to take advantage of you once he was gone."

"That was why he gave me the dagger—and why he sent me to you."

His gaze drifted over her head. After a moment of frowning silence, he said slowly, "There was a time when my brother was in danger of his life and I feared his only safety lay in fleeing the country. I was going to send him to Simon for protection." He gave a heavy sigh. "He would not have failed me the way I have failed him."

"Triston, you haven't—"

"Nay, I have made a miserable botch of your life. Had I not been so high-handed about you and Sir Gavin, you would never have fallen into Raynor's trap. And all because I found it—uncomfortable—to have you near me. Nay," he repeated and lifted her chin when she would have looked away, "you cannot help your face. Have you not told me that time and again? I should have been stronger, I should have been more sane—"

His voice caught in a different way now and Siri felt her breath catch with it.

261

"Sane," he murmured again, then said abruptly, "Perrin has been inconsolable since you left."

The statement was so far detached from their former conversation that it took a moment for her mind to make the shift. "Perrin?"

"He says that I drove you away from us. I do not know how to explain to him, but I think it is time I found a way. Lady Siriol, will you help me, to tell him about his mother?"

"But I do not know anything about—"

"You know enough and have guessed a great deal more, I think. Please." He pulled her suddenly closer. "There is not much time, and if I lose you again, I will lose my son as well."

"Triston, I cannot stay at Vere beyond these twenty-four hours. Not because I want to return to Raynor, but because he has given me no choice."

"Has given us no choice—or so he thinks. Lady Siriol, I will find a way to extricate you from this devilish trap of Raynor's. Let us talk to Perrin, and then we will find my chaplain and—"

"But Triston, I have told you it will do no good. Raynor has—"

"Nay, let us quarrel about this later. I have told Perrin I would bring you to him. He is waiting for us now. Lady Siriol, please."

Love for the child as strong as the love she bore for his father overcame her. She nodded. The inexorable skill of Raynor's trap could be dealt with later. For now, the fear of it vanished away in the grateful warmth of Triston's eyes.

# Chapter 22

Triston watched as Siri sank to her knees and opened her arms to receive the bundle of energy and ebony curls that flew off the bed to greet her. Perrin nearly tumbled her over with the fervor of his embrace.

"Perrin, you promised you would be still if I brought the Lady Siriol to you."

Triston should have been inured by now to the way his son shrank at the sight of him. Perrin cowered into Siri's lap and whimpered, "Lady Siri, make him go away."

Triston's first impulse was to allow these words to send him backing out of the room, but a quick dart from Siri's eyes stayed him.

"Hush," she said to Perrin, "there is nothing to be afraid of."

He saw the tender way she stroked the boy's curls. There was such calmness in her movements, such control. So different from the boy's mother . . .

As was her reaction when she found the bump on the back of his head. "Oh, my," she said in cheerful surprise. "What a splendid lump you have here. Did you get this when you tried to save me on the stairs?"

Perrin had buried his face in her lap, but now he glanced up. After a moment, his small hand flitted to the back of his head. "I knocked it on one of the steps," he said, in the most natural voice Triston had heard him use since the fall. Though it trembled a little, Siri's presence had clearly begun to soothe him.

"It is very handsome," she said admiringly, "a wound worthy of a most valiant knight. It was very brave of you to try to catch me—though not, perhaps, very wise."

Perrin looked pleased. "Acelet says wisdom is for churchmen, that passion and valiant acts are what make a true knight. He must be right, for Father Michel scolds me and tells me I must stay abed until it heals."

"Perhaps the chaplain is right."

"But it is so dull to stay in bed all day. I wouldn't mind so much if Acelet were here to tell me stories. He knows the best stories, Lady Siri. He told me some the time I fell from the tree and Mamma made me stay in bed for days and days. They quieted Mamma, too." Perrin stopped with a sigh, then added plaintively, "Acelet has been gone a long time. Do you know where he is? Why did he go away?"

"We are not sure," Siri replied. "But as soon as I see him again, I will tell him how much you miss him. Now Father Michel is right, you must get back into bed."

"You were hurt too," Perrin protested, "and you are up."

"Yes, but I received a mere scratch to my forehead. It is nothing like the bump you suffered. Now come, shall I have your Papa carry you to your bed or—"

Triston flinched even before Perrin flew into his predictable response.

"No! I don't want Papa here! Lady Siri, make him go away!"

"Perrin—"

"No, no, no! He will hurt you again! Make him go away before he does!"

Triston said hoarsely, "This was a mistake," and wrenched at the latch on the door.

"Triston, stop!" Siri said. "Stay where you are. Perrin, your papa is not going to hurt anyone."

"He will!" Tears flowed down the boy's too pale cheeks. "He pushed you down the stairs, just like he pushed Mamma! I saw him!"

"Lady Siri," Triston said, "he will make himself ill. We should wait until his head has healed."

"There is not time. I will not be here that long. Now, Perrin—"

But even in his fright, Perrin's ears were quick. "Not be here? Lady Siri, you are not leaving again! Promise me you won't leave me again!" He flung his boyish arms around her neck and burst into sobs.

Without thinking, Triston fell to his knees beside them. He reached out to touch his son, but pulled sharply back before he did. He would only make things worse—if worse they could be—but he could not bear to see his son so lost and afraid.

"Perrin," he pled, "please stop crying. I will not let her leave us. I swear—"

"Triston, don't," Siri said sternly. "You make too many oaths, and this is one you may not be able to keep. Now, Perrin, look at me. Look at me!" She pushed the boy away and took his face between her hands. "You know that I love you. I would never lie to you. You know that, don't you?" The boy hiccupped tearfully. "Don't you?"

Perrin hesitated, then nodded. The tears still flowed, but the wracking sobs quieted.

"Why do you think I went away?"

Perrin's answer was never in doubt. He jabbed a finger at Triston and said with flashing eyes, "Because of him!" And Triston did the worst thing he could—he stood up and backed away.

Siri gave a despairing shake of her head before she returned her attention to Perrin. "Yes, Perrin, I went because of your papa, but not because I was afraid of him."

"But he pushed you down the stairs. I saw him!"

She shook her head again, this time at Perrin. "No. Do you remember Sir Raynor? How I helped tend to him after he was injured by a robber outside Vere's walls? It was he who pushed your papa and made him fall into me. Your papa tried to catch me but he missed, and that is how I fell down the stairs."

"But—" Perrin's eyes narrowed suspiciously "—why would Sir Raynor push Papa?"

"Because he was angry at him, Perrin, and wanted to hurt him by hurting me."

The boy frowned. "I don't understand."

"No." She pulled him back into her arms and laid her cheek against his dark curls. "No, I don't suppose you do. But when you are older you will. For now all you need to believe is that your papa did not mean me harm. Can you believe that?" When the boy did not answer, she turned and said, "Triston, give me your hand."

Triston hesitated, then bent down to take her outstretched fingers.

"No, no, take off that mail and give me your hand."

He stripped the mail glove from off his right hand. Then he dropped to one knee and tentatively took Siri's fingers in his.

"Look," she said to Perrin. She slid her fingers up and laced them with Triston's.

Even in the muted light, Triston observed how white they were against his tanned skin, how delicately small yet how surprisingly and pleasingly strong they were as they twined securely into his hold.

"Perrin, I am not afraid of your papa, and you must not be either."

Perrin huddled down closer into Siri's lap at seeing his father so near. It was clear that Siri's confidence in Triston's touch had given him pause, but—

"Wh–What about Mamma?"

Siri's fingers twisted tighter to prevent Triston from pulling away. This was the moment he had dreaded most of all. The moment he had avoided since the night of Clothilde's death.

The message in Siri's eyes was clear. *You must tell him.* Seeing his son quiet and waiting, Triston took a deep breath and ventured his first uncertain step.

"Perrin," he said, "tell me what you saw that night."

Perrin stared for several moments at Siri's hand entwined with Triston's before he answered. "I heard you shouting at Mamma. And I heard her screaming, the way she did sometimes when she was upset, and I came out to see what was wrong." He paused and glanced at Siri. She gave him an encouraging smile. "You were both standing right by the steps. You were holding onto Mamma and she was trying to pull away and— and then you p–pushed her—"

"Perrin!" Siri exclaimed. "You saw your father push her?"

"I—" The boy hesitated. He seemed to find it easier to tell the rest to Siri rather than his father. "It was dark. I wasn't sure. Afterwards I ran back to my bed and lay there under the covers and prayed and prayed that it was only a dream. But the next morning, when Father Michel came and told me that Mamma had died, I knew what I saw was real."

"What did you see?"

"I saw Mamma fall, but I wasn't sure how. But then Acelet came out of the shadows and ran down the stairs and I heard him screaming at Papa. He said—He said—" Triston closed his eyes and listened again to the words burned as deeply into his mind as they had been burned into Perrin's. "He said, 'She is dead! You killed her!'" Perrin gave a sob and repeated, "'You k–killed her . . .'"

Only Siri's firm yank on his hand brought Triston out of the wrenching memories of that night. He opened his eyes and saw Perrin weeping once more in Siri's lap. Triston's fingers tightened on hers, drawing strength from her strength for the words he had to speak next.

"Perrin. You must listen to me now, son, for I am going to tell you something that you will find difficult to understand. It is something that even your cousin Acelet did not want to believe. But you are a very intelligent boy and if you think about it, you will know that what I say is the truth."

Siri stroked Perrin's hair until his sobs quieted again. Then she nodded at Triston with a sober little smile, and Triston took a deep breath and told his son the truth about his mother.

⤘

Triston paced for what seemed an eternity outside his son's chamber door. Perrin had listened to much of Triston's speech with his face still buried in Siri's lap, so that Triston had not been able to gauge his son's reaction or degree of comprehension of his words. They had been the most difficult of his life. To explain to a child of seven that his mother had been so unstable of mind that she had become a danger to herself and others, was a task that had required every shred of adroitness and tact that he had possessed.

When he had seen Perrin's fingers tighten on Siri's gown, he'd known that Clothilde's shrieking outbursts had not gone unnoticed by the boy. Triston did not try to explain their immediate source, though he had hinted, he realized now, more bitterly than cautiously at the origins of abuse received in her mother's house. It had taken a frown from Siri to bring him back out of those memories and return his focus to the present. Or rather, to Perrin's need to learn about that night.

The night his mother had died. As gently as he could, Triston told him about the dagger his mother had seized, of how Triston had been afraid that she would harm herself or another. Perhaps it had been the tremor in his voice when he described their wrestle at the head of the stairs and its tragic result, which made his son look up at last. He had seen the tears still glistening on Perrin's cheeks and knew they must have been flowing freely throughout his story. And the unspoken question still hung in the air between them. *What about Acelet?*

It was Siri who came to Triston's rescue there. Acelet, she said, must have been as confused about what he saw as Perrin had been. He too had been watching from the shadows and it must have been too dark for him to see what really occurred. Aye, Triston said, and Acelet had loved Perrin's mamma too, and had been grief-stricken at her death. Acelet had spoken hastily, bitterly, from the pain and sorrow of his heart.

Perrin had gazed at his father another moment, then put his head back in Siri's lap. But Siri's smile at Triston had been one of approval, and when he tilted his head towards the door, she had nodded and allowed him to leave.

He paced a few more steps, then stopped and leaned against the wall. He was not sure whether his heart was pounding with relief that his encounter with his son was over or with some other emotion, with Siri at its center, when she finally came out of the room. He did not turn his head to look at her, nor did he straighten from his slump against the wall.

"Do you think he understood?" he asked of Perrin.

"I think he will when he considers your words a little more. He cried a long while after you left, but when he finally wore himself out, he let me put him to bed and then he stared at the ceiling and said—" She hesitated, but Triston did not move, and after a moment she finished, "He said he knew his mamma had been unhappy for a long time. And he confided in me that sometimes he was frightened of her screaming. You must give him time to let his memories work."

But Triston felt a blaze of self-anger run through him. "I should not have left him like that. I do not want him to remember his mother with fear! I should have tempered my words with— with—" He waved a frustrated hand. "Something gentler. She was not constantly mad. She had quiet times, tender times, when she loved both Perrin—and me."

He stopped and pressed a hand to his eyes.

"Later it will be kind to remind him of those happier days," she said, her clear, sweet voice subdued in a way he had seldom heard it. "But just now he needs to face the harder truth."

Triston let his hand fall away. "How did you learn to be so wise, my lady? One would think you had been mother to a veritable brood of children."

Her voice went wistful. "It is one of my few regrets that I never had any. I think I would have made a very good mother."

"A splendid mother," he agreed. His mouth curved slowly up as he turned his head to look at her. "What is it?" he asked at the startled expression on her face.

"N–Nothing. It's just—I have never seen you smile that way before."

He raised his brows. "Did you think me incapable of smiling?"

"Of course not. Only you do not do it very often, and when you do it is either very sad or . . . "

"Or what?"

"Or, well, bitter."

Triston fancied he had good reason to feel bitter now, or sad. Reliving the memories with Perrin had been difficult. But just at this moment, both emotions seemed curiously distant.

He reached out and took her hand. His smile deepened. "Tell me, Lady Siriol, when I kiss you, do you go blazingly angry or fall into a chill?"

"Neither," she whispered with a blush, "you know I do neither. And I have kissed you far more often than you have kissed me."

"Are you sure? I have not kept a strict accounting. Perhaps you had better refresh my memory." He heard her breath catch as he pulled her a little closer.

"Well," she said, "you kissed me first, when you first saw me in your hall. And again at Perrin's bedside that first night. But I kissed you back, which was most unladylike, for I didn't even know you, and I know it shocked you because of the way you thrust me away."

"Surprised, not shocked me," he corrected. "Clo's kisses were never so—frank—as yours. But that is twice, my lady, and you cannot deny that I initiated them both."

"But I kissed you after we quarreled about Sir Gavin."

"Aye, that you did, though I bravely shouldered the blame for it against Lady Lucianna's rebuke." He pulled her another step closer. "And I kissed you first that night we quarreled about Raynor, and again the next day in the garden. And I have wanted to kiss you innumerable times in between. So which of us is truly the most shameless and bold?"

This confession seemed to drive everything out of her head but a kind of shy confusion. "Did you, Triston? Did you truly want to kiss me?"

"If you want the answer to that, you must come one step closer. But you must take it yourself, for I will not stand accused of coercing—"

She was in his arms before he could finish. "I like you better this way," she laughed. "Slumping against the wall, you are not so tall—" her fingers fluttered to his lips and her blue eyes darkened "—not so far away . . ."

"But I cannot do it properly like this," he murmured, and straightened so that he could take her more firmly into his embrace.

He should not have been surprised that she rose up on her toes to meet his kiss. Siri had never been shy about reciprocating his passion, however muddled he might have been about it in his own mind. But this time he thrust away every thought, every sensation but pleasure. He let his mouth linger over hers, drinking from her strength, her vibrance, the honey-sweet essence of her soul . . .

She seemed to sense his need to take this first kiss slowly, to let him find his way through the flood of emotions. Or perhaps she was merely afraid of shocking him again. After the first eager response of her mouth, everything in her went still.

She murmured a protest when he drew away, but he did so only so that he could gather her face in his hands and indulge himself with another kiss. This one was more insistent, for suddenly he did not want her quiet and demure, but her own energetic, ingenuous self. But while her arms wound a little more tightly around his waist, she returned the kiss as hesitantly as before.

He raised his head with a frustrated breath. "She is not here," he whispered. "There is nothing to be afraid of. Now kiss me, the way you did beside Perrin's bed, the way you did in the yard in the dark—"

He thought she gave a little gasp, but he could not be sure since he claimed her mouth again so quickly. All in an instant she warmed, then quivered into a flame. He could not remember the last time a woman had kissed him like this, if one ever had. Certainly not his wife— Nay, he would not spoil this pleasure with those tortured memories. It was Siri he held now, Siri whose zealous kiss swirled his mind into transports, Siri whom he longed to keep kissing until life and eternity slipped away . . .

But they had not an eternity. At least, not yet. He dropped his hands to her shoulders before he loosed her lips, then held her tightly against his chest so that she would not think he had rebuffed her yet again. He rubbed his bare thumb across her lips and felt them still warm from the heat of his own.

"Three kisses," he whispered. "A magic number. Perhaps they will bring us luck."

Her hand stole up to his cheek and he turned his head to nestle his lips against her palm.

"Come," he said. "Let us speak to Father Michel."

For a moment she looked dazed. Then her eyes darted away, but not before he caught a gleam in them of something glistening and moist. A tear? He lifted her face, but her lids slid shut before he could find it again.

"I think we should look for Acelet first," she said. "You told Raynor that you had seen him in the woods. Should we not try to find him while the light still holds?"

He did not answer. He held her face until a tiny trickle leaked out of the corner of her eye. He raised a finger to wipe it away.

"Siri."

Her mouth trembled and at the risk of spoiling the magic, he kissed her again.

She pushed him away. "Oh, don't. Why do you have to love me now?"

She backed away from him, then stopped and covered her face with her hands.

Triston stared at her. *Love.* He had not spoken the word, he had not even thought it. But he knew at the echo of her voice that it was the emotion now swelling in his breast. And some corner of his mind had known it too, yesterday in the woods when he had sought in vain to draw Clothilde's face, but had only been able to see Siri's.

When had it happened? He had been so sure that it was only Clothilde who lay in his heart when he and Siri had spoken at Perrin's bedside after her and Perrin's fall down the stairs. He had just spent an agonizing night pacing the floor beside his son's bed, terrified lest some unknown injuries lingered inside the small body. But when exhaustion had finally lowered him to doze fretfully in the chair, the images that had swirled around him had all had been of Clothilde, of her madness and violent death, and his guilt that he had been unable to save her from either.

She had still been in his mind when Siri had come in, looking so like the way his wife had once looked in her innocence and sweetness. Still overwhelmed by the tormenting dreams and the renewed pangs of loss they'd stirred, he had rebuffed Siri with what had seemed such a finality to them both that he had sent her flying headlong into the malicious arms of his enemy.

But he was not dreaming now and for a few precious, priceless hours he had brought her back home. And though he knew he would never entirely escape his grief for Clothilde, the loss had been flooded out by Siri's spirit, so bright, so strong that he wondered how it had not vanished at their first kiss.

"Siri—"

"No," she cried, her voice muffled behind her hands, "do not say it. Do not say you love me. Triston, I cannot stay with you."

"Sweetheart, we will find a way."

"There is no way. He has got Lucianna!"

"What?"

"Raynor has locked Lucianna in one of his towers. He says if I do not return and bring him Acelet, he will— he will h–hurt her."

Triston felt his mouth go grim. "We will save Lucianna. Once the chaplain has absolved me of the oath, I will be free to act."

"But what if he won't?" She lowered her hands and he saw the silver tears on her cheeks. "What if the chaplain will not absolve you? Triston, what will you do then?"

He did not answer for a moment. He would have flung his own soul to hell to save Siri. But Raynor had cunningly entrapped him with another's instead. The oath still burned in his ears: *May your mother's soul never come to paradise, may she eternally suffer the torments of her sins in the purgatory of the accursed, and may your prayers and those of your brother never bring her mercy from the flames.*

Surely God could not be so cruel as to punish the innocent for the crimes of the guilty. Yet if one's prayers could ease the dead's suffering, might not one's actions on earth bind the dead to that suffering, as well? The mere possibility conjured up such an image that a sweat broke out on Triston's palms. It was a risk he dared not take. His mother had been everything to him in his childhood, filling the hunger of his mind with her learning and the malleability of his youthful soul with her doubtless faith.

It was that faith he needed now, faith that he could find some way out of this darkened maze. For he knew that to fail either his mother or Siri would leave him to suffer a living hell as racking as anything the eternal worlds could devise.

"Sweetheart." He drew her to him again. "There is an escape for us. Somehow we will find it. Nay—" he lifted her chin when she sought to turn her face away "—we will find it. I will not lose you again."

Her hands curled into the cloth against his chest. "I do not want you to break your oath for me. Promise me you will not."

He brushed his thumb across the tears on her cheek. "Let us speak to Father Michel."

"No. Triston, there is not time. We must find Acelet. But first you must promise me—"

"Acelet can wait—and you do not need to ask me to keep the vows I speak."

"Then you will not try to stop me from returning to Belle Noir?"

"The blazes I won't. I am going to do considerably more than try."

In a burst of evident frustration, Siri released his tunic and struck her fists against his chest. "Haven't you heard me? I must return for Lucianna! And I must take Acelet with me! Triston, I do not want to go. It is slaying me to know that I must go! I never thought you would look at me, smile at me, kiss me the way you did today. I never thought that you would—"

"—love you?" he finished softly, and bent his head towards her lips.

But she pulled away before he could even catch a sip of their nectar. "Oh, don't! If you kiss me again I will die!"

Triston laughed at this unlikely prediction. "I'm afraid I am willing to take that risk," he said and reached for her again.

But she danced out of his hands. "No. And don't do that. Don't laugh as if you are happy. I never thought I would hear that sound, either, and how shall I have the strength to go when I see the last of my dreams fulfilled?"

"Sweetheart—"

"No, no, no! Do not say another word! Just take me to find Acelet. Please."

He hesitated. He wanted to go straight to the chaplain, to settle this matter of his oath so that he could ride forth and conclude once and for all this insidious feud with Raynor. But Siri's desperation checked him. Raynor's threat to Lucianna had terrified her, and Triston guessed that Acelet was the price of Lucianna's freedom. Triston had acted with a certain cunning of his own when he had pled for Siri's release to lure

Acelet out of the woods.

"He's afraid of my cousin, isn't he? Afraid Acelet might convince Lord Fauke that Raynor's charges against me are lies, that Raynor is the one who knew of conspiracy between the Young King and our barons and kept silent."

"He is going to make Acelet say you are the traitor."

Triston gave a scornful grunt. "Acelet won't do it. Raynor laid his trap for me too well. Now Acelet is caught in it too, and as shatterbrained as he is, that boy is not so stupid as to put his own neck in a noose."

"I pray you are right," Siri said, "but I must return to Belle Noir tomorrow with Acelet at my side, or Raynor will harm Lucianna."

Triston searched her frightened face, then gave a curt nod. "Very well. If it will ease your mind, we will find Acelet first and speak to the chaplain second. Come."

He took her hand and with their fingers tightly tangled together, he led her out of the keep.

## Chapter 23

Triston's heart sank when he parted the bushes and pulled Siri into his former trysting place, only to find it empty.

"I promised to meet Acelet here at noon," he said. "But we lingered rather long with Perrin, and it's well past noon now. Acelet must have grown tired of waiting."

"But surely he would realize you may have been detained and return to look for you?"

Nothing was sure where Acelet was concerned, and Triston could only shrug his shoulders in response.

Siri let go of his hand and paced across the clearing. Anxiety paled the roses in her cheeks. He saw her fear for Lucianna betrayed in the quivering of her lip, but before he could speak to reassure her, her teeth bit down to still the trembling. Her delicate chin lifted, as though in defiance of her own doubts. A curious kind of pleasure wove through him at the sight, pride for her strength, her courage. But he trusted she was not so strong that she would not welcome a man's supporting arms around her, nor so brave that she would not find her courage buoyed by a comforting embrace.

He stepped forward, intending to intercept her agitated movements as she swept across the clearing and back, but before he could catch her, she stopped suddenly beside the tree stump. Triston's breath caught. For an instant, his newfound reality and joy blinked away. *Nay, not there,* his mind gasped. *Of all things, do not stand there draped in blue as you are, with your hair tumbling down your back and your eyes glowing like two muted jewels in the shade of the trees . . .* The vision enveloped him like a suffocating cloud. He saw her hands flutter together and apart again. Then they closed on the folds of her skirts and she lowered herself to sit on the stump.

He strangled the protest that surged up into his throat, but failed to suppress a muffled groan. The sound made her look up.

"What is it? Triston, what's wrong?"

He shook his head, praying his expression did not reveal what he knew it did.

Siri shrank. The remaining color fled from her cheeks and she threw a horrified glance around the clearing. She sprang up from the stump as though it had been set afire.

"Oh! This is your place, isn't it? Yours and hers?"

He could not deny it, could not deny the memory that had threatened to choke him at the sight of her sitting on Clothilde's moss-covered throne. With a look of mortified panic, Siri tried to run past him out of the clearing.

He caught her arm. "Siri, wait. I loved her here once, aye, but—"

"And she is still here. You still see her here! Do not lie. The truth is in your face."

She tried to back away but he held onto her arm and drew her inexorably closer. Slowly he lowered his head until he found and mastered the unhappy wobbling of her mouth. A subtle scent of lavender wreathed upward through his senses. Lavender. Clo had always smelled of violets.

"Come," he coaxed, "do not be afraid. I know she is gone, I know you are Siri. But I will not deny that this place had meaning for us. This is where I found her after her betrothal to Merval, wearing a gown of blue—" he saw her glance down at her own blue sleeve "—her hair sweeping her shoulders in a golden stream, her sweet face so sad and afraid—" he lifted her chin "—despairing, the way you looked a moment ago when I knew you were thinking of Lucianna."

Gently, he set a kiss to the crease between her brows, then sighed and allowed his gaze to drift back across the clearing. "I found her there, sitting on that stump, and I knelt before her in the grass and dried her tears and took her hands in mine—and uttered the first words of love I had ever spoken to a woman. And she put her arms around my neck and wept that she loved me too." Again his voice went husky. "Aye, this place has meaning for me. But," he looked down at Siri, "it does not alter what I now feel for you."

She hid her face against his breast. "How can I believe that, when I still see the memory in your eyes?"

"Then help me forget. Do not wear blue and do not sit in her place. Sit anywhere but on that stump, and there will be no one in my eyes but you."

She tightened her hold on the tunic that overlaid his mail. "I can await Acelet sitting in the grass. But I'm afraid I am wearing blue and I can think of no decorous way to change it."

Her coy words made him laugh, and hearing his reaction, she chuckled too. He ran his hands down the cloth on her arms—she wore linen, not silk like Clothilde's gown had been—until he found her hands.

"Come, then, let us do as you say and sit in the grass. For there is something more I must tell you . . . about my past."

She rolled back her head, caution returned to her eyes. "Something more about Clothilde?"

"Nay," he answered, the playful humor chased away by the grimness of the confession he knew he owed her. "Something about Osanne."

He felt her fingers stiffen. This time when she backed away, he made no attempt to stop her, though she allowed the very tips of her fingers to remain clasped in his.

"I see you have heard the rumors," he said.

"Tell me they are no more than that and I will believe you."

He heard the hopeful little catch in her voice. How he ached to give her the response she wanted! But a lie would destroy the fragile foundation he had begun to build between them this day. The truth might prove equally damaging, but she deserved no less. He could not ask her to entrust her love and life to him, in ignorance of an offense so black as to make any virtuous woman recoil in justifiable horror.

Still, he spoke tentatively, testing the waters of her possible reaction. "Gossip can be an insidious viper," he owned, "a vicious destroyer of lives. Raynor proved that with his malicious slander about me and the village wench."

"I did not think that could be true," she replied with a promptness that both relieved and shamed him for the depths that it spoke of her faith in his character, if not fully yet his heart.

"And Isobel was also a lie," she continued. "I mean about the child. Triston, why did you not tell the truth then and forestall all this grief with Raynor?"

The reluctance he had known to speak of Isobel at the bridge now became a welcome diversion from the darker confession that hovered oppressively on his tongue. He was glad enough to swallow the latter for the moment and say instead, "Because Isobel persuaded me to make one of my foolish oaths to conceal her secret."

Siri shook her head slightly, then slid her hands back into his and drew him down to sit with her in the grass. "Tell me the rest."

He loosed her clasp to pluck a wildflower that sprouted near his knee. He twirled it restlessly as he spoke. "I had told her that it was over between us, that I would not betray my friendship with her brother by despoiling her innocence. Her innocence!" The word came out like a jeer. "What a shacklebrained fool I was. It took her not a week to find herself a less scrupulous lover than I. She came to me in tears after he deserted her and pled with me to help her deflect her brother Drogo's anger. And I, young idiot that I was, had my head so filled with the gallant ideals of the newly knighted that I saw only a lady in distress. I said I would speak with Drogo and named her a day and time."

Siri must have seen the angry clenching of his hand, for she leaned forward and removed the flower before he could crush it. He watched her place it artfully behind her ear, a splash of deep orange against her bright hair. But the seething memory of Isobel robbed him of pleasure at the sight.

"What did her brother say when you confronted him?" she asked when he sat too long silent in his resentment.

"I never did confront him. Isobel and Raynor were waiting for me when I rode across the bridge. Raynor was in a rage and ordered me to dismount and when I did, Isobel weepingly accused me of being her lover. I was stunned, but when she spoke of the child, her game became blindingly clear. Until that moment I had not known there was a babe involved, but I saw at once what she hoped to do. Her real lover had deserted her. Raynor had seen her and I together in a compromising embrace. It was too easy for him to believe the lie, and she thought if she shouted it loud enough that perhaps I would marry her to prevent a scandal being attached to my name. But she reckoned without my temper and when she threw herself in my arms and started kissing me—"

"But Triston," she interrupted, no doubt hoping to preempt the tragic ending already known too well to them both, "all this does not explain why you did not tell Raynor the truth."

"I did. But when I would not name her true lover, he called my story a sham and refused to believe me. But Isobel had confided the name to me only on oath that I would not repeat it or challenge her seducer." He paused, then admitted somewhat grudgingly, "In all honesty, I think she meant it for my protection. Had I pursued the dastard as my instincts urged, it might well have brought disaster on myself and my house. Nay, do not give me that inquiring look. All I will say is this: he is one of Duke Richard's men. But his name I will not speak."

He waited for her to chide him, to remind him that Isobel was dead, to insist that it was foolish and needless to continue to honor such an oath. Her gaze on his face was weighing. But after several moments all she said was, "Then tell me about Osanne."

He looked away. He had rather relive each scene with Isobel a hundred times than speak of this to Siri. But there could be no avoiding it. Rumor had ensured that the one guilt he had thought he'd successfully buried should now be the one to stand most ominously between them.

He said in a rough tumble of words, "She was my father's wife. I seduced her. It was a sin against both him and God, a sin my father never forgave me for."

He waited in rigid dread for her reaction. Horror, revulsion, loathing—He braced himself to endure them all. But there came nothing but silence. It stretched so deep and long that he thought his lungs would burst from holding his breath. Then, just as he was about to shout at her to say something, she startled him with a flash of quiet comprehension.

"But God forgave you, didn't he?"

He glanced up and saw her eyes had narrowed on his face.

"The way you said that—'my father never forgave me'—it is his condemnation that continues to haunt you, not God's. Whatever you did, you have made your peace with Heaven about it, haven't you?"

He sighed. "It seems the only thing I have made peace about in my life."

"Then if you do not wish to tell me . . ."

He knew from the smallness of her voice that she was trying to be forbearing, but he knew that if he did not tell her, she would always wonder. Questions would turn into doubts and doubts into suspicions, gnawing their destructive way into the bonds of their trust until it crumbled away like a rotted bridge.

"Was she the seducer, or was I?" he murmured. "The most pathetic part of the story is that to this day, I do not know the answer myself."

Siri's skirts rustled as she drew up her knees. She wrapped her arms around them and hugged them to her chest. Was she withdrawing from him? Shrinking? But she only watched him steadily and waited for the rest.

"I told you when I returned from my pilgrimage and learned that Clothilde had married Merval, I tried to confront her, but she turned me away. So I went home to Vere and drank myself into a stupor. Or at least, that's what I meant to do. Only after weeks of wallowing in my drunken haze, I sobered up to hear my father's screaming accusations that I had defiled his new young wife. Osanne confessed to it, and there were just enough foggy images in my mind to make me fear it was true."

"But you don't remember?"

His mouth tightened and he stared across the clearing, seeing again Osanne's smug smile, his father's livid rage. "All I remember is that my father's trust in me was shattered. No tears, no repentance, no pleas of mine were able to restore it to the day of his death. But I had no reason not to believe it was true. Osanne was beautiful and she had been fluttering her eyes at me since the day I returned to Vere and found her married to my father. My behavior would have been lamentable enough had she been anyone else— But she was my father's wife, and that was a sin not easily absolved."

"Aye," Siri said in vigorous agreement, "'a vile sin,' as Lucianna would say. Yet you seem to be remarkably calm about it now."

His muscles tensed at the hint of recrimination in her tones. He felt a ruffling of his temper, which he made haste to snap back under control. "'Twas not a calmness easily or lightly won. The knowledge of my crime lay heavy with me. My father would not heed my tears. His chaplain had died, and the village priest only shrugged and assigned me some meaningless penance. I had nowhere to turn for relief of my sickened soul, until it came to me to offer my tears and repentance directly to God. I spent long hours in Vere's chapel imploring His pardon—difficult, anguished hours of regret and shame. And in the end I promised Him, swore to Him upon a solemn oath that if He would forgive me, I should never again raise a cup of wine to my lips nor touch a woman—" He checked and glanced at her.

She gasped. If she had not recoiled before, she did so now. "'Nor touch a woman . . . ?' You have taken a vow of *celibacy?"*

Triston made haste to reassure her.

"Nay. Oh, it was undoubtedly the vow I intended to make when I knelt before the altar in Vere's chapel. But even as the words trembled on my lips, I remembered Clothilde. Some small, desperate part of me still clung to her. She was still my wife, and the thought came to me, 'What if I should someday win her back?' I found I was not prepared to forgo the pleasures of my lawful marriage. And so I amended my oath to fall thus: 'to the day of my death, I shall touch no woman save she who is in Thy sight my wife.' I had nearly forgotten the wording of it, until Father Michel reminded me shortly after you arrived. I had meant it to refer only to Clothilde and when she died—I thought all hope of love had died with her."

He hesitated, then reached out and took one of Siri's hands, unlinking it from where it was still clasped with its twin around her knees. To his relief, she did not try to draw away.

"My father's bitterness will always pain me. But I have adhered to my two vows most strictly and I trust in God's forgiveness so long as I continue to do so. Aye, I have made my peace with Heaven in the matter of Osanne. But you, sweet Siriol." He felt her fingers tremble in his grasp. "Is your wonderful magnanimity of spirit sufficient to allow you to forgive me too?"

What the trembling signified he dared not try to surmise, but after a moment she went very still. She averted her face from his searching gaze and sat in solemn silence. His hopes sank as the minutes pulsed by and at last, slowly, sorrowfully, he released her hand. He was about to rise when her voice finally stayed him, low and intensely even.

"I am not your judge, Triston de Brielle. And I will not quarrel with Heaven's pardon."

Hope leapt in him anew. He reached for her fingers again, but she snatched them away and added more breathlessly, "Nor will I tempt you to lose it. You said that your oath was meant only for Clothilde."

But Triston seized her retreating fingers and carried them to his lips. "Aye," he murmured, so awash with relief that it left him feeling weak. "That was the intent in my heart when I spoke the words. But it was not the way the words fell. Heaven was merciful to me, sweet Siriol, more merciful than I deserved. It inspired me to form my oath in such a way that I need not close my life to love, so long as it be given its proper place."

"But—" her steady voice quavered now and threatened to break "— is not the intent of the heart what matters to God?"

He tilted her face up to his and gazed deep into her glorious, tear-brimming eyes. "So I long believed," he murmured. "But when Heaven intervenes to turn one's oath another way, we would be ungrateful not to avail ourselves of its compassion. And Father Michel has assured me that it would be no sin—were I to marry again."

Her swimming eyes widened. "Triston, are you—"

"Aye. Siriol de Calendri, I am asking you to be my wife."

# Chapter 24

**I**t took every ounce of strength that Siri possessed to choke back her joy and answer as she must.

"But, Triston, I cannot marry you." The surprise on his face blurred through her tears. "You have promised my hand to Raynor."

His face flushed and his eyes flashed black fire. "The day that villain lays another hand on you, is the last day he gazes upon the sun."

She felt her heart cracking. "But your oath—"

"I swear another oath, here and now, that I will—"

"No!" She pressed her hands, quick and hard, against his mouth. "Do not say it! Do not say anything! Remember your mother's soul and be still!"

That checked him, as she had known it would. But he caught her wrists and pressed kisses, warm and urgent, into her palms. "I will not lose you."

"Triston—"

"I will not! Tell me only this—if I can find a way to keep you without breaking my oath, will you have me for your husband?"

Surely he could not doubt her answer. She breathed it out on a sob. "Yes. Oh, yes, yes, yes . . ."

She might have whispered the word unceasingly had his swift kiss not silenced her. She wound her arms tight around his neck and returned his passion fiercely. Then, she indulged an impulse too long refrained. She slid her hands into his ebony curls and found them as thick and silky as she had dreamed.

After several moments, he pulled away, and his rueful smile set her heart thudding. "You are altogether too tempting, my lovely Siri."

"Don't stop yet." She wound her hands more tightly into his hair. "I cannot bear to leave you yet."

Desire burned bright and deep in his eyes. He set his lips lightly to one corner and then the other of her trembling mouth, then closed the shells of her lids over her eyes. Warm and gentle, his lips hovered against each lid before pressing into the little space between her brows. Slowly, the speed of his kisses began to increase, until quick and teasing, they rained down upon her cheeks, her chin, across her brow . . .

She gasped and pulled him down with her into the grass. She was not one to accept such enravishing caresses with meek and grateful passivity. She retaliated against his provocative attack by attempting to return it in kind. But it took a greater skill than she thought. One of her kisses landed just below his eye, while another fell with a smack on his eyebrow.

Triston laughed, his voice thick with amusement mingled with a husky passion. "Slowly, sweetheart. It takes practice to master this art. One must learn it first in steps. The eyes of one's beloved are closed thus—" he demonstrated again, more lingeringly "—and one must aim just so to find that spot between the brows which makes a woman shiver . . ."

She blissfully obliged him with a delicate tremor. A soft, seductive heat spread through her body. She did not want him to stop, but . . .

"Triston—"

"I know." He lifted his mouth. "You are more delicious than honey, sweet Siriol, and if I am not careful, I will devour every inch of you here and now. Just one more, and then we will return to the castle and seek Father Michel's counsel about Raynor's cursed oath."

He possessed her lips in a quick, fervent kiss. She wound her arms around his neck again. She wanted only to succumb, to lie forever in his embrace and—

*Snap.*

Her eyes, closed against their passion, flew open at the brittle crack of a twig. She saw a blur of movement over their heads, an arm swinging in the air and a glint of steel . . .

She wrenched her lips away and screamed. Triston tensed instantly, but his reaction came too late. The arm swooped down and she heard a horrible thud as something cracked into Triston's skull.

Her second scream was one of pure panic. His body slumped atop her and pinned her in a limp, suffocating weight. That glint of steel, she knew, had betokened a sword, and now Triston . . .

A shudder of terror slammed through her. Frantically she tried to free herself, wild with dread of what she might see when she did, but desperate to know how grievously he had been wounded. He was so heavy, so limp!

She had wriggled herself halfway out from under him when hands grabbed her by the shoulders and dragged her the rest of the way to set her on her feet.

"Come, he's not dead. I struck him only with the hilt of my sword. He'll have a raging headache when he awakens, I'll warrant, one I trust will keep him muddled enough to prevent him from coming after us too soon. We must be well clear of Belle Noir, carissima, before he—"

It was that endearment, spoken in mockingly familiar tones, that broke through her terror. She sent her heels flying back against her captor's shins, and followed this attack by stomping furiously on his feet. Her captor gave a yelp of pain. He freed her shoulders, but the shove that struck her in the small of her back knocked the breath from her and sent her face down into the grass.

"Cat," the voice above her hissed. "I am going to clip those nasty claws of yours before I am done."

Siri arched away from the ground and spit the grass out of her mouth. She rolled and started up, her hand on her dagger, then dropped back in horror. Raynor had not come alone. Six men stood at his back, all with swords drawn. At a signal from their master, two of them moved to stand threateningly over Triston. But it was a seventh man, held between the remaining four, that made her blood run cold. A dirty, bearded Acelet stood with blazing eyes, a gag stuffed into his mouth, and his arms pulled behind him at such an unlikely angle that she could only assume that he was bound as well.

Raynor followed her stricken gaze. "As you see, I have no further need to hold to my bargain with Triston. My erstwhile young friend has fallen into my hands betimes, thanks to you."

"You followed me," she cried. "You never meant to keep your word to Triston, to give me twenty-four hours with him. You followed us here, hoping we would lead you to Acelet."

"Of course I followed you. Did you honestly think I would give Triston a chance to despoil my bride before our wedding?"

His gleaming eyes raked her disheveled form. Her cheeks burned as she recalled the tangled embrace she and Triston had been locked in when Raynor had come upon them.

"I own," he added, in a sardonic drawl that carried a subtly withering edge, "it was the promised night I was most concerned about. I saw the way he looked at you on the riverbank, the murder in his eyes when I kissed you. He is in love with you, carissima, and from what I've just witnessed, he is hungry for you, as well. Too hungry, it would seem, to wait for the veiling modesty of night."

"Triston was not despoiling me. He has never assailed my virtue, either by day or by night. He swore you an oath, Raynor, and he would not have broken it."

"No? Then he is a better man than I. Which is, I'm afraid, more the pity for you."

He leaned down, grabbed her by the arm and hauled her roughly to her feet. His sneering smile widened as her fingers gripped her dagger, then withdrew from the hilt in defeat. She dared not defy him while his henchmen hovered over Triston's defenseless body.

He reached out a hand to pluck the orange flower from her hair and tossed it away. "Come," he said, "Lady Lucianna is waiting for you at Belle Noir, and then you and I are off to Poitiers."

"Poitiers? What do you mean to do with me there?"

"I mean to marry you, my sweet, a union even Triston will not dare to challenge."

"You are a fool if you believe that. When he realizes the dastardly way you have tricked him, he will come after us. He would not have broken his oath, had you let us be, but now that you have broken your word to him, he will no longer be bound by his."

"I would not be so sure of that," Raynor said. "I agreed to release you to him, aye, but I did not do it on oath, while Triston made his pledge before God. Triston may find it harder than he thinks to find a way out for his conscience."

He began pulling her towards the bushes that surrounded the clearing. She dug her heels into the ground, trying to resist him. She did not want to leave without first assuring herself that Triston was indeed alive and safe, but Raynor overcame her struggles with a few brisk tugs. He pushed the bushes aside and dragged her into the trees.

A grunting sound made her glance over her shoulder. She saw Acelet being shoved rudely out of the clearing by Raynor's men. One of them held the point of his sword to the young man's side, but that did not prevent Acelet from lashing out with a foot against one of his captors. He connected a well-aimed kick, but the next instant crumpled to his knees, his face twisting in pain, as the man with the sword rammed the hilt of it into his ribs.

Raynor dragged her the remaining distance to a cluster of horses.

"I trust I will not have to bind and gag you, as well," he warned. He tossed her up onto one of the beasts and mounted quickly behind her. "Get him up!"

His snapping command manifested no sympathy for Acelet's gasping attempts to reclaim the breath that had evidently been knocked out of him.

"Sir," one of his men ventured, "what are we going to do with him? He knows too much about our forays on the road, our attacks on Duke Richard's men. If Lord Fauke knew that we were the ones who—"

"Leave Lord Fauke to me," Raynor growled, "and the whelp, as well. I will deal with Master Acelet back at Belle Noir."

He gave a quick flick of the reins and galloped out of the trees, Siri trapped between his arms.

Lucianna stood in the center of Belle Noir's great hall, her auburn hair unveiled and loose about her shoulders, as it had been the last time Siri had seen her. Siri ran to her and gave her a fierce hug.

"Lucianna, I have been so worried about you. Raynor said—"

"Si, I can just imagine what that *farabutto* said," Lucianna cut her off with flaming eyes. "Give me your dagger, carissima, and I will show him—"

Siri struck her hand away from the blade. Raynor and his men had followed her into the hall, and they grinned with mocking leers at the older woman's anger.

"Do not provoke them, Lucianna," Siri said. "I have suffered no harm from them, and Triston will rescue us before I do."

That prompted a loud laugh from Raynor. "First he will have to find you. If he comes after you as you hope, he will seek you here at Belle Noir and will waste a good many days besieging these walls before he realizes I have taken you elsewhere."

Siri threw him a scornful glance. "It will not matter. As long as I am Triston's ward, you cannot marry me without his consent. Once his chaplain absolves him of that cheating oath you made him swear—"

Raynor strolled across the floor and took her chin in his hand. "Ah, now, but there may be the rub. Are you Triston's ward, or are you not?"

Her eyes widened. "Of course I am his ward! It is why you had to make him swear the oath."

"I thought the oath expedient to bind him in the event that my suspicions should come to naught. However, it may very well be, carissima, that your hand is not Triston's to give at all, but the duke's."

Even Lucianna was struck speechless by this statement for a moment, but she rallied before Siri did. "How is that possible? Donna Siri would have to be heiress to some Poitevin land."

Raynor withdrew his hand. "The answer, I trust, lies in Poitiers in the court of Duke Richard. Lord Fauke has gone there to sound the matter out, but we will not know the truth until your lady is brought there as well. I suggest you make her ready for the journey. We leave as soon as fresh horses have been saddled." To one of his men, he said, "Escort them to their chamber and wait for them while they gather their belongings."

He turned to leave, then paused and glanced back. "One more thing, carissima. See that you bring along Lord Fauke's manuscript. He has taken it in mind to make a gift of it to the duke, as soon as you have completed the illuminations. And allow me to lend you a warning. Lord Fauke is not as forbearing as I. When you are alone with him on our wedding night, either plunge your dagger straight into his heart or submit to his embrace without a murmur. Pull on him just one of the tricks you have played on me this day, and he will make you regret it with a brutal vengeance that I assure you, you've no wish to taste."

His amber eyes almost softened for a moment with an emotion Siri could not quite identify . . . sorrow? guilt? Surely not repentance, for they hardened again almost at once before he turned and strode out of the hall.

It did not take Siri and Lucianna long to gather the few belongings they had brought with them from Vere. Siri moved about the chamber mechanically, picking up a ribbon here, a stocking there, handing Lucianna her comb and mirror . . .

Despite the journey looming before them, despite Raynor's hints of an unknown inheritance, her mind slid away from the future back to the vision of Triston unconscious in the woods. Surely he had recovered by now, surely he had guessed what had happened, and where and by whom she had been taken? He would come thundering after her any moment. He would rescue her like the brave, valiant knight he was. Except—

She tried and failed to quash the practical little voice that whispered in her ear. Except that he had had no horse nearby. He would have to walk back to Vere to rouse the garrison. Surely the blow to his head would make his trek, at the very least, slow and unsteady, at the worst— She tried desperately not to think of the worst, not to think of him still lying on the forest floor, hurt and possibly bleeding, unable to rise at all.

She sank onto the bed and pressed a hand to her forehead.

"What is it, carissima?" Lucianna laid aside the gown she had been folding and came to sit beside Siri on the bed.

"Oh, Lucianna," Siri whispered, "what if he cannot come?"

"Who, carissima?"

"Triston. What if Raynor has injured him so badly that he cannot come after me?" She tried hard to still her quivering lips. "And what is this about an inheritance which would give my wardship into Duke Richard's hands? You do not think that can be true, do you?"

Lucianna frowned but lifted her handsome shoulders in a shrug. "I do not know, carissima. But there were always rumors about your father's birth, that he came of noble stock."

"But they were never anymore than rumors. Had there been land or wealth awaiting him here, he would have told Simon. And when Simon knew he was dying, he would have told me. He would not have sent me to Triston, but to—to—" Siri waved a helpless hand "—to wherever our inheritance lay."

"I do not know," Lucianna said again. "Your mother never confided the truth to me, if she knew it. But of one thing you may be sure." She left the bed to fetch a piece of white linen and carried it with the comb across to Siri. "If your hand lies within the duke's prerogative to bestow, you may be certain it will not be on Triston de Brielle."

These words so startled Siri that she did not even wince when Lucianna dropped the veil on the bed and pulled back her hair, tugging the skin around the gash in her forehead.

Lucianna was right. Duke Richard would never grant her hand to Triston, a man whom he had viewed with the deepest suspicion even before Raynor's scheming accusations of treason. Surely, *surely,* all this talk of inheritance was but another of Raynor's lies. How would she bear it to have come so near the fulfillment of Triston's love, only to have it snatched away for some bit of land or wealth that she had never desired or even heard of?

She looked up at the click of the door and tensed.

"Carissima." The word was as mocking in Raynor's mouth as it was tender in Lucianna's. "I fear you will have to leave the packing to your companion. It appears I have need of you elsewhere just now."

"Diavolo!" Lucianna dropped the comb and made another swipe for Siri's dagger.

Raynor moved swiftly to catch her wrist. He shoved Lucianna across the room as he pulled Siri off the bed, then dragged Siri into the passageway and slammed the door.

"Keep that shrew locked within," he commanded the man who stood guard outside. "If she gives you any trouble, you may deal with her however you like."

"Where are you taking me?" Siri demanded.

Raynor did not answer. She stumbled along beside him as he dragged her down the passageway to a set of stone stairs contained within a corner tower. They mounted perhaps two dozen steps, then he stopped and reached out to touch a point on the wall. Nay, it was a door, painted grey like the stones of the wall in which it was tucked.

The door swung open and Raynor pulled her into yet another, narrower passageway. There was not room for them to walk side by side, but he kept a firm grip on her wrist as he pulled her along behind him. She guessed it to be meant as a hidden means of escape in the event that an attacker burst through the outer walls to breach the keep. During a confused mêlée to defend the stairs, a knowledgeable inmate might be able to slip quickly and unseen through that covert door and flee through this slit in the wall.

There must have been hidden vents carved into the stones, for Siri could feel small drafts of air about them. The darkness was relieved by a glow, which she took to be a torch awaiting them up ahead. She scanned the walls as they reached the light and detected another painted door, positioned just to the left of the torch.

Raynor drew a key from his belt and slid it into the lock. From the way it grated and creaked as he turned it, she guessed this door to have been long forgotten, or at the very least neglected, by the castle's inhabitants. He replaced the key in his belt before he pushed the door open and pulled her inside to the chamber beyond.

Chamber? It was more like a cell. No more than four, perhaps five paces square. The only defense against an inky darkness was a single, low-burning candle set in one corner. Beside it a prisoner sat, his arms wrapped around his knees, his head bent forward to hide his face.

"I have brought you a visitor." Raynor's voice rang hollowly against the stone walls of the tiny chamber. "I trust she can make you see sense. I do not intend to tarry much longer for your decision. The horses are waiting in the bailey."

The prisoner raised his head and shouted, "You have my answer, you traitor! I am not going to put my head in the noose for you!"

"Acelet!" Siri cried. Raynor allowed her to slip away from his hold to kneel beside the young man.

"Lady Siri!" Acelet gasped, then flashed at Raynor, "You devil, why have you brought her here?"

"Because I have not the time to resort to other means. You may thank the saints, my young friend, that I am in a hurry, else you would be lying not here, but in a chamber below with one of my henchmen employing a few hot irons to persuade you to loosen your tongue. My lady, his choice is this—journey with us to Poitiers and agree to speak there the words I require of him, or remain in this cell, locked away for eternity. I am told starvation is an ugly way to die. Aye, carissima, I would counsel him very carefully—and quickly."

She took Acelet's icy fingers and squeezed them. To Raynor, she said, "You would not dare to carry out that threat. He has family and friends who will demand to know where he is."

"Few friends, I think. He has not seen fit to mingle much with the other young men of these parts. And his reputation among his own kin for dizzy, impulsive dreams is such that I imagine it would not be difficult to convince them that has simply run off to seek his fortune elsewhere."

"But you said you could not prove Triston's guilt without a confession from Acelet. If you leave him here—"

"Nay, it will be more difficult, is all. But I shall find some way to prove it. I could forge a written confession and attach Acelet's name to it.

Aye, then I could say he had fled in shame and fear of his life. Thank you, carissima, that is an excellent idea. It seems there is no reason to linger here further."

"No!" Siri shrank away from his reaching hand, even as she realized it was but a mocking feint. He did not really intend to take her away yet. A written confession might be challenged. But Acelet standing before the duke, admitting his guilt and accusing Triston—that was evidence the duke would not be able to ignore.

"Then convince him to come with us, carissima," Raynor said. "But do not take too long. I will not give Triston a chance to surround these walls again."

"Nothing she can say is going to convince me to—"

"Acelet, hush," she scolded. She was not prepared to underestimate Raynor's ruthless resolve at this point. She had to get Acelet safely out of this cell. Then together, perhaps, they could plan an escape. "Let me talk with him alone," she said to Raynor. "Just a few minutes. I will persuade him. But Raynor, you must give him a better choice than death at your hand or the duke's."

"Such as? I will not see him set free to recant his words and lay at my feet a charge of highway robbery and treason."

"Then let him be imprisoned at the duke's discretion."

Raynor shook his head. "Even had I the power to name such a judgment, it would be fraught with the same dangers for me. As long as he has a tongue with which to speak, I would stand at risk of exposure. Nay, I will not intercede for him other than to ask Lord Fauke to plead him a more merciful execution than the standard traitor's fate. For his free confession, he may win himself a simple hanging. I assure you, that would be preferable to either being drawn and quartered—" she felt Acelet shudder "—or left to waste miserably away in this cell."

Despite his display of dread, Acelet began a defiant response, but Siri shushed him again. "You see?" she said. "He will not listen to me while you are standing there. Go away. Give me a few minutes alone with him and I promise he will not defy you further."

Raynor hesitated. Siri had to press Acelet's fingers hard to keep him quiet.

"Very well," Raynor said at last. "But do not take long. I will be waiting just outside the door."

He closed it behind him with a bang and Siri heard the scrape of the key as he locked them in.

The chamber seemed to become smaller, more oppressively dismal and dank once she realized how thoroughly they were sealed off from the rest of the world. The terrors of existing in a place like this for long would become suffocating, then maddening. To be abandoned, forgotten, left to rot out one's days in darkness and silence, to know that rescue was vain and hope a delusion . . . Surely those horrors would overwhelm one long before the pangs of hunger or thirst!

"Acelet." She did not know why she whispered, except that her throat suddenly seemed painfully constricted. "You cannot stay here."

"I'm not going to go to Poitiers. I'm not going to say what he wants me to." If Raynor's threats had intimidated him, it did not show in his stubborn response.

She tried to swallow and found that she could not. "Acelet—"

"Lady Siri, he wants me to call Triston a traitor, but Raynor is the blackest traitor of all! I thought he followed the Young King for love, but it was only profit he wanted, as it was only profit he sought when he attacked all those travelers on the road. He told me he did it in the Young King's name, to harass Duke Richard's bullying henchmen, but it was all a lie. It was only their gold he wanted. He confessed it when he came before."

"Before?"

"After they took you and me in the woods. Raynor had two of his men bring me to this cell and lock me up in the dark. Then Raynor brought a candle and told me what he wanted me to do. He is going to betray the Young King's secrets, and he wants me to help him do it. Well, I won't! I am not a coward and I won't be bullied into informing on my lord."

From the fervor of his words, Siri knew it would do no good to remind him that the Young King was not, in fact, his lord.

"How long have you known that there was a conspiracy?" she asked, then held her breath for his answer. If it should be revealed to the duke that there was a plot and that Acelet had known of it and kept silent, the consequences for this impulsive young man would be dire indeed.

"Raynor told me. When he came here to threaten me earlier."

Then he had not known from the beginning. Good. There was a chance to turn the tables on Raynor yet. She let out her breath, then took another, deeper one. She knew her next words were going to meet with resistance.

"Acelet, you have got to come with us to Poitiers. We will make a preemptive strike. You will tell the duke what Raynor has revealed to you, that he is part of the conspiracy. The duke's wrath will then fall where it belongs, on Raynor rather than you and Triston."

She was not surprised to see Acelet shake his head. "Whatever the Young King is planning, I will not be the one to expose it. Nay, I will raise my own sword to his cause when he returns to free us from Richard the tyrant."

Siri had to lace her fingers together to stop herself from slapping him for this foolish reply. "The only thing talk like that is going to win you is a ride to the gallows. Weren't you listening to Raynor? If you do not speak first, he will see you hanged for his own guilty knowledge, and Triston—" Now she was the one who shuddered. "Acelet, you have got to do it. If you tell them everything Raynor has told you, if you give them names and—"

"But I don't know any names. Raynor did not give me any details. I suppose he thinks it better for his own safety to wait until we are in Poitiers, until just before I make my 'confession,' to confide such information to me—so that I cannot do exactly what you're asking me to do."

There was a hint of reproof in his voice, as if he could not expect her to understand the demands of manly loyalty, but was nevertheless disappointed that she did not.

Siri bowed her head, frustration and despair tickling over her flesh. She knew there would be no changing his mind. That left them only one option.

"I will not allow you to destroy yourself and Triston to serve a hopeless cause," she said. "We must get you away from Belle Noir. We must get you back to Vere."

Acelet gave a harsh laugh. "I don't think Raynor is of a mind to let me go."

"You must pretend that I have persuaded you to come with us to Poitiers. We will find a way for you to escape along the way."

"Even if we did, I would not abandon you to his dastardly hands."

She reached out and brushed her fingers against his cheek. His stubble of beard startled her for a moment, but she did not draw away, even when he caught her wrist and turned his head to press his lips into her palm.

"Acelet," she said more softly, "I appreciate your devotion, but I need your courage to serve me in another way now."

"Devotion? Lady Siri, you know it is more than that. I love—"

"Do not say it. It is not love you feel for me. Yes, I know you think otherwise now, but one day when you feel your heart take flight at the smile of some winsome lass, you will realize how silly you have been. And you will be very glad then that I had the good sense to remain only your friend."

"You are wrong." His voice came muffled, a hot breath inside her hand. "I would lay down my life for you."

She smiled. "I do not doubt that. Just as I do not doubt the depths of unselfishness you revealed when you tried to help Raynor win my hand at the expense of your own emotions. Nay, do not chide yourself for it now. You could not know what Raynor had in mind."

"He swore he would cherish you like a priceless pearl. The way—The way I always wanted to cherish Clothilde. Only I knew—that she did not love me anymore than you do." His voice cracked. "I was so angry at Triston for failing her, so certain that he would fail you too—"

"I know." She stroked his bearded cheek. "It took a strong, selfless heart to support another man's suit, when I know how much you wished to win me for yourself. And that is why I know that I can trust you now—"

"—to go to Triston," Acelet finished. He turned her hand about and kissed her fingers, then let her go. "He does love you, you know? I mean he loves *you.*"

*Pray heaven, let it be true,* Siri thought. Then she felt a quickened patter in her breast, a whisper of doubt that startled and unnerved her.

She was thankful for the darkness to hide her guilty blush and said, before Acelet could pursue the topic of his cousin's affections, "We have not much time to lay a plan. Raynor will be returning any moment. If you are to escape, you will need a weapon." She slid her jeweled dagger out of its sheath and pressed it into Acelet's hands. "Take this. Have you somewhere about you that you can hide it?"

She felt Acelet start. "And leave you undefended? Nay!"

"It is of no use to me. Raynor watches me too closely. What about here, in your boot?" She pulled the soft leather away from his calf.

He slid it tentatively in. "They will see it," he said.

"Not if you put it on the inside of your leg, like this. At least it will be less noticeable there. But you must push the hilt all the way down so they can't see the jewels. Gently! You will cut yourself!"

Acelet positioned it as she suggested. The weapon, designed by her brother for his diminutive sister, was smaller than a man's weapon. That made its concealment easier. Raynor would not see it in the dim light of the passageway, and hopefully his guards would not notice it either.

"I don't like it," Acelet said. "I don't like the thought of leaving you behind with Raynor."

"You cannot save me alone. You will need help, and only Triston can give you that."

"But—"

There was a grating sound, a click, and the door swung open.

"Time's up, carissima. What is our young friend's decision?"

She stood up and calmly shook out her skirts. "He is coming with us, of course."

"Well done." She stiffened as Raynor's arm slid around her waist. "One wonders how you managed to persuade him. I trust you have done nothing to make me jealous. I'm sure Acelet would have enjoyed a few furtive kisses in the dark." He laughed. "Not that I think so smitten a sapling as he would have the slightest clue of how to enjoy a woman like you. I have offered to introduce him to a village wench or two, but he prefers his own bemused dreams."

Acelet shot to his feet. "I'll show you how bemused I am. I am not going to Poitiers! And if you don't get your dirty hands off of her—"

"Acelet, don't!" Siri cried.

Raynor's sneering voice took on a malicious edge. "Alas, carissima, perhaps you should have given him more than kisses. I said your time was up. If he does not come with us, so be it. He will he stay. And may Heaven have mercy on his lonely cries, for they shall find none from—"

Siri felt rather than saw the blur of Acelet's fist as it whizzed past her face in the dark and silenced the rest of this threat. There was an earsplitting crack and Raynor's arm sprang free from her waist. An instant later, she heard the thud of his body as it landed in the passageway outside the open door.

Amazed, not only by Acelet's bold action, but by the speed and accuracy of his blow, she stepped across the threshold to view the damage. The light of the torch revealed Raynor slumped on the floor against the opposite wall, so stunned an expression on his face that Siri knew instantly that Acelet's escape lay, not along the road, but in this very moment.

"Run!" She grabbed Acelet's arm and dragged him into the passageway, then gave him a desperate push. "*Run!*"

"But— I—" He caught her hand. "Come with me."

Panic lent her the strength to pull away. "Nay, I will slow you down. Go! Go!"

Acelet hesitated, then turned on his heel and fled down the passageway.

Raynor clambered to his feet, the surprise on his face flooded out by a deadly fury. He let loose an explosive curse. Once he reached the stairs and sounded an alarm, Acelet would be lost.

Siri grabbed the torch out of its bracket and swished it warningly at Raynor, blocking the way that Acelet had gone. "Stay back, or I will singe your face black to match your heart."

Raynor sprang back with another startled, angry oath. "You are heaping sins upon your head, carissima. My hand will fall sore on you for this."

"We shall see who is sore when I set you aflame." She made a jab with the torch, careful not to actually touch him, but reveling in the way her feint made him flinch.

She could not tell, as he recovered himself, whether it was the fire or rage that made his face so red.

"You are doing that whelp no service. My men will cut him down in the yard."

"Not without your command, I think. They may try to stop him, but he has surprise on his side and I am guessing that his feet are as swift as his fist."

"Aye, he took me unawares, but I do not make the same mistake twice. And in case you were wondering where the remainder of this passageway leads, there is more than one exit and one set of stairs that leads away from this cell."

He turned away sharply from her threatening flame and strode off into the darkness.

Siri had no choice but to follow him. She did not have the nerve to actually set him on fire, which was the only way she could think of stopping him.

Obviously aware of the time he had lost in his confrontation with her and her torch, Raynor increased his speed to a lope and then a run. Siri soon wished she had left the torch in its bracket. The narrow walls made it difficult to hold the flame at a comfortable distance to her side and impossible to safely run with it. She would set her own hair on fire! She walked as swiftly as she dared while maneuvering the torch the best she could, but her cheeks were throbbing with heat and sweat rolled off her brow by the time she reached the door.

Raynor was nowhere in sight on the stairs. Siri paused for the length of a single breath, but it seemed obvious where both he and Acelet had gone. Unless Acelet knew of a secret postern gate like the one at Vere, there would be only one way out of Belle Noir.

By the time Siri reached the bailey still carrying her torch, the yard was in chaos. Raynor stood cursing and shouting frantic commands at his men, who again and again lunged in vain at the flaxen-haired young man who zigged and zagged with remarkable speed and success around them. The gate stood open in expectation of Raynor's departure for Poitiers, and the only thing Acelet yet lacked to make good his escape was a horse.

Raynor's men must have been awaiting their master dismounted, for all sought to block Acelet's path on foot. Siri watched as he bolted towards an abandoned palfrey.

"Stop him! You fools! You idiots! If he gets away, I shall have every one of you flayed!"

Raynor's bellowing threat sent another cluster of men flying after Acelet. Siri watched with horror as one of them outstripped the others and reached his target at the same moment that Acelet set his foot to the stirrup.

The man spun Acelet away from the horse, then whirled a great broadsword at his head. Siri screamed and dropped her torch. Her hands flew over her eyes. Ah, saints! He could not have evaded such a deadly thrust! Could he?

Sick with dread, she hesitantly spread her fingers and peeked at where she was certain she would see Acelet lying in a pool of blood.

But Acelet was still on his feet. How he had dodged the blow she would never know, but the swiftness with which he now darted down and came back up with her dagger hinted at the answer. His newly revealed talent for speed again stood him in good stead. The sword sliced again over his ducking head, then Acelet made a lunge of his own. He and his attacker locked together. Then the blade fell from the swordsman's hand. He stumbled two steps backwards, clutching at a spreading red stain on his chest, fell into the horse, and slumped like water onto the ground.

Still holding the dagger in his right hand, Acelet grabbed up his fallen opponent's blade with his left and whirled about just in time to swing a parallel arc to the ground of sufficient force and menace to send a group of would-be captors springing back out of reach. Acelet sprang over the fallen man's body, leapt into the saddle, and set the steed thundering across the yard.

"Curse you, lower the gate!"

A jarring whine of machinery responded to Raynor's order. As Acelet galloped between the twin towers of the gatehouse, great iron-tipped spikes soared downwards to close off his path. Acelet wore no spurs, but Siri saw him pounding his booted heels into the horse's flanks. One second slower and he and his horse might have been snapped in half. But instead they flew across the drawbridge, and the portcullis banged down in the dust of the steed's flashing heels.

# Chapter 25

Triston waited. His vision had cleared since he'd regained consciousness in the woods, but sickening waves of pain still slapped back and forth inside his skull. He stood, steadying himself with one hand against the small chapel's altar, confident that he was about to receive the absolution he needed to find Siri and fetch her safely back to Vere.

"I am sorry, my son. But deceitfully compelled or not, the words were nevertheless spoken to God. I'm afraid I cannot release you from your vow."

Triston thought for a moment that the roar in his ears must have muddled his understanding of the chaplain's response. "Father . . . after all I have told you, surely you are not suggesting that I surrender the Lady Siri to Raynor?"

"You said you swore to their marriage on your oath." The sadness in the chaplain's face was rivaled only by his quiet resolve. "I did not know your mother, my son, but your servants speak of a gentle, pious woman who well served her husband and sons. Nevertheless, even the most pious of us fall short of the perfection of God and require the purification of the flames of purgatory 'ere we become worthy of His kingdom. I am not suggesting that the wording of the oath imposed upon you holds such power as to actually bind your mother to that suffering forever. But Saint Augustine taught clearly the exquisite anguish of the purgatorial flames, even upon those whose sins were light, as well as the power of the prayers of the living on behalf of the deceased, to shorten the time of their suffering. If you care not for the risk to your own soul should you break such an oath, I would counsel you to consider carefully your mother's pains before you—"

"Blazes," Triston exploded, "I do not need a sermon about the nature of purgatory or the consequences awaiting my mother's soul if you do not release me from this oath!"

He let go of the altar to pace an unsteady line across the chapel floor and back. A muscle twitched furiously away in his jaw. He locked his hands behind him in a numbing grip. He longed to seize Father Michel and forcibly shake from him the answer he wanted to hear, but he knew neither sympathy nor coercion would cause the chaplain to speak otherwise than his conscience bade him. Devil take his honest priest!

Even through the still-throbbing haze of his brain, Triston realized what had happened in the woods. Raynor must have followed them, intent on catching Acelet and making off with Siri before Triston could think of a way to stop him. The blow of the chaplain's rejection of Triston's argument that Raynor had broken his word and that thereby Triston should be released from his, reverberated as strongly through every cell of Triston's body as the pounding in his head. As if from a distance he heard Father Michel dolefully reasserting that where Triston had sworn to his words on an oath, Raynor had done no more than make a simple promise. It was dishonorable of him to break it, yes, but it placed no one's soul at risk, least of all Raynor's own.

Triston impatiently waved the chaplain's words away, then stopped and raised a hand to the swelling on the back of his head. What the devil had Raynor struck him with? He winced, then pressed his palms against his temples. *Blazes,* there was not time for this! He had to think clearly, to reach beyond this throbbing pain. The hot fury in his breast threatened to drive him again to Belle Noir's walls and to scale them in fire and blood. But Raynor would be expecting that. Triston saw again the awful vision of Siri dangling over the castle's walls, sustained only by his enemy's vengeful hand. Even had Triston been prepared to forsake his oath, a frontal assault on Belle Noir would likely only provoke another savage threat to Siri's safety.

But he could not just stand here and do nothing. Siri needed him. Her sweet face had become the breath of life and hope for him. Without her, the grief, the guilt, the oppressive despair of loneliness would overwhelm him finally and forever. She had become the saving light in his otherwise empty life, and if he were to lose her now, what would there be left for him to live for?

"Papa?"

Triston turned as the breathless, childish voice seemed to answer his aching question.

"Perrin."

The boy stood in the doorway, his blue eyes bright with an excitement that had him fairly bouncing on the threshold. Triston dropped to one knee and held out his arms. He saw how they shook and struggled to master himself. Would the boy come to him?

"Perrin—"

"Papa . . ."

The boy took a few tentative steps towards his father, hesitated, then apparently overcome by whatever had excited him so, ran the few remaining steps between them.

Triston could not stop himself. He caught the boy and crushed him to his chest. Perrin squirmed. Triston squeezed his eyes shut against the sudden stinging beneath his lids. He clutched his son in his arms a long moment, pleading with the Heavens that the struggles might still, that he might feel the small arms encircle his neck, that he might cradle his son quiet and trusting and loving . . .

But Perrin continued to wiggle and mumble into Triston's breast. He wanted loose. He was still afraid. Triston smothered a broken sigh and let him go.

". . . and it looks like he is wearing rags and his face is funny and . . ."

The rest of Perrin's panted words were lost in Triston's surprise. His son did not look panicked. His cheeks were so rosy as to be almost flushed, his eyes glowed, not with fear but with excitement, and his spilling words were not a frantic plea for escape, but—

"Perrin, wait. Slow down. What are you talking about?"

"I have been trying to tell you, if you would let me breathe," Perrin said. "Papa, Acelet has come home."

"Acelet?"

"I saw him from the window, riding through the gates on a big grey horse. Yes, I know I was supposed to be in bed, but—"

"Perrin, you cannot see the gates from your window."

"I know, but I can from Siri's. I mean the one in her workshop. I wanted to talk to her, but I couldn't find her, and I couldn't find you either, so I waited for her in her workshop. I was looking through her big book with all the pictures that she draws. And then I heard some shouting and went to the window to see what was happening in the yard, and Acelet was just riding through the gate and Sir Balduin was limping to meet him and—"

"Perrin—" Triston grabbed the boy by the shoulders "—are you sure it was Acelet you saw?"

"Of course I'm sure."

Acelet had been hiding in the woods on foot. Why would he be returning to Vere on a horse?

"You said his face looked funny. Might it have been someone else?"

Perrin shook his head. "It's Acelet. I think he is growing a beard. And his clothes are all torn and with his long hair, he looks like a wild man. But I know it is he."

Triston was halfway to the door before he felt Perrin on his heels. He stopped and turned to his son. "I want you to stay here with Father Michel."

"But I want to see Acelet too."

"Not now."

"But he might know something about Siri." Perrin's bright blue eyes turned sober now and worried. "She didn't come back with you, did she? After you told me about Mama—" his voice quavered, but to Triston's relief, the blue eyes remained dry "—and Siri put me to bed, you went off somewhere together. And now you are here, but she's still gone. And she said she couldn't stay with us anymore. Maybe Acelet will know why.

Papa, please let me come."

He caught Triston's hand and pulled pleadingly on it. Triston hesitated, torn between wanting to cling to this evidence of newfound trust by his son and wanting to shield him from whatever dark news Acelet might carry of Siri.

"Perrin," Father Michel said, "do not quarrel with your father. If Acelet brings word of the Lady Siri, I'm sure your father will tell you. Come, I will take you back to your bed."

Perrin let go of Triston's hand and turned on the chaplain with a flash of temper Triston knew his son had inherited from himself.

"I don't want to go to bed! I'm not sick!"

The chaplain answered calmly, "Well, let us test that, then. You have suffered a nasty bump on your head. Let us see how badly it has scrambled your brain. Can you tell me the Latin verb for 'obey'?

Triston smiled, but Perrin's face went sulky, for he was quick enough to catch the rebuke in the question. He mumbled something.

"I beg your pardon," the chaplain said. "I didn't quite understand your answer."

"It is *parere,*" Perrin repeated loudly.

"Excellent. And the conjugations? You may begin with the present indicative active in the singular form."

*"Pareo, pares, paret."*

"And the plural?"

*"Paremus, paretis—"*

Triston went out on *parent,* marveling that one form of the Latin verb for obedience should be so similar to the French word for the begetters of a child.

Later he would reflect on the significance of that, but just now— He quickened his pace, his long strides carrying him swiftly out to the bailey. He arrived in time to see Sir Balduin steering a bedraggled-looking Acelet across the yard.

Acelet caught sight of Triston and began to run. "Cousin!"

"Acelet."

Triston caught him by the shoulders and held him at arms-length. He remembered the beard from their encounter in the woods and now, in the unfiltered light of the sun, took full inventory of his cousin's stained and tattered clothes. His long, flaxen hair had become a nest for a variety of leaves, twigs, and grass. Acelet had always been of slender build, but now he was even thinner. Forest life clearly had not agreed with him.

"You return to Vere well mounted." Triston nodded at the champing grey horse whose reins were being held by one of his grooms.

"I took it from one of Sir Raynor's men," Acelet gasped. "I had to— I—"

At first, Triston thought Acelet was merely out of breath. Then he felt the shudder that ran through his cousin's body.

"What is it?"

"The horse— I had to fight the man for it. I–I think I may have killed him." Acelet's hand shook as he drew a familiar jeweled dagger from his belt. "Siri gave me this. He would have killed me if I hadn't used it. B–but—"

Triston took one glance at the bloodied blade and returned his gaze to his cousin's white face. Acelet's eyes fell, as if he were ashamed of his display of emotion. His voice hoarsened into a whisper.

"It slid into him so easily. I did not even think what I was doing. Suddenly the blade was just in him. And his face, just before he fell—"

Triston pressed his shoulders, trying to steady him. Triston had wielded his blade strongly and lethally in defense of both his home and his duke, but that first time—that first life taken—was a memory one never forgot.

He took Acelet's arm and guided him towards the keep.

"It is better not to have time to think at moments like that," Triston said. "Killing is never easy, even in battle. But it is too often one of the demands of those who bear the arms of knighthood. You will be twenty-one soon, Acelet. You are going to have to decide just how badly you wish to win those arms."

Acelet said nothing more until they reached the great hall. The best thing Triston could do for Acelet now, he knew, was to turn his cousin's thoughts away from the man in Belle Noir's yard. Triston sent Sir Balduin off to fetch some wine, then seated Acelet in his own carved chair on the dais.

"What news do you bring?" Triston asked then. "I presume Siri is in Raynor's hands?"

Siri's name appeared to shake Acelet from his gloominess. "Aye. He is taking her to Poitiers."

"Poitiers? What does he mean to do with her there?"

"He means to marry her." Acelet's blue eyes flashed and some of the color returned to his face. "In the duke's court. And he says that you will not be able to stop him."

Triston thought of his oath. Siri, the oath, his mother's soul . . . Frustration welled into his mouth again. There had to be a way to answer the demands of them all.

"You'll go after her, won't you?"

Triston moved to stare out one of the barred windows into the courtyard. It was nearly dusk and Sir Rollo was just disbanding his drill with another group of serving boys.

"Aye." Triston wrapped his fingers around one of the cold, iron bars. In the fading light, his clenched knuckles shone pale as ivory. "I will go to Poitiers. But how to stop this marriage—I know not."

Triston heard the scraping of the chair as Acelet sprang to his feet. "You're not going to let him do it? Marry her himself, then give her to Lord Fauke?"

"Lord Fauke?" Triston swung around. "What about Lord Fauke?"

"Raynor taunted me with it before he brought Siri to my cell. He has promised Lord Fauke *jus primae noctis* with her, in return for his support of their marriage."

"The devil he has!" Triston took a step towards the dais with a snarl that sent Acelet darting behind the chair.

"Aye." Acelet recovered himself as Triston stopped. "And he says you cannot stop him because her hand is no longer yours to give."

Raynor must have been thinking of Triston's oath when he said that. The fox thought he had his enemy squarely backed into a corner. But if he believed Triston would stand by and allow Lord Fauke to ravish Siri—

Triston did not know what expression came into his face when the world shifted into a blood-red mist, as it did for him now, but he saw Acelet clutch the back of the chair as though he thought he might need it for some sort of shield. Then the image of Acelet blinked out, replaced by a vision of Triston's hands wrapped around Raynor's throat and his dagger in Lord Fauke's heart.

Fire scorched through his veins at the prospect of turning vision into truth. He snapped about on his heel.

*Remember what your temper wrought with Isobel.*

Stubbornly, he pushed the whispering voice aside. His steel sword hissed as he pulled it from the scabbard at his side. He strode towards the arched exit way of the hall, a single intent raging in his heart. Before another day passed, he would see Raynor's blood in the dust.

If Raynor rested the night at Belle Noir, Triston would meet him when he rode through his gates in the morning.

*Remember Isobel.*

If he had already started for Poitiers, Triston and his men would ride to cut them off.

*Remember Isobel.*

Once and for all, he would end this feud, and when he was through, there would not be enough of Raynor left for men to recall that he had ever walked upon the earth. He would strike the villain once for Clothilde.

*Remember . . .*

Once for the days of trust he had lost with his son.

*Remember . . .*

And he would strike the deathblow for Siri…

*Remember . . .*

. . . for Siri . . .

"No!" Triston slammed his sword against the arched frame of the exit way, sparks flying at the violent contact of steel striking stone.

"What is it?" Acelet had followed Triston across the floor and stood staring at the trembling sword in his hand.

"I can't."

"What do you mean, you can't?"

Triston plunged his free hand into his hair and squeezed shut his eyes. *Blazes, where are my senses?* Raynor would not venture out of Belle Noir without Siri by his side, and Triston dared not attack him while she was still in his hands. That obstinate whisper had been right. An impulsive burst of anger had cost Isobel de Molinet her life. Reacting now, while in another rage, could well cost Siri the same. He must not allow himself to forget her crumpled body at the foot of the stairs, her dangling form over the walls of Belle Noir. Raynor's hatred for him was absolute. If Triston attacked him directly, there was no telling what further harm his mad revenge might inflict on Siri.

"Triston?"

He ignored Acelet's bewildered voice. It was not rage, but coolheaded judgment he needed now if he were to save her. Slowly, deliberately, he drew in several lungfuls of air. He kept on breathing until his blood began to cool and the red mist faded from before his eyes.

"Triston, what's wrong?"

Slowly, Triston returned his sword to its scabbard. "I have sworn an oath. I cannot challenge Raynor in the matter of the marriage. And I dare not confront him on the road to Poitiers."

Acelet looked incredulous. "But—"

Sir Balduin returned, carrying a tray with a goblet and a bottle of wine. He attempted to hand the cup to Acelet, but Acelet pushed it away so hard that the liquid splashed out and stained Sir Balduin's sleeve.

"You are just going to abandon her?" Acelet cried. "If you're afraid, then give me your sword. I will defend her honor to the last drop of my blood!"

"You have a sword of your own," Triston snapped, "if you can remember where you've laid it."

Acelet colored at the jibe. Triston stopped and took another breath. He would not lose his temper again.

He added more levelly, "Sir Rollo says you know well how to use your sword in theory, but today you have experienced the blade's practical application and witnessed its potentially mortal effects. Are you sure it is an experience you wish to repeat?"

As quickly as he had flushed, Acelet now paled, but after several watchful moments, Triston observed that his cousin's mouth remained firm.

"I will do whatever needs be done," Acelet said, "to save Siri from that treacherous dog."

The passionate words and stalwart stance encouraged Triston. For Siri's sake, Acelet just might make a knight yet.

"There may well be more blood spilled before this is over," Triston said, "and you, as well as I, may have a hand in spilling it. I will welcome your sword at my side. But Acelet, make no mistake. Siri belongs to me. And you must let me decide how and when to bring her home."

Acelet frowned. "But you said you would not challenge the marriage."

Triston watched as Sir Balduin refilled the goblet and handed it to Acelet. Acelet took the cup this time. He hesitated, as though he intended first to pursue this quarrel with his cousin. But the ruby liquid seemed to beckon him powerfully and after a moment of apparent indecision, he gulped the wine down so fast that some of it ran out the corner of his mouth and trickled into his flaxen beard.

Acelet wiped his mouth with the back of his hand, then held out the cup for more and drank as greedily as before. One would think he had had nothing to drink for days. Again, Triston observed how thin he'd grown. His flaxen locks dirty and tangled, his tunic tattered, his hose torn at the knees, one of his boots ripped so badly that it was a wonder it remained on his foot . . .

Triston's eyes narrowed. *A wild man,* Perrin had called Acelet, and so he looked. Wild. Hungry. Exhausted. A sorry state for any man to find himself in. And for a noble-blooded squire to be brought so low—

"You must be famished," Triston said abruptly.

"Aye," Acelet admitted. "I caught a rabbit one day, but mostly I have been subsisting on berries and water from the river. I suppose I should have paid more attention when Etienne tried to show me how to fish."

Triston smiled at this reference to his brother's favorite recreation. "Well, you will not go hungry tonight. Sir Balduin, tell Cook to prepare

Acelet a feast. You may eat to your heart's content, cousin, though I must ask you to go sparingly on the wine. Perhaps Cook will remember how to reproduce one of those fragrant waters Siri introduced at her banquet and has served a time or two since. They really are quite good."

"Triston—"

"Acelet, I said I would bring her home."

"But how?"

Triston studied Acelet's disheveled state another moment. He had begun to see his way.

"Raynor is not the only one with a trick or two in his bag. I take seriously my obligations as head of the de Brielle house, and I do not intend to turn my head to any indignities heaped upon my kin."

Acelet opened his mouth to demand his meaning, but again Triston forestalled him. He turned to Sir Balduin.

"After my cousin has eaten, get him a bath and shave off that beard. He cannot appear in the duke's court looking like some peasant we picked up along the road. And Acelet, before you go to bed, I want a full account of everything that has passed between you and Raynor." He saw his cousin's hesitance and repeated, "Everything. That includes anything you may know about any plot with the Young King. Remember—" he added as Acelet's mouth went mulish— "it is for Siri."

The rebellion did not entirely die out of Acelet's face, but Triston took comfort in its perceptible ebbing. Pray heaven his cousin's devotion to Siri would finally outweigh this dangerous and misguided zealotry of his!

"Sir," Sir Balduin inquired, "will we be riding, then, to Poitiers?"

"Aye. We will leave at dawn, if Acelet can rouse himself by then. Allow him one more cup of wine with his meal and then only water. I know he is thirsty, but I don't want him drunk."

Sir Balduin left to carry out his orders.

Acelet said, "Raynor is not going to wait until dawn. He will be on the road right now and when he gets Siri to Poitiers—"

"He will do nothing. Not until he is certain he can flaunt it in my face. Nay, he will wait until I come there to make his move with her—if he does not decide to make his move against me first."

"He is going to accuse you before the duke."

"I know. But he is missing a rather essential piece of the puzzle, isn't he? He is missing you."

Acelet's head lowered a little. "You were right about him. He was just using me." He paused and his head sank almost to his breast. "I suppose you were right about me too. I've been nothing but a fool."

"Nay," Triston murmured, "you have only been young. And perhaps I should have been a little more patient."

He flung his arm about his cousin's hunched shoulders and led him back to the dais.

# Chapter 26

Raynor and his men rode with their captives through the night. They arrived in Poitiers just after daybreak, clattering into the yard of the ducal palace. Raynor spoke a word and a half-dozen serving maids whisked Siri away from Lucianna's side.

Siri silently cursed Raynor and racked her brains for some way to counter his imminent scheme to destroy Triston. But she had no time alone even to rest from their madcap ride. The maids bore her through a labyrinth of corridors to a chamber where they bathed and attired her in a pearl gray tunic, overlaid with a surcote of delicate blue-green silk with scrolling embroidery worked along the wide cuffs of the sleeves. No sooner had they looped a girdle with amber studs about her hips and set a diaphanous white veil over her braided hair, than a knock fell on the chamber door.

A gentleman stood in the passageway. The quality of his crimson tunic, his smooth ringleted hair, and the badge on his shoulder all proclaimed him to belong to some great man's household. Naturally enough, Siri's artistic curiosity lingered, not on his face, but on the image wrought on his badge.

Startled and appalled, she only just stopped her hand from darting up to sketch the sign of the cross against her breast. On the man's shoulder coiled what she had first taken for a serpent. Now she recognized it as a woman with flowing hair whose voluptuous body dissolved at the waist into a writhing serpentine tail. Any doubt that the image was intended to be demonic was dispelled by a sinisterly embroidered smile and tiny winking eyes of red glass.

"Lady Siriol de Calendri?" the gentleman inquired.

Siri forced her gaze away from the unnerving image he wore. "Yes."

"My master the duke requests that you attend him in his mother's solar. If you would allow me to escort you?"

Siri forced herself not to panic at this politely couched command. She needed to remain calm and clearheaded if she were to thwart Raynor's plan. She placed her hand on the gentleman's crimson sleeve and let him lead her away from the chamber.

A barking command dismissed the gentleman when they reached the queen's solar. Siri sank into a deep curtsy, but not before she had glimpsed a semicircle of unfamiliar gentlemen, together with Lord Fauke and Raynor, standing near a gaily painted chair where sprawled a young man wearing a gold coronet.

Several nerve-racking moments passed before the same voice that had sent the gentleman way, invited her to rise.

"Come forward, Lady Siriol," the rich, baritone voice finally bade her. "Lord Fauke, pray lend the lady your arm."

Siri had no choice but to accept Lord Fauke's quickly proffered arm and allow him to lead her towards the young man in the chair. She took in the rest of the chamber on a glance, the window seats scattered with silken pillows, three more carved and painted chairs, a red padded stool, and an empty hearth. Carved into the stone above the hearth and painted a vibrant red were six flowers with six petals each, connected to one another by swirling, painted green tendrils. The same floral motif garlanded the whitewashed walls just above the floorboards and below the ceiling, completely encircling the room.

Six tapestries completed the scene, each depicting brightly attired couples playfully engaged in a various amorous sports. She remembered Acelet's tales of how Queen Eleanor had conducted her Courts of Love between the walls of this very palace. Might some of her famous judgments have been offered in this room?

Lord Fauke stopped before the young man in the chair and bowed, signaling Siri to make another curtsy.

"Sire, allow me to present to you the Lady Siriol de Calendri, daughter of Lord Walter Geraud."

Siri almost lost her balance on hearing this title spoken before her father's name. She quickly gathered her wits, reminded herself that it was only another one of Raynor's tricks, and completed her curtsy as gracefully as she had begun.

She met the bemused expression in the duke's deep azure eyes as she rose. As he sat for a moment in obvious but silent admiration of her beauty, she took the opportunity to study him as well.

He was a large, muscularly built young man. Gowned in a robe of royal blue silk, jewels flashed from his girdle and his gold-linked collar, while his long, be-ringed fingers fiddled absently with a pendant hanging from a gold chain around his neck. The jewel-studded coronet sat at a rakish angle on hair as richly burnished as Siri's. He sprawled in his chair with a negligent pride she guessed only a prince of recognizably superior birth would dare in the present noble company. Or so she judged the attending gentlemen by their attire. She could not tell the duke's height, but he looked to be long-limbed, and the breadth of his shoulders rivaled Triston's.

He possessed a high brow, ruddy cheeks, and strong, aquiline nose. Behind the bemusement in his eyes, she read a shrewd and alert intelligence. She guessed him to be very near her own age, and while she suspected that petulance was not unknown to his beautifully molded mouth, the cast of it also suggested a tenacious strength of will bordering on the obstinate.

She perceived danger in that mouth. Young as he was, there were already faint lines about his lips that spoke of sensuality indulged, of excesses savored and passions unbridled. And there was arrogance, thinly veiled even now as his lips curved up in amusement.

"I am not accustomed to being so thoroughly perused by the ladies of my court, Lady Siriol. Sir Raynor calls you a termagant, but I like a woman who knows her worth. A woman so bold of eye is bound to be equally bold in matters of love. Do you not agree, my lords?"

Lord Fauke responded with one of his leering grins, Raynor scowled, but the other gentlemen, stocky, grey-bearded men who but for the color of their surcotes were hardly distinguishable from one another, frowned and exchanged disapproving murmurs.

The duke laughed at them, a sound somehow melodious and scornful all at once, then leaned forward to view Siri better. As he did so, he let go of the pendant and she saw that the image he dropped was the same as the serpent-woman she had seen on his servant's badge, albeit this time wrought in jewels and gold.

"It intrigues you?" The duke lifted the pendant by its chain and held it out to allow her a closer inspection.

"It is very skillfully wrought," she said. The inviting lift of one of his dark blond brows prompted her to add, "I was trained in illumination and all such figures of art are of interest to me. I have drawn demons, of course, the serpent in the Garden of Eden, the devil when he tempted our Lord in the desert, the dragon of Saint John's vision, and of course those violent, gnashing demons awaiting the souls of the wicked in the Day of Judgment . . ."

"But this serpent-woman is unknown to you?"

"Yes, my lord."

The duke tilted the pendant so that its ruby eyes and emerald-set scales glittered. "She is Melusine, my infamous ancestress, wife of Count Foulques the Black of Anjou, daughter to the devil himself. It is said that when Foulques uncovered her secret, she let out so ghastly a shriek that it struck some men dead. Then she resumed her true demoness form and flew out the window, leaving behind her a telltale trail of fire and brimstone."

Again that scornful, oddly musical laugh. "Is it any wonder, my lady, that we Angevins live by fire as well, or that we have exchanged brimstone for blood? Familial affinity is unknown to us. My father has been cursed with too many sons, and though he would hope to make it otherwise, only one of us shall succeed him in the end. All of us know it—Henry, Geoffrey, and I. My father thinks to satisfy me with Poitou and Aquitaine, my brother Geoffrey with Brittany, while Henry has England, the richest prize of all. But Henry is not satisfied. And neither, my lady—" his azure eyes gleamed as brightly as the pendant "—am I."

The duke slouched back in his chair and tossed a look at Lord Fauke, permitting Siri a chance to glance at Raynor. The duke's mention of his brother Henry, the Young King, could only mean one thing. He knew of the conspiracy. Raynor had already planted his lies, and Triston was bound to be condemned in the duke's next breath.

But instead he dropped the pendant and waved a careless hand in the air. "Divided my brothers and I are in life. Perhaps in death we shall find some accord. Unfortunately, from the devil we came, and to the devil we shall all no doubt go."

This time Lord Fauke laughed with him, as though he were familiar with this quip from his liege's lips.

Raynor, however, looked impatient. "Sire, Sir Owen has been awaiting your pleasure this good hour. Now that the Lady Siriol is here, should he not be summoned?"

The duke's face darkened at this presumptuous interruption and for a moment Siri thought he was going to blast Raynor for it. The angry lips parted, but one of the grey-haired gentlemen spoke before a rebuke could be uttered.

"Sir Raynor is right, your grace. Your father would deal with this matter expeditiously."

The duke's ruddy cheeks went crimson. He exploded with such a blasphemous oath that Siri crossed herself and whispered a shocked prayer against retribution from the heavens.

"I am governor of these lands," the duke shouted, "and I will deal with this matter as I see fit! My father might welcome counsel from such prattling fools as you, but you are not in my father's court now. And if you wish to keep those grey heads of yours attached to your shoulders, you will hold your tongues in my presence."

"Sire," the same gentleman protested, "it was your father's hope that our counsel might be of aid to you in your youth and inexperience."

"Bah!" the duke spat. "You are nothing more than spies. The Lion thinks to keep a firm hand on my leash by setting you in my court to watch me. But I am lord here, I! And my father will not tell me how to rule!"

Siri sensed that he intended to shout a great deal more, but just then he turned his head and caught her eye. He regarded her for a moment with a glaring frown. Then he muttered something that sounded like another curse and made a sudden jabbing gesture with his hand in the air. "Summon Sir Owen. Let us get this over with."

Lord Fauke bowed and went to the door to speak with a servant, then returned and resumed his place beside Siri. There were a few furtive whispers between the royally appointed advisors, but the duke sat in glowering silence and no one else spoke until the servant returned escorting a frail-looking gentleman leaning on a cane.

Had it not been for that support, Siri would have taken him at a glance for a young man. But a closer scrutiny suggested that he was, in fact, quite old. His shoulder-length hair was not the pale flaxen she had first thought it, but a soft, silver white, such as she fancied Acelet's youthful locks must one day turn. And the face she had first thought smooth, she now saw was brushed with innumerable tiny wrinkles, so subtly woven into his translucent flesh that had the light not been so bright from the windows, she might well not have seen them at all.

"Come forward, Sir Owen," the duke bade him. With typical princely arrogance, he made no apology for keeping the old man waiting. "Behold Sir Raynor's wench. Look her over and tell us what you think."

Siri bristled at this rude invitation to survey her as though she were some item to be haggled over in a market. But given her glimpse of the duke's temper, she held her peace. The old man moved forward. Then he stopped in front of Siri and put up a hand to his eyes, as though to ward off a glare of light.

Except that Siri knew there was no window directly behind her. He seemed confused. Despite her umbrage, she offered the old gentleman a smile and in respect of his age as well as his rank, she acknowledged him with a curtsy.

The hand fell away from his eyes and floated towards her face, hesitated, then gently grasped her chin. His boldness startled her, but she allowed him to tilt up her chin and stare into her countenance. She searched his eyes as he searched hers. They were a deep and jewel-like blue and for an instant their keenness threatened to cut straight through her. Then they softened and grew hazy, and she felt his fingers tremble. That mist in his eyes she had learned too well. It was the mist of recognition, the mist of memory. She had seen it too often in Triston to be mistaken. She held her breath and waited for him to gasp out Clothilde's name.

But the duke thundered first, "Well, Sir Owen? What say you? Is she or is she not your—"

"Ceridwen."

"What?" Siri whispered.

"What?" the duke thundered.

Sir Owen let go of her chin and repeated, "There is no doubt about it. It is Ceridwen."

# Chapter 27

Lady Ceridwen Geraud?" the duke exclaimed. "You are telling us this wench resembles Lord Simon's wife?"

Siri started on hearing her brother's name.

The old man answered in a curiously lilting French. "Resembles, nay. She is Ceridwen's very image, as my beloved niece stood before me forty years ago. There can be only one explanation. Either she is Ceridwen's granddaughter or she is Eluned's."

"Who . . ." Siri began, but Lord Fauke's frown warned her that in the duke's presence she was not to speak unless invited.

Raynor's clearing throat won him a nod from the duke.

"Sire, if he speaks of Eluned, daughter of Dunawd ap Gruffydd, I am acquainted somewhat with a few of her descendants. My neighbor, Lord Laurant, wed her daughter Gwenllian and brought her back to Poitou from Wales. I grew up with the Lady Gwenllian's children—Therri, her son, and her daughters, Clothilde and Heléne. It was my understanding that the Lady Gwenllian's brothers were all younger than she, that they have remained in Wales and that there have been no further unions between Welsh and Poitevin in that branch of the family. Had the Lady Gwenllian a cousin in Poitou, I should think I would have heard it. And yet . . ." He raised his brows at Sir Owen. "Ceridwen, I believe, is a Welsh name?"

"Aye," Sir Owen said, "Ceridwen and I were both Welsh. I still am," he added with a mischievous smile.

"Perhaps, sire," one of the grey-haired counselors suggested to the duke, as though reminding a careless young boy of his manners, "Sir Owen would like a chair."

The duke scowled, but pity for the way the old man was leaning heavily with both hands on his cane appeared to overwhelm his princely pride. He gestured to one of the painted chairs, but Sir Owen moved with his awkward gait over to a window instead.

"If I may, sire, sit here by the light?"

The duke shrugged. "As you wish."

"And if the young lady might sit by me? It is like returning to my youth, to gaze upon her face."

The duke made an exaggerated sweep with his hand. "Lady Siriol."

Siri had to move one of the silk pillows to make room for herself beside Sir Owen on the window seat. The clear, midday light revealed the lines in his face more starkly now and she realized that he was older than she had thought at first. She wrapped her arms around the pillow and hugged it against her chest.

"I have been told I look like Clothilde, the Lady Gwenllian's daughter," she whispered to Sir Owen, "but who is Ceridwen?"

"Perhaps, my lady," the duke said dryly, "you would like to share whatever you are whispering with all of us."

Siri blushed, but Sir Owen merely smiled.

The duke saw it and added a warning. "There is much at stake here, Owen ap Rhys. Neville Geraud left a valuable inheritance of lands and wealth when he died. If the Lady Siriol is truly his heir, we will need more proof than some striking but elusive resemblance to his mother."

Sir Owen shook his head, as though Siri's face were all the proof he needed, but he asked in his gentle, lilting voice, "What is your name, child, and from where do you hail?"

"Siriol de Calendri," she said, then corrected herself. "Siriol Geraud. De Calendri is my married name."

"You are wed?"

"Widowed. I was born in Venice, but my father was Poitevin and after he died, my brother—"

"You have a brother?" Sir Owen interrupted sharply. His jewel-like eyes flashed to the duke. "You did not tell me this."

"The brother is dead," the duke said. "Or so I'm told." He glanced at Raynor.

Raynor nodded. "His name was also Simon, I believe. An illuminator, like his father. Two more mere 'coincidences,' my liege?"

"Is this true, my child?" Sir Owen asked Siri.

"That my brother's name was Simon, yes. That he and my father were illuminators in Venice, yes. And our name was Geraud. But my father never spoke of any inheritance."

"Walter Geraud was your father?"

"Yes."

"And he came from Poitou? And was trained in illumination? And he married a Venetian merchant's daughter, did he not? Elisabetta Gallo?"

Siri was so surprised that she dropped the pillow. "Yes. But how could you know that?"

Sir Owen's smile grew sad. "The Abbot of Les Préaux tried to hush the scandal up, but Lord Simon chose to trumpet his son's sins from the rooftops. Your father never spoke to you of his family?"

"No, never. He very seldom even spoke of Poitou, except—"

"What, child?" he prompted as she hesitated. "Please tell me."

Siri laced her fingers together and stared down at them in her lap. Her father's image swirled into her memory. She saw again his large, skillful hands guiding her small, childish one as he taught her to draw her name, heard his kind words of encouragement at her first attempt to trace a simple flower, felt his reassuring arms around her when her pen slipped and stained the parchment, ruining all her careful labors . . .

Sir Owen's thin hand fluttered over hers and pressed them.

"As my father lay dying," she said, "I heard him tell Simon that 'twas a vow to visit the Holy Land which had brought him from Poitou to Venice in his youth. But while awaiting a ship to transport him and his fellow pilgrims across the sea, he met my mother and fell into a snare of love." She bit her lip. *A snare of love.* She would never forget the longing way her father had looked at her mother when he said it, or the way her mother had held his hand to her heart and wept.

Sir Owen prompted her gently from her sorrow. "So, your father said he was a pilgrim?"

"Yes. Only he met and married my mother and never fulfilled his vow to go to Jerusalem. He said he had never regretted his choice in life, but now as he prepared for death, he feared the wrath of God for his sins. He begged my brother to complete the journey he had strayed from in his youth and to pray with all diligence before the Holy Sepulchre that the Lord might remember him as a pious servant of God, a loving husband and father, an honest artisan. He said God knew his heart and would forgive him if only he could mend his broken vow through Simon."

Sir Owen shook his silver head. "I pray the Lord proves as merciful as Walter hoped, for the opinion of the abbot for the fate of his soul was dire." He squeezed her hands. "Child, your father was no simple lay pilgrim when he met and married your mother. He was a monk of the Abbey of Les Préaux."

This statement struck Siri as so ludicrous that she laughed. Her father a monk! But the old man's face remained sober, as did every other face she quickly surveyed in the room.

Except Raynor's. She saw a smirking smile on his bearded face and sprang to her feet, so angry that if he had been near enough she would have struck him. "Now you have gone too far! How dare you stoop to slander my father like this!"

"Child," Sir Owen said, "it is true—"

"Nay, it is one of his lies! My father was an honorable man, a pious man. He broke one vow, that of a pilgrim. He did not abandon a whole monastery full of vows! And how would you know, anyway? Who are you?"

"I am your father's great uncle," Sir Owen answered, "your great-grandmother's brother. It was I who brought your grandmother as a babe from Wales to Normandy. I stood with her at her marriage to Lord Simon Geraud of Poitou. I witnessed the baptisms of her sons, Neville and Walter, and the offering of Walter as an oblate to the Abbey of Les Préaux when he was four years old. And at his father's request, I traveled to Venice over twenty-five years ago to learn the truth of the charges laid against him there."

"That my father was a runaway monk? That is simply absurd! He would have been forced back to the abbey!"

"Child, if you will sit down, I will explain."

"Nothing you can say is going to convince me that my father was a—"

The duke gave a thundering oath. "Will you be silent, wench? Whether you sit or stand is of no interest to me, but you will be silent!"

Siri saw the duke's hands clenched on the armrests of his chair and the rigid way he leaned forward to glare at her. She backed away from the azure blaze in his eyes and sat down again beside Sir Owen. That the duke had a temper to rival Triston's was evident, but that it could be set off by so small a provocation as her natural shock betrayed no similar effort to master it.

"Sire," Sir Owen ventured, "it is only to be expected that she would find my words distressing."

"Humph!" the duke snorted. "Distressing, if she is who she says she is. Look at me, wench." He held and weighed her gaze. "Six months ago, the Geraud inheritance fell into my hands when Lord Neville Geraud died without a legitimate heir. Now come Lord Fauke and Sir Raynor to my court, insisting that they have discovered a long-lost child of the Geraud house. The disposal of three castles with their adjoining land and considerable other accumulated wealth, not to mention the barony itself, now lies in question. I am not of a mind to surrender my ducal authority over such a windfall easily. But if you are indeed Lord Walter's legitimate daughter—" He flung himself back in his chair. "There will have to be proof. Sir Owen, you said he was a monk. That would seem to exclude any possibility of legitimacy."

"Sire, have I your permission to start at the beginning?"

"Unless this bears on the Poitevin inheritance, I've no interest in any Welsh link."

Sir Owen gave a small bow from the window seat. "I understand, sire, and it is only of the inheritance which I shall speak. Ceridwen's history has no bearing upon that which befell her son. But I must begin with Lord

Walter's birth."

"Very well. But keep it brief."

Again Sir Owen bowed. "I will do my best, sire. As you are well aware, the tradition of inheritance in Poitou is quite different from those in other parts of your father's kingdom. Unlike England, where the eldest son inherits all, here at a man's death his lands pass to his brothers first and only at their deaths may the first brother's sons lay claim."

"Aye," the duke muttered, "an idiotic custom. My brother Geoffrey battles the same shortsighted approach to inheritance in Brittany."

"I fear it may have been my criticism of this Poitevin custom which sealed young Walter's fate at his father's hands," Sir Owen said. "Had I realized the seed I was planting in Lord Simon's mind, I would never have spoken so freely of the custom of England. After Walter's birth, Lord Simon was dissatisfied. He already had one son in Neville and it soon became clear that he wished Neville alone to stand his heir. But custom required that Neville share his rights with Walter, as long as Walter lived. Unless the younger son could somehow be removed."

*Removed.* The word rang so ominous in Siri's ears that her gaze flew to Sir Owen's face.

The old man responded to her alarm with one of his reassuring smiles. "Lord Simon was not a wicked man, my lady, only a hard-headed one. After a short space of consideration, he exclaimed that the answer was obvious. He would donate his younger son to the Abbey of Les Préaux in Normandy, where one of Lord Simon's uncles still lived as a monk. Walter would be raised as an oblate and at the proper age would profess. He would take vows of poverty, chastity, and obedience, and by so doing, would surrender his claims to share in his brother's inheritance. It seemed a harmless enough solution. The boy would be well cared for. He might even be taught a trade. Les Préaux enjoyed some renown for its scriptorium. Lord Simon was so confident in his scheme's success that he even allowed his wife to insist upon the insertion of a clause in the donation which allowed her son to leave the monastery at the age of profession, if he so desired."

"But Lord Walter did profess," the duke said. "You said yourself that he was one of the monks of Les Préaux.”

"So I did." Sir Owen glanced again at Siri before resuming his recital to the duke. "At his mother's request, I called on the boy from time to time. I cannot say that I found him content. Except when in the scriptorium. He had a gift for drawing and painting, and the monks seemed eager to encourage his talent. He appeared happy enough while working there. And he was young. I thought as he grew older, the discontentment would fade and he would find peace in the service he could render through paint and pen.

"Then, shortly after his fifteenth birthday, his mother, the Lady Ceridwen, died. I went to Les Préaux to inform Walter of it, but the monks refused to let me see him. They said he had already professed, that he was now a novice of the abbey and could no longer be troubled with the worldly concerns of his former family. Once or twice in subsequent years I made some effort to contact him, but always I was turned away by the monks."

"Are you suggesting that there was something suspicious about that?" the duke demanded.

"At the time I did not think so, my liege. The purpose of a monastery is to provide a retreat from the world. And there were rumors that Walter was gaining some fame as an illuminator for the abbey. We had no reason to doubt that he had accepted his life among the brothers."

"And so? You promised me brevity, Sir Owen."

"Aye, sire. Then allow me to jump ahead ten years from the Lady Ceridwen's death. After this long period of silence, Lord Simon suddenly received a summons to Les Préaux. We went to the abbey together, only to discover to our considerable shock that Walter was no longer there."

The duke leaned forward. "He had fled the monastery?"

"Not precisely, my liege. But hoping to build on the growing fame of his scriptorium, the abbot had granted special permission for a few of his more talented monks to travel to the Latinate kingdom of Jerusalem, there not only to pray, but to study the Eastern method of illumination from the great master, Basilius. Walter had been one of the monks chosen. But while awaiting a transport ship in Venice to carry them all to the Holy Land, the abbot said Walter deserted his party, abandoned his vows, and took sinful refuge with a Venetian merchant's family. He said Walter was spreading scurrilous lies about the abbey and swore if he did not cease and return to Les Préaux forthwith, that he should find himself excommunicated.

"I do not know who was outraged more, Lord Simon or the abbot. The latter fumed about the affront to his authority, but Lord Simon feared that Walter meant to return to secular life and demand to be restored to his place in the inheritance. Neither seemed particularly concerned for the state of Walter's soul. But I knew the grief his behavior would have caused his mother. I offered to travel to Venice and try to reason with him, to persuade him to confess his errors and return to Les Préaux."

"The abbot would have been within his rights to have him forcibly returned," the duke said. "And if he'd been excommunicated, he would have been denied the sacrament of marriage. Any children born to a union while under such a ban would have been considered illegitimate."

There was no missing his point, for he looked straight at Siri as he said it. She flushed and only the cautioning touch of Sir Owen's hand on her arm prevented her from blurting out an angry protest.

"As I said, sire," Sir Owen resumed, "I went to Venice myself in search of Walter and the truth. I found him as the abbot had said, in the house of a Venetian merchant, Niccolo Gallo. I reminded Walter of his duty to God and begged him to return with me to Normandy. But he rejected my plea and to my astonishment, announced that the abbot held no rule over him for in fact, he was not a monk."

"Not a monk?" the duke exclaimed. "But you said—" He caught the lift of Sir Owen's brows. "Oh, very well, continue your story."

"Walter told me that at the age of fifteen, he refused to profess and announced his desire to return to the world and his family. But the abbot had insisted that paternal oblation was irrevocable and his mother's clause to the donation meaningless. When Walter continued to reject the vows, the abbot had him beaten and confined to a cell. But during his imprisonment, the quality of work in the scriptorium suffered. Patrons began to complain. After several months of discipline, the abbot finally released Walter and allowed him to resume his duties. So long as he conformed outwardly to a monk's life, the abbot agreed to overlook the matter of the vows for the moment. Apparently, Walter said, the abbot hoped that in time divine inspiration would move him to submit where harsher disciplines had failed. Nevertheless, he was kept strictly cut off from the outside world, lest he attempt to escape or send word of his plight to his family."

"You are asking me to believe that Walter Geraud mimicked the life of a monk for ten years without ever taking the vows?" the duke said incredulously.

"Well, sire," Sir Owen said, "Walter had never known any other life, so adhering to the rule's order would not have been difficult for him. And he seemed to have held a deep and genuine love for his work in the scriptorium. But he insisted that he never did profess. He said that he bided his time and observed the rule of the abbey so strictly that most of the monks forgot his transgression and accepted him as a full brother of the order."

"But the abbot would not have forgotten."

"No, sire. But when the abbot decided to send some of his monks to study illumination at Jerusalem, Walter persuaded him to let him be among their number. He suggested that if he were to find anywhere the divine inspiration to move him towards profession, surely it would be in the very land where our Lord had walked. Walter reminded him of his obedience in every other matter but the speaking of the vows. That, and Walter's preeminence among the abbey's artists, at last persuaded the abbot to let him go."

"But why did he wait until Venice to escape?" the duke said. "There must have been numerous other opportunities along the way."

"After ten years, Walter said he was confused, uncertain anymore of what he truly wanted. He said he meant to complete the journey to Jerusalem and there pray for guidance for his soul. But while waiting for the transport ship, he met Elisabetta Gallo and—" Sir Owen's jewel-blue eyes caught Siri's and held them with a gentle smile "—he fell into a snare of love. Aye, I can still hear his words as clearly as if he had spoken them to me this morning. And one night while his fellow monks lay sleeping, Walter, with a hood over his head to conceal his tonsure, stole away to a church with Elisabetta and married her."

The duke snorted, as though thought of the scene amused him in spite of himself. "That must have thrown his fellow monks into an uproar."

"Indeed," Sir Owen said. "One of their number was immediately dispatched back to Les Préaux to inform the abbot of Walter's rebellion. But Walter made shrewd use of the time it required for the messenger to reach Normandy and return to Venice with the abbot's response. With his new father-in-law's support, he appealed his case directly to the Church at Rome. An ecclesiastical court was summoned, and the remaining monks of his traveling party were brought to Rome to testify. Fortunately for Walter, when they racked their memories, they all agreed that to their knowledge, he had never actually repeated the vows of profession. Two of the older monks also recalled hearing the abbot speak scornfully of a clause at Walter's donation permitting his release from the monastery should he choose not to become a novice. Given this evidence, the court agreed that Walter had been improperly held and should be permitted to return to secular life."

"But why did he not return to Poitou?" the duke asked. "He must have known such a judgment would also have restored him to his inheritance."

"He said the inheritance meant nothing to him. He had not seen his father's face for over twenty years, and was bitterly aware of why he had been placed in the monastery to begin with. 'Let my father tell everyone I'm dead,' he told me. 'Let him will his precious lands to my brother. I will build an inheritance of my own here in Venice, and whatever children Elisabetta bears me, I will keep them all close to my heart.'"

Siri remembered again her father's strong arms around her and felt a warm wetness welling up into her eyes.

"I returned this word to his father and the abbot," Sir Owen continued. "The abbot continued to insist that Walter had lied, but when I suggested that he journey to Rome himself and challenge the matter, he rather quickly declined and declared himself well rid of a troublesome monk. He tried to hush the matter up. But Lord Simon would not believe Walter's disinterest in the inheritance. To his dying day he maintained that Walter was a rebellious monk and as such, could never stand joint heir with his brother."

"Then it seems to me," the duke said, "that it is Walter's word against his father's. And both of them are dead. How am I to know whether, in fact, the Lady Siriol is a legitimate heir to the Geraud lands?"

"Because, sire," Sir Owen replied, "I made a point of obtaining a copy of the judgment issued by the court at Rome. In case Walter should ever change his mind and return to Poitou, I knew his mother would wish him restored to his full rights. I have brought the document with me to Poitiers, should you wish to observe it with your own eyes."

"You may be sure of that."

The duke looked slightly disgruntled at this news, and Siri suspected he had been hoping that a lack of proof would enable him to deny her father's status.

"Very well," he said grudgingly, "let us assume that everything you have told us is true, that Walter Geraud made a valid marriage and even sired children. How do we know that this wench is his daughter?"

It was Lord Fauke who suggested, "She must have brought something of her father's with her from Venice. Think, girl, what evidence do you possess to prove that you are Walter Geraud's daughter?"

Siri took this question as an invitation to express her mind and she did so with all the passionate indignation which she had been forced to smother during Sir Owen's lengthy recital to the duke.

"I don't need any proof. I know he was my father. And if he had no use for Lord Simon's inheritance, then I do not want it either! By all means, sire, keep the Geraud castles and lands. I ask only that you honor my late brother's wishes and return me to the guardian he chose for me, Sir Triston de Brielle."

This last she uttered with a defiant glance at Raynor, but the duke gave an impatient snort.

"It's not that simple, girl. If you are the lawful heir, there is no question but what I must return the lands to you. To do otherwise would arouse an uproar from the other barons. Such a precedent would be seen as an arbitrary and dangerous abuse of royal power and would only fuel the fires of rebellion which I know well are already burning."

Siri's heart skipped. She should not have mentioned Triston's name. But the accusation she expected to follow this reference to rebellion did not come.

"Nay," the duke said, "I dare not ignore the ancient customs of inheritance just yet. But—" his azure eyes narrowed on Siri's face "—the royal interests may still be served as well. 'Tis one of my acknowledged prerogatives to claim wardship of underaged or female heirs."

Siri saw Raynor's triumphant smile and his words came back in a horrific rush. *It may very well be, carissima, that your hand is not Triston's to give at all, but the duke's.*

Her mouth went dry. She made a hasty, desperate retreat from her former position. "You are right, I have no proof of my parentage. My brother sold everything before he died to finance my journey to Poitou. I have nothing but a few trinkets of jewelry from my mother, my brother's paints, a page or two of my father's drawings done when I was a child. Nothing that would link him or me to his Poitevin past."

It was true. Except for clinging to the French language and training his apprentices in French methods of illumination, her father's break with his past seemed to have been complete. She could think of nothing she possessed that might prove Sir Owen's story. A sigh of relief escaped her. Without such proof, the duke would have no reason to claim wardship over her. Now if she could only counter Raynor's charges against Triston—

"What about the pattern book?"

Siri's stomach flopped over even before she fully comprehended the implication of Lord Fauke's abrupt question.

"Pattern book?" the duke repeated.

"Aye, she has her father's pattern book. She brought it with her from Venice and I assumed, when she showed it to me, that it originated there. But might it not in fact be a result of her father's work while at Les Préaux? Perhaps someone in the scriptorium there would remember it."

A hot flush of dread enveloped Siri's body.

"Where is it now?" the duke asked.

"At Vere," Lord Fauke replied. "I could send one of my servants for it."

The duke gave a crisp nod. "Do so. And send someone to Les Préaux to fetch one of the monks from the scriptorium. I would have this matter settled no later than week's end."

Lord Fauke bowed. The duke waved a hand at the company, and Siri knew herself dismissed with the rest. Her head spinning, her heart pounding, she managed one last curtsy to the duke. As she turned to leave, she saw him crook a finger at Raynor. She hesitated. Then she lifted her chin to the smug glance Raynor sent her and swept out of the room.

# Chapter 28

Sunlight filtered through the lush, green trees of Queen Eleanor's fruit garden, dappling the flower-sprinkled grass and graveled walkways. In the heat of the afternoon sun, fragrance of fruit and flower hung almost oppressively thick in the air. Hard, golden quinces, and fat, ruddy peaches bowed the branches, while wine red cherries teased just out of reach of Siri's diminutive hand. Not that she had the least interest in gathering any just now, but the taller of her newly assigned maids considerately plucked a few for her and dropped them into her hands.

Siri thanked her and led Lucianna to one of the carved stone benches that dotted the expansive landscape at regular intervals. She had found Lucianna waiting for her outside the queen's solar when Siri and the others had been dismissed. Now she waited until her maids drifted away to enjoy the flowers and fruit before launching without preamble into a rehearsal of Sir Owen's words in the queen's solar.

Siri was not unaware of Lucianna's pleased smile as she listened to the recital. With a prickle of dread, Siri said at the end, "Lucianna, you knew my parents better than even I remember them. Can it be true, do you think?"

"But of course," Lucianna said with a smug toss of her head. "The rumors were thick in Venice at the time of his marriage to your mother that he had noble blood. Poor men's sons do not end up master illuminators in rich French abbeys."

"You knew," Siri gasped, "that my father was a runaway monk? And you never told me?"

Lucianna laughed and plucked a cherry out of Siri's lap. "Carissima, it was all long forgotten by the time you were of an age to understand. It was a great scandal at the time, of course, but once your father won the ruling of the court at Rome, all was forgiven, in Venice, at least. When he died, he was remembered only as a skilled artisan, well respected by his patrons, renowned more for his tenacious fidelity to your mother than for his desertion of some abbey."

*Fidelity.* Siri's heart swelled with pride at hearing the word thus applied to her father, but curiously, the pride came edged with pain. Her father had loved one woman to the day of his death. But it was not her father's fair, handsome face that swirled into her mind. It was Triston's dark, turbulent one. To her dismay, she felt her faith waver. Did he truly love her? Or was it still only her face, the face so like his lost Clothilde's? So like—

"Lucianna, who is Ceridwen?"

Lucianna left off nibbling on the cherry. "Ceridwen?"

"Sir Owen said she was Father's mother and that I look like her. But then how can I also look like Clothilde?"

"Of that I know nothing, carissima. Your father never confided his past to me." She finished off the cherry and spat out the pit. "Do you realize what this will mean? You are now a great lady in your own right! How many castles did you say you stand heir to?"

"Three. But Lucianna, I don't want them."

Lucianna laughed. "Nonsense, carissima. Of course you want them."

"No, I don't! Not if it means—"

Siri stopped, then stood. She walked down one of the gravel paths, past some rose bushes, past a sweep of violets, to a sweet-smelling bed of lavender. She stepped into the middle of the low-spreading flowers, then sank to her knees and started plucking some blooms. Lucianna followed her and stood watching from the edge of the path. Siri bowed her head. Her veil floated softly against her cheeks concealing, she hoped, the silent movement of her lips.

Her father's pattern book. *Oh please,* she prayed, *let it have been created in Venice. Don't let it be the one he made at Les Préaux.* Her hands moved slowly at first to gather the flowers, but as her prayer grew more fervent, her fingers flew more feverishly. *Please, oh, please, don't let it be true! I don't want the castles. I don't want the land. I only want to go home. Home to Vere. Home to Triston!*

A pile of blooms now filled her lap. Their delicate hue blurred through the tears in her eyes. She swept the petals into her hands and raised them to her face, inhaling deeply of their fragrance. *Oh, please.* She squeezed her eyes shut so hard that it sent her tears trickling out the corners. *I don't care whom he sees in me. Just don't take me away from him. Don't take me away from Triston.*

"Carissima."

Her head flew up. It was not Lucianna's voice that called her, but it was Lucianna's angry voice that challenged the man who did.

"Go away, you *cane!* My donna and I are no longer in your power."

Siri saw Raynor throw her companion an annoyed glance. "On the contrary, you old harridan, your lady remains very much in my power. I suggest you pack your bags and return to Venice. You serve no further purpose here."

Siri dropped her flowers and hurried back to the path. "Don't you dare call her a harridan!" she cried. "You are nothing but a dastardly brute! You think you have been so clever, bringing Sir Owen here and making him identify me as some long-lost heiress. But you have finally outsmarted yourself. You are no more important than Triston, and if I am an heiress, then the duke will never give my hand to you!"

"Do not be so sure, carissima." Oh, how she had come to hate that cunning smile! "I am about to rise several rungs in the duke's esteem. I thought you might like to be present when I give him this."

He drew a piece of folded parchment from inside the breast of his tunic and waved it tauntingly in the air.

"What is it?" Siri demanded.

The hateful smile widened. "Acelet's confession. It is time to settle the score."

She made a grab for the parchment, but he swished it out of reach.

"No one is going to believe it," she insisted. "Acelet is free to deny it. You can't win with a forgery now."

"The duke will believe it," Raynor answered easily, "because it is what he wants to believe. In fact, I have already told him what I know. All that remains is the proof. He sent me to my room to retrieve it. And here it is."

He swished it again, teasingly, just out of reach of her fingers.

"No! Raynor, how can you do this to two innocent men?"

His lips drew back on his teeth, turning the smile into a snarl. "Triston is not innocent. He bears my sister's blood on his hands. As for Acelet, he deserves nothing more for his monumental stupidity. The world will never miss him." He slid the parchment into his belt. "Well, my lady, shall you come? The duke does not like to be kept waiting."

Having met Duke Richard, Siri knew how unlikely it was that he would listen to her objections over a man's sworn word. And she had no doubt that Raynor would swear his soul away to avenge himself on Triston. But she could not stand by and allow him to destroy the man she loved without making some effort to defend him.

She swept with Lucianna ahead of Raynor back into the palace, but once inside, they had to stop and let him lead the way. The duke, Raynor told them, was no longer in his mother's solar, but had retired to the Great Hall.

The vast chamber easily dwarfed the hall at Vere. As they passed through the arcaded entryway, they stepped into a crowd of glitteringly attired people, lords and ladies, knights and damsels, clothed in silks, dripping with jewels and gold. The roar of their conversations filled the air, nearly drowning out the melodic strains of the musicians from the galleries above. At the center of the dais sat the duke in the same long-legged sprawl Siri had seen him use in the solar, only this time his chair was gilded and jeweled like a throne.

She caught no more than a glimpse of him before the press of people crowded him from her view. She was actually grateful for Raynor's hand on her arm to guide her through the confusion on the floor. It was all too easy in the press for leering men to turn a seemingly inadvertent bump against her into a suggestive nudge.

"Step back. Clear the way," Raynor snapped. "You there, put your eyes back in your head. Don't try it, sirrah, unless you want those fingers of yours sliced off by my blade!"

Despite his bloody warnings, Siri knew no steel dared be drawn in the duke's presence. Still, she breathed a prayer of thanks for the distraction when it allowed her fingers to flutter unperceived to the parchment in Raynor's belt.

Lucianna, left to guide herself, was soon choked off from behind them. Siri and Raynor finally reached the dais where the duke sat in his slump, his chin in his hand, watching his court with a brooding frown. Beside his chair stood Lord Fauke, dressed in a gown of black and gilded broadcloth that made his red hair blaze like the devil's. His covetous gaze at Siri did not go unnoticed by the sultry woman at his side. Osanne had also come to court. The raven-haired beauty frowned at Lord Fauke and raked Siri with a glance of pure hatred.

She returned Osanne's glare in full measure, until the duke's barking voice snapped her thoughts away from Triston's past to the heart-pounding danger of the present.

"Well, Sir Raynor? You have it, I presume. Proof that de Brielle has been consorting with my brother to depose me?"

Siri winced. He roared the words loud enough for the entire hall to hear. The hall fell silent, all eyes turning towards the dais and their prince.

"Sire." Raynor bowed before the duke. "I have it here, as I promised, written and signed before he escaped my guards. Every detail of his cousin's confess—"

Siri inched her way backwards as his hand reached for the parchment he had tucked in his belt, but the crowd behind her prevented her from retreating too far. Raynor straightened, clearly surprised. He reached all the way around his belt, front and back, then plunged his hand inside the breast of his tunic. Only when his hand came out empty did his face suddenly darken and he swivel around towards her.

"You conniving little cat. What have you done with it?"

"I—" she began, but Raynor seized her by the shoulders and shook her.

"You've taken it, haven't you? Back there in the crowd, while I was trying to protect you! Where is it? So help me, you'll surrender it if I have to strip you bare before this entire company to find it!"

That sent the men in the crowd into raucous laughter.

Siri twisted and lashed out with her toes at Raynor's ankles, but he was familiar with that trick by now. He lifted her off her feet and shook her again, this time in the air.

"De Molinet," the duke thundered, sitting bolt upright from his slouch, "are you telling me you don't have the confession?"

"I have it! She has it! Give it up, you little cat. Give it up!"

Siri's teeth banged together with the force of his next shake. His fury, she knew, only delayed the inevitable. She had not had time to destroy the parchment, or even to hide it well. She had stuffed it up the tight-fitting sleeve of her undertunic. Once he mastered his rage, the most cursory of searches would find it.

"Put her down, you dog, or feel my steel between your ribs!"

The voice wrenched her gaze away from Raynor's angry face. A newcomer strode through the crowd, head and shoulders above the other men. Her eyes locked with his dark, tumultuous gaze. *Triston!* Ah, saints! She should have been relieved to see him forcing his way, hale and fierce, to her rescue. But all she could think of was that he was striding headlong into the disaster of Acelet's so-called confession.

*Acelet.* It belatedly registered that the challenge to Raynor had not issued in Triston's ringing tones, but from somewhere just below her. She stared down to see Acelet's flaxen head. His hand clenched the hilt of his sword. He had the steel halfway out of its scabbard before Triston reached his side. Triston caught Acelet's fist and rammed the blade back home. To draw steel in the royal presence would be tantamount to treason.

Acelet shook his cousin off with a curt nod of understanding. "Put her down, Raynor," he warned again.

Raynor shot a measuring look at Triston, but the glance he spared Acelet held nothing but contempt. His hands tightened on Siri's waist. If anything, he boosted her higher. "And if I don't?"

A loud crack echoed through the watchful silence of the hall. Raynor howled and Siri lurched downward through the air.

Acelet caught her and shoved her into a pair of strong, familiar arms. Triston's strength swept around her like a blanket of safety, muffling Raynor's shout of rage. Triston clutched her convulsively for a moment. Then his hold on her slackened, and she turned her head to follow his anxious gaze back to Acelet.

Acelet had won her freedom with a hard kick to Raynor's shin. Before Raynor could fully straighten from the pain, Acelet drove a fist into Raynor's stomach, then connected a blow to his chin that landed him on his back on the dais, flat at the duke's feet.

The duke shot up with a thunderous oath. "What is the meaning of this? Who is this cursed whelp?"

"I am Acelet de Cary," Acelet flashed, "and I demand satisfaction from this scoundrel de Molinet!"

"Satisfaction?" Something flickered in the duke's azure eyes alongside the outrage. "For what?"

"False imprisonment, for starters. Threatening me with torture. Dishonoring my name with his lies. I come from a noble lineage, my liege. I am a gentleman, a squire, and hope one day soon to become a knight. This fellow has insulted me, attempted to shame me, and such shame can only be purged on the field of battle."

These martial words stunned Siri. This was not the gentle, dreamy, sometimes foolish youth she knew. A simple, elegant tunic, with a light spring mantle tossed over one shoulder, had replaced the extravagant attire he had sported in his cousin's house. His flaxen locks, though tousled from his journey, retained their long, artful ringlets and his flushed cheeks were smooth again. He stood every inch the noble squire he claimed to be. But the loss of the beard made him look younger, more vulnerable to Raynor's fury, despite the sparkling challenge in his eyes as Raynor struggled to his feet.

"What is Acelet doing?" she whispered to Triston. "You must stop him before Raynor accepts his challenge!"

Before Triston could reply, the duke demanded, "Are these charges true, de Molinet?"

Raynor's chest rose and fell in angry breaths. He leveled a deadly look at Acelet, but he clung to his composure. "Of course not, my liege. 'Tis a ploy, a fabrication by de Brielle to divert us from the truth. He has put these lies in his cousin's mouth. Next the youth will be denying his own confession."

"If anyone tried to put words in my mouth," Acelet said, "it was you." He swung around to the duke. "He tried to bully me into accusing Sir Triston by locking me in a stinking cell at Belle Noir and threatening to do harm upon my person if I refused to obey him. But if there is a traitor in this court, it is he." He pointed at Raynor. "Not only has he lied about our part in the conspiracy, but it is he who has led the robber knights of the road in assault upon your grace's most loyal men."

Until then, the duke had looked torn between giving fair ear to Acelet's accusations and reluctance lest doing so might result in acquittal of the charges he so clearly wished to lay at Triston's feet. But now his ruddy cheeks darkened as Raynor's perceptibly paled.

"De Molinet?"

"Lies, I tell you," Raynor insisted. "He has no proof."

Acelet shot back, "Lady Siriol has proof. She has the vial of paint you stole from her and returned the night of her banquet. And I have seen your ill-got booty for myself. Or have you forgotten the smug way you showed off to me Lord Fauke's gold and his jewel-encrusted scabbard after you waylaid him on the road?"

"What?" Lord Fauke roared. He shook Osanne off his arm and started towards Raynor. "De Molinet, you—?"

"Nay!" Raynor looked panicked for a moment, then made a desperate effort to regain control of the situation. "My lord, sire, it is a trick to divert us from the true issue at hand. I am no robber and I will defend my innocence by my sword. Let me meet this whelp in the field and Heaven will reveal which of us is lying."

His tense muscles eased as he sized up his stripling opponent.

"You must stop them," Siri whispered again to Triston. "Acelet can never stand against Raynor."

Triston's arm tightened about her and pulled her back against his chest, but he murmured, "I cannot. I have no other way to save you. I am bound by my oath—but Acelet is not."

She twisted her head to stare up into his face. "Triston, no! You cannot use Acelet like this!"

"The choice is Acelet's own. It is his honor he defends, his freedom and future that he fights for." His free hand brushed her cheek. "But his courage comes from you. Do not try to dissuade him, Siri. Though he speaks the words I taught him, in his heart he will be fighting for you. And if he cannot raise his sword against a rogue like Raynor, he does not deserve to become a knight."

She knew he was right. As fervently as she had prayed that Triston might rescue her, she had been sick with the knowledge that to do so would mean the breaking of his oath. She could not bear to be the cause of yet another guilt upon his conscience, and she did not think that he could long bear it either. One more straw upon the camel's back. She did not want to win his love at the cost of breaking the man.

*Honor. Integrity. Fidelity.* These were the qualities Siri treasured most in him. But *cunning?* That was a word she had connected only with Raynor. Yet it had required nothing less for Triston to find a way around that insidious oath without so much as cracking it. Acelet might stand at the center of the conflict raging before the duke, but clearly it was Triston who pulled his strings. He had set Acelet up to save her, because he could not save her himself.

But it was not cold calculation she saw in his gaze as it rested on Acelet. It was approval, coupled with an anxious anticipation. His plan had a double purpose. Not only to frustrate Raynor's machinations, but to give Acelet a chance to prove himself, and by so doing, win the knighthood he had coveted for so long.

Acelet's challenge had taken courage. Even the duke seemed to admire his show of it. But swords had not yet been crossed and Siri remembered as clearly as she knew Triston did, the swordmaster's assessment of his cousin's skill.

"He cannot win his spurs if Raynor kills him," she said. "Perhaps the duke will stop them."

Duke Richard had silenced Lord Fauke's outrage and now paced the dais in brooding silence. The murmur of the crowd as they watched their prince masked Triston's soft response from any ears but hers.

"The king would stop them, but the duke loves nothing more than a good fight. Physical prowess is how he weighs a man's worth. If Acelet wavers in his challenge now, the duke will interpret it as weakness, and in his eyes weakness is guilt. He will turn his ear once more to Raynor's charges. I gather they have already been laid?"

She nodded numbly. "He forged a confession from Acelet. I have hidden it in my gown, but Raynor knows I have it. When he finds it—"

"We must not give him that chance. If Acelet can best him in battle, the duke will give heed to the other accusations, particularly the one about Raynor being leader of the robber-knights. Acelet says they need only search Belle Noir to find sufficient evidence of Raynor's spoils from the road. And like it or not, once Raynor is discredited, the duke will have to abandon his hopes of discrediting me. At least for now."

Siri pulled his arm tighter around her. But before she could respond, one of the grey-haired counselors she remembered from the queen's solar pushed himself free of the crowd and stepped onto the dais.

"Sire, your father would forbid this. He would require these men to bring witnesses to testify of their guilt or innocence. Let men be assembled to hear and weigh the merits of their quarrel."

The duke whirled on him. Siri gasped as his eyes flashed with a hatred as deep and violent as anything she had ever seen in Raynor.

"Don't quote my father's laws to me! This is not England, sirrah, and my father is not master here! It is my hand which rules in Poitou, and if you do not want to feel its weight—"

The duke raised one of his powerful hands as if he truly meant to strike the counselor. The man stumbled backwards to escape the impending blow. His ankle twisted over the edge of the dais, buckling his knees. He would have hit the floor had Triston not released Siri and sprung to catch him. Triston bent his head to whisper something into the counselor's ear.

The man nodded and allowed Triston to push him back into the crowd.

As Siri watched him go, she caught sight of Lucianna. Triston and Acelet had not come alone. Sir Balduin stood at Lucianna's side, holding her hand and whispering words Siri was certain were intended to smooth the anxiety from her companion's brow.

"Well spoken, sire."

Siri whirled as Triston's voice rang out the words. In an act of breathtaking brazenness, he placed one foot on the dais. He looked ferociously handsome, his ebony curls disordered by the wind of his ride, his tanned cheeks set in hard, dauntless lines, his dark eyes burning with reckless resolve.

With his arms braced across his knee, he leaned forward to gaze boldly at the duke. "Poitevin quarrels are settled with steel. My cousin's honor has been insulted, and his honor is mine. Let there be no further delay of your justice. We will clear our name on the field of battle, or stand condemned before the eyes of all the world."

Raynor's head snapped round towards Triston. "You put Acelet up to this! It is your way of escaping your oath, of trying to win her back." Raynor closed the space between him and Siri and seized her arm. Black specks of hatred shot from his amber eyes. "You shan't have her, Triston. I swear I would sooner see her dead—"

Siri tried to pull away, but Raynor heard and felt the crinkling beneath his fingers as they tightened on her sleeve. His eyes widened in surprise, then triumph. He pushed the fabric back from her wrist and whisked out the hidden parchment.

He smiled. "Another reprieve for you, carissima." He released her and turned back towards the dais with his prize. "Sire, this—"

"My lord." Triston spoke loudly, the same instant as Raynor. Siri knew he had seen and understood the significance of Raynor's find. He leaned forward more intensely. "This fellow has vilified me and my kin. I demand our rights under Poitevin law."

"Aye," Acelet said, emboldened by Triston's example. "I will prove this dog's infamy by my sword."

Raynor made a sound like a hiss and strode back towards the dais with the parchment extended in his hand, but the duke waved him back.

"Stay," he snapped, and Raynor froze. The duke raised his brows at Triston's arrogant posture and raked him with a glance of repellent dislike, then turned to Acelet. His eyes narrowed and his gaze grew speculative.

"You, stripling." Acelet was only three years younger than the duke himself, but his slender frame made him looked slight, perhaps too slight, to a man of the duke's formidable build. "Are you sure you are equal to this task? Sir Raynor is a man seasoned in battle, while you—" Acelet's face reddened as the duke's gaze turned pitying. "If you wish to withdraw your challenge, I give you leave to do so now."

Acelet responded by spitting an epithet that made Triston gasp and the duke's brows shoot back up.

"The only thing I want to withdraw is my sword from Raynor's chest," Acelet said. "Sire, have we your leave to meet or have we not?"

To Siri's relief, the duke looked amused. He weighed Acelet another moment, then an approving smile curved up his arrogant mouth.

Raynor saw it, and while he flicked at Acelet a contemptuous look, he protested, "Sire, there is no need for this. I have the proof right here of his—"

"De Molinet," the duke interrupted, the smile vanishing into a frown, "are you refusing his challenge? Don't tell me you are afraid of this youth!"

Raynor lowered the parchment, startled. "Of course not, my liege. But if the battle is to prove his and de Brielle's guilt, then I have something better."

He raised the parchment again, but Acelet said, "The guilt is yours, Raynor. You should not have locked me up. You should not have threatened Siri. Triston said he would lop off your hands if you touched her, but I am the one who is going to do it!"

The duke actually laughed, but Lord Fauke, who had been observing the proceedings in simmering silence, muttered, "If I do not skin his thieving hide first."

The duke glanced at him but said, "Enough. De Molinet, whatever that is you are waving in your hand, give it to Lord Fauke. He will hold it until this challenge is settled. Tomorrow at mid-morning, you and this stripling will meet in the field without the city and—"

"Sire," Lord Fauke said abruptly, "set the combat for a week from now."

The duke turned. "A week? Why so long?"

"A week is the time you have allotted to learn the truth of Lady Siriol's birth. You are sending men to fetch her father's pattern book. To reach Vere, they must ride past Belle Noir. Let them investigate Sir Raynor's castle and see what they might find."

Lord Fauke watched Raynor with clear suspicion, but this time Raynor refused panic. He looked smug as he measured the defiant stance of Acelet's slim frame.

"Sire," he said, "I accept the boy's challenge. Let us cross swords at your will. If I defeat him, you and all of Poitou will know that any evidence at my castle was planted by this whelp and his perfidious cousin."

Triston straightened. "Look to yourself, Raynor. For if the victory falls to us, all of Poitou will know that you lied when you called us traitor. And that the spoils in your castle were placed there, not by us, but by you."

"So be it," the duke said, accepting their terms. "De Molinet, de Cary, you shall settle your quarrel by combat. Friday next, you shall meet. My court shall stand witness to Heaven's judgment as to which of you here speaks truth. The winner will stand absolved of all charges. As for the loser, the penalty for either crime, robbery—" his azure gaze held Raynor's "—or conspiracy—" the gaze flicked to Acelet, then shot to Triston and lingered longest there "—is death."

# Chapter 29

*I cried with my whole heart; hear me, O Lord.*

The young shepherd intoning the psalm knelt in a field of white violets, symbols of innocence and purity yet unstained. Behind him on the softly rolling hills, symbolic of his humble past, grazed a scattered flock of snow-fleeced sheep. But the shepherd's robes were red. Innocent and pure, this young man had yet known battle, had shed men's blood and saved a kingdom. As reward, he had been hunted by a jealous, unrighteous king, forced into hiding to save his very life. Behind him, below the grazing sheep, a deep cave yawned. His only refuge. In despair he knelt and wept and poured out his heart to the God he had so long and faithfully served. While above him, unbeknownst to his aching heart, the angels watched and wept too.

"My lady," an awed voice whispered, "how is it that one so beautiful as you has managed to capture such pain?"

She avoided Geoffroi's question, unwilling to admit to the clerk that it was her own pain reflected in her scene of the shepherd-king David. Above the shepherd's head hovered a golden crown with two ruby-colored jewels. She touched the point of her brush to the tiny circle in the center. When she drew it back, another jewel glittered amidst the gold, a breathless sparkle of blue, color of truth and justice.

"The lapis lazuli is most effective when used sparingly," she said.

Her full set of paints had been brought with her father's pattern book

348

from Vere to facilitate her completion of Lord Fauke's psaltery. She welcomed the employment, desperate to occupy her thoughts while she awaited the arrival of the monk of Les Préaux who would confirm or deny her father's link to the Geraud inheritance. Until that matter was settled, she had been ordered by the duke to remain aloof from his court, no doubt to help stem the gossip about her. But the command had had the dual effect of also separating her from Triston.

Geoffroi called her beautiful, but she had seen the dark shadows beneath her eyes when she had gazed in her mirror that morning. How could she sleep at night when her body ached for Triston's arms, her mouth yearned for his kisses? What if she should never taste them again? Perhaps worse, what if she *should* taste them, and find they were not hers after all?

She bit her lip and managed by sheer force of will to master the quiver of her hand. Her father's pattern book and the paints had arrived within days of Acelet's challenge. What might or might not have been found at Belle Noir along the way did not reach her within this secluded chamber set aside for her and Geoffroi's scriptorium. She tried to bury her fears in her art. Fears for what would happen if Acelet failed to defeat Raynor. Fears for her future with Triston if it were proved that her father stood heir to a fortune. Fears that even if they were somehow reunited, her claim to his heart might yet prove too tenuous, that the ghost of Clothilde might rise between them again.

Not until her lip began to sting did she realize her teeth were threatening to pierce the skin. She soothed the soreness with her tongue, then wiped clean her brush and set it aside while she poured onto her wooden mixing board a small pool of black ink and stirred into it a few drops of white lead to make grey. She must turn her thoughts elsewhere. Deftly, she tipped her brush with the new pigment and used it to dart in the wedge-shaped definition of feathers on the wings of her angels.

The door clicked open. She turned her head and stared into Lord Fauke's glittering eyes.

He glanced at the clerk and made a dismissive gesture. Geoffroi hesitated, but when Lord Fauke barked out an order, he left the chamber.

Siri stiffened when she found herself alone with Lord Fauke.

But he only said, "You are summoned by the duke. The monk has arrived from Les Préaux." He raked her with a hot, hungry look. "You have eluded me a long while, my lady, but today is Thursday. By tomorrow night, the duke will have made his decision where to bestow your hand. Then there will be nothing left to stand between the passion you enflame in me—and its long-awaited fulfillment."

Her heart pounded, both at his threat and in fear of what the monk might reveal. But she turned a disdainful back on Lord Fauke's leering grin and swept out of the chamber.

<hr>

"There is no doubt about it, my lord. These drawings were done by Walter Geraud."

The words floating from the queen's solar sent Siri tripping with unladylike haste across the threshold. She glimpsed Sir Owen, standing with Raynor before the duke's chair, together with an unknown man in a monkish robe. Then her eyes locked with Triston's. She stepped towards him, then stopped at the duke's sharp command.

"Come forward, wench. Do you acknowledge this as your father's pattern book?"

Reluctantly, she approached the duke's chair. The monk, the book open in his hands, held it out for her to view. Dare she lie?

She heard a footstep, then Triston spoke at her shoulder. "If your men brought this from Vere, then it is her father's."

She glanced up at him, her cheeks warming. He must have guessed the meaning of her hesitation. But a lie would be useless, if not so obvious as to be dangerous.

"I must hear it from the wench," the duke said. "Well, Lady Siriol?"

She licked her dry lips and forced herself to reply. "Aye, my lord, this book was created by my father's hand."

The duke turned to the monk. "And you, Brother Gaspard, are certain these pictures were drawn by Walter Geraud, Lord Simon's son?"

The monk, an elderly man, replied, "I could not mistake it, my lord. Here—" he shifted the heavy book into one hand and pointed with the other "—are the monkey-demons that gave us all such a fright when he drew them. See how this one beats the drums and that one plays the pipes while their hideous winged fellows drive these weeping sinners down to hell? They were bad enough sketched out here in simple black ink, but when he painted the same into Lord Brian de Savigny's manuscript, with glowing red eyes, distended pink lips, and yellow teeth so long and vicious one could almost hear them chattering—" He shuddered. "Those of us who sat with him in the scriptorium did not sleep soundly for weeks after that commission was completed, so vividly did these images linger with us. But it was praise from Lord Brian for that work which won six of us the abbot's permission to leave Les Préaux to study with Master Basilius in Jerusalem. Walter was one of our number."

"Then you knew Walter well, Brother Gaspard," the duke said. "Well enough, perhaps, to know whether it's true that he never actually professed to the abbey?"

The monk lowered the book. He seemed to hesitate, then worded his answer with evident care.

"I myself was not witness to his profession, nor were any of the brothers with whom I ever spoke. I know that Walter initially resisted speaking the vows, but when he was allowed to resume his duties in the scriptorium, we assumed the abbot's discipline had persuaded him to obedience. But on the road to Venice, Walter confided to me that he had not, in fact, professed, and that he had never given up his dream of escaping monastic life. He said it with a laugh, so that I half believed he spoke in jest—until he eloped with Elisabetta Gallo." He paused and looked at Siri. "This lady is their daughter, yes? She has Walter's bewitching eyes and that same deceptive softness about her chin and mouth. One could not have guessed by looking at his gentle features the stubbornness and strength of his true nature."

"Or Ceridwen's," Sir Owen murmured. "Sire, even Brother Gaspard recognizes that the family resemblance is remarkable. I have spoken with Lady Siriol's companion, the Lady Lucianna, who claims to have been an intimate friend of Elisabetta's. She insists this is indeed Elisabetta's daughter by Walter Geraud. And the girl has possession of Lord Walter's pattern book. What further proof do you need to convince you that she is who we say she is?"

The duke grunted. "Very well, Sir Owen. I shall acquiesce to your judgment. But I shall bestow her hand on a man of my choice, a man of indisputable loyalty to myself and my interests in Poitou."

Siri saw Raynor smile at these words, but when she glanced at the duke, she saw his gaze resting, not on Raynor, but at some point behind her. She turned her head and had to tilt her neck to see around Triston's blocking frame. In the back of the chamber stood the Lady Osanne, locked in a low-voiced quarrel with—

Siri gasped so loudly that Triston turned too and muttered, "What is it?"

She shook her head, but could not stop herself from shrinking against him. A sharp gesture at last sent Osanne swishing from the chamber and Lord Fauke, still scowling, finally joined the circle around the duke.

Triston's hands closed about Siri's shoulders, imparting strength against a horror he could only sense.

That horror, coupled with Triston's beloved touch, galvanized her into braving a confrontation with the unpredictable duke.

"Sire," she said desperately, "surely my brother's will should be considered an extension of my father's wishes? He abandoned all claims to his inheritance before my birth. I pray you again to take it for the Crown, and honor my brother's disposition of me into Sir Triston's hands."

The duke laughed, a dangerous sound without amusement. "I have not maintained my governorship of Poitou by acting the fool. I take your lands, Sir Triston marries you, and then he will accuse me of cheating you of your inheritance. Others will rally around him, eager as always for any pretext to try to wrest Poitou out of the Angevin grasp. But that grasp is going to squeeze the breath from those rebels' necks, beginning with your former guardian's."

"You promised him freedom and safety if Acelet wins his battle against Sir Raynor!"

The duke had leaned forward to glare at Triston, but now he flung himself back in his chair. "Bah! So I did. Not that I think there is much likelihood that the boy can win. But I regret losing so courageous a youth, for if he fails, I must hang him with his cousin."

"Sire—"

"No, silence! You have no permission to speak."

Into the tension-ridden stillness that followed this command, Sir Owen softly ventured, "Sire, if you would permit me to speak with the Lady Siriol, to tell her of her family and explain the duties of her inheritance, perhaps I could bring her around to that quiet obedience you desire."

"There is no question but what she is going to obey me," the duke said with a smoldering gaze on Siri's face. "But if you think your words can tame her froward spirit, then by all means, Sir Owen, take her away." He signaled their dismissal by a wave of his hand. "In fact, away with all of you, save Lord Fauke. He and I have a matter of business to discuss. De Brielle, if I were you, I'd advise your cousin to stop flirting with the ladies of my court and ready himself for tomorrow's battle. And you, de Molinet, I would not take your superior experience too much for granted. That boy has fire in his eye and hatred in his heart. They could prove a more hazardous combination than you think."

Raynor responded to this warning with a contemptuous smirk, whispered something into Lord Fauke's ear, and went out before he saw the baron's calculating smile in reply. But Siri saw it and clutched Triston's hand, hoping the duke would not notice the way she tried to hide their tangled fingers in the folds of her skirt as they followed Sir Owen from the chamber.

But Sir Owen paused outside, leaning on his cane, and observed them both with a gentle smile. "I thought my lady and I could speak in the palace garden. Perhaps, Sir Triston, you would care to join us?"

Triston gave a quick nod and they followed Sir Owen out to the garden.

With the greatest reluctance, Siri surrendered Triston's hand so that Sir Owen could sit beside her on one of the stone benches. She listened with only half an ear as the old man told her of her grandfather, Lord Simon. Any curiosity about her kin had been choked out by the shabby, cold-hearted way her father had been treated by them all. There was only one relative she cared about, and then only so as to solve the mystery that still prevented her from completely trusting Triston's heart.

She laid a hand on Sir Owen's arm, interrupting his description of the prosperous lands once held by her grandfather and uncle. "Tell me about Ceridwen, Lord Simon's wife."

Sir Owen smiled at her. "Your grandmother."

"Yes. You said I look like her."

"So you do."

She resisted an impulse to glance at Triston, who stood near them. "But I am also said to look like the Lady Clothilde, Sir Triston's wife. How can that be true?"

"Perhaps," Sir Owen said with a twinkle in his deep blue eyes, "it is because your father and the Lady Clothilde's mother were cousins."

Triston echoed, "Cousins? I grew up with Clothilde and no word was ever spoken of Welsh cousins in Poitou."

"Probably her mother, the Lady Gwenllian, did not know. I left Wales with Ceridwen while she was still a babe, to escape her father's wrath." The humor faded and Sir Owen sighed. "That was nearly sixty years ago. My weary bones should have found their final rest long before now."

The thick branches spread above them prevented the relentless summer sun from beating down upon the old man's silver head, but he looked very tired. Though the muted light softened the lines in his face, there was a fragility about his thin shoulders that moved Siri with compassion.

"Perhaps you would find it cooler inside?" she offered.

He smiled again. "Nay, child. The duke has kept me standing a long while today, and I am content to rest my tired legs here. But a cup of cool wine from the palace cellars would be welcome."

Triston summoned a servant to send him off for some wine, but before he obeyed, Sir Owen motioned to the young man and whispered something in his ear.

A moment of silence passed when the servant had gone. Siri stilled the impatient wiggling of her feet. "If you wish to await his return before you finish telling me about my grandmother . . ."

But Sir Owen had seen the restless fluttering of her fingers before she laced them firmly in her lap. "Nay, child, I believe you and Sir Triston are eager to know the truth. I cannot blame you. I once met the Lady Clothilde when she was wife to Sir Fulbert de Merval, during the king's wars with his sons."

From the corner of her eye she saw Triston stiffen at this mention of Merval.

"Neville, your father's brother, was lord then," Sir Owen continued. "He sent me to offer our forces as allies in Merval's resistance against King Henry. I spent a single night at Merval's castle, partaking of his and his wife's hospitality. I could scarcely drag my gaze from her then, so striking was her resemblance to my beloved niece, though she seemed timid and frightened, traits I had seldom seen Ceridwen display. But I said nothing of our kinship. I knew my sister wished the matter to remain buried and forgotten."

Though she dared not look into Triston's face, Siri saw the tight curling of his fingers into fists and knew that something in Sir Owen's recital had angered him.

He said, "What sort of matter do you speak of, Sir Owen?"

Sir Owen glanced at Triston, catching whatever expression Siri so carefully avoided. "My sister Margiad was a woman of great beauty, like the Lady Siriol. She drew men like moths to a flame, even after her marriage to the Welsh lord, Dunawd ap Gruffydd. But Dunawd was a jealous man and a violent one. Many was the time I found my sister weeping, her lovely face bruised and swollen, rebuked by her husband for having smiled or spoken a simple word of kindness to some man in their household. The men Dunawd punished with the edge of his sword."

Sir Owen's thin features darkened with his memories. "My sister was terrified of him, as were we all, but none but her husband ever doubted her fidelity to him. At length, she found herself with child. Dunawd's, of course. But on the night of the birthing, she brought forth not one child, but two. Twin daughters. There are many among my people who still believe that twins are sown by two fathers, sure evidence of a wife's unfaithfulness. Certainly her husband was such a man as to believe it. My sister, in panic, talked wildly of casting the second child from her, even—" he hesitated "—of destroying it."

A grating sound made Siri glance down to see the heel of Triston's boot grinding into the graveled walkway. He strode several steps, then stopped, a visible tremor smiting his broad shoulders. She half rose in alarm at the sight, then sank back down as he jerked his shoulders straight again. After a moment, he reached up to pluck a plump, ruddy peach from an overhanging branch, then stood there, staring at it, saying nothing until Sir Owen finally continued.

"One of her women, affrighted by her ravings, brought me to her chamber. I sought to calm her, to reason with her, but she said if she did not do the wicked act, her husband would. I feared it was true. So I agreed to bear one of the babes away, to take her somewhere safe. England, my sister said, was too near. She bade me go to Normandy and gave me a ring, this ruby with a swan etched into the gem." He drew the sparkling red stone from the little finger of his left hand. "The swan is the emblem of my house. It would prove the babe's noble birth to those who would rear her."

He paused as the servant returned with a goblet of wine and held it out with a bow. Sir Owen thanked him and drank the restoring liquid. He returned the cup and motioned the servant away, but not before the servant handed him a scroll of parchment, tied with a red ribbon.

Twins. Siri thought briefly of Raynor and Isobel. How had their father greeted the news of their birth? Less violently than Dunawd ap Gruffydd, it would seem, since they had grown to adulthood together. She glanced at Triston. He still stared down at the peach in his hand, his expression dark and brooding.

Sir Owen watched him a moment too before continuing. "I brought the babe, Ceridwen, to Normandy and placed her in the care of the nuns of Saint-Amand. I found a position nearby as squire to a Norman baron, who later knighted me. I visited Ceridwen often and insisted that the nuns raise her, not as a future novice, but as a lady. They treated her with great kindness. But she remained in their eyes little more than a foundling. And all the time I knew that her twin, Eluned, was growing up the honored daughter of Dunawd ap Gruffydd."

That finally won a glance from Triston. "Eluned. Lady Gwenllian's mother? Clothilde's grandmother?"

Sir Owen nodded. "Aye." He untied the ribbon and rolled out the scroll for Siri to see. "I maintained a pedigree as best I could, though I never dared show it while Dunawd ap Gruffydd lived. Who knows what misguided vengeance he might have sought on my poor sister, had Ceridwen come to his knowledge? As you see, my handwriting is none too elegant, but I believe you can follow the connections."

Her gaze quickly found and fastened on her father's name, with his marriage marked to Elisabetta Gallo. Her own name and her brother's were both starkly absent from the parchment. Until this morning, Sir Owen had not known about their birth, unlike the Lady Clothilde's, whose name appeared on the opposite side of the scroll, alongside her brother's and sister's.

Sir Owen tapped his finger against the name *Eluned,* drawn, like all the other names, in awkwardly squared but discernable letters on the parchment.

"Eluned married a Welsh lord, as you see, but Ceridwen . . . ? Without a dowry, I knew she could not win the kind of marriage her birth entitled her to. So once I was knighted, I set out to make my fortune and hers. I fought in tournaments, hired myself out as a mercenary soldier, sought and hoarded gold in every honest way I could. At length, I came into the service of Lord Simon Geraud. I told him of Ceridwen, who by then was fourteen, and he granted my request to bring her into his house. He fell in love with her at first sight. So enamored was he of her beauty, that he chose to ignore the mystery of her birth, accepting this ring alone as evidence that her blood was noble. He accepted as a dowry the gold I had

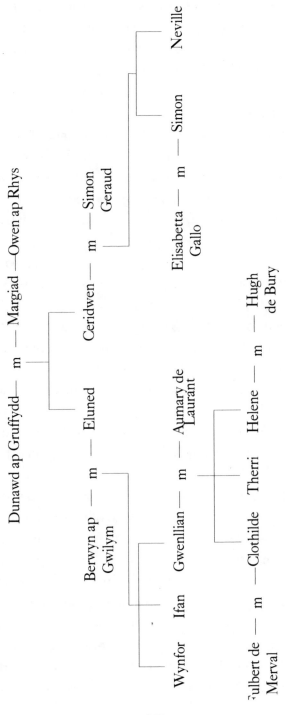

saved and an oath that I would devote my sword to no other cause but his while breath remained in my body. But I think if I had not had a single coin to offer in her behalf, he would still have taken her for his wife."

Siri almost smiled at the romance implied in this tale, until she remembered that the same Lord Simon who had sought love rather than land or gold in marriage, had also plotted and schemed to exclude his younger son from enjoying his rightful inheritance.

Sir Owen must have guessed her thoughts, for he said, "Lord Simon loved his wife deeply. Had she lived, it is more than likely that she would have softened his heart against Walter sufficiently to allow him to come back home."

"You said she died when my father was fifteen. She never knew how unhappy he was at the abbey?"

"No. It would have broken her heart."

Triston said abruptly, "Then why did she let him go? Why did she agree to give him up in the first place?"

Sir Owen looked slightly startled by the rough-voiced questions. "She was a pious woman. 'Tis a privilege to give a child to God, so long as that child is content to serve Him."

"A privilege?" Triston's fingers flexed so hard around the peach that Siri thought he was going to smash it. "Nay, I will tell you what it is. There is a curse to that Welsh blood, a curse of cruelty and selfishness. Your sister abandoned her daughter, who in turn abandoned her son. Out of protection, you say, out of love. But you owned yourself, 'twas not protection your sister first thought of, but murder of her own helpless babe. Such 'protection' Clothilde's mother sought to inflict upon her grandchild, my son, just so she could force Clothilde into marriage with Merval. Heaven intervened to save Perrin, but not to save Clo's sanity."

His voice broke. Siri pressed both her hands to her lips. How she had prayed never to see that look in his eyes again! But there it swirled. The loss, the pain and despair.

Triston drew a loud, shaking breath. "I had thought the Lady Gwenllian an aberration among women, but now you tell me casting children aside is a family tradition. Your sister, your niece, they were no better than

359

she. Their choices robbed Siri and her brother of the lives they should have had, as surely as the Lady Gwenllian robbed me of a life with Clothilde."

Sir Owen said, "I do not know what Gwenllian did to injure you, Sir Triston. I have never met her. But I did not sever all contact with my sister when I came to Normandy. I remember distinctly one message she sent expressing her alarm at her husband's particular affection for their granddaughter, Gwenllian. She feared he was raising her to be as ruthless and ambitious as he. He arranged for her a marriage to what my sister described as 'an ugly old bear of a man' who had lands my brother-in-law coveted. She said that Gwenllian agreed to the match with a smile that chilled my sister's bones. But then one of Gwenllian's brothers brought home a young Poitevin knight he had met in the courts of Count Henry of Anjou, where both had gone to join the struggle to place young Henry on the throne of England."

This last statement seemed to startle Triston so, that for a moment his anger checked. "Poitevin? You mean Laurant? Laurant supported Henry's claim to the throne?"

"Indeed." Sir Owen gave a faint smile. "He was not then Baron Laurant, of course, and Poitou had only recently come under the Angevin sphere with Henry's marriage to Eleanor, heiress of Poitou and Aquitaine. There were many Poitevins who backed Henry's cause then who later turned against him, some who have since returned to the Angevin fold."

Siri guessed that he referred to Laurant. Triston's father, she knew, had died in rebellion against the English crown.

"To my brother-in-law's consternation and fury," Sir Owen continued, "Gwenllian eloped with the Poitevin knight. Dunawd sent men to retrieve them, but they escaped with her brother's help. Later, when she sent to beg Dunawd's forgiveness, she made no claim of having gone for love, but spoke only of the lands and influence her new husband would one day inherit—wealth and power far superior to what she would have gained as wife to her grandfather's choice. My sister said he regretted that power should lie so far from his control, but that he admitted pride in his granddaughter's shrewdness."

"Shrewdness." Triston almost spat the word out. "Ruthless ambition. Do not blame the man for those women's sins. 'Twas the women who cast away their babes to obtain their own selfish ends."

"My sister acted in terror of her life, and the babe's. But Gwenllian knew nothing of the night when her mother and Ceridwen were born. Whatever she might have later done was not the fault of my sister's choice that night."

"No? You said your sister's women heard her ravings the night the twins were born, how she threatened the younger with destruction. How can you know that memories of that night were not whispered down through the years until they finally reached the granddaughter's ears and planted the seed which would later threaten my son?"

Sir Owen began a protest that trailed away. He clearly possessed a general knowledge of significant events that had occurred in Wales after his departure, but he had to have remained ignorant of anything more than his sister had imparted to him through an occasional messenger.

"Your sister," Triston said, his eyes smoldering like two ebony coals, "should have had more courage. And Lady Gwenllian—" He turned and hurled the peach with such force that it splattered against the wall. Again his heel ground into the walkway as he spun and strode out of the garden.

"Triston!" Siri flew up from the bench, but Sir Owen drew her back down.

"Let him go, child. He must deal with his grief in his own way."

"Grief." She could not prevent her voice from trembling on a sob. "Grief for her, for Clothilde. She was his wife and she had my face, and now she is in his heart again." She checked herself. She must not babble her pain in front of Sir Owen. She tried to swallow the too-familiar ache in her throat. She glanced down again at the chart in Sir Owen's lap. "That Clothilde and I are granddaughters of twins, I suppose explains our likeness. But why is it no one ever recognized and wondered at her resemblance to Ceridwen?"

"Ceridwen died before Gwenllian ever came to Poitou," Sir Owen said. "I suppose by the time Gwenllian's daughter had grown to womanhood,

Ceridwen had been forgotten by all but a loving few." He sounded sad and looked even sadder. He rolled up and retied the scroll, then slid the swan-etched ruby ring onto Siri's finger. "Nay," he said when she began a protest, "you are all that is left of Ceridwen. She would have wanted you to have it."

She bit her lip and gazed down at the ring, but its bright glow blurred through her tears.

"Child," Sir Owen murmured, "my eyes have grown dim through the years, but when you came before the duke today and Sir Triston turned and looked at you—well, even I could see how thoroughly in love with you he is. My words raised hurtful memories in him, I fear, but such emotion as I saw in his eyes for you . . ."

"It doesn't matter anymore. I cannot fight her any longer. And the duke is going to give my hand to another man."

A tear splashed onto the ruby ring before her lids squeezed the rest of the flood into a hot stream down her cheeks.

Sir Owen's gentle hand wiped the stream away. "Perhaps not."

Her lids flashed up.

"I watched you before the duke today, as I did when you first arrived. Though you showed dismay at his temper, I was surprised to see no fear. You are a woman of rare strength, Lady Siriol, and I suspect, a woman of great resolve. It will require both strength and resolution to thwart the marriage the duke has in mind for you."

"Thwart? But it is his royal prerogative to name my husband."

"A prerogative with limits. If one knows the way."

She caught her breath. "Do you know the way, Sir Owen?"

"I may. But you are the one who will have to defy the duke. Do you think you have the courage?" He laughed at her fierce nod. "Then listen carefully and I will tell you where to find your answer."

# Chapter 30

All through the night, while Acelet slumbered away at his side like a carefree child, Triston wrestled with the memories so wrenchingly rekindled by Sir Owen's recital. He gasped into the darkness and thrust the sheets away, as if the linen itself were to blame for the weight that threatened to squeeze the breath from his lungs.

Anger flared in him again. Clothilde, her very sanity betrayed by her mother's ambition. An angel-faced demon, her mother had been. He groaned at the violence that pounded in his chest at the thought of that woman. And yet—

He moved a hand against his throat. Rage against her mother never surged in his breast but what his own failures almost immediately eclipsed it. If only he had not gone on pilgrimage, or if he had only forced her to go with him. Had he found some way to make her acknowledge their marriage upon his return, or had he forbidden Raynor welcome to Vere that last, fateful Christmas . . .

Triston had sworn to cherish and love her above all else, but instead he had failed her in every step of the life they had tried to share. And now, in perhaps the greatest betrayal of all, as he lay here in the darkness and sought to envision again her melancholy face, all he could see were merry lips and a golden smile and laughter-crinkled eyes.

All he could see was Siri.

He sat up, smothering a groan, nearly choking on the guilt that filled his throat. Desperately he drew in a loud, ragged breath, loud enough to wake Sir Balduin in the cot he had set up against the wall of the chamber the duke had allotted to the party from Vere.

But Acelet merely murmured and snuggled deeper down into his pillow.

"Sir, are you all right?" Sir Balduin said.

"Aye." Triston's answer came out in a croak. He swung out of bed. "I need some fresh air. I won't be gone long."

"Where are you going? What hour is it?"

"I heard the bells chime lauds some time ago." Triston began to dress in the dark. "Dawn cannot be many hours away. I hope to be back before then, but if I'm not, get Acelet up and dressed. But do not let him leave for the field until I return."

Perhaps a brisk walk in the city streets would help to clear his mind. He pulled his cloak about his shoulders and fastened the strings at the neck.

"Should you not take your sword, or at least a dagger?" Sir Balduin asked.

"Any thieves will have done their night's work and be well abed by now. Don't worry for me, old friend. If you are unable to sleep, then offer a prayer or two for my cousin. Aye, pray that when he wakes we will find that one grain of reality has slipped into that dreamy head of his." Triston paused to gaze down at the slumbering Acelet.

"It'll take more than prayers to even the odds in that boy's favor," Sir Balduin muttered. "Sir Raynor will slaughter him. Sir, is there no other way to win back the Lady Siri?"

Triston's hand found his throat again. Blazes, this guilt was going to strangle him yet! Even if Acelet won the challenge, it would only save Siri from Raynor. Her fate as an heiress still lay at the duke's disposal, and no triumph on Acelet's part, however impressive, would make the duke look kindly on Triston.

But could Acelet win? Events of the past week had made it look more and more doubtful. And if he failed, if Raynor "slaughtered" him as Sir Balduin feared, Triston would have to live with the knowledge that it had been his own attempt at cunning which had cost his cousin his life.

He tried to speak some reassurance to Sir Balduin, but the burning lump in his throat choked off the words. He made a helpless gesture, which Sir Balduin probably could not see in the dark, and went out of the chamber.

≈

Triston wandered the narrow, darkened cobblestone streets, almost regretting the accuracy of his prediction to Sir Balduin. A lively brawl at this hour with a few ruffians would have proved a welcome distraction from the suffocating turn of his thoughts. But the streets remained obstinately empty. Honest citizens slept safe behind bolted doors, while their less honest brethren had ferreted their spoils and returned to their warrens in the twisting, refuse-strewn lanes. Triston pressed his nose into his sleeve to block out the unholy stench. He thought briefly but longingly of the fresh air of Vere, and turned his steps up the slightly wider, less cluttered way of the merchants' shops.

A rat darted across his path, followed by a streaking cat, but otherwise he bore no company but the slowly fading stars overhead. He strolled in no conscious direction, walking past the silent, shuttered shops. He turned past a cold, quiet blacksmith's forge, another turn past the hulking black shape of the guild hall, then came to a stop before a looming stone structure that dwarfed every building in the city but the palace. The Cathedral of Notre-Dame-la-Grande, a glittering jewel-box of a church when the sun bathed it in glory. Though not particularly large as cathedrals go, it was nonetheless the pride of the city. Triston stared up at the twin cone-shaped pinnacles and the triangular gable, with Christ standing in majesty at the center, surrounded by the symbols of the evangelists. Midway up, sheltered in individual archways, stood skillfully carved statues of the twelve apostles. The richly sculpted designs on the portals bespoke an Oriental influence familiar to Triston from his travels in the East.

For a moment, he remembered those hot, dry, sun-baked days in companionship with Simon Geraud. He heard again Simon's hearty laughter, felt himself bristling at Simon's teasing tongue, stared anew to see Simon's mischief replaced by a deep, sober fear for his sister.

*His sister.*

Triston took a deep breath and mounted the cathedral steps.

⁓

Jean aux Bellesmains, the dignified, grey-haired Bishop of Poitiers, listened quietly as Triston confessed the torturous conflict in his heart. The bishop was not unacquainted with the first part of Triston's story. He himself had conducted the wedding of Clothilde to Sir Fulbert de Merval and had belatedly confirmed its annulment, after her prior marriage to Triston had been revealed. The rest he listened to now in silence.

His guilt at last laid bare, Triston awaited the bishop's judgment, hot and flushed with tension where he sat on one of the stone seats attached to the wall in the nave.

"'Tis no sin to love again, my son," the bishop said at last. "It can only be pleasing in the sight of God to provide a kind stepmother for your son and to raise further children to the Lord."

Triston's jaw tightened. Those simple words should have eased his pain, but somehow they did not. The bishop stood with his hands clasped against the background of his dark-colored robe. Triston observed the long, tapered fingers, the smooth skin and beautiful shape of the hands that had won the bishop the sobriquet "Bellesmains."

The bishop frowned at Triston's silence. Then the beautiful hands unfolded and one of them reached out to Triston's shoulder.

"My son, a man has a duty to love and cleave to his wife for as long as she lives. But to grieve inordinately for her after her death is a challenge to God's wisdom and hence, might be viewed as sin."

Triston glanced up. The equation of grief with sin startled him. He met the bishop's steady grey eyes. Then he whispered a hoarse word of thanks and abruptly left the cathedral.

His mind seized upon the thought as a drowning man might clutch at a saving branch. He spared not a glance for the worshippers arriving on horseback as he strode down the steps into the dawn-greyed streets. He walked slowly back to the palace, rehearsing the bishop's words. Grief as sin. Wisdom of God. Wisdom . . . of . . .

When the tentative thought first drifted into his mind, he could not say. Suddenly it was just there, so bold and shocking in its implications that he thrust it away. He stopped when it returned and swept a hand in the air, as though to forcibly strike it from him. But almost immediately it surged back. At last, he drew a shaking breath and forced himself to confront it.

He had blamed Clothilde's mother for his wife's madness. But Clothilde's spirits, he knew, had been precarious from childhood. Either they soared in ecstatic transports or plummeted into the blackest despair. Triston had seldom seen her calmly content about anything. And her fear of the world had been inescapable. As a child, he had watched her shrink from the most mild of her father's horses. As a youth, he had delighted in rescuing her from the overzealous affection of her brother's dogs. The enchanting smiles she rewarded him with instantly made him forget her disturbing, overreactive screams of mere moments before.

But he remembered them now.

Was it possible—?

Again he pushed the thought away, then clenched his jaw and forced himself to complete it. Was it possible that the seeds of imbalance had always been there? That in fact, her mother's act had merely hastened what had always been inevitable?

His mind could not fathom the "wisdom" of God in allowing Clo's sufferings. But perhaps—

He pressed a hand to his suddenly stinging eyes. For more than a year he had anguished over his failure to catch her and prevent her fall that fatal night. But she had been unhappy for so long. Perhaps God's wisdom had prevailed. Perhaps her death had been more than the empty tragedy Triston had always believed it.

Perhaps in an act of mercy and love that Triston only now struggled to comprehend, God had finally brought Clothilde to peace.

❧

The Bishop of Poitiers lifted the massive, leather-bound book out of the small, delicate hands that held it.

"I much regret to disappoint you, my lady, but I do not believe I can allow Gratian's canon to leave the cathedral."

Siri made no attempt to conceal her dismay at this statement. She had come early to the cathedral, arriving just after dawn. But again and again as she had painstakingly studied the pages of the thick, heavy book the bishop now held, her thoughts had returned to the man she had seen striding down the cathedral steps just as she had dismounted from her horse. She had not glimpsed the man's face, but his breathtaking height, the powerful breadth of his shoulders beneath his flowing cloak, his long-legged strides as he vanished down the city street, had put her so forcibly in mind of Triston that she was almost certain it had been he.

What had he been doing at Notre-Dame-la-Grande? Seeking solace from God for his grief? Solace for his lost Clothilde?

How foolish she had been to think their joyful exchange in the forest clearing could last. Clothilde's hold on him remained too powerful. Once Siri had tried to flee from the pain of that knowledge. But her chilling response to Raynor's kisses had made her realize that escape was hopeless. Triston had cast as inexorable a spell over her as Clothilde had cast over him. And if she could not spend her life in Triston's arms, then life would not be worth living. Even if when they loved, it was Clothilde's name he whispered in the dark.

But without the bishop's help, even that bittersweet joy would never be hers.

"But, sir, the duke will never take my word for what Gratian has written," she said. "If I do not have a copy of his *Decretals* myself, he will laugh at me and say I made it up."

"I am sorry, my lady. Perhaps I could have one of my clerks copy out the pertinent section. I believe you were concerned with case twenty-seven, question two?"

He set the book on a table in the cathedral's scriptorium, where they stood. The walls, lined with chests and shelves spilling over with parchment scrolls, stacked with wood- and leather-bound volumes, many gilded and jeweled, reflected a chamber famous for the study and learning of its bishop. Bellesmains flipped through the pages of the book he had taken from Siri, until he came to the section in question. A quick scan of its contents sent his aristocratic eyebrows arching and won her an inquisitive glance.

"Do you hope to quote this passage on your own behalf or another's?"

Siri followed his glance to Lucianna and Sir Balduin, waiting for her in the back of the chamber. She had teased Lucianna for inviting the hobbling knight to accompany them through the streets of Poitiers. Lucianna insisted it was only for their safety, but the way she and Sir Balduin were whispering and blushing now beside a chest of parchment scrolls made the bishop's confusion understandable.

Only an occasional anxious flicker across Sir Balduin's face reminded Siri of her promise that she would have him back at the palace before Acelet left to meet Raynor. Siri intended to be present for that duel too, but it had taken her longer than expected to find the judgment Sir Owen had told her of hidden away in the vast compendium of decretals, conciliar decrees, and patristic texts assembled by the great lawyer-monk Gratian into his famous and authoritative *Decretum*. Created a cardinal for his contributions to canon law, it was unlikely even Duke Richard could deny an opinion penned by Gratian and approved by the Pope.

"It is for myself," Siri said, referring to the passage in question. "I mean to lay it before the duke in the sight of witnesses."

"If you are reluctant to comply with the duke's demands," the bishop said, "you have only to stand firm by your conscience. No priest will force you to act against your will. You do not need to carry this tome to the palace to make your point."

The steady way he watched her prompted her to answer frankly. "I do not want to battle the duke all the way to the church door. I have been told that I have seen only the veriest tip of Duke Richard's temper. If there is a way to preempt another outburst before it starts—"

"Ah. You are afraid his anger will overwhelm you." The bishop smiled ruefully. "A valid fear, my lady. A thoroughly enraged Plantagenet is not a pretty sight. You are wise to try to think of a way to forestall his anger. But this is not likely to do it." He touched the book's page with his finger. "Richard will be enraged when he reads it, and the conflagration will consume even your hardiest resolution."

Siri wished her pursed lips imparted the determination she felt rather than appear the pout she knew they did.

To her surprise, the bishop laughed. "The fire in your eyes betrays your soft features, my lady. But that fire, even coupled with this, may not be enough." His finger tapped the book. He sobered. "It may be that I can help you. But I have found opposing royal prerogatives a most unpleasant business. If I am to do it again, I must be convinced that I am acting on a matter of conscience and not merely to fulfill some woman's contrary whim."

"I assure you, sir—"

The bishop held up a hand, hesitated, then suddenly strode out of the scriptorium.

"May I help you, my lord?" his voice rang out from the nave.

Siri followed him, then stopped so abruptly that Lucianna, at her heels, nearly collided into her.

Lord Fauke, six armed men at his back, replied to the bishop with a thinly veiled sneer. "My companions and I merely thought to enjoy a few moments of quiet contemplation within these peaceful walls."

Sir Balduin limped forward with a growl. "You lie in God's presence. You have not come here to worship, but to steal my master's ward."

"Steal?" Lord Fauke fixed his gaze on Siri. "Nay, rather only to take what is mine."

He put a hand to Sir Balduin's shoulder to turn him out of the way. Sir Balduin jerked back. The high ceilings shuddered as his sword scraped free of its scabbard. Instantly six more swords shrieked against the air.

"Sacrilege!" The bishop strode forward. "Put up your swords! How dare you draw steel in this place?"

Sir Balduin flushed and immediately resheathed his sword, then started to draw it forth again when Lord Fauke's men ignored the bishop's command.

"No." The bishop put out a hand. "Do not compound these men's sins with another of your own. Lord Fauke, you risk Heaven's sore displeasure by threatening violence within these walls."

Lord Fauke gave a signal that caused his men to lower their swords, but not to resheath them. "We will be happy to leave without further ado," he said, "just as soon as you've married me to that lady over there."

The bishop followed his gaze to Siri, who stood too stunned by this pronouncement even to react.

"By what authority do you come seeking the Lady Siriol's hand?" the bishop demanded.

Lord Fauke pulled from his belt a folded sheet of parchment and handed it to the bishop. Siri swept to the bishop's side and saw the red wax seal stamped with a sinister serpent-woman.

The bishop made a face of distaste and muttered something about Richard's devilish humor leading him straight to hell. But aloud he said, "If you wish me to read this, my lord, you will tell your men to put away their swords."

Clearly, the bishop was not a man to be easily intimidated by someone like Lord Fauke. After several moments of enduring the bishop's searing gaze, Lord Fauke's glare turned sullen and he signaled his men to resheath their weapons.

Only then did the bishop break the parchment's seal and read what lay within. When he finished, he gave Lord Fauke a long, measuring look, then handed the parchment to Siri. Inscribed were the duke's orders bestowing her hand, together with the lands she stood to inherit, on Lord Fauke de Vaumâle, signed with the duke's arrogant signature.

"But what about Raynor?" she gasped. "You promised my hand to him!"

Lord Fauke's lip curled back in a snarl. "That thieving dog? I found evidence enough at Belle Noir of his roadside crimes to hang him. Nay, my lady, where once you had nothing to offer me but the sweet pleasures of your beauty, now you bear a noble lineage and bring with you lands and wealth. Why should I not possess all of that, as well as your enticing charms? The duke knows that I will rule it all in his support and thus—" he motioned to the parchment "—agrees that you should be my wife."

"But does the lady agree?" the bishop asked softly.

Lord Fauke looked startled, but Siri stiffened. "I do not!"

The curve of Lord Fauke's mouth grew derisive. "What has that to do with anything? It is by the duke's command."

"Then," the bishop said, "I will speak with the duke. And until I do, there will be no marriage."

"The duke is otherwise occupied this day, and I am not of a mind to wait. You will wed us, sir."

"And if I won't?"

Lord Fauke's hand moved and his men's swords once more rang free. Sir Balduin again grabbed his hilt, but again the bishop signaled him to stop.

"You will not intimidate me with steel," the bishop said, his voice quite level, but his grey eyes glinting. "Put those swords away and leave this place at once."

Lord Fauke looked as though he meant to challenge the bishop. He glanced at his men. Then suddenly, he shrugged. "Very well, sir. If you feel you cannot in good conscience fulfill the duke's request, then I will simply take the lady elsewhere and find a priest who can."

He grabbed Siri before anyone could anticipate his move. She swung a fist at him, but he only laughed and caught her wrist. She heard Lucianna screaming and Sir Balduin and the bishop shouting, but guessed they were being held at bay by Lord Fauke's men. Lord Fauke swept her up into his arms and strode with her unhindered out of the cathedral.

# Chapter 31

Triston watched Acelet lace up his quilted gambeson, then grabbed his cousin's shoulders and turned him about.

"What are you doing?" Acelet said.

"Checking you out."

Triston had returned to the palace just after dawn. Sir Balduin had roused Acelet, then apparently gone off on some errand after having won a promise that Acelet would not leave for the field of battle until Triston returned. Triston frowned at the thought of his delinquent retainer as he worked his fingers across Acelet's shoulders and down his back.

The padded jacket should have been supple but firm. Instead there were lumps in places where the felted hair stuffing had shifted and bunched, with dangerously shallow indentations fanning out around them.

"Blazes, Acelet, I told you to take this to the duke's armorer and have it restuffed."

"I forgot."

"Forgot?" Triston's exasperated shove sent his cousin stumbling forward to fall across the bed. "Don't tell me you didn't repair your mail either?"

Acelet sat up, but he did not seem resentful of the push. "The worn links are in the back of the hauberk. Even so villainous a dog as Raynor would not strike me from behind."

Triston groaned. He must have been mad to think this plan could work. Instead of using the past week to hone his fighting skills, Acelet had squandered the majority of his days in the duke's hall. A bevy of pretty and very young ladies had gathered about him one night after a troubadour's melody had reminded him of a hymn of praise he had heard to the duke's mother. Acelet's hauntingly romantic rendition of the song won him the hearty applause of Duke Richard, the gift of a royal ring, and the sighing adoration of the ladies. Day and night thereafter the girls, none of them over the age of sixteen, gathered around him, trailed him about the hall, and sat in the rushes at his feet, riveted by his tales of chivalry and songs of tragic love.

Only with the greatest reluctance had he allowed Triston to drag him away to practice his fighting technique. Triston had stepped into the role of Raynor to cross swords with him, but to his regret, discovered that his swordmaster's assessment of Acelet's ability had not been misjudged. Acelet clearly possessed the knowledge, as he did speed and skill when striking the air at an opponent he imagined only in his head. But when met with Triston's blade, he tended to panic and retreat. Triston had tried to stiffen his courage, to suggest a trick or two that might take Raynor unawares. But Acelet only shrugged off his timidity, insisted it would be different when he faced Raynor himself, and the first chance he got, returned to those giggling girls in the hall.

"What about this?" Triston ran his fingers over a series of worn links on the breast of Acelet's hauberk. "This lies not on the back, but right over your heart. Raynor's blade would have little difficulty piercing this spot, I think."

"I'll be holding my shield there," Acelet replied. He slid his feet into his mail chausses and pulled them up over his legs, bound them at his waist, then held out his hand for the hauberk. "Don't worry. I am not the one who is going to die today."

He took the mail shirt out of Triston's hand and pulled it over his head. Triston recalled how insulted he had felt on Acelet's behalf when he had first seen the shabby piece of workmanship, a gift from Acelet's father when he'd sent his son to Vere. To this day, Acelet remained blissfully unaware of the scorn implied in his father's gift. And so quickly had Triston come to sympathize with his uncle's aggravation at Acelet's dreamy, rattle-brained ways, that beyond repeatedly telling him to take it to the armorer and have the worn links replaced, he had thought it so unlikely that his cousin would ever find himself in actual need of a good piece of mail, that he had not troubled himself to see if his commands were ever obeyed.

With considerably greater urgency, he had renewed those commands every day this week. He should have known that Acelet would not listen. He should have taken it to the armorer himself.

"Acelet, if you want me to speak with the duke, to request a delay—"

"Why would I want that? Hand me my surcote. You do not think I should wear one with my father's insignia?"

Triston sighed and gave him the forest green surcote emblazoned across the breast with the de Brielle rose. "You are a member of my household now. A slur against your honor is a slur against me, not your father. Remember that, Acelet, it's important."

Acelet nodded absently and arranged his flaxen ringlets over his shoulders. "I'm glad we're not wearing helmets today."

"Under the duke's rules, a strike at the head is forbidden. This is not intended to be a fight to the death. But do not give Raynor a chance to sham a misthrust. He is quite capable of splitting your skull in two and making it appear an unavoidable mistake."

"Maybe I'll split his skull instead."

"Not the way you've been performing this past week. You must not give way before his blows. You must stand firm and return strike for strike. Look for his weaknesses, take advantage of them if you can. Remember what Sir Rollo and I have taught you. And Acelet, above all, you must not look to be afraid."

"Afraid?"

Acelet's eyes flashed, but Triston repeated, "Aye, afraid. Remember the consequences if you lose this fight."

He stopped. He had been about to remind his cousin of Raynor's treason charge, but he recalled Acelet's shuddering dread that day they had spoken of its penalty in the woods. Acelet needed fire to stiffen him, not fear, and Triston had seen that fire flame from only one source.

"Acelet, this is for Siri. If Raynor defeats you, he will make her his wife. And don't forget his bargain with Lord Fauke."

Triston held his breath for Acelet's reaction. He would never have doubted Acelet's response before. But one of those girls in the hall, the shy one with big, soft, adoring eyes like a fawn, had drawn his cousin's particular attention in recent days. Might his passionate loyalty to Siri have ebbed in favor of another?

Triston need not have feared.

Acelet breathed out a curse worthy of Duke Richard himself and exclaimed in gruesome detail exactly how he intended to prevent Raynor from fulfilling his devil's bargain.

Triston admired his cousin's imagination more than he trusted his ability to carry out his threats. But the time was nearly gone. Acelet strapped on his sword and Triston handed him his shield. But when Acelet turned to leave the chamber, Triston caught his arm.

"Acelet, do you remember what we talked about at Vere, when we first agreed that you should challenge Raynor? We couched that challenge carefully in the de Brielle name, so that it might include us both. If you find yourself too hard pressed by Raynor's sword—"

Acelet flushed. "I am not going to surrender my challenge to you!"

"Acelet—"

"I would look like a coward. You said the only way I could win my spurs is to at least fight Raynor to a standstill. And you promised you would knight me yourself if I did."

*A rash promise,* Triston thought. No one else was likely to bestow that honor on this addlepated young man, and with good reason. Even if by some miracle he won his fight with Raynor today, his careless nature would make him a prime target for slaughter in an actual cavalry battle. He would forget to sharpen his sword, or wipe the rust from his mail, or hammer out the dents in his helmet, or any of a dozen other vital preparations for his own defense. Triston felt little better than an accomplice to murder.

"Acelet, I beg you to reconsider. This is not a game. Despite the duke's orders, Raynor may well be out for blood, and the only way to stop him may be to kill him before he kills you. You shed blood once before in Belle Noir's yard. Think on that and tell me truthfully if you are capable of doing it again."

The indignant color faded from Acelet's cheeks, but he answered stoutly, "I have thought of it. And if I can only save Siri by killing Raynor, then that's what I will do."

He turned to leave, but Triston still held his arm. Acelet had been so outraged against Raynor in the immediate aftermath of his escape from Belle Noir, so hot to avenge himself and rescue Siri, that Triston had allowed himself to believe the young man stood an honest chance in battle. But he had not been quite so mad as to place all his hopes on Acelet. They had deliberately worded the challenge so that it might be possible for Triston to step in and complete the fight to save his house's honor. Raynor would know that in fact, he fought for Siri, but the technicality was enough to salve Triston's conscience concerning the oath.

But as long as Acelet refused to surrendered the challenge to him . . .

"Triston, it's time to go," Acelet said. "I don't want them thinking I'm afraid to appear, because you held me here overlong."

It had been their joint fear for Siri that had brought them to this moment, and only Triston's distracting love for her caused him to let go of Acelet's arm. He hesitated, then dealt the young man a light slap, reminiscent of another, crueler blow, but this one playful, almost fond.

"Keep your head up, cousin, and that shield close to those worn links near your heart. Remember, you fight for a knighthood and Siri. If you should fall—"

"I am not going to fall," Acelet said. "But if I do, you will find some other way to save her."

"I pray you are right. But I might actually grieve for you—and miss you if you were gone."

Acelet looked startled, as indeed Triston was by his own words. He overcame the embarrassed moment by steering Acelet out of the chamber while reiterating those bits of fighting advice he thought Acelet might be most prone to remember.

The duke's court turned out in force to witness the engagement. That soft-eyed, adoring girl from the hall shyly tied a favor around Acelet's arm before the duel commenced, but any hope Triston had that her worshipful gaze might spur Acelet on to battle more firmly soon evaporated. Acelet spent most of his time dancing out of reach of Raynor's blade and only occasionally swinging his own. Duke Richard, sitting on a raised wooden platform beneath a fluttering blue canopy, quickly looked disgusted.

Triston struggled with his own frustration. Where was Siri? Her presence might have braced his cousin, fueled his indignation for her and lent courage to his arm. Had Raynor realized that Acelet's courage came from her and somehow contrived to keep her away?

Raynor feinted to one side and then the other, forcing Acelet to twist defensively either way before Raynor sprang at him straight down the center. But whatever else one wished to fault in Acelet, one could not fault his speed. He sprang nimbly out of the way, as he had each time before, leaving Raynor's blade slicing empty air.

But Triston knew that Acelet had to be made to stand still and fight. Only a clear-cut victory would win Siri's safety, and his own and Triston's lives.

Raynor knew it too. He let out a roar and vaulted again towards Acelet. His sword swished so furiously that had the air been made of fabric it would have been sliced into shreds. Acelet stumbled backwards in a desperate attempt to avoid the whirring blade. Raynor lunged harder. Acelet leapt faster. Raynor plunged on unremittingly until he had Acelet hemmed in against the edge of the onlooking crowd.

"Now, you young fool, I have you!"

Raynor made one final thrust. But Acelet hurled himself sideways, so hard that he hit the ground. Raynor, unable to check the force of his advance, plunged, sword swishing, into the crowd.

"Madman!"

"Look out!"

Ladies screamed and men sprang cursing out of Raynor's way.

Acelet rolled to his feet and ran to the other side of the field. Triston took advantage of the confusion to step onto the field and grab his cousin by the shoulder.

"The duke is not going to put up with this farce much longer," he warned. "Blazes, Acelet, you have got to fight."

"I am—fighting," Acelet panted.

"No, you are retreating, and it makes you look like a coward. You have got to meet Raynor steel on steel."

"I thought I could wear him out this way, and then—"

"You'll wear yourself out first, dancing away as you are doing. Besides, the duke has not the patience for your game."

Acelet looked away. "I know this is not the way you would do it."

Triston checked the retort on his tongue. The balance of fighting experience and skill tilted dangerously in Raynor's favor. But though Acelet looked tired, he did not look exhausted. His breathing had already steadied. Time might yet lend Acelet bulk and strength—he was still young—but today, Triston owned, speed undoubtedly stood his greatest ally. To discourage his reliance on it might well prove a fatal mistake.

"No," Triston admitted, "it is not the way I would fight. But your strategy is not without merit. Keep dancing out of Raynor's way. But when Raynor is frustrated and flustered and cursing the air where you stood a moment ago, Acelet, that is when you must raise your sword and strike."

Acelet's face paled, as it had in their chamber when Triston had reminded him of the man he had stabbed in his escape from Belle Noir. Despite Acelet's earlier denials and vivid threats, the prospect of actually shedding another man's blood, even Raynor's, clearly unnerved him.

"Acelet, if you can't do this, then surrender your challenge to me."

Acelet's head flashed up. "No! I'm the one he betrayed and insulted. I spoke the challenge. I'm the one who must—"

"Get off the field, de Brielle," the duke shouted, "and let the boy fight his own battles! And you, de Molinet, if you step outside the bounds again I shall call this combat off. A man who succumbs to recklessness in battle is as dangerous to my cause as the coward who fears to raise his sword at all."

His glare encompassed Acelet on this jibe. Triston glanced at Raynor and saw his fuming gaze locked on Acelet as he strode back across the field. The muscles in Acelet's face betrayed his struggle with Triston's advice. There was no time for more. Triston grabbed Acelet by both shoulders and spoke one last desperate word.

"Siri. Nothing but some foul treachery could have kept her from lending you the support of her presence this day. Think on that when you face Raynor next."

Acelet looked startled. He scanned the crowd, as if only just realizing Siri's absence. Triston stepped hastily off the field before the duke could rebuke him again.

Raynor stopped a sword's length from his opponent and raised his blade. "We end this now, Acelet. Fight like a man or yield like a coward. But stop dancing about like some foolish woman."

Acelet whirled. His sword clanged against Raynor's with such unanticipated force that Raynor actually sprang back in startled reaction.

"Where is she, you devil?"

"Where is who?"

"Siri! What have you done with her?"

Acelet's sword swept up and down again. The speed that had formerly lain in his feet now flashed through his arm and wrist in a sudden flurry of lightning blows. Unprepared for his opponent's swift reversal in tactics, Raynor stumbled into a retreat.

"Devil take you, Acelet!" he shouted. "How should I know where she is?"

"Liar! You've spirited her away somewhere. Admit it! If you have harmed one hair of her head—"

Rage for Siri carried Acelet forward so swiftly that Raynor had not time to recover and revise his own attack. Again and again his sword flashed up to fend off Acelet's blows. The crowd roared, cheering Acelet on. The duke sat forward in his chair, hands clenched around the armrests, his shrewd eyes carefully following each movement of the combatants. Raynor's flushed face betrayed a growing desperation.

Triston smiled, but a sour regret spoiled the completeness of his pleasure. His fingers flexed on the hilt of his own undrawn sword. *Blazes!* It should have been *his* blade beating Raynor back, *his* blade thudding against Raynor's shield, *his* blade swooping with incredible speed to dart around that barrier and land squarely in Raynor's villainous breast—

"Signor Triston! Signor Triston! My donna . . ."

The cry cheated Triston of the satisfaction of seeing Raynor land on his back. He caught only a blur of Raynor's fall from the corner of his eye as his head snapped around towards a frantically waving Lucianna.

"Signor Triston!" she called again.

Triston glimpsed her with Sir Balduin towards the rear of the crowd. He saw the alarm in Lucianna's face, the distress in Sir Balduin's, and the man at their side—the Bishop of Poitiers! What was he doing here?

Lucianna jumped up and down and waved her hands harder than before. "Signor Triston, you must hurry! My donna is in terrible danger!"

Triston's chest clenched. "Siri . . . ?" he shouted.

"Si, it is that *cane, Don* Fauke! He has abducted my donna Si—"

"Aiiieee!"

The woman's scream made even Lucianna blanch. Triston turned and saw Acelet's shy-faced lady swoon away into some older woman's arms. The same instant, the crowd erupted.

"Dastard!"

"Coward!"

"Arrant cur!"

Triston whirled towards the field. Acelet had stepped away from Raynor, towards the crowd, but he seemed to be frozen in mid-step, his face gone curiously blank. Raynor stood behind him. But it was not until Acelet fell that Triston saw Raynor's bloody sword as it pulled free from Acelet's back.

# Chapter 32

For one hideous moment, everything slowed and blurred before Triston's eyes. Acelet's face crumpled, and his sword dropped from limp fingers. His hands flew out in front of him as he fell, clutching the ground, propping himself up ever so slightly before he slumped into the grass. And Raynor stood over him, his fiendish blade dripping with Acelet's blood.

The blur turned red. Triston hurtled across the field and collided into Raynor. He saw Raynor's mouth moving as they hit the ground, but the thunder in Triston's head drowned out the words. His fingers crushed down about Raynor's throat. Raynor's mail bit into Triston's bare hands but provided inadequate resistance against Triston's rage-driven strength. The shudder that slammed through him now mingled the red mist of fury with tears of grief.

"Murderer!" he shouted. "Nay, I'll not throttle you like some helpless babe. You deserve that I should tear you limb from limb!"

He stood up, dragging Raynor with him, still held by the throat. Raynor had dropped his sword to grapple with Triston's stranglehold, but now he whipped his dagger free. Triston loosed one hand and caught Raynor's wrist. He twisted the dagger loose with a wrench that should have made Raynor gasp had Triston's other hand not still been wrapped around his windpipe. His last defense gone together with the air in his lungs, Raynor's knees buckled.

"Let him go, de Brielle!" the duke's voice rang out.

Triston cursed. He swung Raynor about, then flung him back onto the ground. But only so that he could deal out a bloodier punishment than simple strangling.

Triston drew his sword and strode towards where Raynor lay in a sprawl. He would deal a blow for Acelet, a blow for Siri, a blow for Clothilde . . . If he hacked away at Raynor's hauberk hard enough, the mail links would break as surely as Acelet's weakened ones had.

Raynor must have seen the intent in Triston's eye. He groped in vain for some defense, but both sword and shield lay out of reach.

"Triston, no—it was an accident," Raynor croaked.

"An accident? Like Siri's fall down the stairs? Nay, Raynor, you die now and your insidious mischief dies with you!"

Triston's sword flashed down and cut deep into the earth. Only panicked desperation could have lent Raynor the strength to roll out of the way in time.

"Triston, I swear! Acelet demanded that I yield, but before I could do so, he stepped back from me and I thought he was allowing me quarter to fight again. I leapt to my feet, but as I struck at him someone shouted Siri's name and he turned and my blade— Something must have been wrong with his hauberk. My sword should not have cut through his links so easily."

"Liar." Triston slammed down his foot on Raynor's sword as Raynor scrambled to retrieve it. "'Tis a coward who strikes a man in the back. A coward who would strike a man through his women. You deserve to rot in the lowest realms of hell, and I mean to be the one who sends you there." He raised his sword.

"Curse you, Triston." Raynor's hand curled into the ground and came up with a wad of dirt and grass he sent hurling into Triston's face.

Triston stumbled back. His free hand scrubbed at his stinging eyes. By the time he'd wiped away enough to see again, Raynor was on his feet, sword in hand.

"You call me coward? You curse me for the way I've used your women? What about Isobel? What about a man who murders his lover to conceal the shame of his own child?"

Raynor's sword slashed down, but even with his still watery vision Triston deflected the blow.

"Devil take you, Raynor, we were not lovers! The child was not mine."

Their steel rang together again.

"Yours was the only name she ever spoke," Raynor shouted.

"She lied."

A curse followed the swing of Raynor's blade.

"Nay, you are the liar, Triston. I caught the pair of you together, remember? Down by the river?"

"She lied," Triston repeated. Bitterness fed his rage. His blade-tip clipped across Raynor's breast, flinging him backwards. "We never exchanged more than the kisses you saw. When I rejected her, she took a lover, hoping to make me jealous. The babe was his, not mine."

Raynor regained his balance and circled. His lips sneered his disbelief. "And who was this mysterious lover? Why did she never name him? Why did not you?"

Triston turned with Raynor's movements, his sword at the ready. Over Raynor's shoulder he saw that a portion of the crowd had gathered around Acelet, cutting his crumpled body off from Triston's view. He caught a glimpse of Sir Balduin and the duke, standing beside the bishop. The bishop. Was it too late to shrive his poor cousin of his sins?

Raynor lunged in that moment of Triston's inattention. But Triston blocked the stabbing blade with his own and swept them both downward. The points sliced the earth before he forced Raynor's blade up again and disengaged with a powerful shove of his steel's edge.

The movement turned him in the direction of Lucianna, still waving frantically at Triston.

"Well?" Raynor demanded. "You cannot tell me his name because he does not exist!"

Raynor's blade swooped towards Triston again, but Triston caught it with his own and forced it away. He did not need to hear Lucianna. Her former cry flooded back, and with it, panic washed through his grief. Lord

Fauke had taken Siri. Each moment Triston stood here battling Raynor, she raced into greater danger.

Raynor's sword swiped towards Triston's head in a sideways arc. Instead of meeting it this time, Triston ducked almost to the ground, then launched himself like a missile into Raynor's chest. Raynor barreled backwards and hit the ground with Triston atop him.

Triston laid the edge of his blade across Raynor's mail-clad throat. "Drop it."

Raynor spat an obscenity at Triston.

Triston pressed his blade closer. "Drop your sword and yield."

"Never. Kill me if you want. I will never yield to you."

"I have not time to kill you, Raynor. Siri needs me now. We will have to finish this another day."

He slammed his fist into Raynor's face. Then he twisted Raynor's sword away, stood up, and cast it across the field. By the time Raynor recovered and retrieved it, Triston would be gone.

He turned, but felt a tug at the hem of his surcote.

"Triston—"

He glanced down. Raynor looked dazed, but he clung tenaciously to the cloth. Triston wrenched Raynor's hand away. He had no time to linger. Yet some flicker in his enemy's stunned face checked him.

"Raynor, Isobel made me swear I would not speak her lover's name. She did it for my protection and yours. She tried to trap me with the child because her lover deserted her. I could not avenge her dishonor then, for I was bound by the oath. But if I can rescue Siri now, I swear to you—the punishment her abductor suffers at my hand will appease your sister's ghost as well."

Raynor fell back as Triston thrust his hand aside. Triston spun away without further hindrance and strode across the field to Lucianna.

"Where is she?" he demanded.

Tears welled up into Lucianna's eyes. "Ah, signore, I do not know where he has taken her. He abducted her from the cathedral. The bishop refused to marry them, but *Don* Fauke said—"

"Marry?"

"Si, he said that the duke has given him her hand."

Triston swore. He pushed his way through the crowd towards where the horses were tethered.

Lucianna ran after him. "Where are you going? How will you find them?"

"If you do not know where they have gone, I know someone who will. I must return to the palace."

He shoved his foot into the stirrup and swung himself onto his horse. Then he paused to look back over the crowd, but he was too far away and there were too many people to see what might be happening around Acelet now.

"Signore." Lucianna reached up to take his hand. Tears streamed down her face. "If you will only bring my donna back—"

Triston leaned down and pressed her fingers. "I will bring her back," he promised. "And when I do, I shall never let her go again."

⌘

Siri was not the only lady whose absence Triston had observed on the field. His brows rose in surprise when a servant directed him to the scriptorium. But the voices issuing from the chamber as he approached twisted his lips into a cynical smile.

"Away with you, foul wench! You will not tempt me from my vows."

A woman's trilling laughter answered this sharp rebuke. "Perhaps if you had a glimpse of what you are rejecting, you would reconsider?"

Triston stepped into the open doorway. "Osanne."

Osanne whirled, her hands at the wide-cut neck of her gown, one gleaming shoulder peeping from its lowered edge.

"Make yourself decent, woman," Triston said. "I need to speak with you." Then to the clerk, Geoffroi, "If you would permit me a moment alone with my stepmother?"

Geoffroi bowed and slipped from the room with such a look of relief that Triston nearly laughed.

"You wanted me, Triston?" She fairly slithered across the room to him.

Triston jerked her gown up, then pressed his fingers menacingly into her re-clad shoulders. "Where has your devilish lover taken Siri?"

Osanne winced but managed a defiant laugh. "How should I know where he goes to sate his lust?"

He shook her so hard that it snapped the pins from her hair. Luscious black tresses flowed over his hands, but the sensation only fueled his anger.

"I'm warning you, Osanne. I'm in no mood for your games. He took her to the cathedral, but the bishop refused to marry them. Where would he have taken her next?"

"My, but you are fierce." Her lips turned up in a sultry sneer. "It's too late to stop them, and it would do you no good if you did. The duke has given her hand to Fauke, together with her lands. Fauke will find some priest he can bribe into marrying them. No one but Bellesmains is going to defy Duke Richard."

"Then she will find herself a widow 'ere nightfall. Tell me where they've gone."

"Nay." Osanne slid her hands over his chest, then twined her arms around his neck. "Give it up, Triston. The Lady Siriol will never be yours. Let me console you . . ."

She pressed her mouth against his, her lips hot and moist and greedy. The memories flooded back—hazy, drunken images of lust and shame.

"No!" He thrust her away.

She stumbled against one of the tables, scattering pages of paint and script onto the floor.

His breathing came heavy, not with desire, but with revulsion. "I have won forgiveness for my sin with you, Osanne. Your strumpet charms only sicken me now."

Her raven brows swept down in anger. "Forgiveness?" she repeated. "Your father never forgave you!"

"Nay, but God—"

"God?" The anger in her face dissolved slowly into a mocking mirth. "God forgave you for what we did?"

She threw back her head as jeering laughter rolled from her throat.

He glared at her. "I suppose you would find that amusing, a conscienceless witch like you."

She doubled over, laughing so hard that she could scarcely speak. "I suppose I sh–should have known you would weep out your guilt to Heaven. It is j–just like you, Triston. H–How many weeks did you pray? What p–promises did you swear in return for divine pardon? Oh, I hope you did not vow something foolish like lifelong chastity!"

"Laugh at me all you like, Osanne. But do it after I am gone, after you have told me where—"

"But, T–Triston, don't you see how p–pathetically ironic it is?"

"Ironic?"

"A–Aye. Your father died hating you and Heaven forgave you, for a sin you never committed."

Triston stared, but suspicion quickly overwhelmed his shock. "Nay, what game do you play at now? I remember—"

Osanne struggled to overcome her laughter and straightened, her still-bright eyes taunting. "What do you remember?"

"You and me in my chamber. Your hair, your arms . . . your lips . . ."

"And then?"

"Then?"

"Aye, Triston. What do you remember next?" Her laughter at his silence bit like a lash. "Fool. You remember nothing because you were too drunk to commit the sin your father accused you of."

He struggled and failed to clear the hazy images in his mind, to follow them to the completion of the sin he had so long accepted as true.

"I came to you in your chamber that night," Osanne said, looking amused at his confusion. "Your father lingered late in the hall, gambling with his men. You were drunk, but you roused quite delightfully to my kisses at first. That night—ah, Triston, never doubt that there was genuine desire in your heart for me that night."

"Then— Then we did—"

A very unladylike snort cut him off.

"Nay, in the midst of our kisses you pulled away, groaning that you needed more wine, and like a fool I let you fill your cup. I took the opportunity to remove all but my chemise. Your drunken snores made removing any more pointless. None of my caresses could rouse you a second time. I grew so angry that I even slapped you, but you only rolled away muttering your beloved Clothilde's name and sank into a deeper stupor. So I shrugged and settled down beside you, thinking that perhaps you would waken later and I would have more luck. Only I fell asleep as well."

Triston's voice scraped hoarsely through his throat. "I remember waking to my father's screams. You were in my bed and—"

Osanne smiled and drew near enough to trace her finger over his lips. "And you remembered our few moments of passion before your wits deserted you."

He snatched her hand away. "You burst out weeping and told my father that I had seduced you. You he forgave. But me he cursed and hated till the day of his death."

She winced at the tight grip of his hand, but still managed to purr, "Self-preservation, my dear. Besides, I thought if you believed we were already lovers, it would make it easier to seduce you another time. In truth, Triston—" she slid her free hand into the curls that lay against his brow "—I have never desired a man more than I have desired you."

She reached up to kiss him.

He murmured against her mouth, "This much I do remember, Osanne. My father's outrage and my own horror were just what I needed to sober me up for good. I never touched another cup of wine. And once I was no longer drunk, I recognized your lewd charms for the vulgar dross they are."

She jerked her hand out of his hair and slapped him.

Triston fought hard against the quivering violence that spread from his stomach to the tips of his fingers. He wrenched her wrist backwards, forcing her to her knees.

"Ah!" Tears started to her eyes. "Triston, stop! You will crush my fingers!"

"I should crush the whole of you to the dust. Do you have any idea what I have suffered for your lie?"

"Nay!" She tried to pull her hand away, but clearly it only heightened her agony. "Nay, it was not all a lie! You did lust for me!"

"Lust for you?"

Only the sour truth of that made him fling her away. He should have felt relief. Lust was a far lesser sin than actually seducing his father's wife. But the flashing thought that his pleas for his father's forgiveness, the endless hours of repentance, his double oath of abstinence from wine and women—the thought that all of that had been for naught flickered out as quickly as it sprang into his mind. He had allowed pain to blind him and self-pity to overwhelm his reason with wine. Sober, he would never have looked twice at Osanne, not with Clothilde still in his heart. But drunk, Osanne had become a temptation. It had not been honor or self-mastery that had restrained him from making love to her, as it had with Isobel. Nay, it had merely been one too many cups of wine.

His shame remained as real now as his vows remained valid. But his weakness did not excuse the trick that Osanne had played on him. The bonds of his father's affection and trust, always so tenuous, had been finally and irrevocably destroyed by this deceitful woman. And that memory Triston would have to live with for the rest of his life.

Osanne huddled on the floor amidst the scattered pages of Siri's manuscript. She pressed her injured wrist to her breast and glared at Triston, but there was fear in her eyes when he knelt beside her. The jewel tones of one of Siri's miniatures seemed to leap at him from off the floor. *Siri.* What would she say to him now? How would she advise him in this moment of revelation and rage?

He brushed his fingers against the lustrous scene her talent had created. The scarlet-robed shepherd, the snow-fleeced sheep, the weeping angels. He drew a deep breath, but his voice still came out with a dangerous tremor.

"Aye," he said to Osanne, "well might you look afraid. If you know where Siri is, you had better tell me quickly, before my rage overtakes what remains of my reason."

"Triston—"

"No, Osanne." He slid a finger beneath her chin and lifted her face to his. "I am trying hard not to think of my father and the curses he flung at me before he died. But they are coming back rapidly. You know that I am not a man of great patience. Nor have I much self-control when I am angry. Tell me where Siri has gone and I might let you leave here in one piece."

"You would not dare to harm me. Fauke—"

"Lord Fauke is not here to protect you now, and I suspect if he has his way with Siri, he will never look your way again. In fact—" He released her and rose with a shrug. "Why don't I call one of the king's grey-haired counselors and remind him of the part you played in my father's treason. Let us see whether or not Lord Fauke will rush from Siri's side to deliver you from the judgment you should have suffered three years ago." Her eyes challenged him another moment. "The king pardoned me for my father's crime, but you? Only Lord Fauke has stood between you and the fire they save for female traitors. If you believe he will continue to protect you, then you have nothing to fear. I will summon the counselor—"

He moved towards the door.

"Wait!"

He turned and saw the shudder that ran through Osanne.

"Tell me where Lord Fauke has taken Siri," he said, "and you have until I return with her to make your escape from Poitiers."

Her eyes finally fell from his. "Fauke said as soon as they were married, he would ride to claim her chief castle."

"Which is?"

"Dauvillier, northwest, near the borders of Touraine. If the bishop has refused him, then he will find some other priest to marry them along the way."

He nodded curtly, strode to the door, and wrenched it open.

And nearly collided with Raynor on the other side. He tried to shoulder Raynor aside, but Raynor stood fast where he was.

"Out of my way, de Molinet," Triston growled. "I've not time to resume our quarrel now."

Raynor spoke stiffly. "I thought you might want to know that Acelet is not dead."

Triston had set a hand to Raynor's breast, intending to push him harder, but now he froze.

"Acelet— Are you sure?"

"I saw him carried away from the field and heard the duke shouting orders for his own physician to be summoned. One does not call a physician to tend to a dead man."

Triston dropped his hand but said, "If you think this bit of luck on Acelet's part will absolve you of your cowardly strike at my cousin, or of anything else—"

"Nay, I've not come here to grovel or to seek your forgiveness. I've come because I want the truth about you and Isobel."

"I have told you the truth a dozen times. You refused to believe me."

"Tell me again, and this time, name her lover."

Triston shook his head. "I cannot. I swore an oath to her, and you, of all men, know that I will not break my oaths." He thrust his hand again at Raynor and this time shoved him out of the way.

But Raynor whirled and caught Triston by the arm. "Wait! Then tell me this. What did you mean when you said you could appease my sister's ghost by punishing Siri's abductor? Who has taken her?"

But Triston saw quickly through that trap. "Nay, Raynor—"

"Tell me! Or at least—" his grip tightened, then eased. He released Triston's arm and stepped back. "At least, let me come with you. For Siri's sake," he added as Triston shook his head again. "I care about her too."

Triston hesitated. He had sworn not to name Isobel's lover or seek retribution for her dishonor. But he had never sworn not to protect Siri. Raynor knew that, and he was clearly determined to take advantage of it.

"Triston—please."

There was no bravado now in Raynor's plea, and precious little cunning in his face. Triston saw in Raynor's amber eyes a reflection of that agony that had once seared his own soul. Raynor still grieved for Isobel the way Triston had for Clothilde. Grief had bred bitterness and hatred on both sides and now lay an insurmountable barrier between them. But Triston could not scorn Raynor's pain, any more than he could dismiss it. And it did not require forgiveness to respond with pity to his request.

"Very well, then," Triston said curtly. "Come. We ride for Siri. But

Raynor, she and her abductor both belong to me."

Raynor's lips twitched into something that might have been a smile. But he only nodded and followed Triston out of the palace.

＊

Lord Fauke slammed the door shut behind the protesting merchant and his companions, turned out of their room by the greedy innkeeper in exchange for Lord Fauke's gold. Lord Fauke had spent the last several miles breathing threatenings into Siri's ear, warning her to keep her tongue quiet. Thus far, her cries of abduction along their journey had failed to result in any rescue from the villages and peasants they'd passed. Not even the blacksmith in the forge where they had been forced to pause to reshoe Lord Fauke's horse, had dared to defy the baron's orders to ignore her pleas for help.

Neither that failure nor Lord Fauke's threats prevented her from appealing yet again to the innkeeper, as they'd ridden into the yard of this dilapidated roadside inn. But a flash of Lord Fauke's purse, a clink of coins, and Siri had been whisked into the inn and up the stairs, while the innkeeper's son scurried off to fetch a priest.

She stared now about the room, appalled. Broken shutters hung at a dizzying angle from their hinges on the window. Large cracks yawned in the wooden planks of the walls. The chamber could scarcely have housed five men comfortably, far less the seven of the merchant's company. But that they had been prepared to make the best of their squalid surroundings was attested by a platter of hard bread and cheese on the table near the window, together with several abandoned mugs of ale.

She approached the bed cautiously. Four people, with difficulty, might have been able to squeeze into its width, but the rest of the merchant's party would have had to sleep on the dust-laden floor. The bed sagged in the middle and when she leaned forward to test the mattress, it prickled beneath her hand. Straw stuffing, and very coarse straw, at that. The stained and rumpled sheets with their strong, fetid odor made her recoil.

"My lord, this is outrageous," she said. "If you mean to lock me up while you wait for a priest, I demand a better prison than this."

Lord Fauke flicked a distasteful glance around the room, but said, "Unfortunately, this is the only prison I have." With a flick of his hand, he slid the bolt on the door into place.

Siri's stomach flopped. Lord Fauke raked her with so lewd a gaze that even the mantle she wrapped closer about her felt as though it had grown transparent. She stepped back and bumped against the bed.

She squeezed shut her eyes to quell her panic, then opened them again. "I don't care what Duke Richard has commanded or how much you pay the priest. I will never consent to marry you. And without my consent, you cannot make me your wife. So you may as well just take me back to Poitiers and find yourself some other heiress to wed."

Lord Fauke shook his head and tapped his breast. The duke's letter, which she had seen him slide into his tunic, crackled beneath his hand.

"Nay, you are the heiress I want, and this is the only consent I need. When the priest comes, you will speak the vows he bids you."

"I will not. I will tell him that you have abducted me, and—"

She broke off as his fingers gripped her chin.

"You will say 'yea' and 'yea' and 'I will my good lord obey.' The words will, after all, be mere formality, for I do not mean to wait for the priest to enjoy my wedding rights."

He forced her head back and she saw the hungry leer on his lips as they lowered towards hers. Her left hand closed on the bed sheets behind her. Her right hand flew up to slap him. Though her blow checked him only momentarily, it was time enough for her to drag the sheets free and throw them into his face.

"Pah!" He gagged at the reek of the cloth and let her go.

She ran to the window and wrenched open the slanting shutters. The yard lay two stories below them. She pulled herself into the window and leaned out towards the branch of a tree that grew a few feet away. If she could only reach that swaying limb . . .

But even as her fingers brushed the leaves, a wave a nausea hit her. Siri had never been frightened of heights before Raynor had threatened to throw her from the walls of his castle. But now this two story perch soared into the memory of that sheer, thirty-foot drop.

*No,* her mind gasped. *This is not the wall of Belle Noir. You are not going to fall. Don't freeze!*

But every ounce of blood seemed to drain away to her toes. Her reaching fingers turned to ice and refused to close around the extended branch. Nausea gave way to a chilling dizziness. Faster and faster the yard below her spun. Seized with a terrifying paralysis, she felt herself pitching forward . . .

"Nay, you'll not escape me so easily, wench."

Lord Fauke grabbed her from behind and dragged her back into the room. He slammed the broken shutters closed and threw her on the bed. Weak with relief, trembling at her sudden safety, Siri had no strength at first to struggle as he pinned her down.

But protruding straws from the mattress stabbed into her back, awakening her to the horror of her failure. The rank odor of the bed threatened to make her sick, almost as sick as the feel of Lord Fauke pressing her further into the reek. She writhed beneath him, but though not as large as Triston, his strength was sufficient to hold her trapped

"Let me up—" A gag choked off her plea. Her stomach flopped again, then gave a heave.

Lord Fauke interpreted her protest as mere disgust at the bed. Without shifting his weight, he pulled the veil from her head and held it to his nose. "Ah, lavender. You chose your scent well, my lady. I hope you have bathed in it, too."

He thrust the veil aside and buried his face in her streaming hair. His mouth sought the scented skin of her throat through the silken mane.

"Aye." His voice slurred with a dangerous thickness. "When I am through, I think you will be glad enough to speak the vows which will turn you from my mistress into my wife."

# Chapter 33

$iri's vociferous protests of abduction made it easy for Triston to trace her and Lord Fauke's movements past the handful of villages that lay along the road. In one of the villages, Triston learned that Lord Fauke had lost a few hours at a blacksmith's forge. Hopefully the delay had given Triston and Raynor time to close the distance between them.

Triston glanced at the lowering sun as they rode into the yard of a dilapidated roadside inn. By this hour, Lord Fauke must be searching for a place to bed for the night. The door to the inn opened and a small man with beadlike eyes and ferret features emerged to greet Triston and his companion in the yard.

"Is there aught I can do for you, my lords?"

Raynor answered before Triston could speak. "We are looking for a lady with golden hair and sapphire eyes. She is with a red-haired gentleman. Have you seen them?"

"I—" The man glanced back at the doorway of the inn. "Nay, my lords. I—"

Triston caught the poor attempt at dissemblance, and swung himself off his horse to grab the man by the front of his tunic.

"Where are they?" he demanded.

The man looked frightened. "My lord, if there is aught amiss, I swear I did not know—"

*"Where are they?"*

"Don't hurt me! I thought him an honest man when he asked me to find him a priest."

Triston drug the man onto his toes. "A priest has been here?"

The tiny eyes went wide with terror. "Nay! Nay! Milord, please! If the gentleman with her meant foul by her, I swear I did not know it!"

Triston shared the cynicism of Raynor's grunt. "I'm only going to ask you one more time—"

The man's arm flew out, pointing to the door behind him. "She's there! Up the stairs, down the corridor, third door—"

Triston tossed the man aside and strode into the inn.

⁓

Siri's throat ached with suffocated screams. Lord Fauke held her silent with one lustful kiss after another. So sickened was she, that she did not feel his hands at the neck of her surcote until it was too late. He gave a sharp tug, the cloth shrieked, and he pushed the torn shreds apart. Unable to gasp, she struck frantically at his hands as they dug next into the soft cloth of her tunic. He only grunted with impatience against her mouth and ripped the tunic's neck as easily as he had the surcote's. That left only the barrier of her chemise. Terrified, hopeless sobs vied with the screams in her throbbing throat, all trapped to bursting there by Lord Fauke's brutish kisses.

Then suddenly, her mouth was free. Lord Fauke jerked his head towards the door. She did not comprehend at first the sound that checked him. She took one gulping breath of air. And then the screams raced past the sobs to claw their way out of her throat.

"Siri?"

Triston's voice thundered her name almost as loudly as the reverberating thud that followed it. Her screams strangled into sobs of relief. Lord Fauke rolled off the bed. She sat up, gathering together the shreds of her tunic with shaking hands. She expected to see the door crashed off its hinges. But the bolt held it fast—for now. The way the door trembled at the sound of a second blow, she knew that the wood was not as thick as

397

the doors at Vere. A few more strikes and the bolt would break. What was Triston hammering against it? It sounded like his body.

"Siri—"

"Triston, I'm here!"

Again a thud. She actually saw the door bow that time and a few splinters flew off from the edges. Lord Fauke snarled a curse, then gave a fiendish grimace and drew his sword. He stepped to the side of the door and positioned himself to greet Triston with a deadly thrust the moment he burst across the threshold.

There was no time to shout a warning. One more strike and the door would break. Siri scrambled off the bed. She grabbed the tray of food from the table near the window and threw it, contents and all, at Lord Fauke's head.

He never saw the missile coming. The tray hit him in the side of the head, tumbling him with cheese and bread. He staggered in front of the door, then stumbled aside just in time to escape being crushed as the door finally exploded with a shower of splinters and banged down against the floor.

"Triston!" She hurled herself into his arms so hard that she only narrowly missed being speared by his sword.

His arms locked around her waist and lifted her off her feet. "Sweetheart."

He groaned the endearment in her ear. She buried her face against his neck, gasping and sobbing and savoring the familiar, beloved smell of him that betokened safety to her frightened senses.

If he felt her hot tears against his skin, he had no time to react to it. A shuffling of feet signaled Lord Fauke's recovery, but even as Triston tensed and started to put her down, a voice thundered from behind him.

"Lord Fauke? It was Lord Fauke with Isobel?"

Siri continued to cling to Triston as he set her on her feet, but she turned her head and saw Raynor standing on the doorless threshold. The stunned look in his amber eyes melted into disbelieving wrath as he stared at the flame-haired baron across the room.

"Triston?" Raynor growled.

"We have come here for Siri," Triston snapped back. "And I told you I would deal with her abductor."

"You're not going anywhere with her, de Brielle," Lord Fauke warned. "I have the duke's warrant for our marriage." He pulled the letter from his tunic and waved it triumphantly in the air.

"Cheat," Raynor spat across the room. "You promised her to me."

"Aye," Lord Fauke said, "when I thought she was a nobody and coveted her only for her beauty. But now I want her lands as well, and the duke has given me both."

"You would never have known of her inheritance, if it weren't for me," Raynor said. "I gave you her name and told you to investigate the Geraud family. You owe me something for that, my lord."

"I suppose you think I should reverse our bargain and lend her to you on my wedding night?" Lord Fauke mocked.

Raynor glanced at Siri. She saw a smoldering light in his eyes, but he only said, "I would rather have the truth about you and my sister."

"Your sister?" The baron's fiery eyebrows lifted. "Isabeau? Isabette? How was it again?"

"Isobel." Raynor's hand gripped the hilt of his sword. He stepped towards Lord Fauke, but Triston caught Raynor's arm and held him back.

"Ah," Lord Fauke said, "Isobel. I remember now. It was during that interminably tedious trip my great-uncle dragged me on through his domains just after I became his heir. The only thing that made that journey tolerable were those few nights we spent at Belle Noir. Your sister proved wonderfully accommodating, I recall, in relieving my boredom."

"You seduced her!"

Lord Fauke sneered. "'Twas no seduction. She came to me willingly. She made love like a common harlot. Of course that should not surprise me, knowing that her brother is nothing more than a common thief."

"This common thief is going to cut out your bowels for this. Had I known you were the father of Isobel's child, I would never have let you out of that peasant's hovel alive."

Lord Fauke's face reddened at this reminder of his humiliating seizure by Raynor's band of roadside bandits.

"I swore I'd see you flayed alive for that, de Molinet. Come then." Lord Fauke raised his sword. "And I will—"

Raynor tore free of Triston's hold and cut off the rest of Lord Fauke's threat with a clash of steel. Triston took a step as though he meant to intervene, then stopped and turned to Siri.

"Wait for us downstairs—" He broke off, his gaze suddenly riveted on the shredded neck of her tunic. The oath that burst from his lips made her cringe.

He whirled about and grabbed Raynor's shoulder. With a flash of speed that rivaled Acelet's, he twisted Raynor out of the way, then slashed his own sword down on Lord Fauke's blade.

"Devil take you, Triston!" Raynor shouted.

"I told you he was mine," Triston said. "And the only one disemboweling him is going to be me, for what he has done to Siri!"

Lord Fauke cursed them both and vigorously returned Triston's attack. Raynor stood watching them, breathing heavily, face flushed, clearly resentful of Triston's interference. But he made no move to stop it.

Lord Fauke met Triston's onslaught bravely, but he was no match for Triston's enraged strength. Triston beat him back against the bed. Lord Fauke sprang up onto the mattress, apparently hoping height might give him an advantage. Instead, the uneven surface proved his undoing. His ankle turned as he warded off one of Triston's blows. He fell over, hitting the bed so hard that the whole frame shuddered and groaned.

Triston's sword swooped up in the air.

Siri's mind reeled with a vision of Duke Richard's wrath if that blade flashed down into Lord Fauke's heart.

"Triston," she screamed, "he did not ravish me! Don't kill him!"

The blade hovered in the air only an instant. Then the angle of the blade shifted and Triston brought down the hilt into Lord Fauke's head.

Siri shivered at the awful thud and the baron slumped into silence.

"That was a mistake, Triston," Raynor said. "When he wakes up, he'll go raging to the duke. When Richard learns that you've assaulted one of his most loyal supporters, he will call it further evidence of treason."

"He's not going to rage anywhere just yet." Triston glared down at

Lord Fauke's prone body and touched the point of his sword to the baron's exposed throat. "Siri, tell me straightly. What did this felon do to you?"

She saw the deadly fury that still lingered in his face. One misspoken word, and that sword tip would pierce Lord Fauke's flesh. She drew the shreds of her tunic across her breast and held them there with fingers grown cold with memory. "He k–kissed me—and t–tore my gown—and threatened to r–ravish me. He said I would be glad to marry him then."

"Threatened—only?"

She heard the strain in his voice. "Yes. I swear. Oh, Triston . . ." His name broke from her lips on a sob.

He turned from the bed, then thrust his sword into its scabbard and crossed the room to embrace her. She caught his head and pulled it down to hers. She kissed his mouth frantically, over and over with quick, snatching kisses, desperate to drive away the foul taste of Lord Fauke's lips.

"Ahem!"

Raynor's rough protest echoed a thousand miles away, and memories of Lord Fauke faded nearly as far. Triston had mastered her frenzied mouth now, stilling her with a single, powerful kiss. His strong arms wrapped her tightly to his chest as she wound her arms around his neck.

The moan sounded dimly from across the room and scarcely registered against her passionate relief and pleasure in Triston's embrace. Some corner of her mind laid the sound again at Raynor's door. Had Triston not abruptly released her mouth to nuzzle a kiss at the base of her ear, she might not have opened her eyes to the awful truth of the growl that followed.

Lord Fauke, his senses recovered, staggered off the bed, his sword raised high and aimed for Triston's back.

"No!" Siri screamed.

Triston had not time to turn, much less to draw his sword in defense. But she saw a flash of motion from Raynor. Lord Fauke lurched forward, then sideways, then pitched face down across the floor.

A red stain spread between his shoulder blades. Raynor's sword dripped with blood.

Triston gave a sharp gasp, then knelt beside the baron and rolled him over. Lord Fauke's eyes stared, glassy and unseeing. Triston felt for a pulse, bent an ear to the baron's chest.

"He's dead." Triston's voice shook.

"I saved your life," Raynor said. "Is it too much to expect a little gratitude?" His face darkened. "Now Isobel may rest in peace."

If his words touched a chord in Triston, Siri saw no sign of it.

"You stabbed Lord Fauke in the back, like Acelet. You have no more honor than a craven cur!"

Triston lunged at him, knocking the sword out of Raynor's hand and hitting him so hard with his fist that Raynor slammed against the wall.

"Curse you, Triston." Raynor recovered from the blow and dodged over to the window before Triston could reach him again. "I told you that was an accident. Acelet turned before I could check my strike."

Siri stood frozen by the fury in Triston's face and the horrible implications of his accusation. Until this moment, she had not had time to wonder about the outcome of Acelet's duel with Raynor. What dreadful thing had Raynor done that Triston should now look ready to murder him?

"An accident," Triston snorted. He strode towards Raynor. "Like you accidentally poisoned Clothilde's mind against me and accidentally threatened to throw Siri from your castle walls? Nay, Raynor—"

Lacking the defense of his sword, Raynor braced his hands against the windowsill and drove Triston back with a hard kick to the stomach. Triston stumbled away, doubled over. Raynor seized the opportunity to try to reclaim his sword, but Triston saw his movement and lurched to intercept him.

They locked together as Raynor's hand closed on his sword's hilt.

"Let me go," Raynor panted.

But Triston only swung him around and tried to wrestle the sword away. They stumbled together over the fallen door. Both landed on their knees, then struggled up again as one.

"Triston, stop!" Raynor shouted. "I wronged you, I admit it. My behavior with Clothilde was despicable. It is too late to make amends for that, but I can rectify my lies to the duke."

Triston gave a humorless laugh and forced Raynor back against the bed.

"Nay," Raynor said, "I can! Return to the duke and tell him that it is I, not you, who hold knowledge of conspiracy by the barons with his brother, the Young King. Tell him that I am the dishonorable robber-knight who waylaid his men along the road. Tell him that I murdered Lord Fauke because I coveted the Lady Siriol."

"And what is there to make the duke believe me? Nay, Raynor, if I let you live, it'll be so that I can drag you back to the duke to tell him yourself."

Triston finally wrenched the sword away, but when he grabbed Raynor by the collar, Raynor's eyes widened in alarm. He rammed the palm of his hand beneath Triston's chin, then pulled away just enough to enable himself to swing his fist into Triston's jaw.

There was a loud crack of knuckles hitting bone and Raynor finally pulled free. He retreated again to the window and laid his hand on the table beside it.

"I am not going back to the noose and the knife," he said. "But I'll give you evidence enough to convince the duke that what you testify against me is true."

Triston, only momentarily deflected by Raynor's blow, stepped towards him again with a skeptical grunt.

Raynor picked up the table. He bashed it into Triston's body with such force that two of the legs splintered and broke.

Triston staggered and dropped to one knee. Raynor tossed the broken table aside, joined his hands together, and brought them down with a crack on the base of Triston's skull.

Triston hit the floor. He groaned, but immediately tried to push himself back up. Raynor drove a foot into his back, again knocking the breath from him and forcing him flat on the floor.

"Forgive me," Raynor muttered, "but it is for your own good."

Dismayed, Siri ran across the room and tried to push him away. "Let him up! Triston was right! You are nothing but a coward to attack him in this arrant way!"

"If you'd felt his hands around your throat, you'd drive him back any way you could, as well," Raynor retorted. He hunched down and snapped his fist into the back of Triston's head, this time knocking him into unconsciousness. Then Raynor stood, picked Siri up, and threw her over his shoulder.

"What are you doing?" she squealed.

"Absconding with you, carissima. When Triston returns to court without you, the duke will believe that I murdered Lord Fauke so that I could steal you away. He will then be forced to believe the rest of the truth as well, and Triston may return to Vere with his honor and lands safely intact."

She beat her fists against his back. "You are not doing this for Triston. You are not that unselfish, Raynor. This is a trick to somehow win my lands."

Raynor's laugh was bitter. "That is less than likely. I've struck two men in the back—though Acelet was an accident and Lord Fauke would have stabbed Triston in the back if I hadn't struck him first. But men will still call me coward, as you have done. My honor has been indelibly stained. And as if that weren't bad enough, they've found proof of my thievery at Belle Noir and Acelet knows of my involvement in the conspiracy against the duke. My knightly title is sullied, the duke will seize my lands. There is no place or safety for me left in Poitou. But I am not leaving here without at least one prize."

He strode to the door with her, but Siri reached out and grabbed the doorframe.

"Put me down! If you think I am going with you after everything you've done—"

"I will make it all up to you, carissima, I promise. You almost loved me once. I swear I will make you do so again."

He tried to yank her away, but she held on hard. He turned and tried to pry her fingers loose. Desperation lent her strength. He had to use both hands to finally pull her free, but that weakened his hold on her legs. She kicked and rolled her way off his shoulder, but his arms were there to catch her.

"Carissima—" He sounded annoyed and started to swing her back up.

Then he lurched and they both hit the wall on the opposite side of the corridor.

Siri slid down the wall, out of Raynor's abruptly relaxed hold. Raynor twisted about, swearing. A somewhat dazed-looking Triston had crawled to the doorway and caught hold of Raynor's ankle, tripping him. Raynor tried to kick him loose, but renewed fury was fast replacing the haze in Triston's eyes.

"We end this now, Raynor."

He let go of Raynor's ankle and struggled up onto his knees. By the time he reached his feet, he had pulled his dagger free.

"Triston—"

"No. I am losing no more women to your endless, insidious guile."

Raynor leapt up, too, his face flushed. "Clothilde and Isobel would both be alive today if you had only told me the truth about Lord Fauke."

He pulled out his own dagger, and none too soon. Triston's blade swooped towards Raynor's throat. Raynor deflected the strike so narrowly that Siri had to blink several times to assure herself that no blood stained the tip of Triston's weapon.

Triston hissed something that Siri could not hear. Raynor's blade locked with his, but Triston disengaged and drove Raynor back with a blow of his hilt-clenched fist. Siri scrambled up just in time to avoid being trampled by Raynor's staggering boots.

But Raynor righted almost at once. The two men circled one another as best they could in the narrow corridor of the inn.

"Curse you, Raynor," Triston said, "there is no excuse for what you did. Have you any idea what Clothilde suffered because of what you said and did that Christmas-tide?"

"What she suffered?" Raynor exclaimed. "What about what I have suffered? What about your mad, reckless temper? What about Isobel?"

Siri moved out of their way, back towards the stairs, but she scarcely heard Raynor's words through the stab of anguish in her heart. The air shuddered with a sudden flurry of striking metal, but the flashing ferocity of both men's daggers only punctuated her pain. Nothing had changed. She had been abducted, frightened halfway out of her wits and nearly ravished, and all Triston could think about even now was Clothilde.

As the two men lunged and parried one another's strikes, she saw through her blur of tears Raynor's amber eyes glistening with a furious kind of grief. She could not bear to look at Triston, to see Raynor's agony reflected, as she knew it would be, so much deeper in Triston's eyes.

She turned and gazed down the stairs, anything rather than watch them kill each other in their grief. The narrow wooden steps fell away more steeply than the wide, stone stairs at Vere, so steeply that she felt a flicker of her newfound panic of heights. She moved back a pace and felt safer. The entryway to the inn was empty, but she could hear loud, raucous laughter from somewhere below. The merchant's party was probably too occupied with getting drunk to hear the sounds of the battle raging above stairs.

"To hell with your precious oaths!" Raynor shouted amidst the shuffling of feet and clanging steel. "You should have told me the truth! I'd have cut the cur down and left him to wallow in his blood!"

"Blazes, Raynor," Triston retorted, "that's why Isobel made me swear. She lured the oath from me as much for your sake as mine. Fauke was already a trusted member of the duke's circle, and heir to both our families' liege lord. Attacking him would have brought vengeance not only upon you and me, but upon both our houses."

"Do you think fear of retaliation would have stopped me from avenging my sister's honor?"

A thud and a grunt betrayed flesh striking flesh again, before steel scraped once more.

"Nay." Triston sounded a little breathless. "I'd have cut him down myself, had she not made me swear. Isobel loved you, Raynor, more than her own life. I realize now, that is why she also made me swear not to repeat Lord Fauke's name, so that you should not learn of it and do something which could only have ended in your own disaster."

"Disaster," Raynor repeated. "That's what I'm at the center of now, isn't it?"

The scraping ceased and the irony in his voice turned Siri's head about. She saw Triston step back from him, his eyes narrowed on Raynor's face.

Raynor stood with his back to Siri. She could not see his expression, but his battle-tense shoulders seemed to slump a little.

"If I return to court with you, Triston," Raynor said, "do you suppose they will give me a choice of execution? Hanging for thievery or murder would be preferable to being hanged and drawn for conspiracy."

Triston's dagger lowered a fraction, then raised again. "If you think to win some pity from me—"

"Nay, I am only considering my options. Going back would be the honorable thing to do, would it not? Return and atone for my sins? Or shall I flee and live the rest of my life branded a traitor and a coward?" Raynor paused. "What do you suppose Isobel would want me to do?"

Triston answered harshly. "She was your twin, and you always said that twins' hearts beat alike. How honorable was she when she lied about me fathering her child? Nay, I know you, Raynor. And I know you will not come back of your own accord."

Raynor's shoulders straightened. "You are right. Nor will I let myself be dragged back by you. I have lost much today, Triston, but I am not going to lose it all."

He lunged at Triston. Triston reacted with an instinctive feint, but Raynor dodged it and barreled his body into Triston's chest. Triston flew backwards several feet down the corridor before hitting the floor. Raynor righted and stood over him, dagger still in hand.

Siri, her mind fresh with Raynor's arrant attack on Triston in the chamber, ran down the corridor towards them.

But Raynor intercepted her before she could reach Triston. "Nay, carissima, it is time for us to go."

"Raynor," she gasped, "I am not—"

He silenced her with a kiss so hard and quick that she had not time to react. "Ah," he murmured, "that will have to suffice for now. Now come, before Triston finds his feet."

Raynor dragged her towards the stairs, her heels scraping on the wooden floor as she struggled to resist and pull away.

"No! Raynor, let me go!"

"Raynor."

The name thundered from behind them. Raynor quickened his pace. He swung her about in front of him as they reached the stairs, as though he meant to force her down the steps before him.

Panic at the sight of the sharp descent made her mouth go dry. She twisted about and grabbed at Raynor. "I can't—"

He checked at the look on her face, but said, "Carissima, we must hurry."

She might have made her way down the steps slowly, but to run down them as he obviously wanted her to— "Raynor, I can't. Please . . ."

Raynor cursed, but it was not her plea that made him draw back. Triston's hand clamped on his shoulder, wrenching him away from her. With eyes flaming like two ebony torches, Triston's fist flashed like a ball of light, smashing into Raynor's face.

The blow hurled Raynor away from the stairs, but his foot lashed out as he fell. It caught Siri's ankle and flipped her off balance.

"Siri!"

She thought it was Triston who screamed her name, but the roar of terror in her ears quickly drowned out any other sound. She groped wildly for some support to break her fall down the stairs, but felt only hideously open space before her. The steps tilted and whirled. Air rushed past her cheeks. At least there was no child's face to greet her this time. But how many times could one escape the same potential tragedy?

*Oh, please, dear God,* she prayed, *don't let me break my neck.*

It was the last thing she thought before terror swirled away into blackness.

# Chapter 34

The pounding of Triston's heart matched the desperation of his lunge as he vaulted over Raynor's prostrate body. Like before, he grabbed for her hair, her sleeve, her skirt, anything to stop her. Like before, all fluttered out of reach. One moment he almost had her in his hands. The next, she was gone, her stumbling feet pitching her into a headlong fall down the stairs.

*Merciful heavens, please—*

He uttered one last fervent prayer, then threw his body forward with a speed and force that tumbled him into a dangerous fall of his own. It closed the distance between them, but he saw the stairs rising up to meet them both. He scooped her up and rolled his body under hers one instant before he hit the steps in a full-length sprawl.

The stairs banged into his shoulder, then scraped along his back as he twisted to hold her atop him. His head bumped down twice, amplifying the pain of the lump put there by Raynor's fist. The ceiling spun in a sickening whirl. He closed his eyes and hung doggedly onto consciousness. He could hear her gasping. If he broke his neck now, at least she would be alive.

But the throbbing ache in his body as he finally skidded to a stop at the foot of the stairs attested to his continued vitality. He lay there a moment, stunned, struggling to absorb both the physical pain and the emotional shock of relief.

Siri . . .

He dragged himself into a sitting position, shifting her into his lap, then gingerly lifted her head. Her blue eyes stared dazedly back at him. Her mouth wobbled.

Then the corners curved up in a tremulous smile. "You caught me. Triston, you caught me."

He closed his eyes with a groan and rolled his forehead against hers. A hot wetness welled up behind his lids. "This time," he whispered. "This time."

She gave a little gasp, followed by a sob. But her arms slid around his neck.

"Great heavens, Triston, is she all right?"

Triston's head snapped up at the sound of Raynor's voice. Raynor stood at the top of the stairs, his face nearly as pale as Triston imagined his own must be. The trembling in Triston's body slid from relief into rage and a too familiar reddish mist tinged his vision.

"Curse you, Raynor—"

"Triston—"

"—how many times do you think I'm going to let you get away with throwing her down the stairs?"

"Devil take you, Triston, if you hadn't come flying after me like the madman you are—"

Triston pushed Siri away and sprang to his feet. Aches forgotten, he leapt up the steps, hands flexing for Raynor's throat. Only briefly did it flash through his mind that Raynor might have thrown him back down the stairs with a kick. But Raynor made no such move of defense, and Triston's hands found their target unhindered.

"Triston, no!"

Siri's cry echoed dimly against his fury. He slammed Raynor against the wall.

Raynor groped wildly at his crushing hands.

"Triston, please!" she cried. He felt her urgent pull on his arm. "This time it was an accident. I saw his foot fly out as you knocked him down, and I think you saw it too."

The memory flickered defiantly into Triston's mind, but he kept his hands locked stubbornly in place. "What about your fall at Vere? What about the walls of Belle Noir? What about Clo? Am I to forgive him for all of that?"

She gave a sound like a broken sob. Her delicate hand reached up to his pressing fingers. "Killing him will not end your grief, and it will not bring back Clothilde. Let him go. For your own sake, let him go."

Her hand withdrew on another, louder sob. It was the utter despair in that sound that loosened his fingers and turned him to stare at her. She scrubbed away the tears on her cheeks and averted her face quickly from his gaze. He slid one hand down to Raynor's chest and held him pinned hard against the wall. His other hand reached out to tilt up her quivering chin.

Raynor's chest heaved beneath his hand in a ragged gasp for air, but he made no effort to break away.

"Curse you, Triston," he croaked. "We both have grudges. I regret my sister's lies which led me to suspect you in Lord Fauke's stead. You had every right to be angry—but you did not need to cast Isobel off so hard."

Triston felt a surge of color in his face. "It was an accident. I never meant to hurt her."

"Yet she is still gone, isn't she?"

"Aye . . . like Clothilde."

Triston could not deny the pain that still stirred in his heart at the thought of Clo. Yet the emotion came tinged with a startling perception. In a curious way he realized that the pain was no longer so much for his loss, as regret for the sufferings of her unhappy, anguished mind. An anguish he was no longer convinced had ever lain in his power to ease.

His hand slid from Siri's chin to caress her cheek. She held her lower lip tight between her teeth to prevent, he guessed, any more betraying sobs, but the tears spilt out again from her closed eyes and splashed against his fingers. What was she thinking? And perhaps more importantly, what did she think *he* was thinking?

Raynor's voice came rough, whether from an aching throat or from his own lingering grief, Triston could not tell.

"I cannot restore your wife, Triston, anymore than you can restore my sister. So, what do we do now?"

"Let him go," Siri whispered again.

Triston curled his hand into a fist on Raynor's tunic. How could he let Raynor go after all he had done? Triston saw again Siri's crumpled body at the foot of Vere's stairs, Raynor's vengeful hand dangling her over his castle walls, and Acelet . . . Acelet . . .

He started as Siri's fingers fluttered up to his eyes.

"Triston," she said, "you must let them go, too. The anger, the hatred . . . they will destroy you if you don't. You must let them all go. It is the only way you will ever find peace."

Peace. He had known it in childhood, while his mother lived, and had lost it on the day he had bound himself to Clothilde. He saw it offered him anew at Siri's hands—but could he bring himself to pay the price? When he looked at Raynor he felt only violence and a driving thirst for revenge.

"There is no other way to win it," she said. "Let him go. Forgive him. As God forgave you for the Lady Osanne."

He felt his mouth curl bitterly at the irony of her plea. She did not know the truth. He started to speak, then clamped his mouth shut. This was not the time to tell her of that mistake. But . . .

"I do not know if I can be as merciful as God."

She reached up a hand again to his fist. He hesitated. Then he allowed her to pull his hand away from Raynor's breast.

"I will help you," she said, with that sweet strength that even her saddest tears never seemed to dim. She turned to Raynor. "My fall at Vere and the fright you inflicted upon me at Belle Noir . . . those are mine to forgive." She grasped Triston's hand. "I will never trust you, Raynor, and I will never forget what you did. But I will not allow hate and bitterness to consume me. You have my leave to go from us now in peace."

If Raynor were touched by her magnanimity, he gave no outward sign of it. He studied her a moment, his face impassive, then shifted his gaze to Triston. "And you? Are you willing to pardon me for Clothilde?"

Triston's hand tightened so hard on Siri's that he heard her gasp. For an instant he saw Raynor and Clothilde again. The pain of that scene and its aftermath sliced through him like a chilling blade. But vision and pain both dulled quickly. Clothilde's madness had not been caused by Raynor's lies. Had she lived, she would be suffering still.

Nay, it was Siri's sufferings he wanted to punish Raynor for now. How could she be so willing to forgive Raynor for them? He glanced down at her and saw her eyes closed again, her cheeks wet, the beautiful planes of her face drawn tight with what could only be some pain of her own.

And suddenly he knew what she was thinking.

If he refused to pardon Raynor, she would believe it was because of Clothilde. Even after his declaration in the clearing, she still did not trust his heart. And how could he blame her? He had clung to his blindness for so long, had wounded her so many times. How could he ever convince her that she alone now lay in his heart?

He dried her cheeks with the back of his hand, hesitated, then lightly traced his fingers over her brow, down the curve of her cheek and across her chin. He ran his thumb across her silken lips, then brushed a finger to the damp corner of her eye.

He took a deep breath. Then he moved back a pace from Raynor. "Go."

Siri's eyes flew open.

Raynor did not move and Triston dared not look at him. He said more loudly, "Go. Now, before I change my mind."

Raynor hesitated another moment, then started down the stairs. But halfway down, he paused and turned.

"Triston—"

Triston tensed. His hand went to the hilt of his sword. Did Raynor intend to reward his generosity with yet another trick?

"—about Acelet's . . . hurt."

His grip tightened on the hilt. Why hadn't Raynor just gone? Triston felt his mercy flowing away at the memory of his cousin.

Raynor met Triston's eyes, his amber gaze level and steady. "I have little use for oaths of the sort you have chosen to bind your life with, but I will swear you such an one now as even you will not be able to doubt.

Acelet fell as I told you he did, by a misstroke from my blade. He turned before I could check my strike. I swear this is true—by my sister Isobel's grave."

Triston's breath came in sharply. As dishonorable as Raynor had proven himself to be, Triston knew he would never swear a false oath by those words. Triston did not release his sword, but some of the tension left his fingers.

Raynor turned away.

"I will tell that to the duke."

Raynor swung around, as startled at the words as Triston was. But Triston had heard his own voice speaking them.

Raynor flushed. "Thank you. But too many people witnessed the blow. They will interpret it as a strike of cowardice. Your words will not change that."

"Nevertheless, I will tell him."

Raynor hesitated, then nodded. He continued down the stairs, but when he reached the bottom, he stopped. Triston saw the way his shoulders lifted with the breath he drew before he turned around again.

"My sword is upstairs with Lord Fauke," Raynor said. "Show it to the duke and tell him that I murdered his man in my attempt to steal Lady Siri. Tell him that I fled to avoid punishment for that, as well as for my theft and conspiracy. Tell him—" a glimmer of the old cunning flickered in his amber eyes "—that he can catch me if he can."

Triston groaned at the audacious challenge, but when Raynor turned away, he stopped him again.

"Wait. Then you had better take this." He drew out his sword and extended it, hilt first, towards Raynor. "In case you encounter any of Lord Fauke's men along the way."

Raynor looked startled, but the hilt never wavered. Slowly, he reached out a hand and took the blade. And as it left Triston's fingers, Triston felt a desolating weight lift suddenly from his chest.

"My thanks," Raynor said gruffly. He saluted Triston with the sword, then looked at Siri. "Carissima, I thank you for your forgiveness, but it warms me more to know that you will not forget me. Guard her well,

Triston, for the day just may come when we will meet again."

Triston slid his arm around Siri and pulled her against his side. Together, they watched as Raynor strode out of the inn.

≈

Siri set her hand on the door to push it open, but paused when she saw how violently her fingers still trembled. Raynor had called Triston a madman, but true madness still raged in the palace hall.

It had been well after dark before she and Triston had returned to Poitiers. The duke had already retired to his bed, and Siri could only imagine his reaction at being roused to listen to Triston's account of Lord Fauke's death.

"Let me come with you," she had pleaded. "I will tell him—"

But Triston cut her off. "Nay, you should know our duke better than that by now. He will not receive evidence from a woman."

He sent her firmly away to her chamber with a tearfully relieved Lucianna, promising they would broach the matter of marriage in a few days, when the duke's shock and anger over Lord Fauke had faded a bit.

But something in his interview with the duke must have provoked Triston to speak of it sooner. With the first light of dawn, Siri had been summoned to the duke's presence. Summoned to a nightmare, would be a more apt description. Sir Owen and the bishop had been there to support her, but she would much rather have had Triston beside her, lending her his strength against the ugly tirade. But Triston had been banished to another part of the palace, and Siri had had naught but her own courage to see her through.

She shuddered again at the memory. When the duke, still cursing, had finally dismissed her, Sir Owen had whispered to her to look for Triston here. She tried to still the trembling in her hand before she finally pushed open the door.

Two sighs, equally dreamy, wreathing together as one, floated across the small bedchamber. The drawn bed curtains allowed Siri a clear view of the young man in the blankets. He lay on his side, propped up on his

415

elbow, but she could see the bandages wrapped around his upper body. His flaxen, slightly disheveled ringlets tumbled over his naked shoulders. The young lady in the chair beside the bed returned his languishing gaze with softly adoring eyes.

A plump, good-natured matron, observing the young couple above her embroidery frame from the window seat, caught sight of Siri first.

"My lady." The matron rose and dropped Siri a curtsy.

Her greeting roused the young man's attention. "Siri!"

He started to sit up, then fell back against the pillows, gasping.

"Oh!" the young lady cried. She flew up from the chair. "You have hurt yourself. Shame on you, sir. I told you that you must lie very still."

But his dreamy eyes brightened even through his obvious pain and he ignored her to reach out an unsteady hand. "Siri."

Siri saw the way the young lady's face fell at his snub. She was a pretty girl, with gentle, delicate features and shining brown hair that fell over her shoulders in thick, soft curls.

Siri offered her a smile as she moved to the bed and took the young man's hand. "You should listen to this lady, Acelet. After all the trouble the duke's physician has taken to save you, it would be most inconsiderate of you to pull your wound open and die on us now."

He gave a shaky laugh, but the weakness of his fingers on hers attested, as did his pallor, to the seriousness of his wound. Impulsively, she leaned down and kissed his cheek.

"The court is abuzz with how valiantly you fought in my name," she said. "You have saved your cousin's honor, for the duke has condemned Raynor's final blow and named you victor. And whatever else the duke might be—" she shivered again at the memory of her recent interview "—he appears to be a man of his word."

Acelet made a wry face. "Triston said it is only because the duke spoke the promise before so many witnesses, that he has absolved us both of Raynor's charges."

Siri's pulses quickened. "So Triston has been here?"

"All morning." An encouraging tinge of color flushed Acelet's pale cheeks. "And he didn't even rebuke me once. I thought he might for letting Raynor hit me the way I did. I know it was foolish to turn away merely because I heard Triston shout your name, but I didn't think—" He paused and the faint color deepened slightly. "I know that's what Triston wanted to say. I just don't think. But he didn't. In fact . . ."

"What?" Siri asked. Her feet twitched in her eagerness to go find his cousin, but Acelet looked disturbed, an expression that puzzled her given his next statement.

"Triston actually praised me for the way I fought. He said the duke was impressed with me too, and that the duke wants me to stay in Poitiers and finish my training for knighthood with his own men-at-arms."

Siri stared. She could hardly reconcile such generosity with the monster she had just left in the hall. "Are you going to stay?"

"I—I don't know. I wish it were the Young King who was extending me the offer. Only, even if it were, I . . ."

"What?" she asked again as he trailed off.

He looked away as if he were somehow embarrassed or ashamed. "I—I'm not sure I want to be a knight anymore."

He rolled onto his side again, shifting his weight from the wound in his back. The young lady gave a worried murmur when his face screwed up in pain, but his free hand waved her back. "I'm all right. But thank you."

The rather gruff addition restored the shy smile to her face.

Siri did not know what to say. For Acelet to give up such a long-held dream! Raynor's blow must have struck much deeper than mere flesh.

She covered the awkward moment by plumping the pillows behind him. "I think this young lady is right. You need to lie still and rest. Everything may look different when you are well again."

He sighed and nodded. But she saw his dejection and tried to divert his mind with a gentle rebuke.

"You have not introduced me to your guests yet, Acelet."

"What?" He glanced at the young lady. "Oh. This is—"

Siri shook her head and tossed a pointed glance at the matron. To her surprise, Acelet took the hint.

"Lady Siri, this—" he nodded toward the older woman "—is Lady Eloise, and this is her daughter, the Lady Lisette."

"I am pleased to meet you both," Siri said. "And I am Siriol—Lady Siriol de Calendri," she corrected herself. She blushed a little, for while accustomed to hearing the title on others' lips, it felt absurd on her own.

"The new heiress," Lady Eloise said with a beaming smile. "We are most pleased to meet you, Lady Siriol. Lisette, show the Lady Siriol your curtsy."

Lisette did so very prettily, but Siri caught the girl's quick glance from herself to Acelet. Poor Lisette! Acelet appeared quite oblivious to her jealousy.

"I see you are in very good hands here, Acelet," Siri said. "I know I need have no fears about leaving you in them while I go to speak with you cousin. If you will tell me where he is?"

Acelet sighed and laid down, his arm folded under his head. "He told me to tell you he would be waiting for you in the scriptorium."

The scriptorium? Why would Triston wait for her there? She thanked him and excused herself to the ladies. Lisette sat down as Siri turned to leave, and on her way to the door, she heard Lisette say brightly, "Shall I finish the story now? You must tell me if I've learned it aright. Mylisant promised to be Rauolin's love and to come to him every evening to that spot beside the river where she had saved him. But Rauolin must never speak her name or boast of her beauty. For many long months—"

"Years," Acelet corrected. "It was years."

Siri glanced over her shoulder. Lisette's face glowed at having retrieved his attention to herself. Acelet looked tired, but he seemed to cheer a little at hearing his own story recited so enthusiastically back to him and his gaze as it rested on Lisette was undeniably fond.

"You are right, it was years," Lisette said. "For many long years Rauolin kept her faith, but one day . . ."

Siri left the room smiling.

⁂

But her smile faded when she entered the scriptorium. So this was why Triston had chosen to await her here. He had gone looking for parchment and pens. He had gone someplace where he could draw *her.*

He sat on a bench at one of the long wooden tables, surrounded by piles of Siri's own handiwork. She stood for a moment in silence, watching the deft movement of his hand as he guided his pen across the sheet. She tried to speak, but there was a lump in her throat and she had to clear it away.

The sound made Triston look up.

"Ah." He turned around on the bench and held out a hand to her. "So, you have survived your confrontation with the duke. Do we to marry or do we not?"

She did not move from her position near the door. "Yes, we can marry. As soon as you like."

His brows frowned in puzzlement when she failed to take his hand, but Siri would not move. She would not cross to the table where his drawing of Clothilde lay.

"Was it so bad?" he queried gently, apparently blaming her reluctance on her encounter with the duke.

That memory momentarily overwhelmed her hurt. She shuddered. "Oh, Triston, it was awful! I was so terrified I thought I would dissolve into a whimpering puddle of tears."

"You let him see your tears?" he asked sharply.

"No, but only because I was too terrified even to cry."

Triston laughed and held out his arms. She struggled hard to resist again, but suddenly she ached for his comfort. Hesitantly, she crossed the room and allowed him to pull her into his lap. If she leaned her head into his shoulder just so, she could not see the drawing on the table.

"What did Duke Richard do?" he asked her.

She snuggled warmly into the security of his embrace before she answered. "He screamed and screamed at me. He called me horrible, shameful names, but I still refused to bend to his will. But when his face turned from red to purple and he started sputtering instead of shouting and I saw the flecks of froth on his lips . . ."

Triston stroked her shivering shoulder.

"I thought he might fall down in a fit," she said. "But the bishop gave me a firm, warning look, so I stood fast by my resolve. Then the duke began to roar again. He pulled two of the tapestries from the walls and shredded them with his bare hands. Then he strode so near to me that I could smell the sour wine on his breath and he shouted the most horrible threats. If the bishop had not come to stand behind me, I'm quite sure I would have fallen to my knees and wept out my assent to anything, just to make him stop."

Triston held her closer. "I wish I might have been there to shield you from the ugliness. The Plantagenets have the devil's own temper."

"He made you look like a positive lamb."

Triston laughed again. "I am usually wise enough to guard my own temper before him. But I'm afraid I let it slip last night. I expected him to reject my explanation of Raynor's strike at Acelet, but I wasn't prepared to have him turn so abruptly from rage at Lord Fauke's death to suddenly ticking off a list of eligible candidates who might take the baron's place as your future husband. When I blurted out a protest, he screamed me out of his presence. I think it was only because he was so certain he could browbeat you into forswearing me, that he did not eject me from the palace, as well."

"I very nearly did forswear you," she admitted. "I did not care what the duke threatened to do to me, but when he started threatening you . . ." She shivered more deeply still. "It was only because Sir Owen caught my eye and gave me that sharp shake of his head, that I found courage to bite my tongue."

"Thank heaven Sir Owen was there. But you said the duke has agreed to let us marry? I may no longer be at risk of a treason charge, but I am no more worthy of an heiress's hand than I was before."

She nestled one hand against his strongly beating heart. She knew how it galled him to have been unable to win this battle for her. But Heaven had brought other champions to her aid. "The bishop and I gave him no choice. I steadfastly refused to marry anyone but you, and the bishop showed him Gratian's *Decretum* with the Church's decree on required consent in marriage. The duke reminded me that as his ward, neither could I marry without his consent. But I said that then I would not marry at all, and that I should retire to a nunnery and bequeath all my lands to the Church."

"A nunnery?" Triston gave a shout of laughter. "I wish I might have seen the duke's face when you said that!"

She glanced up at him. If only that light might brighten his eyes forever. Too soon, she knew, the laughter would be gone, replaced by soberness and sorrow again.

"It did rather take the wind out of his rage a bit," she said. "I know he wanted to shout that he would never allow me to do any such thing. But the bishop had already heard my words and the duke must have known that the bishop had power to fight him for so rich a bequest to the Church as my inheritance."

"So rather than forfeit your inheritance altogether, he agreed to let us wed."

"Yes. But only if you agree to publicly renew your oath of fealty to him and swear to use both my wealth and your sword to support his claims in Poitou."

The laughter fled from Triston's face, but it was not sorrow which replaced it. Her heartbeat quickened at his frown. Surely he would not refuse the duke's demand?

"I have already sworn two such oaths," he said. "To force me to swear a third implies that I am not to be trusted with the first. If he thinks I am going to humiliate myself before all the barons of this county—"

"You won't do it?"

She could see his almost physical struggle to swallow his pride.

"Nay, I will do it," he ground out at last, "if it is the only way to win you."

He shifted her from his lap onto the bench beside him. She tried not to show her dismay at this distancing move. She linked her hands in her lap and forced herself to speak calmly.

"Then just as soon as the oath is sworn, the bishop has promised to marry us. When do you think . . . ?"

"The words will taste no sweeter a week from now than they will today. If the duke agrees, I will renew my oath this afternoon. Surely there are enough noblemen gathered at this court, together with his father's counselors, to witness my swearing."

"And then?"

He shifted about to face her and cupped her chin in his hand. Resentment eased from his features, replaced with a warm anticipation. "Then we will be married, sweet Siriol. For I will not willingly pass one more night without you in my arms."

She tried to push her doubts aside and surrender to the promise in his kiss. The night could not come soon enough.

It took a moment when the kiss ended for her to summon sufficient breath to speak. "Then let us go to him now."

She took him by the hand, but he did not rise with her. She tugged at his fingers, impatient at his resistance.

"Triston—"

"Wait, sweetheart. First I want you to see this." He reached behind him for the parchment sheet.

She released his hand and sprang back. "No. I do not want to see it. I do not need to see it. Let us just go to the duke and—"

He stood and held out the sheet to her. "I think you should look."

She turned away to avoid that very thing. "Please," she said, unable to control the trembling in her voice. "I know that you loved her and always will. I know that I can never replace her in your heart. I am willing to live with that, if that is the only way I can have you. But please—" she twisted her fingers together "—do not make me look."

She felt his hand on her shoulder.

"Please," she whispered again.

But he turned her around.

The drawing blurred through her tears. Her own face stared back at her, yet she knew it was not her own. Clothilde's eyes, Clothilde's nose, Clothilde's lips smiling with a mischief and joy she must have known in the carefree days of her youth. The smile that had won Triston's heart so long ago and still held so inexorably, eternally bound.

"It is you."

She glanced up at his simple words. In a burst of sudden anger, she struck the sheet away. "Nay, I will endure the truth, but not a lie. That is not me."

"Siri—"

"Nay, it is she. I heard the way your voice broke on her name when you fought Raynor in her memory. She is still in your heart and she always will be."

"Aye," he said softly. "I thought that is what you feared." The parchment crackled slightly as he extended it towards her again. "That is why I drew this today. So that you might see the truth."

The truth. She sought it, not in the lines on the parchment, but in the dark depths of his eyes. For several long moments she searched them, but seek as she would, behind the sadness she saw only a strong and steady warmth.

"My memory is where she is," he said, "and where she will remain. Aye, it yet grieves me when I think how Raynor twisted her tortured mind to wound me, when I recall how frightened and vulnerable and unhappy she was those months before she died. But I cannot change the past—and I will not lose the future. Look again." He pointed, first at the woman's crinkling eyes, then at her merry smile. "I knew Clothilde all my life, and Acelet was right—Clo never looked as happy as this."

Siri bit her lip and forced herself to study the drawing anew. Dared she believe that joyous face could be her own? The image fluttered away, floating to the floor as it slipped from Triston's hand. He slid a finger beneath her chin and lifted it. The corners of his mouth gave a tantalizing twitch.

"She never kissed me like this, either."

He set his teasing mouth to hers. All her determination to resist him failed. Her arms wound around his neck and she returned his kiss with such a shameless passion that when he finally pulled away, his husky laugh betrayed his triumph.

"There, you see? How could I ever confuse you in my mind with her when you kiss me back like that?"

His dark eyes were alight now with laughter and longing. She quivered with the thought that both might truly be for herself alone.

"Triston, are you sure it is me you see?"

"I have seen no one else for a long while, now. Sweet Siriol." His voice caressed her as surely as his hands. "I love you. I want you. I need all the things you bring me. Your laughter, your strength, your wisdom . . ." His hands encircled her face. "You were right about Raynor. Clothilde and Isobel—I will leave those judgments with God."

"I thought you might be angry with me because I made you let him go."

"Nay, since I let Raynor walk out of that inn, I have felt more peace than I have known since the night my mother died. I pray that Isobel is finally at peace as well. I know that Clothilde is." He kissed her again, sweetly, tenderly. "You have given me back my life. I don't know what I can give you in return for all the remarkable things you have brought me, but—"

"This." She brushed her fingers across his eyes. "This is all I ever wanted. To see your eyes lit with happiness, rather than anguish."

"If there is light in my eyes, it is you who put it there."

She gasped when his arms wound around her waist and lifted her off her feet. The oddity of having her toes dangle in the air through his kiss was quickly submerged in the pleasure of being so thoroughly crushed against his chest.

"Perrin will be glad to have a mother again," he murmured against her mouth. He shifted to brush his lips against her cheek. "He let me hold him before I left Vere. I promised him I would bring you back—and he put his arms around my neck and let me hold him." His voice shook a little.

"I am glad you have reconciled," she whispered. "He is a sweet boy."

"Aye. But I think a few brothers and sisters will do him good."

She wondered if he felt the thrill that ran through her. She closed his eyes with her kisses so that he might not see her blush.

"What shall you do about Acelet?" she murmured.

"Acelet?" He sounded for all the world as though he hadn't a clue who Acelet was.

She giggled and found some delight in further distracting him by reaching around to nuzzle his ear. She had to desist when the arms around her waist suddenly threatened to squeeze the breath from her.

"Yes," she gasped out, "Acelet. I think he is having second thoughts about becoming a knight." She leaned as far away as his strong arms would allow her while they still held her suspended in the air.

"Oh—Acelet." He looked disappointed at her withdrawal, but managed this time to focus on her question. "I own, that boy has more fire and talent in him than I thought. But he has not the mental discipline for knighthood. To have allowed himself to be distracted in the midst of a sword fight by the shout of a woman's name! But I have promised myself I would not chide him for that. Nay, I think knighthood is not for him. But he would make an excellent troubadour."

"A troubadour? You would agree to that?"

"Music and poetry are honored traditions in Poitou. Our queen's own grandfather was famed for his verses and songs. That Acelet should tread in William the Troubadour's footsteps would bring as much honor to our house as a knighthood. If that's what he wants, I will lend him my support."

She wondered if Triston would also support Acelet's budding affection for Lisette. But she only sighed and leaned forward again to resume her nuzzling of his ear. He held her more lightly this time, perhaps to prolong the pleasure.

"How long are you going to hold me in the air like this?" she asked at last.

He answered huskily, "As long as it takes to convince you that you are the only one in my mind and my heart."

She glanced at the drawing on the floor. *My face. My smile.* If she had had any doubts left, his fierce response to the kiss she pressed to his mouth would have banished them.

"I believe you, Triston. And I love you too."

# Glossary of Medieval Terms

**Angevin**: One who hails from the Anjou region of present-day France; the birthplace of King Henry II of England.

**Aquitaine**: A region of southwest France that was ruled by Henry II of England in the Middle Ages.

**Bailey:** The courtyard of a castle.

**Battlements:** The **crenellated** top of a castle wall.

**Bestiary:** A collection of drawings or paintings of animals, real or imagined, accompanied by their physical and allegorical descriptions.

**Chausses**: That portion of the chain **mail** that covered the feet, legs, and body below the waist.

**Chemise**: A woman's loose undergarment.

**Crenel**: A gap or notch between two **merlons** on the top of a castle wall. Used for firing arrows and for launching other types of ammunition.

**Crenellated**: Provided with gaps or notches—as in the top of a castle wall—for firing arrows, etc.

**Crespin**: A decorative hairnet worn by women.

**Curtain wall**: The outer wall that lies between the towers of a castle.

**Dais**: A raised platform in a castle **hall.**

**Drawbridge**: A bridge that can be raised or lowered to permit access across a ditch or moat into a castle's **bailey.**

**Drawing board**: A portable wooden board with a deerskin thong to hold sheets of parchment in place.

**Fealty**: The loyalty sworn by oath by a knight to his lord.

**Gambeson**: A quilted jacket worn beneath a knight's armor to cushion the blows of battle.

**Gatehouse**: The heavily fortified entrance to a castle complex.

**Girdle**: A belt worn around the waist.

**Gradual psalms**: Psalms 119–133, recited by pilgrims traveling to Jerusalem.

**Hauberk**: A long tunic made of chain **mail** that covers the upper body.

**High table**: The table on the **dais** in the castle **hall**, where the most important people sit.

**Illumination**: The medieval art of decorating books with miniatures or ornamental designs painted in brilliant colors or silver or gold leaf to "illuminate" or bring light to the pages.

**Keep**: The central tower and main residence area of the castle.

**Lapis lazuli**: A stone mined in Persia and Afghanistan, from which a blue pigment was extracted and used in painting illuminated manuscripts in the medieval era.

**Lawn**: A very fine fabric made of linen.

**Liege lord**: The king or lord to whom a man of lower rank owed **fealty.**

**Mail**: A flexible armor made of small, overlapping metal rings.

**Mead**: A medieval garden designed to imitate a small meadow.

**Merlon**: The part of the fortified castle wall that juts up between two **crenels** (gaps or open areas).

**Mural chamber**: A chamber built inside the thickness of a castle's wall.

**Mural tower**: A tower built into a castle's walls.

**Oblate**: A child "donated" to a monastery by his parents to be brought up in the religious life.

**Parchment**: Material made from animal skin; used for the pages of books or other writing.

**Poitevin**: A resident of **Poitou.**

**Poitiers**: The capitol city of **Poitou.**

**Poitou**: A region of west-central France, ruled by Henry II of England during the Middle Ages.

**Portcullis**: A grated gate usually ending in spikes that dropped vertically to seal off the entrance through a castle's **gatehouse.**

**Postern**: A hidden door in a castle's **curtain wall.**

**Primogeniture**: The custom or law by which the eldest son inherits all of his parents' property.

**Profession**: The act of taking special vows of poverty, chastity, and obedience, signifying a man or woman's commitment to give up a secular life for a life dedicated to God.

**Psalter/psaltery**: A book containing the book of Psalms from the Bible.

**Romance**: A long, narrative tale recounting marvelous adventures and deeds of chivalry.

**Smock**: A loose, blouse-like garment.

**Solar**: A small, well-lit room, usually the domain of the lady of the castle.

**Surcote**: Also known as the surcoat or super-tunic; a secondary **tunic** worn over an under **tunic**, usually more elaborately decorated.

**The hall or great hall**: The central living space of the castle inside the **keep**; the ceremonial and legal center.

**Trenchers**: Large slices of stale bread, cut either round or square, and used as "plates" for medieval dining.

**Tunic**: A sleeved, loose-fitting outer garment worn by both men and women; could be worn alone or under a **surcote**; for a man, could be knee or ankle length.

**Vassal**: A man who owes military service to one of higher rank, in return for land and protection.

**Vellum**: A very thin, fine form of **parchment** made from calfskin; also known as "veal parchment."

**Wall-walk**: The walking space behind the fortifications (**merlons** and **crenels**) on the **battlements**; also known as the allure.

# Suggested Reading List

**Duke William (Guilliaume) IX of Aquitaine, "The Troubadour"**

Lyrics of the Troubadours and Trouveres: An Anthology and a History. Translations and introductions by Frederick Goldin. Gloucester, MA: Peter Smith, 1983.

**Queen Eleanor's Courts of Love**

Kelly, Amy. Eleanor of Aquitaine and the Four Kings. Cambridge, Mass: Harvard University Press, 1950.

Owen, D.D.R. Eleanor of Aquitaine: Queen & Legend. Oxford: Blackwell Publishers, 1993.

**Duke Richard's Rule of Aquitaine and Poitou; Rivalry between and Personalities of Henry the Young King and Duke Richard of Aquitaine; Siege of Chateauneuf, Pons, and Battle of Taillebourg; Jean aux Bellesmains, Bishop of Poitiers**

Bridge, Antony. Richard the Lionheart. New York: M. Evans & Company, 1989.

Warren, W.L. Henry II. Berkley and Los Angeles: University of California Press, 1973.

**Tradition of Inheritance in Poitou and Acquitaine**

Warren, W.L. Henry II. Berkley and Los Angeles: University of California Press, 1973.

**Illuminated Manuscripts**

Gill, D.M. Illuminated Manuscripts. New York: Barnes & Noble Books, 1996.

Shailor, Barbara A. The Medieval Book. Toronto: The University of Toronto Press, 1991.

**Bees in Medieval Lore**

Payne, Ann. Medieval Beasts. New York: New Amsterdam Books, 1990.

**Purgatory**

Hanna, Edward J. "Purgatory." The Original Catholic Encyclopedia. 2009. See
http://oce.catholic.com/index.php?title=Purgatory

**Oblates: "Donating" Children to the Church**

Boswell, John. The Kindness of Strangers: The Abandonment of Children in Western Europe from Late Antiquity to the Renaissance. New York: Pantheon Books, 1988.

**Medieval Beliefs about Twins**

Shahar, Shylamith. Childhood in the Middle Ages. London and New York: Routledge, 1996.

**Gratian's Decretals—Consent in Marriage**

Gies, Frances and Joseph. Marriage and the Family in the Middle Ages. New York: Harper & Row, 1987.

# Author Bio

Joyce DiPastena moved from Utah to Arizona at the age of two, and grew up to be a died-in-the-fur desert rat. She first fell in love with the Middle Ages when she read Thomas B. Costain's *The Conquering Family* in high school. She attended the University of Arizona, where she graduated with a degree specializing in medieval history.

Joyce has taught piano lessons to children and adults of all ages for over twenty years. She loves to play the piano and sing for her own amusement, and sings in her church choir. Other interests include reading, spending time with her sister, trying out new restaurants, and, unfortunately, buying new clothes. The highlight of her year is attending the Arizona Renaissance Festival, which she has not missed once in its twenty-one years of existence.

Joyce has been owned and loved by many cats, the most recent being Clio (who helps her with her website), and Glinka Rimsky-Korsokov (that's all one cat).

*Illuminations of the Heart* tells the story of Triston, a character from Joyce's first medieval novel, *Loyalty's Web*. Joyce enjoys hearing from her readers and may be contacted at jdipastena@yahoo.com. You can also visit her on her website at www.joyce-dipastena.com and her JDP NEWS blog at http://jdp-news.blogspot.com.

# Excerpt from *Loyalty's Web*

## Poitou, France—Spring 1176

"Can you see him yet? What does he look like? Is he tall and slender? Is he as handsome as they say? Oh, tell me, Heléne, tell me quickly! I am like to die from trepidation!"

Heléne glanced at her sister, waiting anxiously beside the bed. Agitation only deepened the bloom in her glorious cheeks, while an almost feverish dread lent a dazzling fire to her brilliant eyes. Clothilde de Merval was a heart-stopping beauty. Golden hair streamed over her shoulders in shimmering, luxurious waves, and her chemise of fine lawn graced a figure so tantalizing as to have driven men to distraction for miles around.

She stood now, her fair hands clasped to her shapely bosom, her tender face a tortuous mirror of hope and fear. She looked, Heléne thought, more like a maid awaiting her bridal night than a twenty-one year-old woman who, not eighteen months past, had seen her husband's body laid in the grave.

"If you are so curious," Heléne said, "why don't you come and see for yourself?"

Clothilde shrank delicately from the thought. "Oh, I could not. It would be so bold. What if he saw me? What would he think?"

"He would think you as curious about him as he must be about you. Do not be such a goose."

Clothilde's bow-like mouth drooped at her sister's chiding, but she made no move to join Heléne at the window. Heléne tried hard not to feel impatient with Clothilde, but felt no compunction herself about spying on events in the bailey below. She knelt on the cushioned window seat . . . heedless of her own state of undress, and leaned forward again to look through the recessed opening looped into the castle's thick stone wall.

Dozens of men had ridden into the yard below. Heléne saw the colorful flash of rich mantles, a flurry of yellows and blues and reds. At least thirty knights mingled with the men of her father's court, but even amid this miscellany of aristocratic rank, she easily singled out the Earl of Gunthar. She had glimpsed him once before, arrayed in full battle armor in her father's hall. He had been oblivious to her presence then, and she had been hastily bustled away by her mother before he could become aware of her. But even though he wore no armor now, she had no trouble recognizing him.

He stood head and shoulders above the others, and even from the distance of her second-story window, she saw the proud loftiness of his stance. She watched with scorn as her father acknowledged the earl with a low, self-effacing bow.

"Heléne—" her sister's voice floated once more across the room— "please tell me what you see."

"I see a yard full of knights come to pay court to our father."

"But the earl? Can you tell which one is he?"

"Of course. He is the one Papa is groveling before."

It had been over a year since the Peace of Montlouis wherein the king had made peace with his sons, and her father, like the other rebels, had renewed his oath of loyalty to the Crown. . . . Her father was a man of honor, and it was unfair that the king should continue to punish her family for their support of the princes.

Her voice took on a crisp note of anger. "It is not enough that the king has ordered Gunthar to take our brother away and make him little better than a hostage. He insists on humiliating us with this insulting offer of marriage."

*Offer?* she thought. It was a command devised by the king to ensure their family's loyalty. And her father simply bowed and consented!

"Were the king to bear such a dictate to me, I would—"

"Heléne, is he fat?"

Heléne turned her head, biting her tongue on an exasperated response. What on earth had that to do with anything?

Clothilde gave a despairing shudder, and too late Heléne understood the urgency of her sister's question.

"No, no," she said quickly as Clothilde raised trembling hands to her face. "He is just as you hoped. He is very tall and lean and—and handsome." She added this last though in fact she had not yet seen his face. "Come, Clo, see for yourself. He will never know we are looking."

She turned back towards the window and leaned out over the courtyard once more. Only then did she realize the inaccuracy of her last statement. The Earl of Gunthar had turned away from her father and, as if sensing her gaze, suddenly glanced up at the window.

Heléne expected to feel again the rush of hatred she had known when she had seen him in her father's hall, his features concealed by a fearsomely crested helmet. Instead she gasped. His face, exposed to her now, was hawkishly proud, though not exactly handsome. His eyes, grey and piercing beneath thick, lowering brows, met her contemptuous stare with a powerful, probing regard. For a moment it transfixed her so thoroughly that she felt as though she had ceased to breathe, had been frozen into some curiously fashioned image, laid open—every favor and flaw—to his uncompromising gaze.

Then one of his heavy eyebrows lifted and his cold, unyielding mouth curved upwards into a quizzical smile.

With that first glimmer of unexpected charm, Heléne remembered her awkward state of undress. Like her sister, she wore only a sleeveless chemise, with her pale gold braid spilling over her shoulder. With belated modesty, she drew back and leaned against the cold stones that ensconced the window seat. She pulled up her knees and twisted her arms around them, trying desperately to quiet the wild thudding of a heart that had but a moment ago been so inexplicably still.

To read the rest of the first chapter of *Loyalty's Web,* visit
http://walnutspringspress.blogspot.com